LANA KORTCHIK grew up in two opposite corners of the Soviet Union – a snow-white Siberian town and the golden-domed Ukrainian capital. At the age of sixteen, she moved to Australia with her mother. Lana and her family live on the Central Coast of NSW, where it never snows and is always summer-warm. She loves books, martial arts, the ocean and Napoleonic history. Her short stories have appeared in many magazines and anthologies, and she was the winner of the Historical Novel Society Autumn 2012 Short Fiction competition. In 2020 she became a *USA Today* bestseller with her debut historical novel, *Sisters of War*.

Also by Lana Kortchik

Sisters of War
Daughters of the Resistance

The
COUNTESS
of the
REVOLUTION

LANA KORTCHIK

ONE PLACE. MANY STORIES

HQ
An imprint of HarperCollins*Publishers* Ltd
1 London Bridge Street
London SE1 9GF

www.harpercollins.co.uk

HarperCollins*Publishers*
Macken House, 39/40 Mayor Street Upper,
Dublin 1, D01 C9W8

This paperback edition 2022

1

First published in Great Britain by
HQ, an imprint of HarperCollins*Publishers* Ltd 2022

Copyright © Lana Kortchik 2022

Lana Kortchik asserts the moral right to be
identified as the author of this work.
A catalogue record for this book is
available from the British Library.

ISBN: 9780008512613

This book is produced from independently certified FSC™ paper
to ensure responsible forest management.

For more information visit: www.harpercollins.co.uk/green

Printed and bound in Great Britain using 100% Renewable Electricity by
CPI Group (UK) Ltd, Croydon, CRO 4YY

For Christopher and Sophie, the loves of my life

'A year will come, the year of Russia, last,
When the monarchs' crown will be cast;
Mob will forget its former love and faith,
And food of many will be blood and death.'

Mikhail Lermontov

PART ONE

Chapter 1

March 1917

All of Petrograd had been invited to Sophia Orlova's twenty-third birthday, but when the clock struck seven, not a single guest turned up. Sophia's husband of five years always insisted on celebrating her birthdays in style. She never argued. If he wanted to prove his love by doing something she didn't want, who was she to stop him? The evening had been planned to perfection – the food, the music, the gown and entertainment. The house sparkled like a diamond, with flowers from Moldova and candles from Denmark, delivered especially for the occasion. Dinner was waiting – shrimp and lobster from the Bering Sea, roast suckling pigs with apples in their mouths, cold meats and Russian cakes, waffles, blinis, pastries and fruit. Count Dmitry Orlov wanted people to talk about the event long after the lights had gone out. Everything had to be memorable. And on the fateful day of the fifteenth of March 1917, when rifle shots cracked like fireworks outside, it certainly was.

Sophia knelt on the floor of her salon in the dress she had received from Paris the week before, blue silk, tulle and ribbons that made her look like a princess and feel like an actress on stage playing a part that wasn't hers, a wind-up doll that didn't belong. Her face pressed to her mother's favourite icon, she clasped her hands together and prayed, tears rolling down her cheeks. 'It's the flowers,' she told her husband when he asked if she was all right. 'They make my eyes water.' But they both knew she was lying.

The sun had gone down but it was bright as day outside. The eerie light of the fires devouring Petrograd burst through the gap in the curtains. She wanted to scream to Dmitry to shut the blinds because she couldn't bear seeing what was happening to the streets of her childhood. She closed her eyes and put her hands over her ears, so she couldn't hear the gunshots and explosions.

'Don't worry, my dear. They won't come here.' Dmitry stepped away from the window and pulled the curtains shut. Darkness fell but she could still hear the sound of war. 'They would need to break the door down and …'

Before he finished talking, she heard an awful crash that reminded her of a bridge collapsing over the Neva when she was a child, then a deafening gunshot. Finally, another sound, the most terrifying of all. Heavy boots on the marble floors of her house, getting closer. Drunken shouts, resonating through her pristine dining room, her orangery and, finally, her boudoir – only two doors down the hall. Any moment they would be here, in her happy place, where she had always felt safe – until now. And then what? She wanted to scream in fear, but when she opened her mouth, no sound came. And only her hand remained on the gilded frame of Our Lady of Kazan.

Dmitry took her hand and brought it to his lips. 'Courage!' he whispered. His fingers were trembling. The putrid smoke reached her from the streets, making the back of her throat burn. Outside, bulletproof vehicles armed with machine guns rattled past. It rained bullets, from every street corner and every roof. The sprawling Kazan Cathedral, the symbol of Russia's victory over Napoleon, of freedom and sacrifice, of bravery and spirit, sported a red revolutionary flag. And the mob was looting. Men and women scurried in every direction, their arms full of expensive clothes, art and jewellery, furniture and books, until they either made it to safety with their loot or someone forcibly took it away from them.

Sophia thought she was living through the worst day of her life, her worst nightmare that by some dark magic had come alive on this cool spring evening. For the first time in her life, she was truly afraid, not just for herself, but for everyone she loved and for all innocent people of Petrograd.

Somewhere, a door slammed and a woman whimpered. It sounded pitiful, like a kitten in pain. Glass shattered. Was it outside on the frenzied streets or was it here, in what was supposed to be her safe haven, inside her beautiful home?

Her husband's voice made her shudder, even though he spoke softly. 'Get up, we need to go. We can still get away through the back door.' Dmitry was throwing everything he could get his hands on into a large trunk – their clothes, his books and her musical instruments.

'Get away and then what? We have nowhere to go.' A volley of gunshots was heard, coming from Nevsky Avenue. She couldn't hear herself over the terrible noise and for a moment she was quiet. Finally, she added, 'There are soldiers everywhere.'

Dmitry was like a caged lion, edgy and agitated, ready to throw himself out the window into the mayhem outside. Finally, he stopped packing and put his arms around her. 'I won't let anything happen to you, Sophochka, you know that. I will protect you with everything I have.'

She extricated herself from his embrace and glanced towards the door. 'You are but one man, Dima. What can you possibly do against the mob?'

'I'm going to take you to my cousin's house on Ligovsky.'

'Your cousin evacuated weeks ago. Like we should have evacuated.' She tried to hide the reproach in her voice. Until the last minute, Dmitry didn't take the threat seriously. Any moment he expected the gendarmes to descend on the unruly mob and disperse them. She wanted to remind him that for the past few weeks she'd been begging him to take her away from Petrograd. This insurrection felt different to the ones before. It felt *all-encompassing*, unlikely to pass like a summer storm and be forgotten a few weeks later. He hadn't believed her and now it was too late. She wanted to say, *I told you so*. But as she looked into his panicked face and saw her own fear reflected back at her, she didn't say a word. She didn't want to be a nagging wife at twenty-three.

'I have the keys to their house. We might be safer there.'

'And how are you planning to get there without some trigger-happy sailor using us for target practice?'

The crowd sounded like an enraged ocean at storm. It was buzzing dangerously, quieter one moment, louder the next. When she glanced outside earlier that day, all she could see was a human river of drunken faces twisted in anger and greed, soldiers' uniforms, officers' epaulettes, rifles pointed at the windows of her house. She had recoiled in horror and didn't look again, avoiding windows from fear of a stray bullet. She had never felt so exposed.

'The sailors will soon be here, inside our house,' said Dmitry and his shoulders slumped. He looked defeated, unsure what to do or how to protect what he loved most in the world – his wife. He was unkempt, his hair pointing in different directions like feathers of a pigeon in the rain, a dark stubble making his face appear grim. His clothes, although perfectly tailored, were wrinkled and mismatched. His valet was no longer there to help him dress every morning. A barber no longer came to the house to shave him. Almost all the members of their household had left and joined the revolutionaries at the first rumble of trouble in Petrograd. Although Dmitry refused to admit it, Sophia knew he had been forced to hire outside help to organise her birthday. He looked like he hadn't slept, the worry of the last few days making him appear older than he was.

She put her head in her hands and cried. Dmitry knelt next

6

to her, kissing her softly on her cheek. 'Don't cry, darling. It will be all right, one way or another.'

'How?' she whispered. A gunshot sounded nearby, and Sophia could swear it had come from inside the house. She shuddered. 'I haven't heard from Regina for five days. It's the longest we've gone without talking. What if something is wrong?'

'Perhaps we could stop by her house on the way and see if she's at home.'

'I went there yesterday. There was no one there. I'm so scared, Dima.'

'We can try again. But we have to hurry. We need to leave *now*, before it's too late.' Dmitry guided her towards the door, leaving the half-filled trunk behind.

Sophia looked at her silk dresses, laid out carefully by her beloved Nanny. She looked at the expensive furniture and tall ceilings, granite and oak, gilt candlesticks and soft satin poufs, her favourite paintings by Aivazovsky and books by Tolstoy. The tears in her eyes made everything appear fuzzy, as if it was disappearing in front of her eyes, as if she was losing it all.

And then three short blows were heard and the door to the salon collapsed. A light blinded her. Behind the light, a dark shadow loomed.

A shadow of a man with a torch and a rifle in his hands.

*

The man reeked of alcohol and sweat, the unsavoury smell of the revolution – it seemed over the last week or so the streets had become flooded with people smelling and looking just like that: loud, obnoxious and angry. The man barged in, his greasy fingers touching their exquisite furniture and expensive tapestries with possessive fascination, while his red-rimmed eyes widened at the sight of art the likes of which he had never seen before. His clothes were dirty, his back hunched, making him appear shorter than he was. The ash hung off the tip of his cigarette as he breathed smoke and the stench of stale cheese into Sophia's face.

From fear and disgust, she recoiled from him, taking a few steps inside the room, straightening her back, trying to appear taller, more imposing. More noble. This evening, like every evening, she was a picture of poise and grace. She was perfectly presented, like her world had not fallen apart overnight. But the man didn't seem intimidated by her appearance. He turned away from the statue of Apollo and leered at her, his eyes roaming over her face and body, making her feel queasy and unwell.

'Excusez-moi, madame, monsieur!' His French was bad and his eyes twinkled at this mockery of how the nobility spoke. 'I must conduct you to the cellar.' He slurred his words. It didn't come as a surprise to Sophia. This was what the revolution sounded like to her: thousands of intoxicated men and women – sailors, soldiers, escaped convicts, students and factory workers – singing the Marseillaise in drunken, overeager, too-loud-for-comfort voices. 'Orders from our leader.'

'And who might that be?' demanded Dmitry, sounding composed and self-assured. Only his right cheek was twitching, a sure indication of his distress.

'It's not your place to ask questions. From now on, you are to stay in the cellar where the rotten remains of the old regime such as yourselves belong.'

'This is our house. You can't do this to us,' cried Sophia. Dmitry pulled her by the hand, whispering to her to be quiet.

The man raised his rifle and pointed the muzzle at her. 'It's our house now. We can do whatever we want.'

Sophia followed her husband out of the room and down the sprawling marble stairway to the cellar, the hairs on the back of her neck rising in horror, at the revolutionary hordes everywhere she looked, at the unfamiliar smells that made her stomach twist, at the indignity of being marched through her house like a common criminal, as if she had done something wrong. These people who

8

had taken her house over by force believed that she had. Her crime was having everything while they had nothing, having been born into luxury while their whole lives they had struggled to put bread on the table. Accident of birth. Did they think they could put things right by running riot around Petrograd, murdering, looting and destroying everything in sight?

The house no longer felt like it belonged to them. It was alien, unfamiliar.

At the bottom of the stairs a small figure dressed in black leapt in their direction and Sophia stifled a cry of panic.

'Sophochka! Thank God you're all right! They wouldn't let me go in and see you.'

Sophia breathed a sigh of relief when she recognised Nanny, the woman who had nursed her and rocked her to sleep when she was a baby, who was like a second mother to her. In Nanny's embrace, she felt her fear momentarily dissolve. 'I'm all right, Nanny, darling. And you? You are so pale. Your face …' Nanny looked as if she had aged years since the morning. Her skin seemed grey in the dim light of the torch and there were dark circles under her eyes.

'Move it, all of you!' shouted the man, lifting his rifle, and the sad procession ambled slowly forward.

'Don't cry, Nanny,' whispered Sophia. 'Don't give them the satisfaction.' But she too struggled to hold back tears. She bit her lip and clasped her fists but it wasn't enough – the tears kept coming. Fortunately, it was dark and no one was looking at her.

When they reached the cellar, the man motioned towards the heavy wooden door and ordered Dmitry to open it. Dmitry's hands shook so badly, he couldn't fit the key into the old rusty lock.

'Hurry,' shouted the revolutionary. 'Do I look like I've got all night?'

He shined his torch into Dmitry's face, making him blink and shield his eyes. Sophia could see beads of perspiration on her husband's forehead. She wanted to help him but couldn't move. Her hands and legs felt heavy and unresponsive, like they belonged to someone else. She was afraid of the horrible man behind her, of the gunshots outside and the angry murmur of the crowd, but most of all she was afraid of the darkness that lay behind this door. She couldn't force herself to take the key from Dmitry and open it.

'Move it!' repeated their jailer.

'Why don't you try?' snapped Dmitry and a moment later cried out in pain as the butt of the rifle descended on his back. Finally, the door gave way with a heavy sigh. One after another they stepped inside and the heavy lock screeched back into place.

The darkness swallowed them.

★

When Sophia was a little girl, she had often played hide-and-seek with her best friend Regina at her parents' house on the other side of the Neva. Once, she had hid in the cellar because she knew for a fact her friend wasn't brave enough to look for her there. Laughing to herself, Sophia waited, wondering if it was time to come out, if Regina had given up yet. She was thinking of ways to tease her friend for losing the game when she heard squeaking sounds nearby. Something large ran over her foot. Little Sophia stormed out of the cellar screaming. She had never gone into one since. Sometimes she still had nightmares about it.

As she sat on the floor next to Nanny and Dmitry, she felt a little bit like that. The same heart-stopping panic, a shriek of fear stuck in her throat. The difference was, she couldn't run because there was nowhere for her to go.

She couldn't stop shaking, from the cold, from the terror of it all. As Nanny cradled her head and covered her hair with kisses, Sophia felt her body begin to shake. No matter how hard she tried, she couldn't get enough oxygen into her lungs. Her breathing came out in short, petrified puffs. Were there rats here?

Did they bite humans, feast on their flesh while they slept? Were they going to come out in hundreds and thousands the minute she closed her eyes? She thought she could hear their hungry yelps. She could sense her nightmares lurking here, closing in on her, even though the rational part of her brain understood that everything she had to fear was not inside the dark cellar but roaming free through her house and beyond. It wasn't the four-legged creatures she had to be afraid of but the two-legged variety that had descended on them like locusts.

They had been in the cellar for hours and through the walls she'd been hearing the distant hum of voices, cheering, singing, shouting, furniture crashing, glass breaking, guns barking like rabid dogs. The upheaval they were witnessing, was it limited to Petrograd or was it more than that? As they sat on the rocky floor of their dungeon, was it spreading all over Russia like cancer? Was their motherland under threat not just from the Germans but from the enemy within? She had no way of knowing. There had been no newspapers since it had all begun. No news, no explanation, just a mad torrent sweeping through the city she loved.

While the mob demanded equality for all and the end to war, they got their hands on everything they could carry. How many of them believed in the revolutionary slogans they were brandishing and how many were along for the ride to see what they could get?

Weary and breathless, her eyes wide, Sophia stared into nothingness. There was no way she could sleep, not in the dank cellar while the unthinkable was happening outside. And yet, she was so tired, she could barely sit up straight. Nanny sang a lullaby under her breath as she stroked her hand. Sophia could hardly hear it but the familiarity of it brought comfort. The soft sounds transported her back in time, to when she was a child, carefree and safe, when all she had to fear was her teacher Madame Antonova's temper or her father's displeasure, when she would hide from them all in Nanny's loving embrace. No one could take the pain away quite like Nanny. Not her father, ruling her

11

childhood home like he did the courtroom he presided over; not her mother, too busy with her love affair to care for her only daughter; and definitely not Dmitry, scared for his life, for her life, trapped in his own worst nightmare.

As she fought sleep, she saw herself as she once was, young and happy and unafraid, with her whole life ahead of her, the life of ballrooms and dinner parties, of quadrille, mazurka and waltz, of joyful trips to their summer house and rooms filled with friends, of poker and poems and romance novels. Her future had been meticulously planned, predictable and enjoyable, until the end. A trouble-free existence of a girl who was lucky enough to be born with a silver spoon in her mouth. Rich parents who gave her all the freedom she wanted, an even richer husband who adored her and whose feelings she accepted gratefully, like it was her due.

But nothing was predictable about March 1917.

'Are you hungry, darling girl?' whispered Nanny. 'Are they planning to feed us soon? How long are they going to keep us here? Like rats, hidden in this cellar.'

'I'm not hungry, Nanny. Don't worry about me.' Sophia stroked the old woman's hand. By chance or design, the vultures had placed them in the cellar where the wine was stored. The cellar next door had provisions. Sophia tried not to think of cheeses and cold meats hanging off the walls like grapes off the vine. Despite what she had told Nanny, her stomach was rumbling.

'Speak for yourself,' said Dmitry, who was once again pacing in impotent anger. He banged on the door, shouting, 'Let us out, you heartless brutes!'

Sophia wanted to tell him to stop. There was only one thing scarier than being locked in the cellar, and it was seeing the horrible man with his rifle pointing at her. She hoped she would never have to see his hollow eyes and smirking mouth but she knew that for as long as she lived she would not forget that face.

Dmitry gave the door one more feeble shove. 'What do you want from us?' he shouted.

A new fear gripped Sophia. What if the mob forgot them here, left them to die? What if they wasted away in this cellar and no one ever found them? How long would it take? Days? Weeks? How long could a human being live without food and water?

Dmitry sat next to her, whispering under his breath like a man possessed. Sophia couldn't see him but she could sense his presence, could almost touch his fear. 'This house is everything to me,' he said. 'The wretches better not touch anything or else.' Dmitry was a lawyer, like his father and grandfather and great-grandfather before him. He had never lost a case. No matter who his opponent was, he almost always had the last word. Not so at home. His beloved Sophia could have anything she wanted. A new ball gown, even though she already had a wardrobe full of dresses she'd never worn? But of course. A new pair of gloves, new jewellery, a new hat? Why not? He thought he gave her everything she needed but despite the gowns, the gloves, the jewellery and the hats, something was missing. 'When order is restored, they will pay for all of it.'

'That's the problem. They think *they* are the new order,' said Sophia.

'It's my childhood home. So many precious memories and these imbeciles are running riot. No sense of propriety, no conscience, no concept of private property.' He was quiet for a moment. When he spoke again, his voice was softer. 'Remember our first night here as husband and wife?'

'I remember. When I saw this house for the first time, it seemed so safe. Like a fortress.'

'It was the happiest night of my life. Just the two of us, no servants, no family.' He took her hand.

'You tried to carry me over the threshold and dropped me on the floor. To this day I haven't forgiven you.'

They had met a month before their wedding, a week after her father had told her she was to marry the son of his business associate. An obedient daughter, she married not for herself but

13

for her father and his business interests. Her first emotion when she had laid eyes on her future husband was intense and over-whelming relief. He wasn't old. He wasn't ugly. He was pleasant to talk to. Her second emotion, once she got to know him a little, was wonder. This young man looked at her like she was the most beautiful woman in the world. He stuttered a little when he spoke to her, as if he was nervous in her presence, like she was a queen granting him an audience and not an eighteen-year-old girl who'd never been kissed. He composed poems for her and showered her with gifts. He never raised his voice and rushed to execute her every whim. His hands trembled when he touched her and his eyes lit up with happiness at the sight of her. That she could inspire such passion never failed to amaze her. Another thing that amazed her was her husband's blind belief that she loved him back. Once, she had asked Nanny about it. 'When we love someone, we assume that person feels the same way. We can't imagine it any other way,' the older woman had replied.

Sophia had settled into married life as if she was born to it. Fortunately, Dmitry's work took up a big chunk of his time, leaving her with plenty of freedom to pursue her passions – reading, embroidering and dancing the night away.

But recently, something had changed. She had enjoyed the balls when she was a young girl of eighteen, nineteen, twenty. The ballrooms filled with twinkling lights, the silk of her gowns, tight in all the right places, the diamonds in her ears and around her neck, her eyes shining, the brightest jewels of all, twirling for hours with one eligible man after another, basking in their admiration. And no one admired her more than her husband, who, although he never danced, watched her like she was his most precious possession, his eyes narrowing every time another man approached as if he was about to challenge him to a deadly duel.

But at twenty-one, she thought, what was the point? Suddenly, it all felt so empty. They dressed up and danced, they compli-mented one another, they drank champagne and returned home after midnight, dizzy with excitement, only to do it all again another time, another giddy evening. And then what? She couldn't help but think that there should be more to life than small talk and aimless dancing. The balls, the company, the twinkling lights hadn't changed but she had.

Sophia was twenty when the war had started in 1914. Her best friend had invited her to volunteer at a nearby hospital, helping the nurses who looked after the soldiers returning from the front. It was a novelty for Regina, who was all about unusual experiences. The excitement had worn off quickly and soon the dreariness of changing the bandages and washing night pans took its toll. Regina had left but Sophia stayed, not because the suffering and the mind-numbing tasks didn't bring her down but because she felt needed in a way she'd never been before. As she cleaned the infected limbs and tried not to retch at the sight of rotten flesh, she knew she had found her purpose.

The pain and the suffering she had witnessed at the hospital had opened her eyes to the way things truly were in the world. She realised how privileged she was. Most people didn't live the way she lived. They didn't dance their lives away, while their houses were cleaned by others, and their meals and clothes prepared for them. Most people were perpetually hungry, overworked and despondent. Was it any wonder they were marching on the streets, demanding change at any cost, even that of thousands of human lives?

After a few months of volunteering, she began to despise the frivolity of the other side of her life. She still attended the balls because it was expected of her but she did so under duress. Just like her husband, she had stopped dancing and began to read. Voltaire told her society could be changed peacefully through common sense and enlightened thinking. Rousseau stated people could not exist without freedom. Diderot called her to overturn the barriers that reason never elected, questioning the right of one person to hold power over all the rest because it was supposedly

God's will. She longed for a change in her life, for a taste of something different. A glimpse into a different world. Deep in her heart, she approved of their ideas. But, although the maddened crowd on the street shouted slogans that were similar to what she had read over the years, she didn't approve of the havoc and the killings, the looting and the burning. She didn't approve of the chaos of what Petrograd was becoming.

Suddenly, the door opened with a creak. A man Sophia hadn't seen before walked in, a torch in his hand, the flame reflecting off his broad face. He was tall and round, built like the barrels of wine that surrounded them. Sophia looked up, hoping to see a tray of food. But other than the torch and a rifle at his back, the man had nothing.

'Thank God,' cried Nanny. 'Can we have something to eat, please? We've been here for hours with no food or water.'

'Be grateful you're alive. Why should we feed you too?' The man's voice was hoarse, his face grim.

'Even the Germans feed their prisoners of war,' said Dmitry.

'This is not war, comrade. This is the revolution.'

As if there was a difference, thought Sophia. Revolution was war on everything they held dear.

The man looked at the three of them like they were dirt on the soles of his boots. 'No mercy for enemies of the people. You are leeches that drank the blood of the common people for thousands of years. You don't deserve food.' The man reached for a barrel of wine and rolled it out of the cellar, closing the door behind him. Once again, darkness fell. Outside, the voices became louder, meeting the wine with cheers and hurrahs. How much longer? wondered Sophia. How much longer were they to sit here, staring into nothingness, waiting for a miracle?

'Not long now,' said Dmitry, as if he could read her mind. 'The police will round the rascals up.'

'Of course, dear,' said Sophia, even though she didn't believe it.

She must have drifted off to sleep because, when she opened

her eyes, the voices outside had quietened and her head was in Nanny's lap. 'This is punishment for our sins,' said Nanny. 'Our Father, who art in Heaven, hallowed be Thy name,' she whispered urgently, twisting her hands.

'What sins, dear Nanny? You are a saint, the kindest soul I know,' said Sophia.

Nanny pressed Sophia's hand gently and continued to pray, while the gunfire outside never stopped. It reached the cellar as if through cotton wool, muffled by the thick walls but still unmistakeable. Another sound joined it, like a candle crackling. Fireworks! The rebels were celebrating. But celebrating what? What were they hoping to achieve as they razed Petrograd to the ground?

'Whatever happens is God's will, child,' said Nanny. 'He will not abandon us.'

'What kind of God allows something like this? Innocent people murdered in the street for nothing more than being in the wrong place at the wrong time. Properties destroyed. Lives shattered.'

'This is not God's doing, it's the people's.'

Sophia heard a noise outside. The door opened and a light illuminated their prison. The same man who had brought them here walked in, holding his rifle across his chest. For a few seconds he watched them with disdain and then barked, 'Out now! Hands behind backs.' His suspicious eyes were on Dmitry. 'Slow and steady. No sudden movements or I shoot.'

'Where are you taking us?' asked Sophia, her voice only slightly above a whisper. When she rose to her feet, her knees were trembling so much, she had no choice but to lean on Dmitry's arm.

'You'll find out soon enough.'

Were they finally going to give them something to eat? Or better still, release them? Her hope giving her strength, Sophia stood up straight and looked the man in the face. There was no compassion there, only drunken belligerence. It was like looking at a bloodthirsty animal with not a sliver of humanity.

After a night on the cold floor, she felt unsteady on her feet and a little dizzy. It felt good to stretch her legs, to walk out of the damp cellar and up the stairs, to see the dawn painting the sky red through the floor-to-ceiling windows of her ballroom. The murmur of the crowd was like hostile waves hitting the shore – constant, jubilant and threatening. As they made their way through the ground floor, Sophia couldn't believe her eyes. In less than twenty-four hours, the mob had destroyed her beautiful home. The books were discarded on the floor, there were wine stains and cigarette butts on carpets, and their expensive furniture had turned into a pile of broken wood, as if ravaged by a tsunami. Her house that was supposed to have been filled with music and dancing couples was now teeming with men who spoke in angry voices and behaved like nothing was sacred.

And what was that smell? Something was burning. She wanted to bring it to their jailer's attention but the expression on his face stopped her. She would rather talk to a venomous snake.

Still, none of it mattered as long as they were safe.

'Please, can we stop in the kitchen?' asked Dmitry, his voice uncharacteristically cold and withdrawn, as if he no longer cared what happened to them. 'My wife is unwell. We haven't eaten since yesterday.'

'What did I say? Move it,' shouted the man, shoving Sophia with his rifle. She staggered and fell on her husband, who caught her, looking like a cornered deer surrounded by wolfhounds.

'I can't promise you food but I can promise entertainment,' said the man. His laughter sent shivers of terror down Sophia's back. She wondered what he meant but was too afraid to ask.

On her divans and sofas, all over her Persian rugs, in every corner of her house, men were drinking, laughing, singing and playing cards. They wore black, like ravens foretelling unspeakable horrors. Their eyes were on Sophia. They took her in, her breasts, her small waist, her hips accentuated by her beautiful dress. She felt exposed and vulnerable under their spiteful glares, wishing for the first time in her life that she was shorter, not as striking, that her dark hair was not as long. Wishing she was invisible.

'Up the stairs,' commanded the man, pointing with his rifle.

The snow-white stairway was covered in bloodstains and mud. On shaking legs Sophia put one foot in front of the other as if in a stupor, doing her best to avoid the red and brown blotches. A couple of times she slipped and would have fallen if Dmitry didn't catch her. Soon her shoes were stained with blood. When she glanced at the floor, she saw that she was leaving bloody footprints behind her. Her hand flew to her mouth in horror.

Their jailer led them to the balcony, where a group of men cheered at the sight of them. At first Sophia couldn't understand what it was they were chanting. Only when the men formed a circle around them, still shouting, their faces twisted, did she make out the words. 'Death to the enemies of the people,' came out of every twisted mouth.

It wasn't happening. She refused to believe it. These people she didn't even know were not about to kill them. It made no sense to her as she stood trembling under a dozen rifles. She had never done anything to them. In fact, she had never done anything bad in her life to anybody. She wanted to tell them that, wanted to appeal to their human nature but like wild beasts they circled around the three of them, spitting venom. 'Please,' she whispered. 'Have mercy on us!'

Her words were lost in the racket. Nanny threw herself in front of Sophia, as if to protect her. A strong hand pushed her away. 'You are one of us. You can go!'

'I will not leave my child!' cried Nanny, clawing at their arms. But no one paid her any attention. Soon the crowd pushed her away. Sophia could no longer hear her pitiful cries.

The man who had brought them here lifted his rifle and Sophia's heart skipped a beat. A second later, he threw it on the ground. 'Thank you,' she whispered, thinking he had changed his mind. 'Thank you for your kindness.'

But his blood-shot eyes were filled with anger. 'I wouldn't waste a bullet on the likes of you,' he shouted. A long, thin blade appeared in his hand.

Sophia felt her legs give out and she fell on Dmitry, who looked like he was about to faint. She could see the sword in front of her, inches away from her face, reflecting the rising sun. Their tormentor was taunting her, taking his time. As she stared death in the face, the past didn't flash before her eyes. She didn't think of what she had done but, rather, of everything she hadn't. She hadn't finished her training and become a fully qualified nurse. She had never had children. She had never been to Paris and walked with a lover on the banks of the river Seine. She had never been serenaded by a gondolier on a canal boat in Venice or travelled on a train. She had never been in love. And now she never would.

But she wasn't going to beg. She wouldn't give the monsters the satisfaction. Reaching for Dmitry's hand, she clasped it like he was her only hope. But he couldn't help her because in the face of an enraged mob he was just as helpless as she was.

Once again, the man raised his sword. Sophia shut her eyes, preparing for the inevitable blow. This was it. This was how her life was going to end, on the balcony of her beloved house surrounded by monsters who knew no pity. Her whole body was trembling but she wouldn't fall to her knees. She would stand tall and proud until the end. And soon she would be with her parents. One more second and she would see her mother's kind face and her father's loving smile. The thought brought comfort.

Suddenly, a commanding voice filled the balcony, drowning out every other sound. 'What is going on here?'

As if by magic, the crowd fell quiet. The man with the sword staggered backwards, dropping his weapon and taking his hat off. When Sophia looked up, she saw a tall young man standing in the doorway. Her vision blurry from tears, all she could make out was his dark, sparkling eyes and a handsome face. 'Release them immediately. We are not animals. If we behave like this, who is going to believe in our cause?' He turned to Sophia, offering her his hand. 'Please, accept my apologies, madam. Let me take you back to your room.'

As she gratefully leaned on his arm, she heard Dmitry's intake of breath and his quiet, urgent whisper. 'Nikolai!'

The stranger nodded to Dmitry and turned back to her. 'You can have your old rooms back. No one will bother you again. You have my word.'

Behind them, the crowd dispersed with a disappointed sigh. Sophia wanted to thank the young man for saving their lives but her throat was dry and she couldn't get the words out. All she could do was watch him, his tall frame, his broad shoulders, the way he moved with a calm assurance of a born leader. In silence, they followed him back to their rooms, where a stranger was sprawled across her bed, reeking of alcohol and urine. Sophia could see his vomit in the corner. She turned away, fighting a wave of nausea.

The man who had rescued them grabbed the man on the bed and shoved him out of the room. The drunkard barely made a noise and slumped to the floor, unconscious. 'I will send someone to clean up the mess. Once again, accept my apology. My men can be overeager sometimes.'

Sophia wanted to say his men were more than overeager, they were rabid animals in need of muzzles, but she didn't dare. She was lost for words. Swaying from exhaustion, she leaned on Dmitry, who seemed to regain his composure. 'You are the last person I expected to see here,' he said to the unknown man.

'I knew you and your wife would be in danger, so I came to make sure you were safe. Besides, it's my house too.'

Sophia watched them, stunned. Nothing they were saying made sense.

'I didn't ask for your help, Nikolai,' said Dmitry belligerently, as if this man didn't save his life only moments earlier.

21

'And yet you desperately needed it.' Nikolai smiled, seemingly oblivious to Dmitry's coldness. 'Keep it to yourself that we know each other and I will personally answer for your safety. But if anyone finds out we are related, all of us are in danger.'

Without waiting for a response from Dmitry or Sophia, he tipped his hat and went out.

As soon as the door closed behind him, Sophia turned to her husband. 'Who was that?'

'That was my younger brother.'

'I didn't know you had a brother.'

Dmitry ran a hand through his hair. His face was red, his eyes dark. 'He's been estranged from our family for many years. I didn't mention him because, as far as I am concerned, I don't have a brother anymore.'

Sophia sat down on her bed, her eyes on her husband. 'Estranged, why?'

'Father disowned him. His own fault, really. He was always reading forbidden literature, even as a teenager. He'd been arrested three times before he was sixteen, for spreading *Iskra*, the revolutionary newspaper. Last I heard, he was in charge of an underground printing house in Switzerland, producing propaganda material for the Bolsheviks. I had no idea he was in Russia, although I'm not surprised. The first sign of trouble and my brother is in the thick of it. He's always been a dreamer, trying to change the world, as if it was possible. I never thought I'd see him again. If Father were still alive, he would personally escort him out.'

'He's your brother. It's his house as much as yours.'

'Father left it to me when he died. He wouldn't want him here.'

'He wouldn't have had much choice, it seems.'

'Yes, the world has truly gone mad.'

With shaking hands, Sophia stripped the linen off the bed and fell on top of it in her clothes, closing her eyes. She didn't hear a man arrive to clean the vomit off the floor. She didn't know how long she had slept for. It could have been minutes or hours. Through her sleep she felt Dmitry's arms around her. 'Why aren't you in your bed? You need your rest,' she mumbled. All she wanted was to be alone, to sleep for a thousand years, then maybe when she woke up, this nightmare would be over and her life would make sense again.

'I'm not leaving you alone. I will stay here with you, so I can protect you,' he whispered. 'I love you so much. I would do anything for you. You know that, don't you?'

She closed her eyes and pretended to go back to sleep. Sometimes his passion scared her, not so much by its intensity but because she felt that, as a good wife, she was obligated to reciprocate.

'If anything happens to you, I don't know what I'd do,' he added. 'When that man had his sword to you, my heart nearly stopped. I'm so glad you're safe. I'm so glad I'm holding you in my arms.'

She wanted to say she was glad they were safe too but didn't. Yes, they were still alive. But for how long?

There was a quiet knock on the door. Dmitry moved away from her and seconds later Nanny appeared, her face grey with fear. 'Thank God you're safe. Those people looked mad enough to kill you. I was beside myself.' She placed a piece of bread on the bed next to Sophia and kissed her hands. 'Here, I managed to find this in the kitchen when their backs were turned. It was all I could get but I will go back for more. I'm not afraid of them.'

Sophia hugged her. 'Thank you but please don't put yourself in danger. Why don't you have it?'

Nanny looked stooped and frail and extremely tired. 'I can't even look at food. I brought it for you.'

'You need it as much as I do. Here, we can share.' Sophia broke the bread in two. Nanny tried to push it away but Sophia insisted. 'I won't hear of it. You need your strength.' Nanny took the bread and held it in her hands, as if not sure what to do with it. Tears were rolling down her cheeks. Sophia put her arms around her. 'Don't cry, Nanny. We are safe now. The worst is behind us.'

'I think you're wrong. I think it's only just beginning,' muttered Nanny.

Chapter 2

March 1917

Sophia woke the next morning and for a few blissful moments thought all was well in her world. The timid Petrograd sun was peeking through the curtains, reminding her that spring was here, beckoning her outside. Perhaps they could have breakfast on the balcony and call on some friends. Or they could have a picnic and enjoy some wine under the open skies. Or maybe Dmitry felt like riding today. They just had some beautiful horses delivered to the stables.

But then she heard the shouts outside. Somewhere nearby machine guns were firing. A series of short angry sounds like a dog barking. And it all came back to her. There would be no visits to friends, picnics under the open skies, riding or drinking wine. All these things that she had taken for granted were in the past. What would their future bring?

Shivering, she retreated deeper under her duvet and only opened her eyes when she heard noises coming from the other side of the room, of chest drawers and commode doors slamming. All her belongings were on the floor and Dmitry was standing over them, a mad glint in his eyes. 'What are you doing?' she whispered.

'What we should have done a long time ago. Packing.'

'Packing what?'

'Our things.' He pointed at the mountain of clothes on the carpet. 'We can't take much. We'll have to leave most of our belongings to the vultures.' His face was red as if he had been running or exercising. Dmitry never ran and he avoided exercise like a plague. Sophia had never seen him this worked up.

'Where are we going?'

'Anywhere, as long as it's away from here. We could go overseas. I've always wanted to show you Paris. Now is my chance. Imagine us on Champs-Élysées together, having a coffee, looking at the Arc de Triomphe, built by a warrior to commemorate other warriors. We could go on a river cruise on the Seine and have hot chocolate outside Notre Dame. In Paris, we'd be safe. We wouldn't have to worry about anything.'

Wouldn't it be wonderful, to be safe, to not have to worry? What he was describing sounded like a different life, like something out of a fairy tale. It had always been her dream to see the world. Just not like this. Not if it meant leaving their home for good. 'What would we live on?'

'Don't worry. I will get a job. Two jobs if I need to. A good lawyer is always in demand. I will provide for you. You won't want for anything.'

'We'll have to get there first. And that might be difficult.' Impossible, she wanted to add. 'It's not safe out there.'

'It's not safe *here*.' He smiled at her kindly. 'Sleep a little longer. Have some rest while I pack. You'll need your energy. And don't worry about a thing. I will take care of everything.'

She watched him as he moved around the room, muttering under his breath about money and documents and what they would need on the road and whether they would be able to sell their jewellery. She must have drifted off because next thing she knew, Dmitry was sitting on her bed with his hand on her

26

shoulder, whispering. His voice was so low, she had to make an effort to hear him. 'I will go out by myself first to find a coach, and then I will come back for you. Stay here, don't go anywhere and wait for me. Be ready at a moment's notice.'

'How will you leave the house? Those monsters are everywhere.'

'I will climb out the window. Nikolai and I used to do it all the time when we were children. Sneak out so our parents wouldn't notice.'

'Be careful.'

After he was gone, Sophia could no longer stay in bed. She paced like a wild animal in a cage, wondering what was happening outside or if Nanny was safely in her room. Was it her imagination or was it quieter in the house? She went through all her things, choosing the items she couldn't live without, trying to keep in mind what Dmitry had told her, that they could only take the essentials. Wasn't the pearl hair comb her mother had given her for her twelfth birthday essential? And what about the malachite chess set that had been her father's favourite? She couldn't bear leaving any of it behind. Her chest was hurting and tears sprang to her eyes at the sight of the things she loved, at all the precious memories. Maybe she should listen to Dmitry and let him do the packing. Turning away from the pile of belongings on the floor, she sat down and reached for her embroidery. She had started this design only days before their home was invaded but now it seemed like a lifetime ago, irretrievably in the past. She pulled her chair closer to the window so she could see the street and sat with the needle in her hand, staring outside, lost in thought.

An hour passed, then another. She wondered how long it would take to find a coach. Were all the coachmen shouting on street corners with red flags flapping over their heads? Was anyone working in the revolutionary Petrograd?

Finally, she heard a scratch at the window and Dmitry appeared. As soon as she saw his face, she knew something was wrong. She waited till he was safely inside before she asked any questions. 'Did you find a coach?'

He closed and locked the window as if afraid someone would follow him in. Then he shook his head.

'What happened?'

'They were stopping carriages on Anichkov Bridge, looking for the upper class. For people like us.'

She felt her hands shaking. 'Looking for them, why?'

He turned away from her, as if he didn't want to tell her. Moments passed before he said, 'They are forcing everybody outside, shooting some of them, throwing others in the river.'

'They are killing innocent people?' And then she thought, *Why should this surprise me? These are the same people who were ready to stab us in our own house only yesterday.*

He didn't reply. His face looked grim and grey in the light that managed to get in through the tightly drawn curtains.

'We don't need to travel over Anichkov Bridge. We could go the other way, through—'

'And what makes you think the other way is any safer?' he interrupted. 'Even if we get away from the house unnoticed, we won't make it out of Petrograd alive.'

She knew he was right. At the same time, she didn't want to believe it. Her beloved Petrograd, the city of her childhood, the only home she had ever known, had turned on them and was no longer their friend but a deadly enemy. If someone had told her two days ago that she would be desperate to leave, she would not have believed them. Yet, overnight everything had changed.

'We are better off staying here,' concluded Dmitry.

'With the vultures ready to shoot us whenever they feel like it?'

'I know it's not ideal. But it's the lesser of two evils.' She cried and he held her, whispering everything would be all right. 'It's only a temporary delay. We will leave soon, I promise you, darling. When things quieten down a bit.'

'What if things never quieten down?'

'Of course they will.' He stroked her back and rocked her in

28

his arms like a baby. 'Soon everything will go back to normal.'

Did he really believe it or was he just saying it to make her feel better? She suspected it was the latter because what was happening around them felt like the earth under their feet shifting, a blood-thirsty beginning of terrors that they couldn't even imagine.

*

As the days passed and Sophia remained in bed, wanting nothing more than to shut the world out because overnight it had become hostile and cruel, she remembered herself a couple of years ago, dancing a quadrille with a handsome young man on her birthday, happy and full of joy. He had said something to her and it stayed with her for a long time. As they twirled on the dance floor among other carefree couples, he told her he was going to the front the next morning. *This is my last ball*, he had said. *For as long as I live, I hope I never see another.* When she asked him why, he replied that *all this* – and here he pointed at the band bolting out a cheerful tune, at men and women dressed in their best attire, adorned with their best jewellery and smiles, at waiters carrying trays of shrimp and lobster tail – all this wasn't real. But suffering and struggle were real. And that's why he was going off to war. He was done living a fake life.

As much as she had grown to despise it, she wanted that fake life back. She wanted to wake up in the morning and complain to Nanny that nothing exciting ever happened, that it was all the same, day after day. She wanted that monotony back, the boredom and predictability. How happy and safe she had been and she didn't even know it.

Morning after morning, she opened her eyes after another sleepless night and listened to the gunshots outside and the noise of the crowd, shouting, 'Long live the revolution.'

They hadn't left their room or seen their captors, and if it wasn't for the loud voices in the rest of the house, Sophia could pretend they were still safe in the sanctuary of their home. Dmitry never left her side. Every five minutes, he took her hand and placed his palm on her forehead. *Do you want anything, dear? Should I read to you? What can I get you? Would you like a drink or something to eat?* She said no to everything, turning away, wishing he would just go and, at the same time, afraid of being alone. She suspected his solicitous attention was the direct result of his confinement in their two rooms. There was no work or books or newspapers to distract him; there was only her. And so he paced the room back and forth, back and forth, and every few minutes approached her, asking-asking-asking. She smiled with gratitude, trying not to think of what was happening to her city and the innocent people of Petrograd, thinking instead about summers long gone, of boat races and picnics and cherries with cream. She thought about the past not to dwell on the present, not to fret about the future because what future could people like her possibly have in the new Russia lauded by the revolutionaries? There was no place for them here. But if not here, then where? This was their home. The only home they had ever known.

She thought of her patients at the hospital, of Max who had come back from the front with his left leg missing. He had a fiancée in Petrograd but refused to see her because, while Max was at war, fighting for the woman he loved, Amelia had met someone else. The affair had been brief and she swore it was Max she loved but no matter how much she begged, he refused to forgive her. The poor woman spent days in the waiting area, praying for him to change his mind but he was stubborn and wouldn't. Sophia wanted to tell Max that the fact Amelia was there at all was proof of her feelings. Max would need care for the rest of his life, and Amelia didn't abandon him, didn't turn her back on him. She was there for him, despite everything. Sophia wanted to tell Max that people made mistakes. She didn't say a word, of course. It wasn't her place. As she lay in her bed with her fists clasped to her mouth and tried not to cry, as she tried to pretend the incessant popping of rifle shots outside meant nothing, that the low hum of the mob meant nothing, she wondered what would become of Max and others like him now that the revolutionaries had taken over the hospital. Last she heard, they were throwing the patients out onto the street, making room for their own wounded, and shooting all the officers of the Imperial Army.

Feverish and confused, she prayed for Max and for herself and for all of Russia before falling into a troubled sleep.

She woke up when a warm hand touched her forehead. 'You are burning up,' she heard Nanny's voice. Brave Nanny who took no notice of the revolutionaries in the house as if they weren't even there. 'Here, I brought you some fruit and toast. You haven't eaten since yesterday morning. You will make yourself sick with all the worrying.'

Sophia pulled herself up in bed and pushed the food away. 'There's much to worry about.'

'That's why you need your energy. Eat first, worry later.'

Sophia looked into Nanny's face. Her hand on Sophia's wrist was trembling. 'When was the last time you've eaten?'

'If you eat, I'll eat. Agreed?'

Sophia nodded. Nanny cut the toast in two and handed a slice to Sophia, taking a smaller slice for herself. The toast was dry and made her throat ache. There was no butter or jam. She ate it anyway, suddenly realising how hungry she was.

Nanny pumped her pillows, all the while shaking her head. 'They are using your favourite books as ashtrays. And they are burning the furniture, the barbarians.'

'Burning it, why?'

'To keep warm, I suppose.'

'I was wondering what this smell was,' said Sophia, wishing Nanny would spare her the details. If she didn't know what was happening out there, she could pretend a little longer.

'They are like the Mongolian hordes. As if Genghis Khan himself descended on the house.'

'Perhaps if they knew how much the furniture had cost, they would be trying to sell it instead of burning it,' said Dmitry, helplessly watching the mob through the window.

The front door slammed again and again. Sophia heard a car engine splutter and cough. 'What is happening?'

'Nothing, dear,' said Dmitry. By the expression on his face, she knew he was lying. Reluctantly, she got out of bed and joined him by the window.

In the courtyard, parked right next to the front entrance, was a large truck adorned with a red revolutionary flag. The driver was smoking a cigarette and whistling the Marseillaise under his breath. Sophia wondered why the revolutionaries couldn't come up with their own anthem. Why did they have to borrow everything from the French: the music, the ideas, the violence?

Every now and then, the front door opened and a man appeared, carrying a box. He stacked this box next to other similar boxes in the back of the truck. One of them had come undone and with horror Sophia caught a glimpse of her dresses and jewellery boxes. For a few seconds she couldn't speak. 'Are they taking our belongings?' she whispered.

'Don't stand by the window or they will see you,' said Dmitry.

'What are they going to do? Shoot me?' Dmitry walked over to her and tried to pull her away. She resisted, her pale face inches away from the glass. 'What are they doing, taking what doesn't belong to them without asking?'

'And if they asked first, would that make you feel better?' demanded Dmitry.

Nanny crossed herself in silence.

Sophia turned to her husband, grabbing his hand. 'Don't just stand there, do something! Go over there and tell them these are our things.'

'I'm sure they are aware of the fact.'

At the top of another box, she spotted her violin. It was intricately carved in the eighteenth century by a famous violin maker in Italy and had once belonged to her mother and grandmother. The violin was priceless, but it wasn't its monetary value that was important. It was the fact her beloved mother's hands had once touched it. Every morning, when little Sophia woke up, she heard the beautiful sounds coming from her mother's bedroom. The violin was irreplaceable, just like the memories it held. 'Please, Dima. We have to stop them!'

'We can't go out there. Not after these madmen nearly killed us.'

If they got their hands on her violin, safely stored away in the salon, what else did they have in those boxes? 'If you don't, I will.' She raised her head and put her hands on her hips.

'You won't do anything of the sort.'

'Watch me.'

'It's too dangerous. What are you hoping to achieve? They are not going to listen to you. They are the conquerors. As far as they are concerned, it all belongs to them.' He took her under her elbow and steered her towards the bed. 'They're just things, Sophochka. Let them have them. Who cares?'

'They are not just things. They are our life. And I'm not going to stand there and watch them take it all away from us.'

'Are you sure you want to do this, Sophochka?' asked Nanny. 'Dmitry Nikolaevich is right. They are just things and not worth risking your life for.'

Dmitry nodded. 'All that matters is that we are alive and safe.'

A volley of gunshots was heard from outside. Inside, everything was quiet. Two expectant pairs of eyes watched her. 'Do you feel safe? I don't. Not at all.' Sophia pulled her hand away from Dmitry and in three strides crossed the room to her dresser, picking up a hairbrush, running it through her hair, pulling and flinching, finally fixing it in a messy bun on top of her head. Removing her nightgown and pulling her dress on, something she would never normally do in front of her husband, she stormed towards the door barefoot, then retraced her steps and put her slippers on. Dmitry didn't try to stop her. In the doorway she paused, turned around and waited. When he didn't say anything, she cried, 'Please, don't let me do this by myself!'

Hesitantly he trod behind her, while Nanny remained in the room, petrified.

Trying not to show how afraid she was, Sophia walked briskly through the house. She looked straight ahead, her gaze glued to the floor, not wanting to see the havoc the intruders had wreaked after only three days, her furniture burnt, her books and art destroyed, her beige carpets dirty and covered with blood. When she reached the front door, the man was carrying another wooden crate to the truck. She waited for Dmitry to say something, but he didn't. He was hiding behind her, even though she was smaller and a head shorter. She thought she recognised the man as one of their tormentors from the balcony. The sneering, twisted faces were forever etched into her memory. Trembling, she blocked his way. 'Where do you think you are taking these?'

'Just following orders, comrades.'

She winced at the revolutionary address. 'These things belong to us. You have no right to take them. Kindly return everything to its place.'

'Everything in this house belongs to us now,' said the man, turning away and making a move towards the truck.

'Where is Nikolai? We wish to speak to him,' demanded Dmitry, finally emerging from behind her.

The man shrugged as if he had no idea who Dmitry was talking about. When the door slammed behind him, Dmitry pulled her by the arm. 'There is nothing else we can do. I told you these people won't listen. Let's go back.'

'You go,' she replied, marching towards the dining hall without a glance at her husband. For a moment, Dmitry stood still, as if contemplating going back without her. But then he followed in small, uncertain footsteps. As they walked past her garderobe, she stopped in the doorway, glancing inside. The room that had once contained hundreds of gowns, many of which she had never

34

worn, was completely empty. Her many pairs of shoes were gone, her undergarments, her hats, even her ribbons. Her hand on her mouth, she ran to her commode. It was on its side with its legs in the air like a helpless turtle. The lock on the jewellery compartment was broken. The contents were gone. The precious gems that had been in her family for generations, her grandmother's wedding ring, the pearl earrings her mother had given her the day she turned sixteen, the precious rubies and emeralds Dmitry had gifted her over the years. Just like the violin, their value was not in how much they had cost, although it was considerable. It was in the memories they held. When she looked at the earrings, she saw her mother's loving face. When she looked at the ring, she remembered the summers she had spent at her grandmother's estate in Kazan, roaming around with her friends, picking berries, rowing on the lake and listening to her grandparents' stories from a lifetime ago. And now the jewels were gone without a trace.

In the dining hall, a dozen men sat around the table, smoking and drinking. With a shudder she recognised the leader of the group, the man who had locked them in the cellar. Her breath caught and she backed away. Maybe Dmitry was right. Maybe the fact they were still alive was enough and she should forget about the material possessions, even if they represented everything that was dear to her. She was about to turn around and run but the men fell quiet and were staring at her, waiting for her to speak.

Taking a deep breath, she said, 'I would like to speak to your leader, Nikolai.'

'He's in his study,' replied the man, a crooked grin on his face. 'He doesn't want to be disturbed.'

'In his study? You mean, in my husband's study?' Before he had a chance to reply, she walked away, her head held high, trailed by Dmitry, who looked relieved to finally leave the lion's den.

As she strode down the dim corridor, her ancestors watched her from their gilded frames. Haughty eyes, tight corsets, noble faces, once upon a time they had had the world at their feet. Could they ever imagine the havoc of Petrograd in March 1917? Centuries of tradition, gone within days, and here she was, walking through the house that no longer belonged to her, without a hope or a place in the world. What would her ancestors say if they could see her now? What would her parents say had they lived to see this day?

She was surprised and pleased the mob hadn't got their hands on the precious paintings but suspected it was only a matter of time.

'We need to hide the paintings,' she whispered to her husband.

'Hide them where? And how? We can't protect ourselves and you are thinking about the paintings?'

She knew he was right. The intruders were everywhere. They watched their every step. Without a word, she stopped next to a portrait of her mother. The silky blonde hair framed her delicate face and her lips were stretched into a kind smile. This portrait was Sophia's favourite because her mother looked like she was about to step out of the frame and place her loving hand on Sophia's cheek. She looked just like Sophia remembered her. And now, when Sophia needed it the most, she seemed to smile with love and encouragement. *After every rain comes a beautiful rainbow.* She remembered the words her mother often said. She seemed to really believe it, hoping for a happily ever after that had never come.

Dmitry's study, always immaculate, looked like a bomb had exploded inside it. Not just the table, but the floor and the small divan were covered with papers, pamphlets and proclamations. Buried in these papers, his head low, scribbling something in a thick notebook, was Nikolai. The window behind him was open, letting sunlight trickle all over the room. In this light, he looked even darker and more imposing than he did on the balcony, but his face, when he looked up from his work, was kind and welcoming. His eyes twinkled at the sight of them.

Before she had a chance to say something, Dmitry pushed past her. 'They are taking our belongings by the truckload. You must stop this nonsense immediately.'

He was so brave when it was his brother he was dealing with, thought Sophia.

'Good morning to you too, brother,' said Nikolai, glancing from Dmitry to Sophia.

She lowered her eyes. 'My dresses, my jewellery, my personal things, even my musical instruments are gone. We have nothing left.'

'The revolution is an expensive business. The party has many expenditures.'

'You authorised this?' Dmitry demanded, shaking with indignation.

'It wasn't up to me. The house and everything in it had been requisitioned for the benefit of the revolution. I'm sorry to be the one to tell you but it no longer belongs to you.'

'By what authority?'

'By the authority of the newly established Provisional Government. Unfortunately, there is nothing I can do. We are only following orders.'

'So that's it? Just like that, we are left with nothing?' Sophia's hands trembled. She clasped them to her chest to steady them and took a deep breath. 'You march in here and turn our life upside down and then look me in the eye and tell me there is nothing you can do.'

'I know it's hard. But it's for the greater good.'

'You have no idea what it's like to lose everything, to have everything taken away from you in an instant. Don't sit there and pretend you know what we are going through, when you are the reason this is happening to us.'

'I have some idea,' said Nikolai quietly, glancing at Dmitry.

But Sophia didn't hear him. She was trying hard not to cry. The last thing she wanted was to appear weak in front of Nikolai. 'I lost my whole family when I was young. My mother first, then my father. These belongings are all I have to remind me of them.

They mean everything to me.'

He watched her for a moment before replying, 'I'll see what I can do.' The expression on his face changed. There was warmth in his eyes she hadn't seen before. Was he feeling sorry for her? Well, why not? The proud Countess Sophia Orlova was reduced to begging. She was a pauper without a place to call her own. The thought made her shudder.

'Thank you,' she said. 'That's all we ask for.'

Dmitry glared at his brother. 'That's not all we ask for. They keep us in our rooms like prisoners. This is our house. How can you allow this? You are not one of them. You're one of us. What are you doing, supporting these rebels?'

'Here is where you're wrong, brother. I *am* one of them.'

Dmitry pulled himself up as if to make himself appear taller. 'This is ridiculous, absolutely ridiculous. You people think you can march in here and take what isn't yours? You think you can forcefully, unnaturally reconstruct life and society of a country against its will, against human nature? Even a fool can see that you will fail.'

'Against its will? Have you looked outside?' said Nikolai, gesturing towards the street, where the jubilant crowds were celebrating.

'We've had uprisings before. Where are these so-called revolutionaries now? On the scaffold or in jail or in Siberia where they belong. I'm sorry to be the one to tell you, brother, but that's exactly where you are headed.' This time it was Sophia who tried to pull Dmitry away. He paid no attention to her.

'Only time will tell,' said Nikolai, smiling.

'This is the path you chose. We tried to stop you. Father cut you off to teach you a lesson, hoping you would see sense. We tried to oppose you every step of the way, but you took no notice. And now you are hurling head-first towards your own destruction. You must be blind if you can't see that.'

'It seems you are the one who is completely blind,' replied

Nikolai, turning back to his papers.

'This is nothing but a tempest. A storm in a teacup. Before the week is over, things will go back to normal.' Dmitry took Sophia's hand, stroking it as if to reassure her.

'And what do you consider normal, may I ask?' Nikolai sat up straight, as if ready for battle.

'The way it's been ordained for centuries. The way our parents lived, and their parents and many generations before them. The way God intended.'

'Tell it to the starving peasants all over the country and the dying soldiers on the Eastern Front, fighting a war none of them understand. Tell it to the factory workers, killing themselves for a few kopecks and unable to buy bread to feed their starving families. Everywhere you look, people are dying from hunger and suffocating in misery. And you believe this is what God intended? For the minority, perhaps, for people like you.'

'People like you, too.'

'Open your eyes, brother. For one second, stop thinking of yourself and spare a thought for everybody else in the country. Russia cannot go on as it has.'

'The tsar is the father to his people and only he can guide the country out of this crisis.'

'This crisis is not new. Like you said a moment ago, the injustices go back generations. And we are here to fix them.'

'You are fighting a losing battle. You and a handful of your cronies are up against the tide that will soon crush you. Sooner or later the tsar and his army will put an end to this.'

'Believe me, the tide is turning. And as of today, there is no tsar. There is no monarchy. There is only the revolution.'

For a moment, they were silent. Finally, in a tiny voice, Sophia asked, 'What do you mean, there is no tsar?'

'Tsar Nicholas abdicated in favour of his brother, who refused the throne and surrendered the power to the Provisional Government. As of today, there is a new order in Russia.'

The cheering and hurrahs from the soldiers on the streets suddenly made sense. Sophia shuddered.

'You mean, anarchy,' said Dmitry. 'God help us all. God help our country.'

Inexplicably, without her realising, while she was caught up in a whirlwind of dancing and lunches and games of chance, while she played at being a nurse, marvelling at her selflessness and sacrifice, forces had been at work that had turned her life upside down. Until now, she had hope. Until a moment ago, she firmly believed that any minute the royal troops would march through Petrograd and end this madness. The tsar would bring the country to order and life would soon return to normal. Now this hope had been shattered. There was no tsar. There was only the infuriated, bloodthirsty mob drunk on unprecedented power. Russia was a ship without a helm, at the mercy of a horrifying tempest, propelled by a current towards deadly rocks.

Dmitry shook his head and muttered under his breath all the way back to their rooms. 'The country without a strong ruler is an orphaned country. And Russia more than any needs parental guidance. She needs her tsar. They are going to realise it sooner or later.'

'Yes, but what about us? What is going to happen to us?' she whispered.

He didn't give her an answer. She suspected he didn't have one.

*

Sophia was woken the next morning by a loud knock. When Dmitry flung the door open, she saw their nemesis, the man who had taken them to the cellar on that first terrible day, hovering outside with his hat in his hands, looking ill at ease. At his feet were three wooden crates. 'All we could recover,' he said, stepping from foot to foot, as if he would rather be anywhere else but there. As if, like Sophia, he remembered what had happened

40

on the balcony and was ashamed. She wondered if he regretted it. Did the revolutionaries such as himself regret anything? They seemed devoid of human emotion, of kindness and compassion. Sophia turned away from him. She couldn't look at his face. It was the face she saw in her nightmares every night, screaming for her blood.

Dmitry opened the crates and looked inside. 'Just the clothes and the musical instruments. No jewellery?'

'I'm afraid not.'

'Of course. I am not surprised. Once it's in your clutches, why would you let it go?'

'It's not in my clutches, comrade. I have nothing.'

'You or people like you. It makes no difference.'

'I do apologise,' said the man, not sounding at all apologetic. 'But it's the twentieth century. Life is no longer about material possessions. It's about the rights of the people.'

'If life is not about material possessions,' demanded Sophia, still in bed, her face red, hands clasped with barely suppressed anger, 'what are you doing taking ours?'

'Forget about your things. You have to shed your old skin like a snake, comrade,' said the man, who introduced himself as Arsenii. 'Become a progressive new woman of the revolution. Embrace our principles. They are the future. They are going to change the world.' In the doorway, he turned back. 'You can move freely around the house. But you can't leave.'

'We are prisoners here?'

'Orders from above.'

After he was gone, Sophia curled up in bed and cried. Dmitry said, 'Why are you mourning your jewellery like it's a human being?'

Staring into space, she whispered, 'You live your life, day after day, and you don't even realise everything could be taken away from you. Everything and everyone you love, in mere seconds, gone without a trace.'

He held her, whispering, 'You still have me, darling girl. I'm not going anywhere.'

Nanny came in with a tray of food. It seemed she had an understanding with their captors. They didn't bother her and allowed her to come into the kitchen whenever she wanted to. When she saw Sophia in tears, she placed the tray on the bed and sat next to her. 'Don't cry, dear,' she said, stroking her hair. 'They might have the jewellery. But no one can take your memories away. They are inside your heart, forever.'

'While those undeserving imbeciles destroy Russia with our jewellery inside their bottomless pockets.' Dmitry shook with emotion.

Nanny said, 'Remember what your mother – God rest her soul – always said? Possessions come and go. Money comes and goes. It doesn't matter because none of it makes you happy. You know what makes you happy? The people you love.'

Sophia wasn't mourning the jewellery, she realised. The day before on Anichkov Bridge, a group of revolutionaries stabbed an officer of the royal army to death and left his body in the middle of the road for his wife to find. Even from her bedroom, with her windows closed and her head under the pillow, Sophia could hear the woman's screams. In the face of so much misery, the loss of her jewellery was nothing. What she was mourning was the loss of their way of life. *Look at us*, she wanted to say to Nanny, *we have nothing. We are seen as enemies of the people. Where can we go? What future can we have here in the country of our birth that has turned against us?* Nanny, who had never possessed anything of value, wouldn't understand that there was nothing worse than in one petrifying instant losing everything you had taken for granted.

Chapter 3

March 1917

Sophia woke up late and made her way to the kitchen. Long gone were the days when servants in red liveries would prepare an elaborate breakfast in the dining hall for her and Dmitry to enjoy. Only her loyal Nanny remained. And she was more than a servant, she was family.

Nanny was in the kitchen, peeling potatoes. Wearily Sophia sat on the wooden bench next to her. 'Let me do that, Nanny. I can peel potatoes. I know your back is bothering you.'

'The day has not come when I let you peel potatoes, young mistress.'

'Things have changed overnight in this world, it seems. Have a rest. I'm happy to help.'

'Thank you, my dear. I do have some laundry to do.'

'How about from now on we all do our own laundry? The time when I wore a new dress every day is long gone. It's much easier now.'

'Who would have thought?' Nanny laughed. 'The unexpected silver lining in all this.'

'And now you can sit back and relax. When have you ever

43

been able to do that?'

But Nanny looked ill at ease and unsure of what to do with herself. She sat down next to Sophia for a moment, chatting about what she had seen at the market ('The stalls are empty, no one is selling anything, no one seems to want to work and why should they?'), then she jumped up and busied herself with making tea. They still had plenty of tea, even if their other supplies were dwindling. The revolutionaries seemed to prefer vodka and wine. The cellar was almost empty, Nanny told her.

The alien knife seemed to possess a life of its own in Sophia's hand. It took her a long time to peel even one small potato.

'Get up off that bench this instant,' she heard Dmitry's voice. When she looked up, she saw him staring at her from the doorway, a frown on his face. He was clean-shaven and straight-faced this morning. His eyes were dull. 'It's not right.'

'I'm just helping Nanny. She shouldn't be doing everything around here.'

'She's the servant. That's what servants do.'

'She's right here. She can hear you.'

Dmitry didn't acknowledge Nanny and didn't even glance in her direction. 'You are a lady. Let the servants serve.'

'Nanny is not a servant. We don't even pay her anymore. She's here out of the goodness of her heart.'

'You are acting like she's our equal.'

'Didn't the new government just make everybody equal? It's the new law.'

'Like I give a damn about their laws.'

Annoyed, Sophia continued to peel potatoes. With a shrug, Dmitry sat at the table and opened a newspaper. Sophia couldn't look at the publication that had just resumed circulating after a long break. Reading the revolutionary propaganda and seeing the evil caricatures of the royal family made her sick to her stomach. She didn't want to know what the Provisional Government was doing because learning about it meant accepting it and accepting it meant admitting it was here to stay. The front page showed a cartoonish figure of Tsar Nicholas bribing a German general. She tutted and looked away in disgust. 'They are taking our paintings away,' she said softly.

'What did you expect? They took everything else, why not the paintings too?' Dmitry didn't look at her from behind his newspaper.

'What do you think went through the tsar's head when he abdicated?' asked Sophia, adding another badly peeled potato to the small pile in front of her.

Shaking his head, Dmitry replied, 'It must have been a difficult decision to make. It would have broken his heart.'

'But what a relief it must have been. Russia was becoming uncontrollable. Do you think he felt like he was abandoning us to our fate? Like he was betraying his people?'

'He did what he thought his people wanted. The majority of his people. It's not like he had much choice.'

'What is going to happen to him?' whispered Sophia.

'What is going to happen to all of us, I suppose. That's why we need to leave as soon as possible. As soon as it's safe.'

'Don't we need a special permission from the Provisional Government to leave Petrograd? Maybe you could talk to Nikolai, ask him to help us.'

Dmitry's face became guarded. The warmth melted away from his eyes. 'I would rather not ask Nikolai for anything. He turned his back on our family and now he storms in here, acting like the house belongs to him and we are his poor relations whom he allows to stay out of the kindness of his heart.'

'I don't think that's what he's doing. He seems very passionate about his beliefs.'

'The man is a fool. I don't want to owe him anything. If we leave Petrograd, it will be without his help.'

'You already owe him your life. And my life. And we will never leave here without his help.' The thought of travelling through the country gripped by the revolution, through angry mobs, with bullets raining down on them, to start a new life somewhere far, somewhere she had never been before, filled her with terror. It was the unknown that frightened Sophia. It was better to stay here, in their two rooms that were familiar, even if no longer safe. 'Maybe we'll be all right here, where Nikolai can protect us. And maybe the Provisional Government can restore some semblance of order,' she said uncertainly.

'You might be right. You know what I heard? The soldiers are forcing storekeepers to sell butter for one rouble a pound when it cost them two roubles twenty kopecks to buy. They comply; what choice do they have? But people are already unhappy. This madness cannot last. It will only lead to counter-revolution. Hopefully before they arrest us all and throw us in jail.'

'Arrest us? What for?'

'For not being sympathetic to the revolution. For walking on the wrong side of the road. For wearing the wrong expression on our faces. Like they need a reason. The papers are full of stories of arrests and executions.'

Sophia's hand trembled and the knife slipped, cutting her finger. As Nanny and Dmitry rushed to her side, she stared at the angry bloodstains on the floor and thought, *Can this get any worse? We are already prisoners in our own house, afraid for our lives. What more can they possibly want from us?*

*

Sophia had never missed church on Sunday. Growing up, it was a tradition her mother and she had shared. They would wake up early and dress up in their Sunday best, cover their heads with kerchiefs and walk to Kazan Cathedral, only a few blocks from their house. Little Sophia would gape in awe at the icons and the sculptures, tall ceilings and gilded chandeliers, while her mother would light a candle, kneel and pray. Sophia remembered their last visit like it was yesterday. That day, her mother was praying longer than ever before and her eyes looked red, like she had been crying. 'What are you doing, Mama?' asked Sophia.

'I'm talking to God, darling.'

'Can He hear you?'

'Of course. He can hear all of us.'

'Just in church or anywhere?'

'If you speak from your heart, He can hear you anywhere.'

'What do you talk to Him about?'

It was a while before her mother replied. 'I am asking for guidance.'

'Are you lost?'

Mother didn't reply but hugged her close and covered her face with kisses. She didn't let go for a long time and on the way home she bought her a sweet pie. A week later, she left to stay at their estate in Kazan. She had never returned.

Since that day, Father had taken little Sophia to church every Sunday but it wasn't the same. And not just because Father never bought her sweet pies or talked to her the way Mother did, like Sophia was a grown-up. It was because Sophia had lost her faith. Mother had asked God for guidance, only to leave her family for good. Had God advised her to do so? Sophia still went to church but her heart wasn't in it because it was broken.

But now, as life crumbled around her, Sophia craved the comfort of talking to God. She craved the familiar scent of the candles, the choir singing, the kind and reassuring voice of the priest restoring her faith in humanity and giving her hope. What she longed for most of all as she dressed and brushed her hair was the memory of her mother as she held her little hand and sang a cheerful tune while they walked to church.

Telling Dmitry she was going to find Nanny, Sophia slipped out of the room. She tried not to think of what Dmitry had told her, of violent hands dragging innocent people out of carriages, of icy waters of the Neva parting to receive them as they were thrown off the bridge by men reeking of alcohol and reciting Marx's slogans with little understanding but plenty of passion. She was wearing her simple black dress. Her hair was hidden under Nanny's threadbare kerchief. No one would recognise her as belonging to the upper class, would they? Besides, she wasn't going far. She would be all right, she told herself as she ran down the stairs, crossed the dining hall, the salon, the dance hall and approached the back door. Sighing with relief, she turned the handle. The door gave way. Only when she felt the fresh spring air on her face did she realise how much she had missed being outside. How much she had missed her freedom.

'Where do you think you are going?'

She heard the angry voice and paused like a frightened animal caught in torchlight. When she turned around, she saw Arsenii standing in the doorway, looking at her with disgust. 'I wanted to get some air. We are allowed air, are we not?'

'There's perfectly good air inside the house.'

'Even prisoners are allowed a walk every day.'

'Not in this prison. I have orders from my superior to not let you or your husband out of this house.'

'This is our house. And this is our garden. I will walk here if I want to.'

'Not on my watch.'

She felt herself deflate with disappointment. Their home had become their prison and there was nothing she could do about it. She was about to close the door and return to her room when Nikolai appeared. 'Thank you, Arsenii. I will handle this.'

As Arsenii walked away, Sophia turned to Nikolai. 'You ordered them to keep us locked up? Despite what you said, you treat us like criminals. Like we've done something wrong. You should be ashamed of yourself.' She felt her heart racing. The familiar anger swept her up like an ocean wave, making it hard to breathe or talk or think. She couldn't believe it but suddenly she wanted to punch him.

'The streets are not safe for someone like you. I don't want anything to happen to you. My job is to protect you.'

'Your job is to take everything away from us, it seems. To strip us of dignity, to make us beg for a piece of bread. And you are exceptionally good at it. You must be so proud.' She squared her shoulders and glared at him with as much contempt as she could muster.

'That was never my intention. May I ask where you were going?'

'That is none of your business.' She turned her back on him, ready to storm off.

'If you will allow me, I would like to conduct you to your destination.'

Sophia was torn. On one hand, the prospect of spending time with her jailer didn't appeal to her at all. On the other, if she didn't leave this house immediately, she would suffocate. She craved the comfort and peace of the church to stop her heart from breaking, if only for a moment. 'I will be grateful if you could do so,' she said quietly, blushing as if embarrassed, as if by saying yes she was admitting defeat.

'It will be my pleasure.' He smiled but she didn't smile back.

Along Nevsky Avenue, the shops were reopening, while all around chaos reigned. Instead of hope at the sight of people filtering in and out of the store doors, as if nothing out of the ordinary was happening in Petrograd, Sophia felt a sense of doom. It was as if the chaos had become normal.

The stage driver demanded a ridiculous price – five roubles to go five blocks. Nikolai paid without a word. On the corner she could see soldiers with rifles in their hands and a man with a red armband – a member of the newly established militia. Their job was to restore order on the streets of the city. Sophia thought they were not doing very well. She pulled herself inside the carriage to make sure they couldn't see her but remained turned to the window, so she wouldn't have to talk to Nikolai. Nor did he attempt to start a conversation. Instead, he opened a

49

book and began to read. She threw a surreptitious glance at the cover but couldn't make out what it was.

When the coach approached Kazan Cathedral, Sophia saw a large red flag swaying on its roof. For a few moments, she was speechless. She watched with horror, thinking how much she hated red. It was her least favourite colour, of blood, war and aggression. The colour of revolution. She opened the door to disembark but changed her mind, asking the driver to take them to a small church five minutes away instead. It wasn't the cathedral of her childhood with its majestic walls and stunning interior. It was modest and small but didn't her mother tell her that God was everywhere, that He could hear her anywhere?

'I will wait here for you. Take as long as you need,' said Nikolai.

The church was unusually quiet. It seemed everyone was on the streets, marching and shouting, in the chaos of the revolution forgetting all about God. She felt safe here, in the sanctuary of the wooden structure with a golden cupola. Surely the revolutionaries wouldn't storm the little church the way they had stormed her home? What did they want with God when there were houses to loot and the rights of men to defend?

During service, the priest no longer prayed for the tsar and the imperial family. He didn't ask God to grant them long years, nor did he praise the royalty. But he prayed for peace in Russia and for the end of violence and it was good enough for her. She stood in the back and cried silently because peace, once taken for granted, seemed as far away and unattainable as her mother had been when Sophia needed her as a child.

The other parishioners were people like her, dressed in expensive clothes, with trembling hands and solemn faces, praying to God like He was their only hope. Everywhere she looked, Sophia saw fear. 'My husband went out to visit his father. A stray bullet cut him down a hundred metres from our house,' cried a woman on Sophia's left as she placed a burning candle in front of an icon of the Holy Trinity. She was half-hidden by a woolly kerchief and her eyes were damp. 'And when I called on his father to tell him, he was already dead. Stabbed in his own home. I am all alone in the world.'

Whispering how sorry she was, Sophia knelt before the icon, her hands clasped close to her heart, her eyes closed. She prayed for herself. She prayed for Dmitry and Nanny. And she prayed for guidance, just like her mother had once done, because she had never felt so lost.

When she stepped outside into the mild spring air, her heart felt lighter. She felt like she was no longer alone.

Nikolai suggested they walk home instead of waiting for another coach. She tentatively agreed, although she wasn't sure it was such a good idea. The crowds pushed past her, once or twice almost knocking her off her feet. A horse bolted and would have hit her if she didn't step back. A young man popped out of a window behind Sophia, waving a red flag and shouting, 'Long live free Russia!' She recoiled from him, only to see a group of men marching down the embankment with rifles that pointed straight at her. And yet, with Nikolai by her side she didn't feel afraid.

They walked in silence down Nevsky, towards the Fontanka. 'Did it help?' he asked quietly.

She shuddered, as if waking from a dream. 'Did what help?'

'The church.'

'A little.' Now that she was outside among the threatening crowds, her head spinning from the movement and the noise, the feeling of peace and contentment she had experienced inside the church seemed like a distant dream.

Nikolai navigated the crowd with ease. They parted before him as if they could recognise one of their own. Or was it his firm step and the way he didn't back away from them? The mob were like dogs, they could smell fear. His hand was on her elbow as he manoeuvred her through the human river. She felt warmth where his fingers touched her. Not looking at him, she tried as hard as she could to match his pace, often breaking into a run to keep up.

When the crowd quietened for a moment, she asked, 'What will happen to the tsar and his family now that he's abdicated?'

'Nicholas Romanov will live as a private citizen. He has requested a free passage to Tsarskoe Selo, where the family will stay until the children recover from measles. Afterwards, they will go elsewhere.'

'Where?'

'I don't know but I hope it's far from here.'

'Are they in danger?' She shivered, her wary eyes on the crowd. They seemed quieter than the day before, but she knew danger was always lurking under the surface. It was like sleeping on a barrel of gunpowder. All it took was one spark for the whole thing to explode.

'Not everyone is happy to have them so close. Some fear counter-revolution. So yes, if they stay here, they might be in danger.'

'Are we in danger?' she whispered, so softly, she didn't think he heard, and if she was honest with herself, she feared the answer.

'I will help you leave Petrograd. You will need permission to leave the country. I'm working on it.'

Surprised, she looked up. 'Where can we go? Nowhere in Russia is safe.'

'Go overseas. Italy, France. Anywhere you like.'

'When?'

'When things quieten down a little. It's too dangerous to travel right now. Have you heard what's happening on trains? What they are doing to people like you?'

She shook her head. She hadn't heard and she wasn't sure she wanted to.

'It will take me some time to get permissions for the two of you.'

To change the subject, she asked, pointing at the book in his hands, 'What are you reading?' They were walking across Anichkov Bridge, the Fontanka River a dark ribbon under their feet, flowing towards the Gulf of Finland, away from Petrograd in its strife, oblivious to the human drama unfolding all around it.

As they were about to step off the bridge onto Nevsky Avenue, he showed her the book. It was Chernyshevsky, *What Is to Be Done?* 'Chernyshevsky was a true visionary who predicted the events in Russia we are witnessing right now. Have you read it?'

'No, I haven't. Wasn't it banned under the tsarist government?'

'Read it. Let me know what you think.' He pushed the book to her. 'It's a shame Chernyshevsky didn't live to see the revolution. All his ideas, blossoming on the streets of Petrograd. This is a happy time for Russia. An unprecedented time.'

'You call it happy? Look at all the violence,' said Sophia. *Look at us, left with nothing,* she wanted to add but didn't because all around her, the boisterous crowd was cheering. They seemed elated with everything that was happening, just like the man walking by her side.

'For the common working man, this is indeed a happy time.'

'You think all those who died for no reason were a fair sacrifice to the revolution? All these people murdered on the streets last week alone. Kerensky just arrested Shcheglovitov, Protopopov, Shturmer, Goremykin, Makarov, Klimovich, Deitrikh. They are in Petropavlovskaya Fortress as we speak, and for what?'

'How many revolutionaries do you think have died at the hands of tsarist Russia? The difference is, our principles are worth dying for. Despite the murders, despite the violence, Russia is reborn. We are one step closer to the socialist utopia.'

'Doesn't utopia mean something unrealistic and unattainable? It might sound good in theory. But in reality, it will never work.'

Nikolai turned and looked at Sophia, his eyes twinkling with excitement. 'That's why we are here. To make sure it works. You can't possibly argue that the old regime was efficient. It was slavery, pure and simple. The imperial government waged war on its own people and now it's paying for it.'

'You are fighting for equality and quality of life for everyone. All admirable principles. And yet, look around you.'

'You can't overthrow the existing order without violence.

Revolution is an upheaval. It destroys everything in its path. The old doesn't give way to the new without a struggle. There is no peaceful resolution to the revolution. You can't overthrow the government without taking up weapons. You can't stand up to a cannon with a rock. As long as it's worth it, as long as the end justifies the means, we are on the right path.'

'See, that's where you and I differ. I don't think the end justifies the means.'

'Don't worry. The violent period is almost over. Now the real work begins.'

Although Sophia didn't agree with everything Nikolai said, she enjoyed hearing him talk. His face lit up. His voice changed. It was admirable to be so passionate about something, she thought. Dmitry wasn't passionate about anything other than his cigars and bridge with his friends. He had no strong beliefs. The plight of the working class didn't move him. She found it hard to believe the two men were related. Suddenly, she couldn't look at Nikolai anymore and stared instead at the ice floating downstream.

'Dmitry and I were always on the water growing up, swimming and rowing on the Fontanka in summer, ice skating and sledding in winter,' Nikolai was saying.

'Ice skating? Isn't it dangerous? How strong is the ice here?'

'Not strong at all but that was part of the excitement.'

'I can't imagine Dmitry doing something like that.' The man who was too afraid to leave his room because the revolution had come to his house.

'He didn't. When he was little, he stood on the sidelines and cried. When he was older, he often ran home and told our parents.'

'And what did they do?'

'To my mother's horror, our father sometimes joined us.'

'You had a happy childhood.'

'The best.'

'What went wrong? Why did you turn your back on our way of life?'

For a moment he watched the murky water of the river through the parapets, as if lost in thought. 'I suppose our way of life never made sense to me growing up. It didn't seem fair. We had an old servant, Ivan. He was like your Nanny. Always there for me. Always loyal. One day my uncle became convinced he was stealing. He beat the poor man to death. It broke my heart. To this day I hear his screams. And then it turned out it had been someone else all along. Ivan died for nothing. Even when I was ten, it seemed wrong to me that one person should have the power of life and death over another. That incident opened my eyes to a million injustices around us. I had to do something, even if it felt like I wasn't making any difference.'

'What did you do?'

'I started distributing Marxist leaflets among the students at my university. Then I organised a student strike against the government and its interference in the education system. When I got thrown out a month short of graduating, I told my family I wanted to live my life as a revolutionary. My father was furious. He said I would live it on no money because he was cutting me off. He had forbidden the rest of the family from contacting me or helping me financially.'

'How did you survive?'

'I made friends among the revolutionary circles in Europe. They helped me. I stayed with them, wrote for newspapers, delivered talks, brought forbidden literature into Russia, incited insurrections. Soon every gendarme in the country knew my face. I had to spend the last few years in Switzerland. When I heard about the revolution, I came back.'

As they crossed Nevsky Avenue, he asked her about herself. She thought of her own childhood, of hours of piano and violin, of reading and studying while her mother smiled at her with affection. Of crying for days in her bed, hidden away under her pillow, after she realised her mother wasn't coming back. 'I don't have any brothers or sisters, but I have a best friend who is like a sister to me. When I was a child, Papa would lock me in the room and force me to practise my music. Sometimes, Regina would bring a small gardening ladder to my window and help me escape. We would roam the city for hours, riding trams and eating chocolates. Then I would climb the ladder back and sit by the piano, like nothing happened.'

'Were you ever caught?'

'Never. Nanny knew, of course, but she would never say anything and get me in trouble. I think Mama knew too but she was too kind to punish me. She spent the last few years of her life in Kazan. I barely saw her. She died a week before my wedding.' She looked away from him, suddenly too sad to continue.

'You must miss her so much.'

'I do. All I had left of her was her portrait and her jewellery. Now those are gone too, and it breaks my heart.'

Sophia didn't even notice when they arrived back home, so absorbed was she in the conversation. Thanking Nikolai for helping her and saying goodbye, she ran up to her room and hid the book he had given her under her pillow. She knew Dmitry wouldn't approve.

*

Sophia spent the rest of the day helping Nanny, peeling potatoes, learning how to make dough for the cabbage pie and doing the laundry for the first time in her life. She wished it would be the last. After twenty minutes of rubbing soft fabric on the washboard, her arms and shoulders were sore. Her finger, where the knife had cut it, was throbbing. How did women do this for hours and then move on to other chores, day after day, without a minute to themselves and no light at the end of the tunnel? Was it any wonder they were marching on the streets, demanding justice?

After dinner, she sat in the salon, losing herself in Nikolai's book under the light of a kerosene lamp. That was what she loved about books. In minutes she could escape her life and be someplace else, in a different world, a different life. Except, Chernyshevsky's world was dark and foreboding. It was a world of misery and pain. It reminded her too much of what she now saw on the streets of Petrograd every day.

Sophia had always taken it for granted that everything had been done for her. Her clothes were laundered and appeared on her bed as if by magic, crisp and clean and smelling of morning sunshine. Her hair was dressed by a professional every morning. Her house sparkled without her having to lift a finger. Her food was prepared and her dishes were cleared. All she had to do was step out of her bedroom and into the dining hall, where the table was already set. She didn't have to bake the bread or catch the fish or cook the soup. Not once in the not-so-distant past had she thought about the people who were doing it all and what life was like for them.

Was Nikolai right? Was the overhaul of society as they knew it long overdue? And was she selfish for longing for the past to return, so *she* could continue living the life of luxury?

She lost all track of time and didn't even notice when the grandfather clock in the corner struck eleven. Only when she felt a hand on her shoulder did she look up from the book. Dmitry was standing behind her, glancing over her shoulder to see what she was reading. 'Sophochka, where have you been? I've been waiting for you to come to bed.'

With regret, she closed the book. She would have liked to read a little longer. 'I couldn't sleep, so I sat here for a bit, reading.'

He glanced at the cover. 'Chernyshevsky, *What Is to Be Done?* Where did you get this abhorrent thing?' He picked it up with two fingers and held it in the air, looking at it with disgust, like it was a bag of old rubbish, rotten and smelly.

For some reason, she didn't want him to know about her walk with Nikolai. If someone asked her why she didn't tell her husband the truth, she wouldn't be able to say. She hadn't done anything wrong. She needed help and Nikolai was there for her. And yet, for some unfathomable reason she wanted to keep it to herself. 'I found it around. One of the men must have left it.'

'I'm surprised the brutes can read. But I'm not surprised by what they are reading. Why would you find this interesting?'

She shrugged. 'It's no big deal. I'm trying to understand what's happening around us, that's all. It's good to see things from a different point of view.'

'Madness is happening around us. Reading about it won't help you understand it.'

'It's put things in perspective for me, made me realise how lucky we've been. We've led a sheltered life. We had everything we needed. We never went hungry, never knew hard labour. Not like the rest of the population. Under the tsar, peasants had no rights. Nor did the women. The working class was suffering. No wonder they are unhappy. Chernyshevsky captures it perfectly in his writing.'

Dmitry watched her like he didn't know who she was. 'I can't believe what I'm hearing. This book you speak of so highly is nothing but a manual for the revolutionary mob on how to destroy the old regime. It's a political treatise, radical propaganda at its best.'

'I think the author truly cares about the fate of the working people. He advocates for their rights to happiness and equality. He wants to change their lives for the better.'

'Chernyshevsky was sent to a labour camp by the tsarist regime. The only thing he advocates in his book is the demise of that regime. It's nothing but revenge for him. He goes one step further and offers a practical guide on how to achieve the things he's advocating. This book has brainwashed the barely literate proletariat. What we see today is exactly what he wanted – the shootings, the violence, the uprisings.'

'If you say so, dear.' She was in no mood to argue. It was late and she was tired.

'Chernyshevsky teaches his readers that to achieve their goal, anything goes. Anything is allowed. He advocates endless personal freedom. You can do what you want when you want and only then will you be happy. But it doesn't work like that in the real world. They think socialism will bring Paradise. To achieve this ideal, this utopia, they are ready to destroy what is natural, what has long been established, in the most violent of ways.'

'The old regime might be natural for *us* because it benefits us. But *they* might not think it's natural because it oppresses them.'

'I see this rubbish has brainwashed you too. You sound like Nikolai. I don't want you to read this anymore.' He placed the book under his arm and reached for her. 'Come, let's go to bed.'

'I would like to finish it, please, so I can form my own opinion. I am not a child.' Nikolai had trusted her with his book and she wasn't going to let Dmitry take it. She grabbed the book and pulled. For a moment, they were engaged in a tug-of-war.

When Dmitry realised she had no intention of giving up, he brought his candle close to the pages and they caught fire. 'No!' cried Sophia but it was too late. The book was engulfed in flames. She could feel the heat at the tips of her fingers. She let go and the book fell on her Persian carpet and continued to burn. 'Look what you've done! You've left a mark on the carpet.'

'A mark on the carpet hardly makes a difference when the whole house is being torn apart.' She didn't reply, looking with horror at the smouldering book. 'Don't be upset, my dear!' said Dmitry, putting his arm around her. 'That awful book is not worth crying over. I'll take you to your room. It's late.'

She allowed him to lead her away, turning around once and glancing with regret at what was left of Nikolai's book.

In her bedroom, she perched on the edge of her bed, wondering when Dmitry was leaving. She had no energy for small talk or pretence. But he looked like he had no intention of going anywhere. He sat next to her and pulled her close, loosening her hair, watching it fall around her face, kissing the tips of her fingers and the corner of her lips. 'You are so beautiful like this. With your hair down, you look so young. Just like on the day when we first met.'

'I didn't have my hair down when we first met.'

'I remember. I still see you in my mind, so nervous and afraid.'

'I wasn't nervous.'

'For the first week you barely said a word to me,' he whispered, his mouth on her neck.

His fingers played with her dress, ran over her hips and waist, while she sat still like a pillar, without movement, without feeling. Finally, when his hands became more insistent, she prised his fingers off her and moved slightly away. 'I'm tired, Dima. Let's talk tomorrow.'

His breathing was hot on her skin and his hands were fiddling with the buttons of her dress as he whispered sweet nothings to her, how much he loved her, how much he missed her. She knew it wasn't talking that he had in mind.

'Please, not tonight,' she said firmly, buttoning up her dress and standing up.

'What's the matter?' he asked. 'Are you still sad about earlier? Please, don't be. You know I didn't mean to upset you.'

'I just need to sleep. It's been a long day. I can't keep my eyes open. I'm sorry.'

He stood up. 'Of course, darling. Please, forgive me. I'm being selfish. You must be exhausted. Let me help you out of your dress.'

Finally, he left, but even without him there, she felt suffocated, as if heavy metal chains pressed on her chest. She could barely breathe and, as she lay in the dark, listening to the turmoil outside, listening for his footsteps, hoping he wouldn't come back, all she could think of was a quote from Chernyshevsky that had made an impression.

There is no happiness without freedom.

Chapter 4

Petrograd was never quiet, not during the day but especially not at night. It was a churning cauldron of discontent, at war with itself and the outside world. At war with Sophia and everything she loved. Lately she felt like she was a lone boat in the ocean, fragile and lost. Everywhere she turned, she saw conflict and felt more helpless than she had ever felt in her entire life. As she lay in her bed at night, out of the corner of her eye she would catch a glimpse of the fires devastating her city, their reflection visible under the curtains. She would hide under her pillow to escape but would still hear the terrifying murmur of the people.

One night, her stomach hurting from hunger, she walked to the kitchen for a warm glass of milk, leaving Dmitry sleeping peacefully in her bed. Warm milk with a spoonful of honey was her mother's favourite remedy for restless nights. *Here*, her mother would say. *This will make everything better*. If only it could make the revolution better, thought Sophia, opening the pantry doors.

The jar was empty.

'Looking for milk? There isn't any.' The voice came from behind her and made her jump.

She turned around and saw Nikolai at the kitchen table in the corner, a stack of documents in front of him. 'What are you doing here?'

'Reading. Working.'

'In the dark?'

'My candle burnt out. I've been sitting here thinking. What about you? Can't sleep?'

She nodded. 'Sometimes milk is the only thing that helps me. It's been days since we had any. Haven't seen any bread either. The stores aren't selling anything. Everyone is out on the streets celebrating the new order. No one is milking the cows or growing the wheat. Is that what it's going to be like from now on?'

'Eventually things will settle down. The farmers will go back to milking the cows. The bakers will bake the bread.'

'Someone once told me that our life is fake. That it's not real Russia. But if this is real Russia, it's not a pretty sight.'

'Would you like to see real Russia? Come with me tomorrow.' He grinned.

'Come with you where?'

'You'll see. Now, why don't you sit down and I'll make you a cup of tea? I think I still have some camomile left.'

She placed her kerosene lamp on the table and sat down opposite him, glancing at the papers he was working on. It looked like a speech addressed to the factory workers. She looked away. 'I've never had camomile tea before.'

'It's fantastic for sleepless nights.'

Nikolai boiled some water, poured it into a pot and added some flowers from a jar. 'Tell me, what did you think of the book?'

'I found it fascinating. And eye-opening.'

'I thought you might.'

'Chernyshevsky's principles are admirable. I just don't know if *this* …' she pointed outside, 'is the best way to go about achieving them.'

'Is there any other way? To create the new, to change the world order, we must destroy the old.'

'Yes, you have done a great job destroying. But who is going to rebuild?'

'If not us, then our children will reap the benefits of our revolution.'

'I didn't have a chance to finish it. Dmitry ...' She hesitated. 'He took it.' For some reason, she didn't want to tell Nikolai that Dmitry had burnt the book. She was ashamed of her husband's actions as if she was the one responsible.

'I can't imagine he would be happy with you reading something like that.'

She nodded. 'He doesn't really believe in the rights of working men.'

'One thing about Dmitry, he likes to get his own way. And when he doesn't ...' Nikolai fell quiet.

Suddenly, she felt better about everything. 'The two of you don't seem particularly close.'

'We are too different. Even growing up, we were complete opposites. Unlike Dmitry, I believed in the rights of working men too much.'

'I can see that.'

He poured her some tea. 'I have something for you. Wait here a moment.'

Once he was gone, she picked up her cup of tea and inhaled. It smelt of green fields and sun-filled days, of carefree summers of her childhood. She waited a few minutes for the tea to cool down and took a careful sip. The tea was weaker than she was used to but she liked the subtle taste in her mouth. Nikolai was right. It made her feel relaxed and a little drowsy.

She almost finished her tea by the time Nikolai returned. 'Close your eyes,' he said when he sat down next to her. He had the biggest smile on his face.

'You want me to close my eyes?'

'Yes. It's a surprise.'

She closed her eyes. He placed something in her hands that felt like rolled-up paper. With her eyes still closed, she asked, 'What is it? A newspaper? I've seen enough of those to last me a lifetime, thank you very much.'

'It's not a newspaper.'

'One of the articles you've written? Are you trying to convert me?'

'I'm not trying to convert you. If I did, you'd know about it.'

'Can I open my eyes now?'

'Not yet. Let me unwrap it for you first.'

His hands touching her hands, he removed the paper. With her fingertips she traced the rough surface of the object she was holding. It felt like brush strokes on canvas. It couldn't be … She opened her eyes and saw her mother's face. 'My mother's portrait,' she whispered and burst into tears.

'Why are you crying?' he exclaimed. 'If I knew it would make you cry, I wouldn't have given it to you.'

She was unable to speak for a moment, stroking her mother's lips, her face, her blonde curls. 'I never thought I'd see it again. Where did you get it?'

'I traced it to the art dealer who had purchased it and bought it back. I couldn't get the frame but at least I could get the painting. I know how much it means to you.'

'Everything,' she whispered. 'It means everything to me.' She pressed his hand. 'How can I ever thank you?'

'No thanks are necessary. Seeing the expression on your face is enough.'

Taken aback, she watched him as he said goodnight, collected his papers and left. Back in her room, she unrolled the precious painting and pressed her cheek to her mother's face. Once, before her mother's passions had torn their family apart, they had been so happy. Sophia didn't think she had been happy since. Before the revolution, she had thought she had all the time in the world

64

to find happiness. Not anymore. But having her mother's portrait felt like a little bit of her old life was back.

*

It was the evening of the sixteenth of April and almost dark outside, if it wasn't for the fires smouldering all over her city, the smoke making it hard for her to breathe, their glare scaring her. Having waited for Dmitry to fall asleep, Sophia snuck out of the house and was now walking next to Nikolai through the madness of Petrograd, hearing nothing but the sound of stomping feet and a steady hum of the crowd, with the occasional 'Hurrah!' shouted triumphantly and picked up by a hundred voices. Thousands of soldiers were marching past, waving red flags and placards with angry red writing. Trembling in the wind, the signs read, 'Long live the assembly!', 'Long live the freedom!', 'Long live our heroic army!' In front of the soldiers were officers on horseback. They carried no flags or placards, but their backs were straight and their faces triumphant. The band played the Marseillaise, as if they were in Paris parading in front of the Emperor Napoleon.

Twisted faces, enthusiastic mouths, hysterical laughter – women, children, soldiers and students, and suddenly Sophia felt overwhelmed by it all, wishing she was back in the relative peace of her room. She was terrified by this bacchanalian celebration of the collapse of life as she knew it. But when she glanced at Nikolai's face, which she didn't do often because for some reason looking at him made her short of breath and light-headed, she saw excitement and pride. His face was that of a man who looked at his creation and liked what he saw. His was the satisfied face of someone who had toiled long and hard at the masterpiece of his life and finally observed it in action.

It was overcast and the skies were gloomy, unlike the people around them, who were loud and excited. When the noise quietened for a moment, she asked, 'Are we safe here in the crowd?'

'When you are with me, you don't have to worry about anything,' replied Nikolai.

How could she not worry when everywhere she looked, she saw rifles and machine guns pointing at her and Nikolai? 'Where are you taking me? Are you going to tell me?'

'Why don't you wait five minutes and then you will know.'

'I don't like surprises. I'd rather know now. Is it somewhere I will like?'

'If it's not, will you turn around and go back home, leaving me alone in the crowd?'

They crossed the Neva, finally reaching the magnificent Kschessinska mansion with its narrow windows and snow-white marble walls. It seemed like all of Petrograd was here, waiting for something. Miraculously, the two of them managed to push their way to the front and Sophia watched as an unassuming balding man with a beard dressed in an ill-fitting suit stepped out onto the balcony, where he was welcomed by the soldiers, sailors and civilians.

'Who is this man?' she asked.

'Vladimir Lenin.'

'I thought he was still in Switzerland.'

'He was until a few days ago. Now he's here, where the action is.'

The founder of the Bolshevik party stood on the balcony of the palace that had belonged to the famous imperial ballet star Mathilde Kschessinska and raised his hat in the air. Instantly, the expectant crowd fell quiet as if he were a puppet master pulling strings that controlled them all. He was quiet for a few moments himself, as if gathering his thoughts, and then he spoke. Suddenly, there was nothing unassuming or average or small about him. He became larger than life, presiding over the crowd from the balcony, his electrifying energy, his incredible presence commanding everyone's attention. He was a force of nature, a tornado on that platform and just like everybody else, Sophia couldn't take her eyes off him.

Everyone expected the Bolshevik leader to praise the revolution. They were smug in what they had achieved. Surely Lenin would see how much they had gone through and would thank them for their trouble. But to everyone's astonishment, he did no such thing. He was red in the face as he condemned everything that had been done. As the crowd listened in mute disbelief, he called for further action, for another revolution. 'The capitalists, in whose hands the state power now rests, desire a parliamentary bourgeois republic, that is, a state system where there is no tsar but where power remains in the hands of the capitalists who govern the country by means of the old institutions, namely the police, the bureaucracy and the standing army. We desire a different republic, one more in keeping with the interests of the people, more democratic. The workers of all the world look with pride and hope to the revolutionary workers and soldiers of Russia as the vanguard of the world's liberating army of the working class. The revolution, once begun, must be strengthened and carried on. We shall not allow the police to be re-established! All power in the state, from the bottom up, from the remotest little village to every street block of Petrograd, must belong to the Soviets of Workers', Soldiers', Agricultural Labourers', Peasants' and other Deputies. The central state power uniting these local Soviets must be the Constituent Assembly, National Assembly or Council of Soviets – no matter what name you call it. Not the police, not the bureaucracy, who are unanswerable to the people and placed above the people, not the standing army, separated from the people, but the people themselves, universally armed and united in the Soviets, must run the state. It is they who will establish the necessary order, it is they whose authority will not only be obeyed but also respected, by the workers and peasants.'

Not a branch moved in the air, not a leaf. It was as if Petrograd itself was stunned into silence as the Bolshevik leader paced excitedly on the balcony.

'The land must not belong to the landowners. The peasant

67

committees must take the land away at once from the landowners. All of it must belong to the whole nation, and its disposal must be the concern of the local Soviets of Peasants' Deputies. Do not let the state power or the administration of the state pass into the hands of the bureaucracy, who are non-elective, and paid on a bourgeois scale; get together, unite, organise yourselves, trust no one, depend only on your own intelligence and experience – and Russia will be able to move with a firm, measured, unerring tread toward the liberation of both our own country and of all humanity from the yoke of capital as well as from the horrors of war.'

Lenin had achieved the impossible. He had rendered all of Petrograd speechless for a moment. And then all hell broke loose as men and women shouted, some with joy, others with discontent. The crowd trembled and flowed towards the palace, as if to carry the Bolshevik leader away. As Lenin was whisked to safety, the cries of *excellent, well said, madman, raving lunatic* followed him.

On the way back home, as they walked past manicured parks adjacent to the palace, now littered with vodka bottles and cigarette butts, a drunken man pushed Sophia too hard and she almost fell. Nikolai grabbed her by the elbow, helping her up. He didn't let go as he guided her through the crowd, staying close as if to protect her. 'Why did you bring me here?' she asked.

'I wanted you to feel for yourself the tremendous energy of the crowd. I wanted you to understand what new Russia is all about.'

'Thank you. I think I understand it perfectly well.' She rubbed her shoulder where the drunkard had rammed into her.

'What did you think of Lenin? Incredible, wasn't he?'

'Unbelievable! He could have been saying anything and he'd still have everyone enthralled. I think I forgot to breathe while he was talking.'

'The man has been an inspiration to me for many years.'

'I heard his brother was hanged by the tsarist government many

68

years ago. No wonder he's so passionate about the revolution. He wants to overthrow the old regime and avenge his brother,' she said, acutely aware of Nikolai's hand on her elbow.

'I think it's more than that. He's passionate because he truly believes.'

'But the things he proposes! It almost sounds like another revolution.'

'Don't you think one is necessary?'

Looking at the chaos around her, she couldn't agree more. Seeing Nikolai so excited, she didn't want to admit that watching Vladimir Lenin had scared her. Instead of consolidating the gains of the revolution, he called for more chaos and upheaval. As if Petrograd hadn't had enough. To take her mind off it, she said, 'I understand what Lenin does. He gives speeches and incites insurrections. What is it that you do?'

'Just like Lenin, I give speeches and incite insurrections. Earlier this morning I spoke to the workers at the Putilov plant.'

'I wish you'd taken me to that. I'd love to see you speak.'

'You don't want to go there. The men can get rowdy.'

'More rowdy than here?'

'Much more. Not everyone is happy with the Provisional Government. The tensions are rising. There are talks of more conflict. We are trying to calm the tempers and advocate for peaceful demonstrations instead.'

'Is it working?'

'For now.'

Nikolai made sure she was safely inside before saying goodbye and walking away. He had somewhere to be, he said. Perhaps he had more insurrections to incite and more speeches to deliver. She watched from the window of the dance hall as he crossed the road, then turned around and waved. Her heart racing, she waved back.

At breakfast the next morning, she wanted to tell Dmitry about the man who proposed another revolution and how he kept thousands of people mesmerised just by the sound of his voice. But if she told him, she would have to admit she went to see Lenin with Nikolai. And she didn't want to do that.

As she sat down at the table, Dmitry looked up from his newspaper. 'Did you go out last night? I went looking for you and you weren't there.'

'I went to church. I listened to the service. It made me feel better.' She didn't raise her eyes as she said it. She wasn't used to lying. If she glanced his way, he would read the truth in her face.

'Did anyone go with you?'

'No, I went by myself.' Still not looking at him.

His eyes narrowed. 'Why are you lying to me?' he demanded.

'I'm not lying,' she murmured, paling. 'What makes you think I'm lying?'

'I saw you return with Nikolai.'

'I ran into him on the way back. The crowds scared me, so he walked me home.'

Dmitry seemed satisfied with that. His face relaxed and he took her hand. 'I told you it's dangerous. Promise me you won't leave the house again. You have no idea what it's like out there.'

'I promise,' she whispered.

*

A few days later, Lenin's *April Theses* were published, declaring the war predatory and imperialistic, demanding no support for the Provisional Government and for the power to be shifted to the working people, stating that the control over production and distribution must be given to the workers and the banks must be consolidated into one national bank. Not everyone was pleased with Lenin's solution. Even the Bolsheviks were shocked into silence, so radical were the changes proposed by their leader. The Mensheviks were roaring in anger. And so was Dmitry.

'Do you even hear what he's suggesting? The abolition of the army, police, bureaucracy. What lunacy!' he exclaimed at dinner one evening.

Nikolai, who was at the kitchen table writing something in his notebook, lifted his head and said, 'You don't agree with what he's saying? But the liberal bourgeoisie played no role in the revolution. It was initiated and led by the working class. The power should be placed in the hands of the proletariat. The people, not the bourgeoise, should benefit from the revolution.'

'It's primitive anarchism. Lenin is a madman, a fanatic, a danger to Russia. And he surrounds himself with madmen like him, who are trying to throw this country into chaos. What he is proposing will lead to nothing but trouble. It's catastrophic for Russia. It will end in civil war.'

'What he's proposing is a complete overhaul of society as we know it. It goes against everything we know and so you are naturally opposed to it.'

'Exactly. The country is not ready. Perhaps he's been in exile too long and has lost touch with reality. He doesn't know what's going on. He doesn't know our people. The proletariat is not the majority in Russia. How can it assume and hold the power?'

'What do you think, Sophia?' asked Nikolai. 'Can the proletariat hold the power?' He smiled. She blushed.

'Why are you talking to her about politics?' demanded Dmitry. 'What does she know? She's a woman. All she cares about is fashion and embroidery.'

Hurt, Sophia turned away from him.

'I think you underestimate your wife,' said Nikolai.

Quietly she said, 'Lenin makes a good point. Whatever the Provisional Government is doing is not enough. People are unhappy. There is discontent on the streets of Petrograd.'

'Absolutely,' said Nikolai. 'The second stage of the revolution is not only necessary, it's unavoidable. We need to take steps towards socialism and the Marxist revolution. And that's what the Provisional Government will soon learn. Mark my words.

This madman you speak of so derisively is going to change the direction of the revolution.'

*

One morning a week later, Sophia played her violin, doing her best to ignore the noise from outside. She had become good at it – ignoring the noise. She held the violin lovingly, while the sounds of Mozart and Tchaikovsky, of Bach and Beethoven filled the room, making her heart ache, taking her back in time to when she was a little girl, playing her violin for hours until her wrist was sore. She only ever played for herself, never in public, because the music exposed her soul and let everyone read what was in her heart. And she didn't want to bare her soul in front of strangers.

For the first time in her life, the music failed to bring her comfort. She put the violin away and reached for a book. Just before midday, Nanny came to enquire if she wanted some lunch. 'What are you reading?' she asked.

'Not reading. Just staring at pages. Don't seem to be able to concentrate.' She showed her book to Nanny.

'You know I can't read, dear. Especially not in French.'

'It's *The Queen's Necklace* by Dumas. About Marie Antoinette. It takes place nine years before the French Revolution, when she's still unaware of what's in store for her. She has no idea of the impending collapse of life as she knows it, of violent deaths of all her friends and supporters, of imprisonment and execution. On these pages, she is still carefree, frivolous and happy. But not for long.'

'Why don't you read something cheerful? Something to make you laugh.'

'Don't feel like laughing these days.'

'You know what they say. Laughter is the best medicine. Besides, I have something that will cheer you up. Look in the pantry.'

On the otherwise empty shelves, Sophia found a large jar of milk. Next to it was a cup of camomile flowers. Underneath the cup was a note. *For Sophia. If you ever feel sleepless again.* Smiling, she placed the note in the bodice of her dress, picked up the cup and smelt the camomile flowers.

'A secret admirer?' asked Nanny, watching her.

'Of course not,' muttered Sophia, trying – and failing – to stop smiling.

By the look on Nanny's face, Sophia knew she didn't believe her. But she didn't say anything. 'I went to the market today, thinking of buying a chicken.'

'No one sells fresh meat anymore,' said Sophia.

'I was thinking of a live chicken.'

'A live chicken? What would we do with it? What would we feed it?'

'They eat worms and seeds and grain. Anything really. If we had a chicken, we could have fresh eggs for breakfast every day. Imagine that.'

The thought of a real chicken in the house amused Sophia. There were chickens and ducks and even goats at her grandmother's estate in Kazan. When Sophia visited, she had fresh milk every day, straight from the goat, warm, creamy and delicious. The cook prepared fresh omelettes for her every morning. Sometimes she made Sophia's favourite blinis, mixing milk, eggs and some flour. Sophia often thought of those days with longing. If only she could travel back in time, to the carefree days of her early childhood, when she was never hungry or afraid. 'Maybe we *should* get a chicken,' she said. 'Did you find one?'

'I found one. But they wanted me to pay as much as a cow would have cost back in March. I didn't have enough money, so I left. Back in the old days …' Nanny fell quiet, her eyes misty.

'The old days are gone,' said Sophia. 'Forever, it seems.'

'I was going to tell them they were out of their mind, asking for a small fortune for a chicken. But a fire broke out and the women ran off to see what was happening.'

'A fire at the market?'

'At *Pravda* headquarters. They tried to put it out but couldn't. It spread to the nearby houses. Poor people trapped there! I saw them jumping out the windows. They are not even trying to get anybody out. It's too dangerous. Are you all right, dear? You've gone awfully pale.'

'Nikolai mentioned he was going to *Pravda* this morning to hand in the article he's been working on.' *Pravda* was a Bolshevik newspaper Nikolai contributed to sometimes. Sophia jumped to her feet, almost knocking her chair over.

'Where are you going?' cried Nanny. But Sophia didn't reply, rushing down the corridor and through the front door. Thankfully, the corridor was deserted and no one tried to stop her.

Although the trams were running again, they were filled with shouting, drinking, spitting and weapon-wielding revolutionary masses. Sophia hadn't had the courage to board one – until now. This time she jumped in and paid the fare without a second thought. She was the only woman on the tram and there were no seats available. No one offered her one like they would under the tsar. It seemed there were no gentlemen during the revolution.

She willed the tram to move faster but it crawled through the streets of Petrograd like an overexcited, extremely loud snail. She thought of jumping off and walking but the streets were flooded with people. There was no order in the city, no one to tell its inhabitants what to do or how to do it, and so everyone did what they liked. No one wanted to work, so they didn't. Most of the shops remained shut and the factories operated at minimum capacity. No one wanted to fight in the war that, as far as they were concerned, wasn't going anywhere, so they didn't, deserting by the tens of thousands and marching on the streets, drunk and belligerent. It was anarchy, just like Dmitry had predicted.

What did Nikolai see in the revolution that made him so enamoured with it? Did he see past the façade to some secret meaning she couldn't fathom? Her face flushed at the thought of Nikolai. Would she be able to find him? And would she find him alive?

Trembling, she stood on the tram, pressed against other bodies, trying not to inhale their odour or listen to their drunken conversations. 'Faster,' she whispered, drumming the seconds out on her hip. She would have paced if there was space. 'Please, God, faster.'

She could smell the fire before she could see it. And when the tram turned the corner and stopped outside the *Pravda* building, her hand flew to her mouth and for a few moments she remained motionless. Only when the tram started moving again did she cry out to the driver to wait. The tram screeched to a stop and she jumped off, almost falling when her feet touched the ground. Regaining her balance, her hand on her beating heart, she crossed the street to where a large crowd had gathered, gawking at the inferno. Nearby houses had been destroyed completely and the fire had stopped. But the giant flames slithering up the walls of the *Pravda* building, roaring like a wild beast, didn't show any signs of abating.

The fire seemed to render everyone speechless, not just her. While the nearby streets were noisy and boisterous, the crowd around the headquarters was quiet, almost mournful. Other than a few boys with buckets, no one attempted to put the fire out. Throwing buckets of water against a wall of flames was like sending one man with rocks against a squadron of tanks. It made no impact and soon even the most eager of the boys stood back, their faces to the burning building, their mouths agape. Where were the firefighters with their pumps and ladders and barrels? Sophia couldn't help but think that under the tsar the fire would have been conquered a long time ago.

Silent like the rest of the people around her, Sophia watched, unsure what to do.

'What about those trapped inside? Is anyone rescuing them?' she asked finally.

'Have you seen the state of the place? No one is going in there until the fire burns out,' replied a bearded man with his arm in a sling.

'By then it will be too late,' she whispered, her voice cracking.

Fighting tears, she walked around the perimeter of the building, averting her eyes from the deathly flames. If only she could close her ears just as easily to the deafening sound of the inferno as it swallowed walls and banisters. If only she could ignore the heat that hit her face like a wave.

Soon she came to the back exit and saw that some people had in fact been evacuated from the fire. A man with burns on his face and hands was unconscious on a blanket on the grass, while half a dozen others crouched on the ground in silence, their desolate eyes on the building that had once housed the Bolshevik newspaper. Three young women dressed as nurses tended to the pitiful gang, bringing them water, bandaging the burns on their arms and legs and talking soothingly, like they would to children. Their uniforms were charred, as if they had singlehandedly battled the flames to get the men to safety. Sophia suspected the nurses had come from the nearby Winter Palace hospital. She approached one of them. 'Is there anyone left inside the building?'

The nurse was busy and barely glanced at Sophia. A distinguished-looking man in his late forties or early fifties, whose smart suit had been slightly burnt, replied, 'So many people are still in there, dear. Who are you looking for?'

'Nikolai Orlov. He was delivering his new article for tomorrow's edition. He …'

'I know him well. He was with the editor just before the fire started.'

'So he was here?' whispered Sophia.

'I'm sorry, dear,' replied the man. 'Your sweetheart, was it? It's the cursed Mensheviks. They think they can stop Lenin's changes by burning the newspaper that supports him. Well, they are in for a big surprise …'

But Sophia was no longer listening. The smoke and the tears

blinding her, she dashed towards the entrance to the building and through the gap in the wall that had once served as the door. The flames breathed putrid heat in her face.

Nikolai was family. He was her husband's brother. The man who had saved their lives, who protected them every day, who talked to her like she mattered, who bought her mother's portrait just to see a smile on her face could not have died in the fire. She refused to believe it. And she couldn't sit back and do nothing.

Up the smouldering stairs she ran until she couldn't go any further. She stopped helplessly, looking up, barely able to breathe. The smoke made her choke but still she didn't turn back. Suddenly everything went dark and she would have collapsed if a strong pair of arms didn't grab her.

When she came to, it was Nikolai's face that she saw first. He was looking down at her with concern and she thought she was dreaming. Groaning, she closed her eyes. But then she heard his voice. 'Sophia, can you hear me?'

Moaning softly, rubbing her eyes, she sat up and looked around. She was on a blanket on the ground behind the *Pravda* building next to the other injured people. There was a wet cloth on her forehead. In front of her was Nikolai. She blinked. She could hardly believe her eyes.

He leaned over her. 'You are awake, good. How are you feeling? Any dizziness? Shortness of breath?'

She shook her head, watching him with amazement.

He handed her a jug of water. 'Have a drink. I will finish here and then I'll take you home. Maybe then you can explain to me what you were doing, running into the burning building like rabid dogs were at your heels.'

One of the nurses approached them. 'Doctor, we need you. They brought one more person out of the fire.'

'Doctor?' whispered Sophia.

He pressed her hand gently. 'Stay here and get some rest. I'll be right back.'

She watched him walk up to a man on a stretcher, bend down to him, whisper something, check his pulse, ask the nurses for cold water and some linen. The man was badly burnt, his limbs oozing, the skin on his face blistered and red. But Sophia had seen worse. After all, there was a war on, and she had volunteered at one of the busiest hospitals in Petrograd.

Nikolai checked the man's breathing and applied a cold-water compress to the burnt flesh. His hands moved swiftly, as if he had done it a thousand times before. When he returned, Sophia was sitting up on the blanket, no longer dizzy or disoriented. 'I thought you were a revolutionary. I didn't realise you were a doctor.'

'Why can't I be both?'

'Where did you learn how to do that?'

'I attended medical school and then got thrown out a month before I finished my degree. I suppose I picked up a thing or two.'

She didn't even try to keep the admiration from her voice. 'You are a *doctor*. I had no idea.'

'Almost a doctor. I didn't actually graduate. But I don't think these men care about diplomas.'

Nikolai was a whirlwind of activity, attending to a dozen men, two of them unconscious, three with severe burns, others with surface burns. Sophia volunteered to help but she could barely keep up with him. Two hours later, she was out of breath. Her arms ached from carrying heavy buckets of water, her eyes watered from the smoke, her back hurt from bending over the patients, applying dressings and checking pulses. In the evening, the building was no longer burning but smouldering. And still it was too dangerous to go inside. The wind came down strong from the Neva and the temperature dropped. Even in April, with summer just around the corner, the Petrograd air was icy cold.

'We can't leave them here, in the street,' said Nikolai when it got dark. With his cap askew and his suit rumpled, he looked just like Sophia felt – exhausted. 'We need to take them some-where safe.'

'Let's take them home. We have plenty of space. They will be comfortable there.'

'Are you sure?'

'Positive.'

'Will Dmitry be all right with it?'

'Perhaps not. But we won't ask for his permission.'

Nikolai found a horse-driven cart and with the help of a couple of men from the crowd, they lifted five badly injured men and placed them inside. The men groaned but didn't regain consciousness. As the horse started and they peeled away from the kerb, Sophia watched the dancing flames reflected in Nikolai's face. He held the reins firmly, directing the horse through the busy streets with great skill, as if he was born to it. But when they turned the corner, they were trapped in the crowd and could no longer move forward. 'Go back where you came from,' chanted the people, shaking their fists in the air at an invisible enemy.

'Who are they shouting about?' asked Sophia, shivering. The streetlamps were illuminating angry faces and gaping mouths.

'Lenin. They want him to go back to Switzerland and leave Russia alone to go on as she has been. But they are too late. He is here to stay.'

Sophia had to agree – going on as Russia had been sounded like a terrible idea. Would Lenin bring relief to the country that seemed on the brink of a catastrophe? She soon forgot all about Lenin, however, because the screaming crowd was closing in on them, threatening to overturn the cart. She moved closer to Nikolai and closed her eyes in fear. His arm went around her.

As the cart was lifted in the air and the horse neighed in panic, she heard a volley of machine-gun fire. Opening her eyes, she saw two riders trampling the unfortunates that were in their path, shooting in the air. 'Get down,' shouted Nikolai, throwing her next to the wounded and covering her body with his. Instantly, the crowd's anger turned into terror. Women were screaming, while men ran for their lives. A few minutes later, as if by magic, the road before them cleared.

Nikolai seemed to regain his composure, while Sophia was mute with horror, gulping for air. He went back to his seat and she sat up carefully, rubbing her aching temples. Slowly, they proceeded through the quietened streets.

'For all its bravado, the mob are cowards. Look how quickly they disappeared,' said Nikolai.

'Can you blame them?' she asked, her voice hoarse, as if she was coming down with a cold.

'You never answered my question,' said Nikolai calmly, his eyes on the road, as if mere moments ago they didn't fear for their lives. 'What were you doing inside the burning building?'

She looked away, towards the red flags flapping in the wind and the Neva rushing past. He was her husband's brother. She couldn't tell him the truth. But at the same time, she was too tired to pretend, to think of a suitable lie. 'Looking for you. I heard about the fire. I didn't know if you were all right.'

His eyes warmed. He dropped the reins and looked at her. The horse stopped in the middle of the road. 'You came here for me? How did you even get here?'

'I took a tram.'

'You took a tram to find me?' He smiled. 'Thank you. But you shouldn't have. It's dangerous in the city.'

'No, thank *you*. For saving me in that building. And I thought you said the violence was behind us?'

'Clearly, I was wrong.'

A silent house greeted them. While Nikolai attended to the wounded and carried them inside with the help of his men, Sophia found Nanny in the kitchen. Her eyes were red like she'd been crying, an untouched pile of dirty dishes was in front of her and a scarf she was knitting lay forgotten in her lap. When she saw Sophia, she jumped to her feet and the knitting flew to the floor. As fast as she could she ran to her, pulling her into a hug. 'You are alive,' she cried. 'Thank God! It's madness outside.

We thought … We were so worried …'

'I'm fine, Nanny,' said Sophia, patting her back. 'Everything is fine.'

'You've been gone all day. We thought you'd been killed.'

'We were helping the injured. Did you know Nikolai was a doctor?' She tried and failed to keep pride from her voice, as if Nikolai's achievements had something to do with her. 'The state of that building … I'm afraid to think how many people have died.'

Nanny watched her as if waiting for explanation. A few moments passed. She said, 'What are you thinking, my dear? What is on your mind?'

'Nothing, Nanny. I'm just glad to be back home. I'm sorry I made you worry.'

'I've known you your whole life. You might be able to fool your husband, but you can't fool me.'

'I don't know what you are talking about.'

'Your face lights up every time Nikolai comes into the room. When he's around, you are not yourself. Your eyes follow him wherever he goes. But when he looks at you, you can't look at him.' Sophia opened her mouth to argue but Nanny interrupted. 'What I want to know is, what is it that you are hoping for?'

'Nothing, Nanny. You are imagining it.' Sophia sank into a chair.

'Nonsense. You need to pull yourself together, for your husband. Stop this nonsense immediately. Because if you don't, there will be pain for everyone. Heartbreak for everyone. Dmitry. Nikolai. But most of all, you. Remember who he is. And who you are. What you need is a child to distract you. You've been married for five years now. You should have conceived by now.'

'I don't know what you are talking about.' Suddenly she wanted the day to be over. She was too tired to pretend.

'You young people are all the same. You think us older folk are stupid. Love blinds you. Stay away from love if you know what's good for you. I saw what happened to your parents, both dying from broken hearts because she couldn't love him and he couldn't stop loving her. The last thing I want is the same happening to you. Your husband is a good man at heart. Everything you are looking for is right here, with him. What more could you possibly want?'

'I adore my husband. You know I do.'

Sophia closed her eyes and thought of Nikolai. When he had helped her up into the cart, he held her hand and glanced into her eyes for a second too long. And when they were seated side by side, the reins in his hands, the injured behind them, he told her she was a great nurse because she was caring, compassionate and kind. Beautiful not just on the outside but on the inside too.

Dmitry doesn't want me to be a nurse, she had said to him. *He thinks I'm wasting my time.*

Dmitry is blind, he'd replied. *He'll never understand the satisfaction of helping people, of making someone's world a better place. He's not like you.*

He's not like you, either, she'd said to him, blushing, no longer able to look at him as the Petrograd sun set behind them, igniting the Neva.

'Where is Dmitry?' she asked, blinking the memory away.

'He went out hours ago looking for you. We heard the commotion outside, the gunshots, the machine guns, people shouting. We didn't know what to think.'

Sophia thought of the enraged crowd, of the men on horseback brandishing machine guns, of Dmitry walking the streets by himself, searching for her. The man who never left his rooms stepped into the eye of the storm out of love for her. In the havoc of Petrograd streets, anything could happen. The mob could smell nobility a mile away. Her heart skipped with fear for her husband. 'Dmitry shouldn't have gone out. I'll find Nikolai. We'll go and look for him.'

'Don't you dare set foot outside this house. Now that you're back safely, you think I'll let you go anywhere? Dmitry is not you. He is cautious and smart. He'll be fine.'

Sophia kissed Nanny's cheek. 'You don't think I'm smart?'

'You're certainly not cautious.'

'I'll be safe with Nikolai. But Dmitry won't be safe out there on his own. We have to find him.'

'He could be anywhere. You have no idea where to look, so don't even think about it.'

Sophia knew Nanny was right. Going out now would not help Dmitry. It would just put her – and Nikolai – in danger. But Sophia couldn't shake a feeling of dread, a sinking sensation in the pit of her stomach. Dmitry didn't have Nikolai by his side, protecting him. Would he make it back alive?

*

Sophia spent the next hour by the window, watching the fires outside, hoping to see Dmitry's familiar silhouette approaching the front gate. Finally, she decided there was no point in idle waiting. It wasn't doing anyone any good. She would be better off helping Nikolai. At the very least, it would take her mind off her fears.

With the help of Nikolai's men, they were able to transform the dining hall into a makeshift hospital, making five beds out of wood and straw. Once the men were settled, they brought in a table for the medical supplies. Sophia fetched water, boiled bandages and watched Nikolai, admiring his easy smile and manner with his patients. She didn't even notice when the clock struck midnight. Side by side, Sophia and Nikolai sat at the head of one of the beds, exhausted, their eyes on their unconscious patient.

'Your revolution isn't that great if the revolutionaries are turning against each other, trying to kill one another,' said Sophia softly.

'Remember what Lenin said? There is only one way of smashing the resistance of the bourgeoisie, and that is to find, in the society which surrounds us, the forces which can sweep away the old and create the new, and to enlighten and organise themselves for the struggle. Do you see? Struggle, sweeping away, smashing. Violence. The French went through it. Now, it's our turn.'

'The French went through decades of revolutionary wars. Are you saying we have decades of this still ahead of us?'

'That's nothing in the grand scheme of things. It's a fair price to pay for the future generations to see our dreams realised.'

Were decades of unrest a fair price to pay for some faraway and unattainable happiness? She didn't know the answer to that question. She suspected Nikolai didn't either. She looked away from him and placed her hand on an injured man's forehead. 'He's burning up. Do we have anything for the fever?'

'We don't but we will tomorrow. I will bring some quinine and opium for the pain. Their burns are quite severe. For now, we'll continue wrapping them in cool cloth. Hopefully, it will bring the temperature down.'

'What made you want to become a doctor?'

'The same thing that made me want to become a revolutionary, I suppose. I wanted to help people.'

'And you do it remarkably well. Without you, those men would have died.'

'I'm only doing what any doctor would have done in my place. When I was little, my mother always looked for ways to help the peasants. She took their hardships very close to heart. There was no doctor in the village, so she learnt how to heal from books. She made ointments for wounds and collected herbs. Everyone within a hundred-mile radius knew her and came to her with their illnesses. And I was always by her side, helping.'

'She sounds very kind.'

'She was. We were so close, Mama and I. Whenever someone asked me what I wanted to be when I grew up, I told them I wanted to be like Mama. I never wanted to follow in my father's footsteps and become a lawyer. The only future I saw was in the struggle to improve the lot of people. Papa didn't approve, of course. He always told me I should be more like Dmitry.'

84

'Did your mama approve?'

'I'm sure she would have, had she lived long enough. She passed away just before I started university.'

They had that in common, losing their mother at an early age. She wanted to take Nikolai's hand and squeeze it with affection. She wanted to touch his face but didn't dare.

'You should get some sleep,' he said. 'It's late. I'll stay with the men.'

Although she could barely keep her eyes open, Sophia wanted to talk some more, to ask him if he thought of his mother the way she did, every time she felt weak or afraid or in need of advice. She wanted to ask him if it felt like his mother was still with him and whether his heart still ached, all these years later, just like hers. Suddenly, she heard the front door burst open and Dmitry calling her name. Saying goodnight to Nikolai, she rushed to see her husband.

Dmitry stood in the corridor, holding a candle. For a moment he watched her in silence.

She ran to his side, putting her arms around him, hardly able to breathe with relief. Here he was, safe and alive. As he hugged her back, she swore to herself to never put him in danger again. 'I'm so glad you're back. I was so worried.'

He looked dirty and pale and happy to see her. 'You were worried? What about me? I was going out of my mind. When you didn't come home, I thought something terrible happened.'

'I'm fine. Nothing terrible happened. You shouldn't have gone out there.'

He pulled away and looked at her sternly, like she was a naughty child he disapproved of. 'You left me no choice. Where have you been?'

'There was a fire nearby. They needed nurses to help.'

'Why would you risk your life to help those people? And put me through this nightmare. You were gone all day. I thought I lost you.'

'I'm a nurse. This is what I do. We brought five wounded men home with us. They are in the dining hall.'

'Who is we?'

With a great effort she stopped her voice from trembling. 'Nikolai and I.'

'This is our home, not a hospital.'

'You're wrong. It's no longer our home.'

He took her hand and brought it to his lips. She felt his hot breath on her skin. His hands were shaking. 'You know what I saw outside? A dozen revolutionaries were beating a gendarme. They tried to force him to go on all fours and bark like a dog. When he refused, they shot him. This is the kind of people we are dealing with. Insane, unpredictable, idiotic. Do you understand why I was worried about you, out there all by yourself?'

'I understand.'

'You can't even imagine what I went through. I walked the streets like a madman, with people shouting and fighting, gunshots popping, and I didn't know what to do or where to turn. I didn't know if I would ever see you again.'

'I'm sorry I made you worry. It won't happen again.'

'I love you, Sophia. Don't ever put yourself in danger like this. You didn't even tell me you were going out.'

'Would you have come with me if I told you?'

'No, but I would have tried to stop you.'

'That's exactly why I didn't tell you.'

'I honestly don't know what has come over you. You get these ideas into your head sometimes. Just like my brother. You think you can save the world. But who is going to save you when you are in trouble? You will make me go grey before my time and lose my hair like my father and then you won't love me anymore.'

'I'm sorry,' she whispered, stroking his thick dark hair. 'For everything.'

Chapter 5

May 1917

All of a sudden, there was meaning to Sophia's life. No more waking up late and spending hours in bed. No more thinking longingly of the past to avoid thinking of the future, while playing her violin until her wrist felt numb.

'Where are you going so early? Stay in bed,' muttered Dmitry, yawning. It was barely five o'clock.

'I'll be back soon. Sleep.'

'I don't want to sleep without you. I want you with me.'

He pulled her to him. Gently she shook him off and stepped towards the door. 'Then come with me. We can do with some help.'

He shook his head but didn't try to stop her.

In the makeshift hospital, the curtains were drawn closed. To her and Nikolai's relief, four of the injured were feeling better. They were sitting up in bed, eating with appetite, even walking around. But the fifth, Patrick, was not doing so well. She sat by his side, held his hand and read to him as he drifted in and out of consciousness. She changed his dressings, trying not to flinch at the sight of his burns and disfigured flesh.

'Who are you?' he croaked when she brought him some water and a piece of bread.

'I'm a nurse. My name is Sophia. I am here to look after you.'

'Where am I?'

'You are in hospital.' She smoothed his pillow and covered him with a sheet, then helped him sit up and take a few sips of water. He couldn't hold the cup in his burnt hands.

He choked on his water and coughed. When he was able to talk again, he asked, his voice flat, 'Am I going to die?'

'Not if we can help it.'

'I'm fine with it, you know. If I have to die, at least I know I stood up for my principles. I'll be dying for the revolution. Don't you think it's worth it?'

'I don't think anything is worth a human life. Wouldn't you prefer to live a little longer and fight for what you believe in?'

'I suppose so. What about you? What do you believe in?'

She was quiet for a long time as she examined the burns on his face and body. The infection was getting worse. 'I believe young men like you shouldn't be set on fire for their beliefs. I'm here to do what I can to help, to set things right. Even if in the grand scheme of things it makes no real difference. At least I know I've tried.'

Every day more men arrived, with burns, and gunshot and stab wounds. In the first week of May, when the sun shone bright like it was summer, like there was still joy in the world, they had a dozen beds made of straw and wood and a dozen wounded under their supervision. Sophia spent all her time in the hospital, sitting with the men, changing their bandages, holding their hands, fetching water, food and clean linen. She was no longer the countess who had everything done for her. She was serving the men whose lives depended on her and happier for it. Busy feeding the wounded, she barely thought of feeding herself. Sitting by their side until they fell asleep, she hardly slept herself. She had not a minute to herself.

Twice a day, Nikolai would come in to check on the men. She lived for these meetings, for a glimpse of his face, for his smile that was meant only for her. Sometimes he would operate on the wounded, to remove a bullet or stitch a stab wound, and she would assist him, watching him with awe. He would use iodine and vodka as disinfectants, chloroform and opium for anaesthesia, quinine to bring the temperature down. He held lives in his hands but his skilful fingers didn't tremble. What he had was tremendous empathy and kindness and love for his patients. She was most fascinated by his use of herbs. He seemed to possess an encyclopaedic knowledge of local flora and its various uses, which was lucky because they had no access to any other medication. He used tree vinegar as an antiseptic, orangeroot extract as an antibiotic and pine resin to make plasters for the wounds. He recommended treatment for each patient and she made notes, her eyes not leaving his face. When he wasn't there, she would follow her notes to the letter, hoping for a word of praise from him.

'Have you heard of balsam copaivae?' Nikolai asked her one day, a week after the fire. 'It's a miracle cure for inflammation and infection.'

She smelt the concoction. It made her think of spring, late nights and dips in the river. 'What is it made of?'

'A tree found in South America.'

'You learnt all this before you left school?'

'I've been learning my whole life.'

'You are a doctor from God.'

He blushed! Actually blushed! She thought he looked adorable, standing there with a clean dressing in his hands. She couldn't help it, she laughed. He looked like he was about to say something but one of the men called him and he had to turn away.

The house was quiet, but the streets were rowdy. The tension in Petrograd, already at a boiling point, was rising. Sophia didn't know what it meant and couldn't predict what would happen but every day she could feel it more and more, like a volcano shuddering under pressure before it exploded, showering everything in sight with deadly lava, scorching houses and wiping out settlements as if they had never existed. She busied herself with her tasks the way an ostrich buried its head in the sand and ignored what was going on around her. She ignored her husband's forlorn face and the chaos in the city of her childhood. She ignored the murders on the streets and the threatening men occupying her house. She tried not to think of anything beyond the hospital room, to lose herself in the men's needs, and because their needs were so great, it was an easy thing to do.

∗

Sophia was scrubbing the floor, a wet mop in her hands, her old nurse's uniform damp in places, her hair hidden under a kerchief, when she heard voices. She looked up from the floor and saw Arsenii, the man who had locked them up in the cellar and then brought them to the balcony at gunpoint. Brought them to the balcony to die. He was being carried inside on a stretcher. At the sight of the face of her nightmares, the terrifying face that had haunted her since that fateful day in March, she dropped the mop and it fell into the bucket with a loud splash. She was speechless as the men built another makeshift bed for Arsenii and got him comfortable. His tunic was covered in blood and he looked as pale as the sheets he was resting on. He appeared to be unconscious but when she approached, he groaned and opened his eyes, staring straight at Sophia. Her knees trembled under his gaze. As if he could sense her discomfort, he closed his eyes again.

'He's been shot in the shoulder,' said one of the men who had carried the stretcher. He was the size of a large bear and looked just as angry. 'Orlov said you would take care of him.'

The men turned to leave. *Wait*, Sophia wanted to shout. She didn't want to be alone with the villain from her nightmares. She wanted someone there, even if it was two monosyllabic, belligerent men. 'Where is Nikolai?'

'Do I look like his keeper?'

As she examined Arsenii's shoulder, cleaned the wound and applied the anaesthetic and a bandage, she felt a strange sense of displacement. It couldn't be her, trying to save the man who had almost killed her. She hoped Nikolai would come back soon, so he would tell her what to do. It was easier when she had instructions to follow. Then she could go through the motions and not think about it.

Dmitry walked in as she was finishing washing the floor. She thought he looked thinner than before, and his hair had streaks of grey in it. His eyes were dark from lack of sleep. He gazed down at her, not saying anything at first, and then bent over and lifted her up. 'Get off the floor, for goodness' sake. You are a lady. What do you think you're doing?'

'I'm a nurse first.'

'I wish you would stop with this nurse nonsense. It's beneath you. I told you from the start it was a bad idea. I was against it from day one. It seemed harmless enough, but I knew it wouldn't end well. And now look at you.'

'You think helping people is beneath me?'

'They are not people. They are monsters.' He pointed at Arsenii. 'That man tried to kill us. Why would you want to help him?'

'If I don't help them, no one else will.' She looked down into the bucket of murky water.

'You nurse them back to health, so that they can go out there and continue to murder and steal.'

'That's not what they're doing.'

'That's exactly what they're doing. You of all people should know better.'

'My job is not to judge them. It's to make sure they are well. I don't see them as revolutionaries. I see them as human beings.'

'That doesn't change who they are or what they are doing to our country. What, you don't remember how he stood in front of us with his sword, threatening to cut our throats? How his cronies called for our blood? How he looked into your eyes before he was about to stab you? And he would have done so if my brother didn't intervene. How could you forget?'

'I didn't forget. But it doesn't matter.'

'I never see you anymore. You are always in this room, doing God knows what.'

'I'm a nurse,' she whispered. 'This is what I do. I look after the wounded. I sit with them. I make their lives a little bit easier, a little bit brighter.'

'He showed us no mercy. Why should you be merciful to him and the likes of him? What do you get out of cleaning bedpans and bandaging infected limbs? I don't understand.'

Arsenii groaned and called her name. She said to Dmitry, 'I'm sorry but I have work to do. You can help if you like. There's always something to do around here. You can finish mopping the floor while I check on Arsenii.'

'It's not my place to do that. And it's not yours either.' With an exasperated gesture and a roll of his eyes, Dmitry left.

Sophia breathed a sigh of relief, until she remembered Arsenii was in the room with her. Despite what she had said to Dmitry, she couldn't stop thinking of the bloodthirsty expression on his face the first time they met.

When she approached his bed, Arsenii had tears in his eyes. 'It hurts so much. Why does it hurt so much?'

'You've been shot,' she said grimly. 'What did you think it would feel like? A tickle?'

'Can I have something for the pain? Please?'

'I already gave you plenty. Any more opium will kill you.'

'Is that what you want? To kill me? I can't say I blame you.'

'Of course not. *I'm* not a killer.'

His voice was nothing but a whisper when he said, 'I'm sorry. For everything.'

'We all make mistakes,' she said, trying to appear kind and

forgiving, like Nikolai.

'All I want is to go back to Ekaterinburg. My children and grandchildren are waiting for me. This struggle for a higher purpose, this fight for something that might never happen … I'm getting too old for it all …' He groaned. 'Old people need peace, not revolution. If I get through this, I'm leaving Petrograd and going home.'

'You'll get through this. I'll make sure of it. If you need anything, just let me know.'

'I hope you can forgive me one day,' he whispered, closing his eyes. When she looked at him, she no longer saw the monstrous face that haunted her nightmares. What she saw instead was an old man in pain who needed her.

*

One morning a few days later, when the sun was bright and the Neva sparkled with joy like everything was right in the world, Nikolai said to Sophia, 'Would you like to come to town with me this morning? I need your help.'

To town with Nikolai! She tried not to show how excited she was. 'What about the patients? Arsenii is always asking for me. So does Patrick.'

'I know you are indispensable. But the men can spare you for a few hours. Even Patrick and Arsenii.'

He didn't need to ask twice. She was happy to escape the house, if only for a couple of hours. It felt good to be out in the open, to feel the warm breeze on her face, to walk down the street and not feel afraid because she was with him. 'Will you tell me where we are going? Or is it a surprise?'

'We are going around the corner to find a coach.'

'Oh,' she said. She was looking forward to a walk with him. 'And then?'

'You'll see.'

The coach took them across the Neva to a part of Petrograd she had never visited before. When sprawling mansions gave way to dilapidated houses with peeling paint and crooked windows, the coach stopped and Nikolai disembarked, opening Sophia's door and offering his arm. She followed him to a rickety building that looked more like a shed than a house. Accustomed to the luxury of Nevsky Avenue mansions, she couldn't believe human beings could live like this. Nikolai knocked and a stooped old man opened the door. 'Am I glad to see you!' he exclaimed, vigorously shaking Nikolai's hand. 'Anton was screaming in pain all night. But now he's finally asleep, thank God.'

In a bedroom with dirty wallpaper and a threadbare carpet, a young man rested on a pile of cushions on the floor. Every once in a while, he whimpered in his sleep.

'Don't worry, I'm here to check Anton. I'll try not to disturb him. He needs his rest,' said Nikolai, pulling the sheet covering the boy's body. Sophia gasped. The patient was missing his left leg and the stump looked infected. The dressing was red with blood. She forced herself not to look away. Even though she'd seen worse during her time volunteering at the hospital during the war, she felt slightly woozy, like she was about to be sick.

'This is Nurse Orlova,' Nikolai said to the old man. 'My best nurse. She will assist me today.'

'Thank you,' whispered the man. 'God bless you both.' He crossed himself and whispered a prayer over the young man, who stirred and moaned but didn't open his eyes.

Sophia helped Nikolai clean the wound and change the dressing. 'How did he lose his leg?'

'Bullet wound. I operated on him a few days ago. He was in a bad state.'

'Poor boy. What is he going to do? He will need someone to look after him for the rest of his life.'

'It's heartbreaking. But taking the leg away saved his life.'

Before they left, the old man clasped Nikolai's hand and said,

'How can we ever repay you? I wish we had some money to give you.'

'Just look after Anton. And nurse him back to health for me.'

'Here, take this bread. I baked it myself this morning.' The man pushed something wrapped in paper into Nikolai's hands.

Nikolai shook his head. 'Keep it. You need it more than I do. So does Anton.'

Afterwards, they visited ten more houses and saw ten more patients. People with gunshot and stab wounds, broken bones and bad burns, their mutilated bodies a testament to the unrest in Petrograd. Just like Anton's father, they thanked Nikolai and Sophia with tears in their eyes. And just like Anton's father, they wanted to pay but couldn't.

'So that's where you disappear to every chance you get?' Sophia asked, watching him with warmth. 'Everywhere you go, you help people.'

'I do what I can. I wish I could do more.'

On the way home Sophia drifted off, having barely slept in the last few days. When she felt the coach slowing down and finally coming to a stop, she opened her eyes, expecting to see their cobbled driveway winding its way through an alley of poplar trees towards the house. But all she could see through the window was a gilded gate and a tall brick wall she didn't recognise.

Nikolai opened Sophia's door. She stepped out, leaning on his arm. 'Where are we?' she asked.

'I thought we could have lunch before we go back.'

'I *am* a little hungry,' she admitted. She was glad to be out of the house for a bit longer. Even more so to be spending time with him, even if she would never admit it.

He guided her inside the park and she stood still for a moment, transfixed, her hand on her chest. Never in a million years had she expected to find something like this in the middle of Petrograd. As far as the eye could see were tulips of every colour imaginable. White and cream, yellow and pink, blue and purple, almost black.

It was like looking at the rainbow. Sophia blinked. She couldn't believe her eyes. 'What is this place? I've never seen anything like it.'

'People plant tulips here in memory of their loved ones. It's beautiful in spring, isn't it?'

'Stunning.'

'I knew you would like it. Come with me and I'll show you something.'

Side by side they crossed the park until they reached a patch of the flowers that were taller than most, as if reaching for the sky.

'I planted these for my mother. Red tulips were her favourite.'

Sophia felt tears in her eyes. The unexpected beauty in the midst of all the misery and destruction took her breath away. 'She would have loved them.'

'Sometimes I come here when I want to be alone. When everything becomes too much. Being here makes me feel closer to her.'

Sophia felt like she was witnessing a side to Nikolai not many people had seen. In her smallest voice she said, 'Thank you for bringing me here.'

'You are very welcome. I wanted to do something to thank you for all your help with the patients. I couldn't do it without you.'

'You do most of it. I just do the simple things.'

'No, *you* do most of it. It's the simple things that matter the most. Now, we could have lunch on this bench or …' He opened his bag and pulled out a picnic blanket. 'On the grass over there. What do you prefer?'

Sophia clapped excitedly. 'You thought of everything. I can't remember the last time I had a picnic.'

'The grass it is then.' Seconds later the picnic blanket was on the ground. Nikolai motioned for her to sit down. Her hands shook a little. It was the hunger, she told herself. She hadn't had anything to eat that morning, and then they rushed off. They had a busy morning and now it was catching up with her. Her light-headedness had absolutely nothing to do with Nikolai.

As if by magic, bread, cheese and cold meats appeared on the blanket, followed by fruit and a jug of orange juice. 'And last but not least, I brought you this.' Nikolai placed a small box in front of her.

'What is it?'

'Open it.'

Inside was a small cake.

'I can't wait to try some,' she exclaimed. 'Can I have some now?' In this beautiful park with Nikolai, surrounded by a rainbow of tulips, she felt like it was her birthday. Her other life, her patients, even Dmitry suddenly seemed a million miles away.

'Cake before meat and cheese?'

'Cake before everything. I love cake.'

'Then I'm glad I baked it for you.'

'You baked it yourself?'

'It was my mother's recipe. She loved to bake.'

She watched him with astonishment. Then she looked at the cake. 'Can I have some, please? Or did you bring it here just to show me?'

'You can have some.' He cut a small slice with a knife and placed it on a spoon.

She took the spoon, trembling with excitement. Slowly, she placed it in her mouth, relishing the taste. For a few moments, she couldn't talk. 'It tastes like heaven.'

'It's called Napoleon cake. Rumour has it the French Emperor came up with the recipe while paying court to one of his wife's ladies-in-waiting. What do you think about that?' His eyes twinkled.

'I think he must have been very taken with the lady in question. This cake is delicious. But his poor wife! I thought he loved his Josephine!'

'He did. Unfortunately, she didn't love him.' He pushed the box with the remaining cake closer to her across the picnic blanket. 'Would you like some more?'

'I would. But if I eat it all now, I won't have any left for later.'

'Have it. I can always bake more.'

She blushed and looked into her cake. 'You bake, you plant flowers, you cure people. Is there anything you can't do?'

'There is! Ride a bicycle.'

'You can't ride a bicycle?'

'Never learnt how.'

'I'll tell you what. Teach me how to bake and I'll teach you to ride.'

'You've got yourself a deal!'

Soon all the food was gone but they continued to watch the flowers bowing their colourful heads in the breeze. They talked about his mother and her parents, their childhoods and hopes for the future. They didn't sit next to each other on the picnic blanket. There was a space between them big enough to fit a few more people. And yet, she had never felt closer to anyone in her life. For a moment with him, surrounded by breathtaking beauty, she felt like she had been transported to a different world. One where there was no revolution and no fear. One where she could be happy. She didn't want to leave that world.

*

The rain was coming down steadily and the temperature had dropped, as if winter had decided to lay one more claim on Petrograd before ceding territory to summer once and for all. The monotonous sound of the raindrops hitting the roof almost muffled the din of the crowd. Almost but not quite. Sophia could still hear it, over the wounded, who were groaning, snoring or pleading with her. And they were always pleading. *Nurse Orlova, please, can I have some water? Please, can I have something to eat? I'm uncomfortable, could you roll me to my side?* Sophia was grateful for their demands. If they were asking, it meant they were getting better. Of course, not all of them were asking. Arsenii had barely stirred all day. Nikolai had operated on him and told him to rest. Every time Sophia passed his bed, she hoped for a sign of life, but the old man remained motionless and pale, his eyes firmly closed.

Sophia sat by the window, watching the rain, nursing a piece of stale bread in her lap, trying to ignore the distant voices outside. As she was finishing her lunch, she noticed a lone figure of a woman moving slowly down the deserted street. It wasn't unusual to see a woman walking past their house. What was unusual was that this woman was dressed from foot to head in silk according to the latest Parisian fashion. Rainwater ran down her hair, face and body but she didn't seem to notice. She moved with difficulty, pressing her arm to her chest as if in great pain. When she got closer, Sophia noticed that her blue dress was stained with blood. She thought the woman looked familiar. When she turned the corner and walked through the gate and across their front yard, Sophia gasped. The woman with frantic eyes and blood on her dress was her childhood friend Regina.

The wounded began to stir and call for her. Sophia told them she would be right back and ran out of the room and to the front door. The doorbell chimed. She flung the door open. Her friend was standing outside.

Regina was tall, blonde and stunning. Her waist was tiny, her hair long and curly, her face a picture of innocence, an illusion betrayed by her eyes that usually sparkled with mischief. Usually but not today.

'Regina! What happened to you? You are bleeding,' exclaimed Sophia, pulling her friend inside.

Regina opened her mouth to reply but no words came. She swayed and started to slide to the floor. She would have hit her head on the wall if Sophia hadn't caught her.

'Help!' cried Sophia. 'Somebody, help us!'

Dmitry ran out of his study, rushing to the two women. He lifted Regina in his arms and carried her to one of the guest rooms, placing her on the bed.

'She's soaked in blood,' cried Sophia, placing her hand on her friend's forehead. 'Quick, get me a knife.'

Dmitry brought her a knife from the kitchen. Sophia cut the bodice of the dress. There was a stab wound on Regina's left arm, running from her hand to her elbow. 'It looks deep. She might need stitches.'

With Dmitry's help, she cleaned the wound as best she could, applied some iodine and lidocaine for local anaesthesia. As she began stitching, Regina didn't move.

Forgetting her other patients, Sophia sat with Regina, holding her hand. 'You are safe now,' she whispered. 'Before you know it, you will be good as new.'

Regina's lips trembled and her eyes opened. She groaned.

'Do you want anything? Water? Something to eat?'

'Water,' Regina whispered, her voice breaking. Sophia brought a glass of water to her lips. Regina took a few careful sips. 'Sorry to appear like this. I didn't know where else to go.'

'Don't be silly. You did the right thing, coming here.'

'My arm feels numb. I can't move it.'

'You are not supposed to move it for a while. You've been stabbed. I stitched it for you.'

Regina's eyes filled with tears. 'Those murderers came to our house in the middle of the night and told us to get out. Father is gone.'

Sophia gasped. 'They killed your father?'

'I told him not to say anything to them. It's not worth it. Nothing is worth losing your life over, not even our house. But he didn't listen. They stabbed him in the chest. Valentin and I tried to stop them. That's how I got hurt.'

'And Valentin?'

'They took him away. They put him in an armoured car and drove him somewhere.' Regina sobbed in Sophia's arms. 'It happened so quickly. One minute we were sitting down to tea. The next, both my father and brother are gone. I fainted, more from fear than pain, I think. I don't know how long I was unconscious. When I came to, I was outside in the gutter and the doors to my house were locked.'

'I'm so sorry about your father,' whispered Sophia. 'He was wonderful. The kindest man.'

'What will I do without him? I love him so much, what am I going to do? And I have nowhere to go.'

'You can stay here for as long as you want. And Valentin will come back. They didn't kill him. That's a good thing.'

'We've been sitting on our suitcases for weeks, ready to leave at a moment's notice. Father was trying to get permission slips to travel overseas. And now this happened. The bastards have everything. My house, my jewellery, my clothes. I don't even care about any of it. I just want Papa back.' Regina wiped her face and looked at Sophia. 'You and Dmitry are lucky. You still have your home.' She was breathing heavily and making soft sobbing sounds, like a wounded kitten. 'Papa hated the revolutionaries. Ever since it all started, his health became terrible. His heart was failing. I was hoping if we left Petrograd, he would get better. We were thinking of Paris or Rome, the farther from here the better. Kerensky himself promised him passes. And now it's too late.'

'Not for you. It's not too late for you. You can still go. And whoever did this … One day, they are going to pay.'

Regina shook her head. 'Yes, but it won't bring Papa back.'

*

Arsenii wasn't getting better. His breathing became heavier and he had developed a cough that wasn't going away. Sophia spent days and nights by his side, holding his hand and reading to him from her favourite books.

'Thank you,' he croaked, breaking into a cough and spluttering. 'For everything you've done for me. I was wrong about you. You are a good person. A selfless person. Not like the rest of them.'

'Not all of us are spoilt brats, despite what you might think. We don't only care about parties and jewellery and expensive art. Now, try not to talk. It must be hard for you. Are you hungry? It's almost lunchtime. I will bring you something to eat.'

'Don't have much appetite. What about you? You run around this place, but I never see you take a break.'

'Who has time for a break?' Three beds were now empty. Two of their patients had recovered and one had died. The man had never regained consciousness. Sophia mourned this stranger whom she had never spoken to like a member of her family. She had never felt more helpless. Nikolai told her they had done everything they could and she shouldn't blame herself. There were tears in his eyes when he said it.

She was about to run out of the room, fetch some clean cloths, change another bandage, wipe another forehead. Before she had a chance, Arsenii said, 'I have something for you.'

'What is it?'

He tried to move his hand and winced in pain. 'Check my left pocket.'

In his left pocket, she found something wrapped in an old newspaper. She took it out. 'Is this what you wanted to give me?'

'Yes. Open it.'

Inside were the pearl earrings her mother had given her for her sixteenth birthday in her other, happier life that now seemed forever gone. Rubbing the pearls with her fingertips, she whispered, 'These were my mother's. I never thought I'd see them again.'

'I was going to sell them. That's where I was going when I got shot. I could have got a good price for them on the black market. They are one of a kind, unique. But I want you to have them back. I'm so grateful for everything you've done.'

'They mean so much to me, you can't even imagine.' Her hand closed around the earrings. Overcome by emotion, she leaned on his bed for support.

'You must think I'm a monster.'

Sophia said nothing.

'What I did was terrible. I still can't believe it was me on that balcony. I was mad. I wasn't myself. We've been slaves for so long. We had no rights. Nothing was allowed. And suddenly, we could do anything we wanted. We were all drunk with it. The power.'

'Yes, all of Petrograd seems to be drunk on power, destroying everything in sight.'

'I had a good life, all things considered. I had so much love in my life. But sometimes love turns to hate. It eats you alive like cancer.' Sophia sat down on the edge of his bed. It was clear he wanted to talk. And Nikolai had taught her that listening was sometimes the best thing a doctor or a nurse could do. Arsenii didn't seem to notice she was there at all. He was staring into space, as if in his thoughts he was far from the stuffy hospital room, far from Petrograd with its battle cries of unrest. 'I adored my wife from day one. We met when we were both sixteen. I still see her the way she was then. Her hair long, her face innocent. As soon as I saw her, I knew I wanted to spend my life with her. Our parents were against it, so we had to run away together, start a new life far from home. She was everything to me.' His eyes darkened. 'The old regime took her from me.'

'What happened?'

'I stored some forbidden books at home. While I was away, they searched the house and my wife was arrested. They beat her and threw her into a freezing cold cellar. She got frostbite and lost her fingers. She had to quit her job as a machine operator at a factory. With only one person working, we could no longer afford food. She was never herself after that. She died a year later, never got over her ordeal. Her heart gave out. I hate the people who did it to her. Hate the tsar and everyone who supports him. Because of them, I lost the only woman I have ever loved. The only woman who has ever loved me.'

He took her hand and pressed it and for the first time she didn't want to run and hide from him.

*

One evening, a few days after she arrived, Regina came down for dinner. In the black dress Sophia had lent her, with her back straight and her head held high, she looked regal and smart, as if she hadn't lost everything in one short breath of Petrograd's spring air. Nothing in her bearing betrayed what she'd been through but the slight redness around her eyes and the sadness in her smile.

Dmitry was reading his newspaper. It was his favourite pastime these days – to read the revolutionary propaganda and quietly swear under his breath. 'Can you believe it? Milyukov addressed the allies, promising Russia would fight in this war until the end. It upset the soldiers so much, there was another uprising in Petrograd.'

'That explains all the noise we've heard,' said Sophia, motioning for Regina to join them at the table. *It's been months*, she thought. Months of chaos and still no light at the end of the dark tunnel. The newspapers were printed only sporadically. But those that reached them were full of stories about the disarray in the army, the desertion, soldiers walking off the field of battle en masse. No one believed in the war with the Germans, not when their home itself had become a battlefield.

She wanted to ask Nikolai, *Is this what you imagined your revolution to become? Disorder and anarchy everywhere we turn – is this your utopia?* She wondered what the future would bring. Would it all get better, like Nikolai hoped? Or would it get worse, like she feared?

'A whole regiment occupied Mariinsky Palace and the Provisional Government was imprisoned for a few hours. They are kidding themselves if they think Russia will fight in this war. Thousands of soldiers are running from the front. Rumour has it, they have been eating their horses because there is nothing else.'

'What does it matter who defeats us? The Germans or the hordes that have overrun Petrograd?' exclaimed Regina. 'And maybe if the Germans come here, this nightmare will end.'

Sophia knew many people felt this way. They saw a German occupation as salvation. If the Germans invaded, they would put a stop to the revolutionary nonsense that spread through Petrograd and all of Russia. But wasn't it like making a deal with the devil? The Germans didn't have Russia's best interests at heart. But nor, it seemed, did the revolutionaries. 'How are you feeling, my dear?' asked Sophia, trying to change the subject.

'Like I will wake up from this nightmare any minute. And all I can think of is, what happens now? We are still so young. What will the rest of our lives look like?'

'Only time will tell,' said Sophia quietly.

'Sometimes I wake up in the morning and for a few seconds I think everything is fine. That it was all a bad dream, nothing more. Then I remember it's real and wish I never woke up.'

'Maybe things will get better. The Provisional Government might soon bring peace to Petrograd,' said Sophia.

'Do you really believe it? It won't get better. It will only get worse,' said Dmitry, always the pessimist.

How can it possibly get any worse? wondered Sophia. She had long ago stopped reading the newspaper. All she had to do was open the blinds and she could see the devastation for herself. She didn't need to read about it too. But then she thought, *We are still alive. We haven't been arrested. We haven't been murdered or sent to Siberia like so many others. We are lucky.*

She didn't feel lucky. She felt suspended in time and space, without hope, without a future, waiting for something to happen that would change their lives for the better but fearing the worst.

As they were finishing dinner and Sophia was getting ready to return to the hospital rooms, Regina said, 'I need your help, both of you.'

'Of course, anything.' Dmitry looked up from his newspaper and smiled.

'I need to go back to my house, to find out what happened to my brother. Will you take me? I'm too scared to go by myself.'

'You think going back to the house will help you learn what happened to Valentin?' demanded Dmitry.

'I will ask them where they've taken him. I will throw myself on my knees if I need to. I will do anything.'

'What makes you think they'll tell you?'

'I will beg them until they do. He's my brother. I need to know. I can't go on, not knowing.'

'You barely got away with your life. You were almost killed. You shouldn't go back there. It's not safe. And it won't do any good.'

Later, when Regina left to go back to her room, he said to Sophia, 'Don't you dare go with her.'

'She needs our help. How could you say no to her when she's been through so much?'

'Because I'm thinking of her safety. And yours. Now is not the time to be gallivanting around town.'

'You are not thinking of her safety. You are thinking of yours. You should have just said so. You should have told her you are too afraid to leave the house.'

'With good reason. And I forbid you from going with her.'

'What gives you the right to forbid me anything?'

'My love for you.' He rose to his feet and walked towards the door, his newspaper tucked under his arm. In the doorway, he stopped. 'The problem with you is, you are too kind, too trusting for your own good.'

'And that's a bad thing?'

'Of course. People take advantage. Just look at that monster you are helping.'

'I don't know who you are talking about.'

'Your new friend, Arsenii.'

106

'He's not a monster. He had a hard life. Now that I've got to know him better, I can understand and sympathise.'

'You just proved my point.'

*

Nikolai examined Regina's arm, telling her it was healing nicely and the stitches could come out soon. Regina, who managed to look sophisticated and chic even in the simple dress she was wearing, thanked him and pressed his hand gently. Where were the tears, the grim face? It seemed the old Regina was back, with a mischievous sparkle in her eyes and a flirtatious tone in her voice. She was all curves and hair and smiles and suddenly Sophia felt drab and insignificant in her nurse's uniform and the grey kerchief over her head.

'I will never understand the revolutionaries,' said Regina. 'Fighting for an ideal that doesn't exist, risking their lives and for what? And what shocks me the most is that many of them are of noble descent, born into money, position and respect. Like yourself. Tell me, what was lacking in your life that you had to pursue this chimera? You could have been happy like the rest of us.'

'If by happy you mean stagnating in a lovely mansion and dying from boredom, then yes. Humans need struggle to feel truly happy. When humanity doesn't have a goal, it withers away and dies like a flower without water. The best time is now, when we have something to fight for.'

'I don't agree. Give me a carefree existence without struggle anytime.' Regina pouted, not taking her eyes off him.

'What about the greater good? What's best for humanity?'

'And you think your revolution achieves the greater good? Look at us, driven from our homes, with nowhere to go and no means to support ourselves.' A sadness flashed through Regina's eyes. Sophia knew she was thinking of her father and brother. 'When you talk about the greater good, don't we count at all?'

'Of course. But look at the rest of the population. They've been living with no means to support themselves for generations. We are trying to give them these means. Not everyone is born into privilege and wealth. Not everyone has the same start in life.'

'I don't care what you say. I just want things to go back to how they were. I want my house back, my servants, my life. I want balls, frivolity and happiness.' Her voice cracked. 'I want my father and brother back. Everything has been taken away from us. It seems we were born in the most unlucky of times.'

'On the contrary. We are living in unprecedented times. Look at the masses of ordinary people doing extraordinary things. We overthrew the oppressors and are trying to create something new. A different society, a new way of life.'

'We are rolling towards a catastrophe, accompanied by songs and revolutionary marches. Even your Kerensky said in a speech the other day that he wished he had died two months ago. Then he would still have believed in the revolution as an endeavour of free-thinking individuals, not uprising slaves.'

'Kerensky's got to have more faith.'

'It's good to see you haven't lost yours, even with everything that's happening. But it's only a matter of time.'

Sophia nodded in agreement. Petrograd and all of Russia were trembling in their foundations and still Nikolai believed. As they talked, Sophia observed her friend's body language. Every now and then, Regina would lean closer to Nikolai, as if to hear him better. She would laugh a little too loudly at his jokes, her eyes would twinkle her delight at him, her fingers would fiddle with her hair. Sophia felt an unfamiliar feeling of discomfort, as if something wasn't quite right.

*

The two friends were walking down Nevsky in the direction of Regina's house on the Neva. As they approached the majestic

Winter Palace, instead of the Imperial standard, Sophia saw a red flag blowing in the wind, announcing to the world that all that had happened, the upheaval, the abdication and the madness on Petrograd streets, was not a terrible nightmare from which she would soon awaken but an equally terrible reality. When she saw it, she tripped over and almost fell, averting her gaze from the terrifying symbol of the revolution, looking instead at the boats floating peacefully on the Neva.

'Thank you for coming with me,' said Regina. 'I can't sleep, can't think of anything else. I need to know my brother is safe.'

'It's the least I can do. We all love Valentin. I remember when I was twelve and he taught me how to ride a horse. I was afraid of horses and refused to come close. They seemed so big to a small child, like mountains. He told me horses are like dogs. They can sense fear but they can sense love too. The horse will never misbehave if you approach it with love, he said. I have never been afraid since. He was the kindest boy.'

'Please, don't talk about him in the past tense, like he's already gone. I can't bear it. He is the only family I have left, and I have to have hope.'

'We won't stop until we find him. But don't tell Dmitry I went with you. He'll be so mad.'

'Keeping secrets already? You've only been married for five years. Is everything all right between you two?'

'Dmitry and I are doing great. Everything is fine.'

'Then why can't you tell him where you are going?'

'He's so afraid for me. For all of us.'

By the expression on Regina's face, Sophia knew she didn't believe her. 'I heard you at dinner. You thought I left but I heard you fighting. He talked to you like you are his property.'

'So what? All couples fight.'

'If you say so.' Regina stopped in the middle of the street and turned to Sophia. 'His brother is quite something, don't you think?'

Sophia couldn't meet her friend's eyes. 'He's my brother-in-law. I haven't noticed.'

'But I've noticed. Does he have a wife or a sweetheart?'

'I don't know. I never asked.'

'Can you find out for me?' The familiar twinkle in Regina's eyes was back. 'He is the kind of man I could marry one day. Handsome, kind, smart. It's a shame about his political convictions but given time, I could change those.'

They approached Regina's mansion and Sophia's heart skipped with trepidation. The gate was no longer there. It had been torn off its hinges and lay in the dust like a sad reminder of what had once been, of dinner parties and balls, of gilded carriages and carefree guests dressed in their finest. The fence was a mass of twisted metal, as if a tank had pushed its way through it. The two women made their way through the garden in a daze, taking in the shuttered sculptures, the manicured lawn that had turned into a mess of twisted soil and grass, the intricately shaped bushes that had been hacked to pieces. Every window in the house had been smashed and as they walked, Sophia felt something cracking under her feet. She looked down. They were walking on broken glass.

The front door was ajar. Without a word, they made their way inside. There was no furniture left, no paintings or mirrors. The house was a ghost of its former self. Only the walls remained, with wallpaper cut to pieces, hanging down to the floor like wilted flowers.

'It doesn't seem like anyone is staying here anymore,' whispered Sophia.

Regina sank to the floor, her shoulders shaking. 'They took everything. Everything that means so much to me is gone.'

'I'm so sorry, my dear,' said Sophia, on the verge of tears herself.

'I don't really care about any of that. What have they done to my brother?'

*

Regina spent the next two days in bed, a cover over her, only the tip of her nose and her burning eyes visible. Late in the evenings, when all her chores were done, Sophia sat next to her friend and held her hand. Regina didn't seem to notice she was there. She didn't cry and only stared into space without blinking.

'Once, when we were on our estate near Shlisselburg, Valentin and I went to the forest to pick mushrooms,' she said, her eyes flashing in the light of a candle.

'How old were you?' Sophia was glad her friend was talking again, even if her voice was cracking with emotion. Her heart was breaking for her.

'I was ten. He was twelve. We got separated and I couldn't find him. I didn't know my way around the forest. I walked in circles for what seemed like hours, panicking, shouting for help, not knowing which way to turn. It felt like I'd passed the same tree a thousand times. There was no way out. I called for my brother till my throat was sore. I don't think I've ever cried so much. I was afraid, thirsty, hungry and desperate. My imagination played tricks on me. I saw wolves and bears everywhere. Finally, miraculously, I found my way back. Relieved, I ran to my parents, crying from happiness. And then I realised Valentin was still missing. He was still in the forest. And never, not once, had I thought about my brother. All I thought about was myself.'

'Oh no. What happened next?'

'Papa got a search party together. Everyone from the village volunteered to help. We all went looking for him. We were searching for hours. Calling his name. We had dogs. I was careful to stay close to the grown-ups at all times. Then it got dark. I remember torches burning in the dark, people shouting, dogs barking, like a bad dream. Papa and the other men continued searching, while Mama took me to bed. And who do you think we found in his bedroom, sound asleep in his bed?'

'Your brother?'

'While we were looking for him, he was safely at home. He

must have got back while we were out. I was overjoyed.'

Sophia hugged her friend. 'He'll come back to you. When you least expect it, your brother will come back.'

'I don't think so,' whispered Regina. 'I don't think I'll see him again. The cursed revolutionaries. They are monsters, murderers, wild dogs, and I hope they pay for everything.' She cried and shook in Sophia's arms. 'I am all alone in the world.'

Regina slept but Sophia continued to sit by her side, stroking her hand.

Chapter 6

July 1917

It seemed that in the first week of July, Petrograd finally reached its boiling point. There was an intensity to the crowd's mood that hadn't been there before. And not just here – Moscow, Kiev, Ekaterinoslav and other cities were turning into cauldrons of churning discontent, with hundreds of thousands of workers and soldiers joining hunger strikes and demonstrations against the war that had claimed so many Russian lives. Sophia felt the tension but tried to ignore it, hiding from real life in other people's pain and attending to the wounded with Regina's help. As the city became louder and less content, Nikolai became busier, attending meetings at Putilov and other factories where the Bolsheviks tried to dissuade the masses from striking. Sometimes days went by without Sophia seeing him. There were times when she couldn't sleep from worry for his safety. But when he returned, he always had a smile and a kind word for her.

One scorching afternoon, Dmitry, Sophia and Regina were on the balcony, watching with horror as the gathering crowds demanded action from the Bolsheviks, screaming for bread, for the overthrow of the government, berating them for their inaction and proposing nothing short of an armed insurrection. 'We will go to the front only for a revolutionary war,' they chanted. Entire divisions of soldiers had deserted and were now roaming around Petrograd like a pack of strays. They were arrested by the thousand and yet more kept coming, drunk, loud and unhappy, ready, it seemed, for anything.

'You tell us this is an abhorrent capitalist war! And then you order us to go and fight it, risk our lives, for what? Shame on you!' shouted the soldiers.

The enraged men and women were closing in on the handful of the Bolsheviks who were trying to talk some sense into them. Regina pressed Sophia's hand reassuringly but her own hand was shaking. 'Where is Nikolai?' she whispered.

'At Putilov, I think.'

'Is it quieter there?'

'I don't think it's quiet anywhere in the city. Look at it!'

It was like watching a tempest or a tsunami. They couldn't run or hide but they couldn't take their eyes off it either, even as it threatened to sweep them away.

'You are with us or against us! Make a choice now!' the crowd erupted.

'Violence is not an answer,' someone shouted. Sophia recognised Arsenii, his arm in a sling, standing his ground against the enraged crowd.

'It's the only answer. What else is there?'

'A peaceful protest.'

'We don't want peace! We want results!'

Undeterred by rain and thunder, on and on they marched, shouting in anger. Nikolai's efforts were in vain. Sophia could see hundreds of factory workers joining the soldiers, striding past the house, carrying red flags, placards and rifles, demanding the resignation of the Provisional Government. When automobiles drove past, the insurrectionists stopped them, throwing drivers out onto the street, taking their places and honking the horns.

114

'What are you doing, comrades? I'm a working-class man, just like yourselves. This car is all I have,' shouted one unfortunate driver, having just lost his vehicle to an overzealous soldier in a torn and bloody uniform. No one paid him any attention and soon he was lost in the screaming human river. The soldiers walked on, their eyes bulging, some drunk on vodka, others on their anger and hatred. Down the road, Sophia saw a truck with rifles sticking out like spider legs, carrying a placard that proclaimed, 'Away with the capitalist ministers. Down with the Provisional Government! Down with Kerensky! Down with Bloody Alexander!'

It didn't take long for the mob to surround the house. Someone picked up a rock and threw it at the window below. The glass shattered and soon a dozen people were throwing rocks, screaming, 'Down with the hated bourgeoisie!'

A rock fell close to Sophia, almost hitting her. Dmitry directed them off the balcony and inside the house but even here she didn't feel safe. A dishevelled woman with blood on her face suggested to set fire to the bourgeois nest. 'Burn them all alive!' the crowd responded. 'No mercy for the enemies of the people!'

'I wish Nikolai was here,' whispered Regina, desperately clinging to Sophia, like she couldn't stand up unsupported. 'We would be safer with him around. When did he say he was coming back?'

I wish Nikolai was here too, thought Sophia. *I want to make sure he's all right*. 'I wish I knew. I haven't seen him in days.'

She watched through a gap in the curtains as a man lit a torch and marched through the gate towards the house. The crowd followed and soon the front yard was filled with screaming men and women. Arsenii threw himself in front of the crowd, his one good arm extended in front of him. 'Stop, comrades!' he shouted. 'This is the Bolshevik headquarters!'

He might as well have been speaking French. The crowd didn't listen. In an instant, Arsenii disappeared under their feet. When they moved on, he remained motionless on the cobblestones that were no longer white but dark red with blood. 'Arsenii!' exclaimed

Sophia, moving towards the door.

Dmitry caught her. 'Are you out of your mind? Where do you think you are going?'

'He needs me.'

'It's too late. There is nothing you can do.'

Shuddering, she looked down at Arsenii's broken body, at his eyes staring at the oppressive Petrograd sky. 'The bastards stabbed him,' said Dmitry, while Nanny whimpered quietly and mouthed a prayer under her breath.

Sophia screamed. And screamed and screamed, while Dmitry held her in his arms and told her to be quiet before it was too late.

But it was already too late. They heard a crash. Someone broke down the front door and was now running up the stairs. Moments later, a group of men appeared with rifles in their hands, except for the tallest, who was holding a knife dripping with blood. Arsenii's blood. To Sophia they seemed even more ragged, more violent and unpredictable than the mob that had descended on their house in March. This time it was Regina who cried out in fear, while Sophia was petrified into silence.

'What do you want, comrades?' Dmitry asked, sounding calmer than he looked. 'This house is used as a hospital for wounded Bolsheviks. There are women living here, all nurses.'

Miraculously, his words seemed to calm the intruders. A spark of humanity appeared on their enraged faces. 'We came to requisition your automobiles,' said the leader of the group. Sophia couldn't bear to look at the knife in his hands. She gritted her teeth and forced herself to remain still.

'What automobiles? They had been requisitioned months ago,' said Dmitry.

The crowd pushed him aside and ran rampant through the house, grabbing everything they could get their hands on and throwing it into their sacks. It was just like March all over again but this time there was no Nikolai to help them. Dmitry alone was no match for a dozen belligerent soldiers. Sophia heard their slurred words reverberating through the hall. 'Pull the curtains off. We can sell them. And the divan.'

'They are in the bedroom,' she whispered to Regina. 'Taking what little we have left.' She shivered. Her mother's painting was in the bedroom, hidden under her pillow.

'These men are animals. Ferocious animals. You saw what happened to Arsenii. Let them take whatever they want, as long as they leave afterwards,' said Dmitry.

'They won't be here for long. We hardly have anything left to take,' whispered Sophia.

Holding their breath in fear, they remained in the salon, hoping the hordes would leave soon. Miraculously, they did, moving on to the next mansion, but not before setting fire to her books. Helplessly, Sophia watched as her beloved volumes of Pushkin, Lermontov and Tolstoy turned to ashes, while Dmitry, Regina and Nanny fetched buckets of water. Sophia wanted to help but couldn't move. A terrible premonition gripped her, a dark foreboding of worse to come.

And while the tempest raged in her home and all over Petrograd, and maybe all over Russia too, all she could think was, *Where is Nikolai?*

*

At night, Sophia listened to the storm. The howling wind couldn't compete in volume with the murmur of the crowd that only grew louder when the darkness fell, as if in the dark it could unleash all its powers without fear of retribution. It increased in intensity, infiltrating her dreams, making her shoot up in bed and scream in horror. No one and nothing was safe, not a hapless passer-by, nor the shops, nor the nearby houses. Everything was in ruin on the streets of Petrograd. And on the cobblestones outside, Arsenii's body remained, a sad reminder of the destructive powers that had engulfed their city. Dmitry wanted to move him but was too afraid to leave the comparative safety of the house.

In the morning, there was still no sign of Nikolai but the people were as angry and terrifying as the day before.

From behind the curtain, Sophia could see government automobiles and trucks adorned with red flags. The streets were flooded with soldiers who were no longer fighting, workers who were no longer working, triumphant servants, market stall owners and shopkeepers with red ribbons in their buttonholes. Militia on horseback tried to control the crowds but it was like walking into a tornado and ordering it to stop.

Sophia found Nanny on the balcony, examining a bullet lodged in the wall of their house.

'Come inside,' she exclaimed, pulling the petrified woman back. 'It's not safe out here.'

As if to prove her point, they heard a burst of machine-gun fire and an explosion. The crowd wailed.

Nanny crossed herself. 'Will it ever end? Or will it get worse?'

'Much worse,' said Dmitry. 'At least we have our house to shelter in. How long before that is taken away from us?'

Sitting on the floor in the corner, her head in her hands, Regina sobbed softly. Sophia sat next to her. 'Are you all right?'

'This is not going to end well. Any moment they could kill us. What are we going to do?'

'Nothing we can do but wait.'

'Wait for what? I have a bad feeling. It's as if my father had died because he couldn't bear what was about to happen to Russia. As if he knew what was coming and didn't want to see it. It's a bad sign, Sophia.'

At midday, the sound of thunder joined the cacophony of war. The darkened skies grumbled and roared, just like the streets of Petrograd. But even the rain that came down like a wall of icy water was not enough to calm the tempers down. Sophia slumped on the floor, looking into her hands. She didn't want to raise her head and catch a glimpse of Dmitry or Nanny or Regina. She didn't want to see fear on the faces she loved.

Nikolai walked in as the clock chimed three, his clothes torn, smudges of something dark on his face. He looked unhurt but his shoulders were stooped and his face was grim, as if he had seen something so terrible, he couldn't bear thinking about it.

'Thank God you're back,' Regina said, rushing to his side and pressing his hand. 'We were so scared without you. The louts broke in, took our things, burnt our books.'

Sophia didn't rush to his side, nor did she press his hand. All she could do was watch him from a distance. *Thank God you're safe*, she wanted to say.

He didn't speak for a few moments. 'You got off lightly. Kschessinska mansion was completely ransacked yesterday.' Kschessinska Palace, headquarters of the Bolshevik Central Committee and Petrograd Committee, Lenin's residence. Was nothing sacred? Was nothing safe?

'You think you can control the masses. You are fools. It's like trying to control a herd of stampeding horses,' said Dmitry, shaking his head.

'They killed Arsenii,' whispered Regina, holding on to the wall, looking like she was about to collapse.

A shadow ran over Nikolai's face.

'Is it just me or is it quieter outside?' asked Sophia.

'The government dispersed the crowds. They are shooting the leaders, arresting everybody else. The workers are returning to factories from fear of arrest. The strike is over,' said Nikolai.

'Thank God,' exclaimed Regina, crossing herself.

'Wait,' cried Sophia. Something caught her attention. It was the expression on Nikolai's face. He didn't look pleased when he said the strike was over. She thought of the angry crowd, reciting the Bolshevik slogans as it swept through Petrograd like a tsunami, and of Arsenii, bravely stepping in front of them and dying moments later. She thought of Nikolai, standing before soldiers and workers, advocating for a peaceful protest. But a

119

protest, nonetheless. 'What do you mean, shooting the leaders?'

'The government blames the Bolsheviks for the upheaval. Lenin is in hiding. They will be looking for me.'

Sophia gasped and her face twisted in horror. Thankfully, no one was looking at her.

*

After the storm died down, an eerie silence descended on Petrograd. It seemed unnatural and threatening to Sophia, who had forgotten what it was like to wake up in the city that wasn't torn apart by conflict. It was hard to imagine that only yesterday these same streets had been churning like an angry ocean. Sophia knew insurrection could break out again at any moment. It would take more than a handful of arrests to quieten down this particular storm. Once again, it felt like the city was holding its breath, waiting for another momentous event the likes of which seemed to make up the terrible year of 1917. What had to happen to bring Russia much needed peace? She didn't know and neither, it seemed, did those at the helm of this rogue ship that was heading head-first towards its own destruction.

When she looked outside, she saw deserted streets and burnt-down shops, ransacked during the violent events of the last couple of days. Everyone she knew wanted to leave Petrograd. They were like rats running for their lives because their ship had sprung a leak. If only it was so easy. To leave, one needed special permission from the Provisional Government. To get this permission, one had to have connections. And the old nobility didn't have the connections. In every government building across the city, yesterday's counts and princes begged yesterday's farmers and peasants to have mercy on them, to make an exception, to allow them to leave and start a new life somewhere far from here. Somewhere where they would be safe.

Dmitry and Sophia didn't beg or expect a miracle. They stood in the eye of the storm and watched life as they knew it collapse around them.

To leave was inconceivable. To abandon their home felt like admitting defeat. Yet, to stay was also inconceivable because the tidal wave of the insurrection could hit again at any moment and this time who was to say it wouldn't wash everything away, them included?

'I'm going to hide Nikolai in the secret room,' Dmitry told her. 'You don't mind, do you? I know it's dangerous and we could get in trouble. But he's my brother. I can't turn my back on him.'

'Of course,' she replied, relieved. How had she not thought of the secret room herself? It was perfect! 'It's the safest hiding place. No one will ever find him there.'

'I hope you are right. It's worth a try.'

The secret room was located behind the salon and designed in such a way that, unless one knew of its existence, it was practically impossible to find. Sophia's heart felt lighter knowing Nikolai would be safe. His safety was all that mattered. She didn't care if hiding him in their house would put her and Dmitry in danger.

When she took him to his hiding place, he had looked around the tiny space and said, 'A secret room! What do you keep in here? Love letters?'

'Love letters? Of course not. Who would write to me? Dmitry is not a romantic.'

'I would imagine that someone like you has hundreds of admirers.'

Blushing, she said, 'I keep books here.' Thanks to this room, she still had some books left. Not everything had been burnt by the revolutionary masses. 'Why don't you read something? I don't have any revolutionary books though. They are mostly romance novels.'

'I'm not much for romance novels.'

'Memoirs and biographies, then?'

'Sounds good.'

She watched him closely. 'What's the matter? Are you disappointed with the revolution?'

'I am disappointed with our leaders, who completely misunderstand the principles of the revolution.'

As she lay in her cold bed, only two rooms away from him, her hand pressed to her heart, she wondered if he was reading under the light of his kerosene lamp. Was he writing more speeches and proclamations? Or was he sleeping?

She didn't call out, but she couldn't sleep either. The silence outside filled her with dread.

In the morning, before she even had breakfast, she prepared a tray of food – some bread, a slice of cheese, a boiled egg, a small glass of milk. She wished she had more but they hardly had anything left. She walked upstairs and into the salon, approaching the wall that hid the secret room behind it.

'Where are you going, my dear?' asked Dmitry, who was reading on a divan by the window.

'Just bringing Nikolai his breakfast.'

'I'll take it to him,' said Dmitry, snatching the tray from Sophia, who was too weak to argue, and disappearing inside the secret room. She didn't even catch a glimpse of Nikolai.

In the afternoon, Nikolai's right-hand man Ivan arrived, begging them to hide him. Small and fidgety, with a twitching moustache and shifty eyes, he reminded Sophia of a mouse trapped in a corner by a large cat. 'I was in a carriage on Moika Canal when I realised the driver was a militia man,' he said. 'He was taking me in the opposite direction of where I wanted to go. I had to jump out and run all the way here.'

'They didn't follow you, did they?' asked Sophia, concerned for Nikolai.

Ivan shook his head. She took him to the secret room. She didn't want to disclose Nikolai's hiding place to a complete stranger but Nikolai had insisted that the minute Ivan appeared, he had to see him. The room was much too small for the two men to share but they assured her they would manage. 'Beggars can't be choosers,' said Nikolai, who had slept on the floor the night before.

'Trotsky and Lunacharskii have been arrested on Tavricheskaya Street. They have warrants for Lenin, Zinovyev, Kollontai, Raskolnikov, Parvus. And us,' said Ivan.

'They'll be looking for us at train stations and major roads out of the city. For now, we are safe here.'

Ivan shook his head. 'We are no longer safe, no matter where we go. They are accusing us of plotting with the enemy, feeding the Germans information, helping them disorganise the front. They claim the disruptions were part of the plan by the foreign enemy to destroy Russia.'

'They've always had vivid imaginations.'

'They claim we are financed by the German Empire and stamping us out is paramount for Russia's defence. They won't stop at anything.'

'Sounds like the revolution turned its back on its most fervent supporters,' mumbled Dmitry. Everyone ignored him.

Occasionally, men arrived with important papers for Nikolai to read and sign. He asked Sophia for some ink and paper and spent his days writing. Even confined to the tiny room and unable to leave the house, he never stopped working. And neither did Sophia. They had four wounded left in the hospital and during the day, she spent all her time with them. As she toiled to make their burden lighter, with Regina by her side, the weight she carried on her own shoulders seemed a little lighter too. Every morning she scrubbed the floors – Nikolai was a huge believer in the importance of hygiene. She told men who could walk by themselves to exercise in the garden – Nikolai had once told her physical exercise was the best medicine. She changed their bandages and administered the potions the way Nikolai had taught her.

Sometimes Nikolai would ask her for a deck of cards and the five of them would play every game of chance they could think of to pass the time, poker and bridge being everyone's favourites. Sophia would lose one game after another and get teased mercilessly by her husband and Regina and even Ivan but never Nikolai. 'Unlucky in cards, lucky in love,' he would say and her face would turn red. With all those eyes watching her, with her husband watching her, she was unable to glance in Nikolai's direction. She would look to the side of him and only raise her eyes when he was speaking to her directly. But once she caught Dmitry's gaze and wondered if he realised she couldn't look at his brother the way she looked at Regina or Ivan – without blushing.

Sometimes they would read books to each other. Not Chernyshevsky and his revolutionary manual but romantic novels and books by Dumas and Tolstoy. Nikolai's favourite was *War and Peace*. Sophia preferred *Anna Karenina* but she couldn't read past Anna's suicide, after she had fallen in love with a man who was not her husband and lost everything.

And sometimes, not often, because by the time night fell everyone was too tired for anything serious, they played checkers or chess. To Dmitry's chagrin, Sophia almost always won.

'Women are not supposed to be good at chess,' said Dmitry. 'Just my luck, marrying someone smarter than me.'

Nikolai said, 'You are a lucky man.' Once again Sophia blushed. Everything she was feeling was on her face, for the world to see.

'Do you remember how our mother played chess when we were little?' asked Dmitry.

Nikolai beamed. 'She was spectacular. No one could beat her. Except our father.'

'She let him win to make him feel good.'

'I think Papa knew she was letting him win. But he let her believe he didn't because it brought her so much joy to see how excited he got.'

'He *did* get excited, every single time. Like a child.'

'They loved each other so much,' said Nikolai quietly. 'Do you remember how she danced?'

'No one could take their eyes off her.' Dmitry looked at his brother with affection. Then he said to Sophia, 'We were not allowed to leave our bed late at night but Nikolai found a secret passage. Every time our parents entertained, we would sneak out of bed and watch them. They looked so happy. I still remember my mother's laughter. When I was a child, I thought that's what being a grown-up was going to be like. Nothing but happiness, with not a care in the world.'

'Didn't turn out quite like that,' said Nikolai.

'No, not quite.'

One night, when everyone was tired of chess and cards and idle conversation, Nikolai said to Sophia, 'Why don't you play your violin for us?'

She shook her head adamantly, feeling the colour rush to her cheeks. 'Better not. Someone might hear. They might be looking for you.'

'Nonsense. It's too late for patrols.'

'Too late for music, too,' said Sophia. She didn't want to play here, in front of them, with all those pairs of eyes on her. But most of all, she didn't want to play in front of *him*. Music was something she did in private. It was personal, like praying. It exposed the inner workings of her soul, showed the world what she was feeling. What if he heard her play the violin and knew instantly? What if everybody knew? What if they heard her longing and desire in every note she played for him?

'Don't be shy,' he said. 'It's never too late for music.'

She went back to the salon and soon returned with her violin. Sitting in the corner, not looking at him, she played Chopin and Mozart, Beethoven and Bach but not her favourite Tchaikovsky, because for some reason she couldn't hear the beloved sounds without tears in her eyes.

The chords were magic. They transported her away from the cramped, dark hiding place, away from Petrograd and the revolution to a place with wide fields and topaz rivers, where the sun

125

played on the water surface and the birds sang with joy. When she played a popular gypsy ballad, Nikolai started singing.

'*Black eyes, passionate eyes,*
Burning and beautiful eyes!
How I love you, how I fear you,
It seems I met you in an unlucky hour!'

Never had she heard a voice like his before. It was powerful and lyrical at the same time. It soared and plunged into the very depths of her soul. It made her tremble and she could no longer hold the bow in her hand. She stopped playing but on and on he sang.

'You sing so beautifully,' exclaimed Regina, moving closer. 'Where did you learn to do that?'

'Growing up, he drove us all crazy with his singing,' said Dmitry with a good-natured grin on his face. 'Couldn't get a moment of peace.'

'You should have become a singer instead of a revolutionary. You would have been famous,' said Regina.

'He's famous now,' said Ivan. 'All of Petrograd is looking for him.'

'Infamous,' said Dmitry.

'Father would never forgive me if I became a singer.'

'He never forgave you for becoming a revolutionary,' replied Dmitry and Nikolai laughed.

Sophia couldn't say anything, nor could she take her eyes off him.

When their voices fell quiet, they heard a loud knock at the front door.

*

They left the cards, the chess, the violin and filed out of the hiding place, leaving Nikolai and Ivan behind the secret door. Trembling, Sophia threw one last glance at the wall. Unless one

126

knew exactly what to look for, it was impossible to tell another room was there. And yet, she couldn't help feeling afraid.

To her horror, she heard a stern voice from behind the heavy front door. 'Open up. I have a search warrant, orders of the Provisional Government.'

'It didn't take long,' muttered Dmitry.

'They can search. They'll never find them,' whispered Regina, her voice cracking.

The militia man standing outside was tall and imposing. He looked at them from his great height the way a giraffe might look at a fly, with suspicion and contempt. 'I am looking for Nikolai Orlov. He is wanted for his connection to the enemy and we have every reason to believe this is where he is hiding.'

'I haven't seen my brother in weeks,' said Dmitry. 'We are not close. But you are more than welcome to search for yourself.'

The officer walked from room to room, methodically opening every door, checking the kitchen, the cellars, the empty servant quarters. He paused in the dining hall and looked at the wounded.

'These are the sick I am looking after,' said Sophia. 'They can't walk, they can barely talk. Two of them are contagious.'

She was hoping the officer would be scared off by her lie and leave quickly. But he paid her no attention, walking from bed to bed, shining his torch into the men's faces, shaking them awake and asking them questions. Satisfied the person he was searching for wasn't among them, he left the room and, to Sophia's dismay, proceeded upstairs.

When he entered the salon, she was ready to scream. The wanted men were only a thin wall away. If they spoke, the man would hear. If one of them sneezed, he would know instantly they were there and all would be lost. Not only Nikolai and Ivan, but the rest of them would be arrested. Sophia wondered what the punishment was for hiding men wanted by the state. What price did one pay for treason in this new Russia?

Only when the man left the room and proceeded to search

the rest of the house did the three of them relax. Dmitry took Sophia's hand, squeezing it. Regina crossed herself. Sophia could breathe again.

Their relief was short-lived. When the man was done searching the house, he approached Dmitry and Sophia.

'Can I see your identification papers?' he demanded, visibly angry that his search had produced no results. 'You are Nikolai Orlov's brother?'

'I am,' replied Dmitry, standing up straight.

'You and your wife will follow me.'

'You are arresting us?' exclaimed Dmitry. 'On what grounds?'

'We need to ask you a few questions, to assist with our inquiries.'

Regina exclaimed, 'You are arresting a lady? What kind of a man are you?'

'You don't think your tsarist government arrested women revolutionaries?'

'It's not the same. Sophia Orlova is a countess.'

'There is no such thing, comrade. In Russia, everyone is equal.' When Dmitry and Sophia didn't move, he added, 'Please, follow me. Don't make me handcuff you.'

Not saying a word, not looking at each other and not touching, Sophia and Dmitry followed the officer. At the door, Sophia turned around and mouthed to Regina to look after Nikolai. When she stepped out of the house into the still air outside, she realised she was crying.

Chapter 7

July 1917

The police carriage moved swiftly down Nevsky Avenue and over the river Neva that was nothing but a dark shadow running away towards the horizon. Sophia didn't know what awaited them at their destination but she held no illusions. Didn't Ivan say these people would stop at nothing until they found them? They believed Dmitry and Sophia knew where Nikolai was. She shuddered at the thought of what was to come and willed the carriage to move slower. But for once, the streets of Petrograd were almost empty. Where was the screaming crowd when she needed it?

The streetlights blinded Sophia, the occasional fires. The thoughts whirring through her head drove her crazy. Dmitry reached for her, pulling her closer. 'Don't be afraid, Sophochka,' he whispered.

'I'm not afraid.'

'What can they possibly do to us? The Bolsheviks took our house by force, they stole our possessions. Tell them that never in a million years would we ally ourselves with these people. Say you know nothing.'

'Don't worry. I'll never tell them anything.'

'You are a good woman and a good wife. Nikolai is right. I'm lucky to have you.' He kissed her forehead.

'At lease he's safe,' she whispered.

'For now,' replied Dmitry.

'You are not going to tell them, are you?'

Dmitry looked horrified. 'Of course not. We might have our differences but he's still my brother.'

Everything went dark as they passed over Fontanka. Seconds later, another streak of light. Dmitry looked at her with quiet concern. She lowered her eyes, wishing she could hide from him.

The coach groaned and slowed down, finally stopping outside an imposing grey building. When Sophia stepped out onto the cobbled street, her legs trembled so much, she slipped and fell, hurting her ankle. The officer didn't seem to notice. If he did, he didn't offer to help. Instead, he barked for the two of them to follow him. Wincing in pain, she hobbled after him and Dmitry.

The building that housed the newly established militia had served as a police station under the tsarist government. Sophia could see the outline of the royal insignia on the walls where it had been scraped off by the revolutionaries. She was told to wait, while they led Dmitry away. *No*, she wanted to scream. *Please, don't leave me here alone.* But she knew there was no point. The officer didn't seem the type to feel pity for anyone but especially someone like her, in her expensive silk dress, even if it was falling apart. The man at the desk glared at her. Quietly she sat, trying not to pay attention to the drunken voices coming from the cell where they had taken Dmitry.

What time was it? How long had she been there, staring into space, praying for lightning to strike or perhaps an earthquake to destroy the building? The waiting was the worst part. *Let it come quicker*, she thought. Anything was better than this uncertainty. When the officer returned, she was glad to see him. Without a word he took her to an empty cell and brought her a glass of water, and then the metal door closed with a loud bang and she was alone in the dark.

It was the fifth of July, the date of their traditional summer party. This time last year she was dancing the night away in their garden, with not a care in the world. She was watching the fireworks and the stars, drinking champagne and eating lobster, exchanging pleasantries and wondering if there was more to life than this. Wishing for change, for things to be different somehow. For a little bit of drama and excitement. For a purpose, a higher meaning to her life. 'Be careful what you wish for,' she whispered to herself in her tiny cell as she curled up on her uncomfortable bed.

It was cold and she shivered in her light dress. Her stomach hurt from hunger. The thin mattress she was lying on smelt of mould and stale urine, making her feel queasy and unwell. She wished someone was in the cell with her, another human soul to remind her she was still alive and not buried in this place forever, without light or air or hope.

Pinching the soft skin between her fingers, she willed herself to stay awake. The thought of falling asleep here filled her with panic. When they came for her, she wanted to be alert and in possession of her senses. She didn't want to be drowsy and vulnerable. But her exhaustion got the better of her and she started to drift off, just as the heavy lock screeched and the door opened. A rough hand shook her and a harsh voice ordered her to get up. Her tormentor's torch blinded her. She couldn't see who was behind it. She couldn't get up but continued to stare into the light until her eyes hurt.

A pair of hands yanked her up, placing her on her feet. Once again, she was told to follow. She obeyed, slowly and uncertainly. Every step was a struggle.

'Where are you taking me?' she muttered.

'It's up to us to ask questions. It's up to you to answer them,' said the voice. They walked through a long damp corridor lit by a small yellow light. In this light, she saw that the man in front of her was short and round, the militia uniform about to burst from his rotund belly. Instead of reassuring her, his comical appearance made her more afraid. It seemed out of place, and she felt like she was trapped in a terrifying nightmare.

They walked past Dmitry's cell, alive with voices, laughter and vile smells. The criminals sat on the floor, playing cards and cursing. Dmitry was on the bench with his eyes closed. She wanted to say something to him but didn't want to attract the attention of her guard or the other men in the cell. All she could do was reach her hand out as if trying to touch her husband's face through the space between them.

'Through here, please,' said her jailer. She followed him through the open door and found herself in a brightly lit room with a desk and four chairs. Three of the chairs were unoccupied. The fourth contained a grim square-faced man, his hands on the table and expectant eyes on her. So petrified was she by these probing eyes and the hostile expression on his face, his outsized body that made the desk appear smaller, like he was a grown-up sitting on toddler furniture, she wanted to scream at her guard to take her back to her cell, to not leave her alone in the room with this man. But it was too late. The officer saluted the man at the table like he was his superior and walked away.

She made a move towards the door, but it shut in her face.

'Please, take a seat,' said the man calmly, motioning towards a chair opposite him. They were nothing but polite, these revolutionaries, even as they were about to tear you apart, thought Sophia. And she knew this man was going to tear her apart. He was going to break her until she gave in. It was written all over his face. But if he wanted Nikolai's whereabouts, she would rather die than tell him anything. They could torture her and beat her, they could threaten her and kill her but she wouldn't say a word.

Shaking, Sophia fell into the chair.

'No need to look so frightened. We brought you here to ask you a few questions, that is all.' Instead of calming her, these words made her panic more. It was as if he could see right through her. As if he could read her mind. 'You have nothing to worry about. Provided you cooperate, of course.'

And if I don't? she wanted to ask but didn't dare. She was unable to take her petrified eyes off him. He was like a magnet drawing her gaze.

'Please state your full name and address.'

She did so in a voice she didn't recognise.

'Are you a supporter of the revolution?' Sophia didn't know how to answer his question. Was she a supporter of the revolution that had taken everything from them, leaving them with nothing? That had nearly taken their lives? Was she a supporter of mutiny in Petrograd, of the maddened crowd that swallowed Arsenii and spat out his mutilated body, of murders and looting in her once peaceful city? She said nothing, looking inside her hands as if searching for answers. The man moved forward slightly. 'You hesitate. But that's fine. We are not here to investigate your political views.'

'Why *am* I here?'

Without taking his gaze off her, he said, 'We are looking for your brother-in-law, Nikolai Orlov. He is accused of inciting an insurrection against the Provisional Government and plotting its overthrow with the enemy. In other words, treason.'

'Treason? He's done nothing but support the revolution from day one. His life's work is the revolution. And this is how you repay him?'

'There are many factions out there that are looking to use the revolution to grab the power for themselves. Our job is to identify these factions and neutralise them. The Bolsheviks are like children playing with explosives. One careless movement and the whole thing will blow up.'

'All of you are like children playing at power. You can't control Russia. Only the tsar can do that. And I can't help you. I don't know where Nikolai is.'

'Lying to an official and hiding a known criminal is also treason. And with your and your husband's political convictions ...'

'What political convictions? I haven't done anything other than stand back and watch as my house was taken away from me, my valuables, my future, my dignity, my whole life.'

'Given half a chance, you would return to the old regime, would you not?'

'Can you blame me?'

'That's what I thought. The intention to commit treason in itself is treason. People like you and your husband, people who had everything handed to them on a silver platter, who never had to work a day in their lives, are a threat to the revolution. We are here to eliminate this threat.'

'We are no threat. All we want is to be left alone. To be safe. To go on with our lives ...'

'As before? What lengths would you go to to return to what it was like *before*? Would you like to see the tsar restored? The country plunged into the chaos of civil war?'

'As opposed to the chaos of revolution?'

'We are a new government, comrade. We take every threat seriously. We deal with it accordingly. Our prisons are bursting to the seams with people like you. Our labour camps, too.'

'You are threatened because you are weak. People no longer support you.'

He took off his glasses and cleaned them, a smirk on his face, like he was entertained by her, like she had said something amusing. Then he replaced his glasses on the bridge of his nose and watched her in silence, finally clearing his throat and talking softly, almost kindly. 'The choice is yours. You can cooperate and prove your loyalty to us. Or we can put you and your husband on the next train to Kolyma. What will it be?'

'What do you want from us?'

'Just a few words. It will cost you nothing. In return, you can have your life.'

'You call it a life? We have no future here, no place to call our own.'

He lifted his hand as if to interrupt her. 'Where is Nikolai Orlov?'

'I told you. I don't know.'

'You are all the same, you ladies and gentlemen of the Russian nobility. You don't know the value of hard work. Kolyma will be good for you. It will teach you what it's like to get up at dawn and toil in extreme weather for sixteen hours a day, without food or water or a minute's rest. Day after day, year after year, until you die. It will teach you what it's been like for ninety-nine per cent of the population of Russia over thousands of years.' He pulled a paper out of his briefcase. 'Kolyma is the coldest inhabited place on earth. Prisoners die there at an unprecedented rate. Would you like to find out for yourself? All I need to do is sign this paper and you and your husband will find yourselves on an all-expenses-paid holiday to hell on earth.' He reached for a pen, brought the pen to paper. His eyes never left her face. 'But one word from you and I will know you are a loyal citizen of Russia, who embraces the new regime fully and irrevocably. Where is Nikolai Orlov?'

'What will you do to him if you find him?'

'Punishment for treason is death.'

She looked at the terrible face in front of her, at the paper on the table, condemning her and Dmitry to a fate worse than death. One scribble from her tormentor and her life would be over. But one word from her and she would save them both. All she had to do was tell him where Nikolai was.

Nikolai, who put his own interests last in his lifelong struggle to help those less fortunate than him, whose purpose in life was to save people. Once, when they were cleaning and bandaging a gunshot wound, he had said to her, *Knowing how to heal is what makes a good doctor. But knowing how to heal and give the patient hope is what makes a great doctor. How to heal with love.*

Patients are like children because they are so afraid. Our job is to make them less so.

He was the kindest man she had ever met.

There was only one option. She didn't hesitate.

'You can send me to Kolyma. You can kill me if you want to. But I can't tell you something I don't know.' And then she thought, *What if Dmitry betrays him?* The thought made her blood run cold. The stakes were high. What if Dmitry sacrificed Nikolai to save their lives? *No*, she whispered to herself. *No.* It was impossible. Her husband would never condemn his own brother to a certain death. For a moment the man looked angry enough to strike Sophia. He pushed the papers off his table and rang the bell. When the officer appeared, he said, 'Take her away. Bring her husband in.'

As Sophia walked behind the jailer, her insides frozen with fear, she knew her silence wouldn't save Nikolai. Sooner or later, they were going to find him. They wouldn't stop until he was in their clutches. She also knew her silence was going to condemn her and Dmitry. She had seen the determination on her interrogator's face and she was deathly afraid.

This is for him, she repeated to herself as she took step after step down the dank corridor to her tiny cell. *This is for Nikolai.*

*

The next few days were a blur. Feverish and unwell, Sophia picked at dry rice and bricklike black bread and tried not to scream when rats ran over her feet. She was no longer afraid of rats. There were so many other things to be afraid of. She prayed for sleep. She prayed for clarity and strength. But most of all, she prayed for Nikolai.

Was this how her life was going to end? Far from home, in a God-forsaken place that even the sun had forgotten, mining precious metal until she collapsed and died? Would she go insane

136

and forget who she was? And how long would it take? Weeks, months, years? Would Nanny go to church and light a candle for her, while she was forced into an armoured truck that would take her to a train on its way to the hell on earth her interrogator had described with so much glee?

She no longer heard the rowdy prisoners in the cell down the corridor. No longer heard anything other than the thoughts inside her head. Every time the rusty lock screamed in anger and the guard walked in to bring food or take her tray away, she was expecting to be told to get up and come with him. And yet, she waited for a miracle, for someone to take her hand and lead her to safety, away from her tiny cell with its stale air and pungent mattress, into the freshness of a Petrograd night. Because hope was always the last to go. It lived while the heart lived.

The door opened. She didn't raise her head or open her eyes. 'Please, follow me,' she heard the familiar voice say.

Here it was, the moment she was dreading and yet waiting for because she knew it was inevitable. Her heart skipped with horror one moment and hope the next. She welcomed change because anything was better than the uncertainty. She wanted to get off her uncomfortable bed, walk through the doors, step outside, see the dark Petrograd sky, if only for a moment – it was almost freedom. But her petrified body refused to obey and she remained on the bed, staring at the officer.

He approached and unceremoniously lifted her by her arm, dragging her behind him to a desk where her husband was waiting. Dmitry seemed to have aged years in just a few days. His skin looked grey and his cheeks hollow. His clothes were torn and muddy. He looked resigned, as if he knew what was in store for them and had accepted it. She ran into his arms. 'Don't worry, it will be all right. Everything will be all right,' he whispered, squeezing her. 'Whatever happens, I will look after you.'

She knew he was just saying it, to make her feel better, to give her a moment of hope. But she drew closer to him anyway, finding comfort in his warmth. 'I know.'

The man behind the desk disappeared into the room behind him and soon returned with their belongings – Dmitry's portmanteau, her precious pearl earrings and her comb. 'You are free to go,' he said, his unfriendly eyes appraising them.

'You mean, we can leave?' she asked incredulously.

'That's what I said.'

'We can go home?'

'If you'd rather stay here, I'm sure we can arrange it.' The man grinned, exposing a mouth that was missing half its teeth. Sophia shuddered.

Dmitry guided her outside. It was daylight and the sun shone unusually bright for Petrograd, the sky unusually blue, even for spring, taking Sophia by surprise, making her squint, pause for a moment and take everything in – horses neighing, automobiles honking, people shouting. A tram rattled past and a dog barked. She stood motionless, overwhelmed by it all.

In the carriage back home, she broke down in tears. Dmitry held her and stroked her back, whispering in her ear. In a shaking voice, she said, 'That horrible man threatened to send us to Kolyma. But I didn't tell him anything.'

'Nor did I. I'm not sacrificing my brother to those monsters. I don't care what they say.'

'I don't understand. Why did they let us go?'

'Maybe they believed us. We have nothing to do with their political squabbles. They can't punish us for being of noble birth or they'd have to massacre thousands of us.'

'We have to warn Nikolai. We have to tell him he's in grave danger. Did you see that man's eyes? He looked like a wolfhound following a scent.'

'Yes, you're right. Petrograd is not a safe place for Nikolai. He needs to leave, and soon.'

Sophia sat in silence the rest of the way, her face to the window. She could see groups of people meandering past, carrying revolutionary slogans and red flags, their expectant faces alive with emotion. Even through the tiny window of the carriage, she could sense the tension in the air. Arresting Nikolai and the other Bolshevik leaders would not solve the problem, she thought. It wouldn't make people less hungry, less demanding, less disillusioned with the Provisional Government.

Once again, Petrograd streets were busy. The journey that took minutes a few days ago was now taking forever. Sophia trembled with anticipation. Any moment now, the carriage would stop outside their house and she would jump out, walk through the front gates, run up the stairs, into her salon and through the secret door. Any moment now, she would see Nikolai. And she desperately needed to see him. One glimpse of his face would make the last few days melt away as if they had never happened.

Their residence was mute and seemed deserted. The Bolsheviks were in hiding, just like Nikolai. Even the wounded were gone, their empty beds a mess of tangled sheets and bloodied bandages. A grim Regina greeted them in the dining hall. Her face lit up momentarily when she saw them. But moments later the joy was gone. She hugged Sophia with tears in her eyes. 'I didn't know what to think. I didn't know where to look for you. They took you away and no one was telling us anything. And I desperately needed to get in touch with you.'

There was something in her face that caught Sophia's attention. 'Did something happen while we were gone?'

Regina was silent as if she didn't want to tell them. It was Nanny, crying happy tears at the sight of Sophia and Dmitry, who finally said, 'They arrested Nikolai and Ivan.'

Suddenly Sophia couldn't breathe. All oxygen was gone and her throat was burning. 'How did they find them?'

'They burst in here with three German shepherds and searched the house. The dogs found them.'

Dmitry paled. 'When did it happen?'

'This morning at nine.'

'Just before they let us go. I suppose once they had him in their clutches, they had no use for us anymore.' After their ordeal and the news of Nikolai's arrest, Sophia wanted to crawl into bed, hide from the world and be alone. But Regina and Nanny had other ideas. They clucked over her like mother hens. *Do you want something to eat? Something to drink? Do you want us to boil some water for your bath?* Soon she had a tray of food (stale bread and some old potatoes) and a hot cup of tea in front of her. She didn't touch the food, wrapping her fingers around the cup and letting her tea go cold. She was shivering and couldn't get warm, despite a thick blanket Nanny threw over her legs. She wanted to cry but couldn't. She sat in her salon, absentmindedly stroking her mother's portrait, her gaze on the wall that concealed the secret room.

Nikolai was gone and she didn't even get a chance to say goodbye.

*

The house felt empty because Nikolai was no longer there. No more laughter or card games. No more soft chords of the violin in the dark of night, no more singing. No more wounded men to take her mind off her fear. All she could do was sit and wait. But wait for what? If the Provisional Government had Nikolai, they were unlikely to let him go. When she closed her eyes, she still saw the grim face of her interrogator as he talked of death and exile. She knew there was little hope.

Dmitry found out from the few revolutionaries who were still staying in the house that his brother and Ivan had been taken to Kresty, where the most dangerous political prisoners were kept. 'My brother, in prison!' He shook his head. 'Papa always told him this was where he would end up if he didn't change his ways. But for the revolutionaries to imprison him, the irony!'

'You are saying it like it's his fault,' exclaimed Sophia.

'Of course it's his fault. He has no one to blame but himself.'

She was in no mood to argue, so she let it go. 'We have to do something or they are going to kill him.'

'What can we do? We were lucky to get away with our lives.'

'Can we visit him?'

'We have to distance ourselves or they would think we are supporting him. The last thing we need is to be arrested again.'

'But we *are* supporting him,' cried Sophia.

'Speak for yourself. Showing any interest in Nikolai will put all of us in danger.'

'You are worried about yourself,' she said, looking at her husband with reproach. 'But what about Nikolai? What about your brother, who saved our lives? Without him, we wouldn't be here. Shouldn't you be thinking about him, too?'

'I'm thinking about *you*. Your safety is all that matters to me.'

'So much so that you told them about Nikolai?' She couldn't believe her audacity. But she had to ask.

'Of course I didn't tell them. What are you saying? He is my brother.'

'Then why did they let us go without a punishment, even though he was hiding in our house?'

'They know the Bolsheviks took over our house against our will. They don't hold us responsible for this.'

She saw Nikolai's face everywhere. As she walked through the dining hall, touching the empty beds, she blinked and saw him bending over his patients, whispering encouragements, teaching her how to use the herbs at their disposal. As she sat in her husband's study, she saw Nikolai leaning over his documents, his hair covering his face. As she stood in the doorway to the secret room, she saw him with a book in his hands, mesmerised by the sounds of her violin. She roamed aimlessly from room to room, while Dmitry read the newspaper and wrote in his journal, while Nanny cooked and cleaned, while Regina mourned her father and brother. Sophia's helplessness was killing her. If only she could see him one more time. If only she could pick him up and carry him to safety, like he had carried her to safety that day when she rushed head-first into the burning building.

If only she had told him how she felt. She could barely breathe under the weight of her regret.

At breakfast one morning, Sophia asked Regina, 'Where *is* Kresty?'

'Not too far from here. On the other side of the Neva. Didn't take me long on the train.'

That made Sophia sit up and pay attention. 'You went to see him?'

'Yes, but they didn't let me. They said family only.'

'You should have told me you were going. I would have come with you. He is my brother-in-law.'

'They said close family only.' They both looked at Dmitry, who was reading in the corner and not listening to them. 'Besides, I wanted to see him alone.' Regina blushed. 'While you were gone, we spent a lot of time together. We talked, a lot. He is all I can think about and I know he feels the same way.'

Sophia turned away from her friend. She couldn't take the expression on Regina's face. She thought of the last time she had seen Nikolai. When the dreaded knock on the door had sounded that terrible night, she was playing her violin and his eyes were on her. As she placed the violin down, he smiled and whispered, 'Courage!' As if she was the one in danger and not him. As if her safety was what he worried about the most. When she walked out of the room, her hand brushed his hand for a fraction of a second. Would she ever see him again?

She no longer avoided the newspaper like the plague. She didn't care if it upset her. She needed to know what the Provisional Government was thinking. Every morning, she grabbed the paper as soon as it was delivered, before Dmitry could get to it, and carried it to her room. Sinking into an armchair, she devoured page after page, trying to read between the lines of the extensive

142

revolutionary propaganda. That day after breakfast, her heart nearly stopped when she saw that a number of high-ranking Bolsheviks had been shot for treason. She had to read the small paragraph three times before the words made sense. On fabricated charges, without a trial, in bright daylight, the accused had been turned to the wall and shot with machine guns. Numb from horror, she read through the long list of names. Nikolai Orlov was not among them. Relief like a warm ocean wave washed over her. And just as quickly it was gone, giving way to blind panic. Today he was safe. But what about tomorrow?

She was like an apparition moving through the house. She couldn't eat, couldn't talk to Regina, couldn't tell Nanny what was wrong with her, couldn't sit still. Finally, she waited till Dmitry was nowhere to be seen, got dressed, covered her head with a shawl and slipped out of the house, getting a carriage across the Neva to Kresty. The stage driver seemed intent on killing her, driving at a neck-breaking speed, narrowly avoiding streetlights and passers-by. She didn't care. She wished he would go faster. Her face to the window, she watched as Petrograd flew past.

They crossed the Liteyniy Bridge, going over the deepest place of the Neva, and drove a few more blocks past the train station and the hospital, finally pulling up in front of the grimy walls of Kresty Prison. She paid and disembarked, hiding her trembling lips and pale face behind her shawl.

For a long time, she watched the gloomy building, searching for the courage to walk through the visitor entrance and into the front yard. The face of her interrogator flashed before her and she started to shake. She hadn't felt safe since March, since four months ago when it all had started, but standing here, exposed and alone, made her feel like she was voluntarily stepping into the jaws of a shark. She almost turned around and ran back home but the thought of Nikolai in grave danger, possibly facing execution, made her stay. Dmitry might have turned his back on his brother but she could not. He was not alone and she wanted him to know that.

Trembling, Sophia gave her name and Nikolai's name to the sentry and sleepwalked after him down a long corridor. The lock screeched, a deafening, petrifying noise, and she felt a shiver of premonition, like her soul went dark the minute she stepped inside. It was as if she herself had become a prisoner.

Nikolai was sitting on a narrow iron bed, his face unshaven, his eyes dull, dressed in dirty, torn cotton pants and a shirt. He looked thin and unkempt, his face dark with stubble, but when he saw her, his eyes lit up and he said her name. It was the way he said it that filled her heart with joy, lovingly, like a caress.

'Nikolai,' she whispered, wishing she could run to him and take him in her arms. Instead, she leaned on the cold wall and waited for the sentry to leave.

'You have five minutes,' the oversized, angry man barked before slamming the door shut.

The cell was a small rectangle with an iron bed, a tiny wooden chair and a wobbly table. Her knees shook so much, she couldn't continue to stand in front of him. She sank onto the bed, while Nikolai moved closer and took her hands in his. There was a square window covered in cobwebs. Through this window, a small ray of light peeked through, not enough to brighten the cell. There was no other light, no kerosene lamp or candle.

'My God, Nikolai! Are you all right? You look terrible.'

'I'm fine. Better now that I'm seeing you. How did they let you in here?'

'We have the same last name. I told them I was your wife.' As she said it, she couldn't meet his eyes. She could feel her cheeks burning. She hoped he wouldn't notice in the dark but when she looked up, there was such warmth in his eyes, she forgot for a moment what she was about to say. 'I hate seeing you like this. You don't deserve to be here ...'

'They think I do. And at the moment, what they think is what matters. Does Dmitry know you are here?'

'Of course not. He's afraid of everything. He doesn't want me to leave the house. Doesn't want to visit you in case it gets us in trouble.'

Nikolai nodded. 'You shouldn't have come. It's too dangerous.'

'How could I not come to see you?' she whispered.

'Regina told me about the arrest. I was so worried.'

'It was nothing. It's over now.'

'Believe me, it's far from over. And you need to be careful.'

'They questioned me about you. Threatened terrible things if I didn't tell them where you were. But I didn't say a word.'

'I knew you wouldn't. But Dmitry is right. You can't show them that you support me in any way. If they come to question you again, distance yourself and pretend you don't know who I am. Don't try to defend me. It's too late for that.'

She gulped in fear. 'What are they going to do to you?'

'Only time will tell.'

She wanted to curl into a ball and cry. But she wasn't going to do it here, in front of him. She would wait till she got home. 'Do you get enough food? Do they let you out for a walk?'

'I get a little food. Don't worry, they won't let me starve.'

'Yes, because they intend to kill you themselves,' she murmured, her heart breaking. She didn't think he heard her. 'What do you do here day in and day out?'

'Try not to go out of my mind with boredom. Yesterday, I was attempting to prove the Pythagoras theorem from memory.' He pointed at the wall, where formulas and calculations were scribbled with something sharp.

'I didn't realise you knew the Pythagoras theorem. How did it go?'

'Great, to the fury of my jailer.' He pulled his shirt up and turned around. Down the left side of his back ran a long, angry scar.

She shuddered. 'They whipped you?'

'Apparently, geometry is not allowed at Kresty. Nor is drawing

145

on the walls and damaging state property.'

'I'm so sorry this happened to you.' She wanted to touch the bleeding wound. Wanted to press her lips to the damaged skin, make it all better, make it all go away. 'It must be so terrible here for you.' It had been terrible for her in a tiny cell on a dank mattress and she hadn't been physically threatened or hurt. 'Do they allow you books? Writing? Newspapers?'

He shook his head. 'All I do is think and sleep. I've never been more rested in my life.' And yet, she had never seen him look more exhausted. 'I made some chess pieces out of bread the other day,' he continued. 'Had a great game of chess with myself until they put a stop to it. No chess allowed, either. It was a shame. I was starting to win.' A trace of a smile curled his lips upwards. 'They don't bring me bread anymore. They tell me I'm not to be trusted.'

'I brought some food and some of your favourite books but they took it all away. I had cabbage pies for you. I baked them myself.'

'You baked me pies?'

'With Nanny's help. I've never baked anything in my life. I think they turned out all right. A little salty.'

'I like salty.' He looked at her, blinking fast, as if fighting an emotion he was trying to hide. 'I can't believe you baked me pies.'

'I'm sorry I couldn't give them to you. Those people outside were like vicious dogs. I'm surprised they let me in to see you in one piece.'

'I'm so glad they did. It was worth getting locked up just to have you bake your first pie for me.'

'Can I just point out that I was right and you were wrong?' Through her tears she tried to smile.

'In what way?'

'Your revolution. It isn't so glorious or magnificent after all. It's murderous and destructive. It devours everything in its path. It's trying to devour you, its most fervent defender. How can that be?'

146

'It seems our ideas of the revolution are different. The government sees it one way. We see it another way. Don't worry. It's an honour to be jailed for my beliefs.'

'Is it an honour to be killed for your beliefs? Because that's what they are doing to your comrades.' There was so much she wanted to tell him. So much to say but she couldn't find the right words. They watched each other in silence. It was that helplessness again. It was destroying her. 'How can we help you? Who can we talk to? Maybe if I speak to them, I will explain and they will see what they are accusing you of is absurd. And they will let you go. Then you can come home.'

'They know better than anyone what they are accusing me of is absurd. They are the ones who came up with the accusation. But they don't care.'

'There must be something we can do.'

'They are fighting for their lives because they are threatened. Like a wounded animal, they will destroy everything in their death throes. All they want is us out of the way, so they can continue to betray the revolution.'

'When you say out of the way ...' Her lips went white. She couldn't continue.

He took her hands in his and lowered his head as if he was about to kiss the tips of her fingers. 'You are no longer safe in Petrograd. No one can predict what will happen next.' His shoulders were stooped and his face solemn.

'This is our home. Where can we go?' Feeling him so close, his hands on her hands, she couldn't think straight.

'The next few months will be chaos. What you've seen so far, that was just the preview. The real revolution is still to come.'

'*That* was the preview?'

'God willing, we are planning to overthrow the Provisional Government and will not stop at anything. There will be more uprisings, more hunger. Petrograd is not a safe place for you right now. And more than anything I want you to be safe.'

'You are planning to overthrow the government from jail?'

'Listen to me. Staying in Petrograd is like standing inside the crater of a volcano. At any moment it could erupt. Why risk your life? What for? While I'm in jail, I can't protect you.'

'But who will protect you?' Looking into his face, she added in a tiny voice, 'I don't want to leave without you. I don't want to leave and not know if you're safe.'

'I know, Sophia,' he whispered urgently, leaning closer, as if he was about to kiss her. Holding her breath, she waited. He pulled away. 'I'm like a madman who can't think of anything else. I never knew I could feel this way and I don't know what to do or say. I'm afraid of saying the wrong thing. Of scaring you off somehow.'

'Nothing you say could scare me off.'

'I'm terrified of you. Terrified of this feeling. I've never met anyone like you before. You are selfless, kind, an angel. And married to my brother.' Nikolai pressed her to him. 'God, what are we going to do?'

He was about to say something else when the heavy door opened and the jailer appeared. 'Time,' he shouted.

'Please, promise me you'll be safe. Promise me you'll leave the city if you get a chance,' he said.

'Without you? Never!'

'Please, Sophia. Everything will be easier if I know you're safe. You asked how you could help me. This is how.'

She touched his face, traced his stubble with her fingers, left her hand on his chest so that she could feel his heartbeat with the tips of her fingers. The jailer pulled her by the arm and shouted, 'Let's go!'

She had no choice but to walk away. Shaking all over, she moved reluctantly, with her back to the door and her eyes on Nikolai. For a moment, he looked like he wanted to go after her. He stepped after her but the jailer screamed at him to stay where he was and Nikolai remained on the bed.

'I will come back and see you as soon as I can,' she said before the door closed, shutting him away from her. 'Stay safe and look after yourself.'

On the way back, she didn't get another carriage but walked home through the streets that seemed petrified into silence. Summer had truly come to Petrograd that week, and the air was stiff. Even the breeze from the river carried the heat in it, but Sophia couldn't stop trembling like she was cold. And all she could think of as she pushed her way through a group of disgruntled soldiers was, *What if this was the last time I saw him?*

*

When she returned home, she could hear voices coming from the dance hall. On a silk divan, a wedding present from her parents that had miraculously survived the invasion, she saw the round shape of one of Dmitry's closest friends, Count Alexei Strelnikov. Before she could greet him, Dmitry grabbed her by the arm and led her outside. 'Where have you been? I was worried sick.'

She reddened. 'I'm sorry you were worried. I had a few errands to run.'

'This is not the time to be out on your own. You know that.'

'It won't happen again.'

'If you need to go out, tell me and I'll come with you. It would kill me if anything happened to you.'

She couldn't bear seeing the worry and affection on her husband's face. Looking away from him, she followed him to the dance hall, her guilty heart beating violently.

A few years older than Dmitry, Count Alexei was red in the face with a mouth that pointed downwards, giving him an expression of a discontented bulldog. 'Could you ever imagine anything like this?' he demanded, waving his cup of tea in the air like he had once waved a glass of the best sherry money could buy.

'Only in my worst nightmares,' replied Dmitry, sitting opposite his friend and motioning for Sophia to join him.

'They were shooting near Moscow train station this morning. I barely got away with my life. Sometimes it surprises me that I am still alive, after everything I've been through.'

'How *have* you been these last few months?' asked Dmitry.

'Bad, very bad.' Alexei shook his head. His greasy moustache twitched. 'At first they ordered me to leave my house. I was forced to stay with my cousin and I can't stand him. A week later we were told to leave again. So we moved in with my aunt on the outskirts of Petrograd, only to find the rest of the family already there. There was hardly any space for us and then the Bolsheviks arrived and made the place their headquarters. Just like here.' Alexei glanced at the broken furniture and the stains on the walls. 'I know Kerensky personally. He is a childhood friend. We grew up together. I went to him and asked if I could have my house back. And he said no! Can you believe it?'

'I can believe it,' said Dmitry.

'But he offered me a pass to travel overseas. I'm thinking of going to Paris. I have family there.'

'You would leave Russia?' asked Sophia. Frankly, she wasn't surprised at Alexei's decision. If it wasn't for Nikolai in prison, she would be the first on the train out of Petrograd. It hadn't felt like home since that fateful day in March when their house was taken from them.

'Absolutely. I am no longer enamoured with it the way I was before the revolution. And you should come with me. I can arrange for permissions for you.'

They spoke a little more about the revolution. It was like the weather, always something to talk about. And they spoke about a better future elsewhere, of safety and peace, so desirable and unattainable, and yet, if only they managed to secure a permission slip to leave the city, everything would be different … Sophia smiled and nodded in all the right places but she wasn't listening. She was miles away – in a tiny cell in Kresty across the Neva.

As she was getting ready for bed that evening, brushing her

long hair, Dmitry walked into the room. For a second he watched her, finally coming closer and putting his arms around her. 'You are so beautiful like this, with your hair down.' He kissed her cheek. Moments later, his lips found her lips. She allowed him to kiss her but didn't kiss him back. 'What do you think about Alexei's proposal?' he asked. 'We should be leaving Petrograd. It's not safe here.'

'You want to leave our home?'

'Look what's happening around us. The whole country is drunk on power and soon they will slit each other's throats. Let's not be here to see it. I don't want any part of it.'

'Where would we go?'

'Somewhere far. Somewhere the revolution hasn't reached yet.'

'Is there such a place?'

'Of course. The whole world hasn't gone mad. There must be somewhere you and I can be safe. With Nikolai in prison, how long before they come for us? They've arrested us once; they'll do it again in a heartbeat. They see all of us as a threat to their revolution.'

'You want to abandon Nikolai to his fate, while you run to save your own skin?'

'To save you. That's the only thing that matters to me. Besides, we can't help him. What can we possibly do?'

'I don't want to leave while he's in jail,' she said. 'He saved our lives. If we leave, we'll never know what happened to him.'

His eyes narrowed. He was no longer smiling or touching her. 'My number one priority is you. Leaving Nikolai here is the price I'm willing to pay.'

'I'm not willing to pay that price,' she whispered. By the expression on his face, she knew Dmitry had made up his mind. But so had she. She didn't care if her husband found out how she felt. If he wanted to go, he would have to do so without her because she wasn't leaving without Nikolai.

When she closed her eyes that night, it was Nikolai's words

she heard inside her head. *I'm like a madman who can't think of anything else*, he had said to her just before the guard interfered and they were dragged away from each other. She breathed those words, lived through them as she thrashed sleepless in her bed, a madwoman consumed by what she was feeling.

Sophia knew she couldn't leave Dmitry. She could never be disloyal to him the way her mother had been disloyal to her father. But she also knew she had to talk to Nikolai, even if she couldn't promise him anything.

In the morning, she hurried to Kresty. For the first time in months, she noticed the beauty around her. The birds chirped their happiness at being alive. The sun played on the river and the boats bobbed cheerfully. The flowers in the Mikhailovsky Garden were a kaleidoscope of yellow, red and pink. Sophia inhaled the balmy morning air and increased her pace, her heart soaring at the thought of seeing him again.

This time, she didn't bring food or books. She had spent forever getting ready, brushing her hair until it was shiny and smooth and fixing it in a fetching bun, curls framing her face. She put rouge on her cheeks and tinted her eyelashes. She would have worn a different dress, one that wasn't torn at the elbows, but didn't have one. To compensate, she wore her best hat and gloves and silk ribbons in her hair. She wanted to look her best when she told him she loved him.

Inside the horrifying prison, it was damp and dark, just like before. Once again, she shuddered when she walked through the gate. She approached the man behind the desk. 'I'm here to see Nikolai Orlov.' Her voice trembled. Was it her imagination or did the man look at her with pity?

'No visitors allowed,' he barked.

'I was here yesterday. I saw him yesterday. You must have it in your records. Please. My name is Sophia Orlova.'

The man didn't flinch. 'Visitors are no longer allowed.'

Her hands twisted in anguish. 'Please, I need to see Nikolai.

Just for a moment. I have to tell him something.'

The man looked down from his desk at Sophia. 'Go home, comrade. Orlov is not allowed visitors. Orders from authority higher than myself. There is nothing I can do.'

'What authority? Can I speak to your superior?'

The guard lowered his voice to a terrifying whisper. 'That won't do you any good. You can't see Orlov. Orlov is dead.'

'What?' She paled and grabbed the wall. For a moment all she could hear was the ringing in her ears.

'That's right. He was executed this morning. I'm very sorry.'

The hat she was holding fell to the floor. Leaving it behind, she recoiled from the desk and the man who watched her with curiosity and, grasping the wall, stumbled out of jail. Outside, she slid onto the grass and stared at the fortress with unseeing eyes. She bit her lips till they bled but didn't even notice. No one helped her up. No one even glanced in her direction. People were used to heartbreak on the streets of Petrograd.

How long she stayed there or how she got back home, she didn't know. She might have walked, she might have caught the tram. At home, she went straight to the secret room and collapsed on the pile of clothes that had served as Nikolai's bed. His pillow still smelt of him. She clasped it to her chest, buried her face in it and wept.

'Please, don't leave me,' she whispered over and over. 'Please, don't leave me.'

She tried to remember herself before she had met Nikolai and couldn't. The woman without a care in the world no longer existed. She thought of the last time she saw him, of the way his body moved in her direction when the guard separated them, as if he was reluctant to see her go. Did he know this was to be the last time they saw each other?

She felt someone's warm hand on her forehead. Moments later, she heard Nanny's kind voice. 'What's wrong? We were waiting for you to come for lunch. Dmitry is frantic with worry.'

She couldn't speak at first. Curling into a ball, she sobbed in Nanny's arms, while the older woman stroked her head, like she often did when Sophia was a child. 'What is it, my dear? What happened?'

In a stifled voice, barely able to get the words out, Sophia told her.

Nanny gasped and crossed herself. For a few moments she couldn't speak. 'I'm so sorry, dear. The cursed revolutionists. One day they will pay for everything.' She wiped Sophia's tears away, kissing her forehead.

'Those monsters murdered him. The best man I've ever met. The most wonderful man.'

'Yes, darling, he was kind and selfless. He always wanted the best for everyone. Everybody loved him.'

'He saved us. But we couldn't save him. And I didn't even get to say goodbye.'

'Don't cry, dear. And don't blame yourself. None of it is your fault.'

'He was all alone when he died. He must have been so scared.'

She leaned into Nanny's large shoulder, but Nanny's embrace no longer brought comfort. Only Nikolai could do that. And he was gone.

'You need to pull yourself together,' Nanny said. 'Don't let Dmitry see you like this. What is he going to think?'

'Dmitry doesn't know yet. How can I tell him? I don't want to be the one to tell him.'

'You need to be strong. For Dmitry and for you. You need to save yourself, to get away from here and find a new life elsewhere. Time will help. In time it will hurt less.'

Sophia shook her head. She couldn't imagine it ever hurting less.

Nanny left and soon returned with a cup of steaming hot tea. When Sophia saw that it was the camomile Nikolai had once given her, she collapsed on the bed, groaning in agony. She couldn't even sit up.

'Please, drink this. You need your strength. Did you hear? Count Alexei has our permission slips. Dmitry wants to leave first thing tomorrow.'

'I'm not going anywhere.'

'You can't stay here. It's not safe.'

'It doesn't matter. Nothing matters anymore.'

'Please, don't say that.' Once again, Nanny's arms were around her. 'He would have wanted you to live,' she whispered.

She had thought she had lost everything when the revolution had started. She had thought *then* her life was over. How naïve she had been.

*

Dmitry's room was a whirlwind of clothes, books and newspaper clippings. Two trunks were open on his bed and he was hurling more and more items inside, not bothering to fold his clothes or straighten the papers. In the corner of the room, on a small table, was a kerosene lamp that threw shadows on the walls, on the chaos all around, on Dmitry's frantic face. He packed as if hungry wolves were at his heels, like his life depended on it.

Sophia stood in the doorway mutely. She couldn't speak, could barely hold herself up without falling.

'Have you finished packing?' asked Dmitry when he saw her. 'Alexei says there is a queue of people at the station every day. If we want to get on the train, we have to leave early tomorrow. Before dawn.'

Sophia might have said no, she might have shaken her head. She couldn't take her eyes off the half-empty trunks. Nikolai was dead and they were leaving. It was inconceivable, like they had already forgotten him.

'Where have you been?' Dmitry demanded, not looking at her and throwing more things inside the trunks. Some of it landed on the floor but he didn't stop to pick it up. 'I was looking for you. Nanny told me you went to church.'

'I didn't go to church.'

He looked up from a pile of notebooks he was trying to shove into a briefcase. 'You've got to stop doing that. Going out alone. It's not safe.'

'I went to see Nikolai in jail.'

'You went to see him alone? Why?'

'We are leaving. I wanted to say goodbye,' she lied. She would have told him the truth. She didn't care anymore. Except, he was her husband and he loved her. He didn't deserve any of this.

'Why didn't you tell me? I would have come with you.'

'I tried to. You told me to keep my distance, that seeing him now was too dangerous.' She tried and failed to keep the bitterness out of her voice.

'You are right. We are leaving. We should say goodbye. It's the least we can do.'

'It's been a week since he was arrested. In that week, you haven't visited him once. I didn't think you would be interested.'

'He's my brother. Of course I'd be interested. And I went to see him two days ago.'

'Why didn't you take me with you?'

'I didn't realise you wanted to see him so badly.'

She sank onto her husband's bed and groaned out loud. Dmitry was busy going through documents in his desk and didn't seem to hear. She didn't have the strength to continue this conversation and yet, she hadn't told him the hardest part. 'How did it go? Your visit?' she asked.

'Fine. He was in good spirits, talking about getting out of jail and turning Russia on its head. He should see this as a lesson but no, it's never enough for him. Nikolai is one of those people who are never satisfied with the order of things. He's never happy.'

'Are *you* satisfied with the order of things?'

'No. But I'm not going to risk my life trying to challenge the existing regime. I'm no fool.'

'No, of course not.'

'I'll tell you something. I've never met a man as stupid and stubborn as my brother. He thinks he can change the world. He's a lunatic. As if one man could ever do that.'

Before she stepped into this room, she had promised herself she wouldn't cry in front of Dmitry. She would steel herself for this conversation and walk out with her head held high. But now, as she heard him speak of his brother like this, she couldn't stop the tears from falling. 'He is hardly one man. He believes in something and fights for it. He will only be happy when everyone around him is happy. That's the type of person he is. He cares about others.'

'What did you two talk about when you saw him?' he asked, still focused on his papers, throwing some of them on the floor and others into one of the trunks. 'What can you possibly have in common? A countess and a revolutionary. He's trying to destroy everything that is dear to you. And you act like you don't even care.'

She leaned on the bed for support. Somehow, she didn't know how, she got the words out. 'I didn't see him. The sentry told me he was dead. He was shot this morning.'

Dmitry dropped the papers and staggered back. His face went white. 'There was nothing about it in the papers,' he said finally. She put her face in her hands and wept. Dmitry was silent for a long time, as if he had forgotten she was there. Then he put his arm around her and said, 'Please, don't cry. My brother died fighting for something he believed in. He died doing something he loved. Which is more than I can say for most people. My brother is lucky.'

He's gone, she wanted to scream. She wanted to throw his arm off and push him away, to run from his room and hide. She felt like she couldn't breathe, like she was underwater struggling for her life. *How can you say he's lucky when he was killed and we*

157

weren't even there for him? How can you say he's lucky when he was all alone when he died? she wanted to scream to her husband.

*

Regina had tears in her eyes when they said goodbye. 'Stay safe,' said Sophia, who was like an apparition that morning, without emotion, without feeling. It was the only way she could get through the day – by pretending it was all happening to someone else.

'I'll do my best.' Regina hugged her. 'You too. Look after yourself.'

'I don't feel right leaving you. Why don't you come? It's not too late.'

'I need to find out what happened to my brother. You know I can't leave until I know.'

'It's not safe in the city.'

'It's not safe anywhere in Russia. Besides, I don't care about anything anymore. Nikolai is gone. Just like everyone else I loved.' Regina had taken the news about Nikolai badly. She screamed and sobbed, while Sophia stood in the corner of the room and watched mutely, having herself screamed and sobbed in her bed through the longest night of her life.

The clock at Moscow train station struck six when Sophia, Dmitry and Nanny arrived. Sophia didn't think of the morning sunlight reflected off the Neva, the Summer Garden and Nevsky Avenue, the streets of her childhood she was leaving behind, perhaps forever. All she could think about was his anguished face when he told her he loved her.

The coach deposited them two blocks away from the station because the road was blocked by pedestrians. Everyone, it seemed, wanted to get inside. A red flag was flapping in the wind, announcing to the world the immense change that had occurred here in the last few months. But the change was evident

158

in many other ways. Rubbish littered the street that would have been immaculate under the tsar. A group of soldiers were drinking in broad daylight, in view of everyone, cursing and shouting. In the entrance, two sailors were fighting. No one paid them any attention. At the corner opposite, a dozen university students sat solemnly, drinking beer, eating sunflower seeds and every now and then spitting on the pavement, grim observers of the mayhem around them.

Sophia stood as if rooted to the spot, fighting the urge to turn around and run. She felt out of place here in her simple black dress and long gloves, her fashionable hat and perfect hair. Everyone, it seemed, was staring at her.

She would have stayed home. All she wanted was to close her eyes and sleep for eternity, until this thing she was feeling, this unbearable pain that was tearing her apart, was gone. But the last thing Nikolai had said to her was that he wanted her to leave the city. Who was she to go against his last wish? He wanted her to keep herself safe. And she would, for him.

There was no timetable, no indication of when the next train would arrive. The man who sold them tickets after examining their permission slips had no information. Nor did the conductor. All they could do was wait, like everyone else at the station.

Dmitry pulled her by the hand. 'Sophochka, are you all right? You are so pale. You are not yourself this morning.'

She shrugged. She couldn't talk even if she wanted to. If she opened her mouth, she would break down.

Nanny said, patting her hand, 'Poor child, leaving her home behind forever, she must be heartbroken.'

'It's not forever. Only for a little while. This madness will not last and we'll be back before we know it.' Sophia wondered if he really believed it. He seemed in good spirits this morning, not at all like someone who had received the devastating news of his brother's death the night before. 'It's a new beginning, a new chapter in our life.' He kissed her on the cheek.

When the train finally arrived, it was so busy, only a few people could get on. Sophia, Dmitry and Nanny were among the lucky ones. They stood mutely in the dark corridor, pushed into a corner by a wall of bodies. Sophia could smell sweat and stale urine coming from the men around her. She pressed her fist to her mouth and held her breath.

'I'm not putting our trunks in the luggage compartment. We'll never see them again,' said Dmitry.

'There's no space for them here,' said Nanny. 'Barely any space for us.'

'We'll find space. Follow me.'

They pushed their way from one compartment to another until they found one that wasn't filled to the brim. They left their trunks by the wall.

Before the train started moving, more soldiers piled in. They burst into their compartment and shook a crooked finger at Sophia, Dmitry and Nanny. 'You don't look like you should be on this train. It belongs to the people now.'

'We are people too, aren't we?' said Dmitry, sounding deflated and small.

'Haven't you heard, comrades? We have the power now. Everything belongs to us.'

One of the soldiers opened the carriage window, another one picked up one of their trunks and without a word threw it onto the pavement. Another trunk followed, falling on the ground with a thump. Sophia stifled a cry. She was going to protest but soon she forgot all about the trunks because the soldier turned to her with an evil glint in his eyes. 'Your turn now.'

Dirty hands reached for her. Sophia could smell his disgusting breath on her face. Onions and alcohol. His eyes were slits of amused anger.

Raising her hand, she slapped him hard across the face. 'Kindly leave me alone,' she said. It was the first words she had uttered since they had left home.

The soldier looked stunned. For a few moments, there was silence in the compartment. And then all hell broke loose. The women were screaming, the men swearing, a fight broke out near the entrance.

Dmitry stepped between Sophia and the soldier. 'Excuse me, comrades. We are leaving.' He pulled Sophia and Nanny behind him. As quickly as they could, they made their way outside.

'What were you thinking?' Dmitry berated her as they walked. 'Those men could kill us all and not even blink. What is it with you this morning?'

'Leave the poor child alone,' said Nanny. 'She's upset enough.'

Dmitry took Sophia's hand. When he spoke again, he sounded calmer. 'You need to be more careful. You put all our lives in danger by doing that.'

'Maybe it's not meant to be. Maybe it's a sign we shouldn't leave Petrograd,' said Sophia. And then she fell quiet. Nikolai was gone. There was no reason to stay in Petrograd at all.

'Nonsense. Next time we'll be lucky. And when we get to the Caucasus, we'll be safe. No one will bother us there.' He collected their trunks and checked to make sure the locks were safe. 'Did you know it never snows in Kislovodsk? It has the healthiest climate on earth. There are mineral springs, parks and rivers to swim in. They say spring water can heal anything.'

Not everything, thought Sophia. Nothing could heal what was wrong with her, not even spring water.

'We will live a normal life. And who knows, maybe from there we'll be able to go overseas. How would you like to live in Paris, the city of love?'

She shrugged, wearily perching on one of the trunks.

'Or Rome, the Eternal City of Tibullus and Caesar. We will see the Colosseum, where the gladiators fought for their lives. Would you like that?'

Once, she would have. Now, she was barely listening.

As Dmitry talked about their future, Sophia stared into space, at the mayhem of the station, at the river of people praying for the train to come so they could escape the revolution. When darkness fell and she felt ready to fall down from exhaustion, another train arrived. Sophia was shocked at the state of it. Every compartment, designed for four people, had at least twenty in it. The seats had been damaged, revolutionary slogans written on every surface. The door handles were missing, the lamps broken. Everything was grimy with dirt and everywhere she looked, she could see spit and spilled beer. Even if she could sit down, she wouldn't want to. She stood with her hands pressed to her chest, ready at any moment to be thrown off, like before.

But just like Dmitry predicted, this time they got lucky. The train started moving and they were still on it.

'Will we ever see Petrograd again? Will we see our home?' whispered Nanny.

As the train carried Sophia away from the city, she looked out the window at the familiar streets, her old life slipping quietly away. What would she have preferred? To live her life not knowing this feeling, content and peaceful, calm sailing until the end with a husband who could never break her heart? Or to have her soul soar with joy, to have her chest expand with unrestrained happiness and know it would only last a moment and then she would have to pay? And then she would have nothing? Nikolai was the only man she had ever loved. And now she would never be free. Her heart bound her to him more firmly than marriage vows ever could.

They were in the hospital together, bandaging a wound. She watched his expert fingers, watched the concentration on his face. 'The revolution has taken so many lives. Do you really believe it's worth it?' she asked him as the sun went down behind the Neva, sending its last rays like a wave goodbye through the windows.

'It's a difficult question to answer right now. Is it worth dying for? In theory, yes, it is. But we don't know what it will look like in practice until everything is in place, until we are living the principles

we are advocating.'

'Would you give your life for the revolution?'

'Gladly. If I knew I made a difference, if I knew my principles would live on and it was not in vain, if people had a better life because of me, because of what I'd done, I would gladly give my life for the revolution.'

'You are only saying that because you are all alone in the world. If you had a family, if you had someone who loved you, you wouldn't think this way.'

'Perhaps you're right. Perhaps if I had someone who loved me, I wouldn't think this way,' he said to her, and in his eyes she saw her own longing reflected back at her.

PART TWO

Chapter 8

November 1917

In the resort town of Kislovodsk, named after its world-famous mineral springs, on Kabardinskaya Street, in a tiny apartment on the first floor that smelt of mould and dirt no matter how hard she scrubbed it, Sophia was mixing flour, water and yeast. A spoonful of sugar, a pinch of salt – she was being careful with her salt – and the dough was almost ready. This morning she was able to get some cabbage and carrots at the market but no meat of any kind. The revolution might not have reached Kislovodsk but the food shortages certainly had.

It was a long cry from the luxury they had grown up with. Sophia and her husband had two rooms to themselves, while Nanny slept on a folding bed in the living room. But it was all theirs and that was all that mattered. Even here, in the mountains of Caucasus, the rumours of upheaval reached them all the way from Petrograd. All around her, voices whispered with fear, while Sophia did her best to ignore them. She was grateful because there were no men in black that smelt of smoke and alcohol inside their apartment. Every morning she would open her windows, look at the rocky giants – the Caucasus Mountains, reaching for the sky – inhale the crisp, clean air that made her chest expand and thank God for delivering them from the nightmare that was Petrograd in March 1917.

Here, no one knew who they were. No one treated them like enemies of the people. Sophia could leave her house and not fear for her life. She could walk to the store and buy some flour and eggs and sugar, come back home and bake a pie for lunch and not worry about enraged crowds bursting in, smashing everything in their path. She could read and walk and swim and not be afraid. It was freedom. It was almost like having her life back.

In other rented places around town, other noble families from Petrograd, from Moscow, from all over Russia hid and waited out the revolution, biding their time and trying to pretend their lives had not been turned upside down by the sudden storm that was still howling in anger in most of the country now, eight months later.

Sophia placed the dough in a bowl and covered it with a kitchen towel, shaking flour off her hands. She baked for Dmitry and Nanny but every time she took her pies out of the oven, she thought of Nikolai. Every now and then, something would remind her of him, a song she would hear on her walk, a broad-shouldered man strolling past, a whispered conversation, and she would forget where she was going and stand in the middle of the street, lost and confused, her hand on her heart. Every night as Sophia fell asleep, she saw his face.

In Kislovodsk, the days passed in a blur of lunches, formal dinners and promenades by the river. Even though their apart-ments were barely fit for human habitation and instead of lobster and steak, all they had was bread and potatoes, the former nobility acted as if nothing in their lives had changed. Hidden away between the Black and Caspian Seas, two thousand kilometres from Petrograd, society ladies wore their rubies, diamonds and sapphires as if they were still holding court in their mansions on Fontanka, while their husbands smoked cheap cigarettes and drank cheap wine, reminiscing of the times when they had Cuban cigars and the best whisky money could buy. They lived on what little money they had managed to take with them, bit by bit selling their jewellery, not thinking of the day in a not-so-distant future when they would have nothing left. They drank and ate what little food they could get and were merry, trying to forget the recent past, clinging with everything they had to the past long gone.

Sophia was indifferent to the glitter of fallen society. She was no longer excited by new faces, small talk and pretence. Sometimes at parties, as the sun set behind the mountains, she looked at those around her, their grandeur diminished somewhat but their egos unabated, listened to their voices like echoes of times past and wondered what she was doing there.

Putting her face close to the dough, Sophia inhaled the yeasty smell, the smell of her childhood. She wondered if she could get away with staying at home today, with her books and her embroidery and her dough resting on the big Russian stove. Just like she knew he would, Dmitry poked his head through the door and asked her why she wasn't dressed for lunch yet. He hated being late and making people wait. Most of all, he hated missing out on the small talk and pleasantries that Sophia despised. Because she disliked the social gatherings he insisted they attended, she always left getting ready to the last moment and they were always late, which invariably put him in a bad mood.

'I think I'll stay home today or these pies will never be finished and then we'll have no dinner,' she replied.

'The dough needs time to rise, doesn't it? We'll be back in time to bake your pies.'

'I would rather do something else. Read or sew or go for a walk. All this revolutionary talk tires me out. Go without me, darling.'

'Nonsense,' said Dmitry, who lived for the revolutionary talk. Now that he was free to almost be himself, he was almost happy. And he expected her to be happy too, to live her life as if the revolution had never happened. 'Our friends will miss you if you don't come.'

'They are your friends, not mine. It's you they want. They won't even notice I'm not there.'

'If I show up on my own, they might think we have marital problems.' He chuckled as if the mere thought was ridiculous. 'Put your best dress on and let's go. It won't take long. It's only lunch.'

'You mean my only dress?'

Reluctantly, she got dressed and put on her mother's earrings, all the while thinking, *What is the point? Who are we trying to fool?*

Hand in hand, they walked to the Sudakovs' apartment by the river. It was a mild November day, and while Dmitry pulled her by the hand, she looked in amazement at the mineral springs, the park filled with fruit trees and the amphitheatre of the Caucasus Mountains. Kislovodsk was exile and it would never feel like home. But it was a beautiful exile.

Once upon a time, they had twirled underneath the twinkling lights, while the band played 'Waltz of the Flowers'. They had reached for canapes, while singers dressed in black serenaded them with sad gypsy ballads of love and betrayal. They no longer did that here, in Kislovodsk. Instead, they gathered on benches in public squares because their apartments were too small for guests. When Sophia and Dmitry were seated with a glass of wine in their hands, Princess Anna Sudakova approached them, accompanied by a thin young man in glasses. Just like the Orlovs, Princess Anna had lost everything in the revolution, but you couldn't tell just by looking at her. Her posture was straight, her head held high. Every time she saw her, Sophia couldn't help but think that nobility had nothing to do with money and everything to do with breeding and attitude.

'I would like to introduce my cousin, Count Alexander Pesherskii, fresh from Petrograd,' said Anna. 'Our new friends, Count Dmitry Orlov and his wife, Countess Sophia.'

Sophia smiled sadly, while Alexander bent his head and kissed her hand. Only here in Kislovodsk, they remained counts and

170

princes and dukes. In the rest of the country, they were the enemy. After pleasantries and bows were exchanged, Alexander reached into his pocket and pulled out an envelope. 'I have a letter for you. From Petrograd.'

Sophia watched with amazement as Alexander gave the letter to Dmitry, who placed it in his pocket without looking at it. It was the first letter they had ever received in Kislovodsk. 'How *is* Petrograd?' asked Dmitry.

'The city is hanging by a thread. Any second now, the thread will break and everything will hurl into the abyss.'

'It's already in the abyss, young man. We are lucky to have escaped with our lives.'

Alexander bowed politely. 'Indeed. Petrograd is like a barrel of gunpowder, about to explode.'

'We heard there were no more trains out of the city,' said Anna.

'I was lucky to get away when I did. The next day, the railroad workers went on strike. The city looks lost, like an orphan, like it no longer belongs to anyone. There is no authority, no food, no electricity. Trams are not running any longer. You can't walk down the street without bullets flying past. Everyone is abandoning the city like rats.'

'Can you blame them? Kerensky is an idealist who's lost his grip on reality. The Bolsheviks are openly preparing Petrograd for an uprising. The government knows about it, lives in fear of it but does nothing at all to stop it,' said Anna. 'Everyone is waiting for it like it's going to change everything.'

'If the Provisional Government took matters into its own hands during the July uprising and eliminated the Bolsheviks, this upheaval would never have happened,' said Alexander.

Sophia paled. Nikolai had been arrested and killed after the July uprisings. She leaned back into her seat, wishing she was anywhere but here, listening to these people who thought they knew everything but knew nothing.

'Are you all right, my dear? You look like you've seen a ghost,' whispered Anna, touching her hand.

'I'm fine, thank you, Anna. Just warm, that's all.'

'I know what you mean. I will never get used to these mild winters. I miss snow, miss feeling the ice in the air. I don't know about you but I can't wait to go home.'

'Will that day ever come?' asked Sophia.

As always when they spoke about the revolution, Sophia smiled and nodded politely. Maybe if she stopped listening, she could pretend the revolution wasn't even happening. It was an easy thing to do here, in Kislovodsk, where the winters were mild and the streets quiet, where the birds chirped, the sun played on her face and the mountains like giants watched over them. Taking a sip of wine, she looked at the stunning Beshtau, partly obscured by clouds, and thought of the streets of her childhood, the place where she grew up, so different but no less beautiful. How she wished she could see the Winter Palace rising majestically over the Neva, the royal Peterhof with its magnificent parks and fountains, the wide thoroughfare of Nevsky Avenue and the stunning Summer Garden. How she loved walking through Petrograd in summer, when at midnight it was bright as day.

At home, she followed Dmitry to his room just as he was about to open the letter. 'Who is it from?' she asked.

'Count Butylov. He's saying how lucky we are to be away from Petrograd. How he wishes he'd been clever like us and got away before it was too late. What did I tell you? Coming here was a wonderful idea.'

'A brilliant idea, darling.' Her eyes remained on the letter.

She watched as Dmitry finished reading and placed the letter inside his drawer, on top of his other documents, as if wanting to shield it from her gaze.

In the evening, after the sun had disappeared behind the mountains, after the pies had been eaten and praised and the daily newspaper read and discussed, Sophia locked herself in her room and pulled out the only note Nikolai had ever written her. *If you ever feel sleepless again*, she read, trembling. Was it her imagination or did the writing on the envelope Dmitry had hidden away look similar to the writing on the note? How could it be possible? Was she going insane? Telling herself she was being silly, she went to bed but couldn't get the letter out of her head. Half an hour later, she heard Dmitry's snoring through the paper-thin wall separating the two rooms. Quiet as a mouse, she picked up a candle and tiptoed into his bedroom, opening the drawer next to his bed and looking through the papers inside.

The letter was gone.

*

More than anything in Kislovodsk, Sophia craved solitude. She was grateful for her husband, grateful for his familiar and reassuring presence. But day after day, even if it was raining, she walked the streets of her new home on her own, exploring the picturesque alleyways and broad thoroughfares, studying the local architecture, glancing into gardens filled with flowers, laundry and dishes, laughing children and playing dogs. What she enjoyed most of all was accidentally catching a glimpse of other people's lives and for a moment escaping into an existence that was different from hers.

She loved the green parks, the flowers, the ripening fruit, the sprawling residences. She watched the boats on the river and dreamt that she was on one of them, floating away from here. Somewhere she had never been before, perhaps, to a new and unknown future. As she strolled past the river, she imagined the blue canals of Venice and the steeples of Parisian churches, the ancient ruins of Athens and the Roman Colosseum.

In the first week of November, despite what Dmitry had told her at the station, the first snow fell, enveloping the city in a white blanket and making everything look fresh and shiny. Her breath a puff of icy cold air, bundled into an old winter coat, Sophia walked towards Narzan Gallery through an alley of poplar trees, when she saw a carriage pull up and a woman disembark, followed by three large trunks, thrown onto the street by an angry coach driver. The woman, just as angry, shook her fist and shouted something at the coach that, having deposited its load, sped off down the road. The graceful curve of the neck, the way the woman held her head, the way she wore her hair looked familiar, but Sophia didn't think twice about it. Lately, she saw the people she loved everywhere she looked. Her mother, her childhood friends, but most of all Nikolai, were like ghosts haunting her in this alien place, reminding her of everything she had left behind.

When the woman turned around and Sophia could see her face, she cried out with delight. She recognised Regina, whom she had said goodbye to on the porch of her house in Petrograd all those months ago and wasn't expecting to see again anytime soon. Regina didn't seem to notice Sophia as she stepped from foot to foot in frustration, her three trunks abandoned in the snow.

'Regina! Is that you?' exclaimed Sophia, running down the street, holding her long skirt in one hand and her hat in another and finally reaching her friend and putting her arms around her. 'Or am I imagining you?' Sophia fought an impulse to pinch herself and Regina.

Her friend's face lit up with pleasure. 'Sophochka! I had no idea where to find you and here you are, the first person I meet in this cursed town.'

'What happened to you? Where are you going?'

'I was going to …' Regina glanced at the piece of paper she was clutching. 'Emiratovskaya Street to rent a room. But the coach driver had other ideas. He threw me out.'

'What did you say to him?' Sophia kissed her friend on both cheeks. She wanted to dance on the spot with joy.

'I told him he was driving so fast, he was going to break both our necks. And he pulled over and told me to get out. Can you believe the nerve of these people? They behave like they are our equal.'

'And now they are, by law.' The two women smiled. Sophia took Regina's hands in hers. 'Forget Emiratovskaya Street. Our building has rooms for rent. Come and stay with us.'

They flagged down a new coach and watched the coach driver as he loaded the trunks. When the horse started moving, Sophia whispered, her eyes twinkling, 'Whatever you do, don't say a word to the driver. I can't take it if we are thrown out.'

'This one is barely moving. His horse looks like it's on its last legs. At this rate, we'll get there by tomorrow.'

'But we'll get there in one piece.'

Regina turned to Sophia, looking her up and down. 'You look stunning. This milder climate agrees with you. It's minus twenty in Petrograd, raining bullets.'

'Is that why you left? We hear rumours of what's happening there but we don't know anything for sure. We don't know what to believe.'

'There's an armed insurrection in Petrograd as we speak. There is no heating and the water pipes have frozen. Everyone is starving. People queue in the shops for hours, only to leave empty-handed. Not even any cats or dogs are left in the city.'

'What happened to them?'

'They've all been eaten.'

For a moment, both women were quiet, lost in thought. As they drove through the serene streets of Kislovodsk, Sophia found it hard to imagine the things Regina was describing. It was like a different life, even though they themselves had lived through it only a few short months ago. 'Any news of your brother?'

Regina's eyes sparkled with happiness. 'You are not going to believe it, but Valentin is fine! He was in prison but, thanks to Nikolai, they let him go. He chose to stay in Petrograd but insisted that I leave. It was getting too dangerous in the city. I will always be grateful to Nikolai, you know. He gave me my life back when he found my brother for me. That man is pure gold. I don't know how I can ever thank him. Are you all right? You went white.'

Sophia couldn't speak. She could do nothing but stare at her friend in silence, her eyes round like saucers. What did she just say about Nikolai? Did Sophia imagine it?

'Wait. You didn't know Nikolai was alive?' asked Regina.

'I didn't know Nikolai was alive,' whispered Sophia, her hands trembling as she twisted her handkerchief with the Orlov family crest on it.

'He's written a few times to you and Dmitry. When he got no reply, he realised the post must not be getting through to Kislovodsk, so he passed a letter with one of his friends. You didn't receive it?'

Sophia shook her head, remembering the letter Dmitry had hidden in his drawer. The letter that had later mysteriously disappeared. Had her husband been lying to her? And why? Her heart was racing. She found it hard to breathe. 'Nikolai is alive.' Incredulously she repeated the words, as if saying them out loud would make them seem more real.

'He was released in September after the Kornilov affair. It was him who got me a permission slip to travel here and put me on the train. And lucky he did so. The next day the trains stopped running.'

After the coach driver unloaded Regina's trunks and left them on the road, Sophia helped her friend tug them to the building, where they talked to the building manager, a balding man called Kirill with a beer belly and a red face of someone who was partial to drink. He showed them the only room he had available, a tiny space with a bed and a table. Regina rented it on the spot, saying she was too tired to look for anything else and all she wanted was to fall into the bed and sleep for a thousand years. 'You won't believe what I went through on the way. It took days to get here. The soldiers on the trains are out of control. They threw me out of my compartment and I had to stand the whole way. I stood for ten hours!'

'Thank God you are here safely.'

'I begged Nikolai to come with me, if only halfway. "Who will protect me on the road if you are not with me?" I asked him. But he had too much to do in Petrograd and couldn't. I'm almost glad. I don't want him to see me like this, all dirty and dishevelled. I haven't had a bath in a week.'

'You are in the right town for a bath. The mineral springs here are quite something. In summer, we swim outdoors. When it's too cold to swim, we go to the bathhouse not far from here. I will take you tomorrow.'

Regina stretched on her bed, surveying the pitiful room. 'A long cry from the way we grew up,' she said quietly.

'It is. But at least we are safe.'

'Yes, but for how long? Do you really think the revolution isn't coming to Kislovodsk?'

Sophia didn't want to think about the revolution. Having said goodbye to Nikolai, having mourned him for five months and thought of nothing but him, her fake smile had been firmly in place for the world to see, while inside she was crumbling. Suddenly finding out he was alive, she was so overwhelmed with it all, she could barely talk and couldn't look at her friend at all, in case Regina read everything she was feeling on her pale and exhausted face.

She had never believed in miracles. Until now.

*

After she said goodbye to Regina, Sophia returned home. The apartment was empty. Nanny must be at the market and Dmitry at one of his lunches, Sophia thought. He would be angry she had been delayed and couldn't join him. But she didn't care. She was glad to have the apartment to herself. She needed space to think.

Walking into Dmitry's bedroom and closing the door behind her, she approached his commode. Drawer after drawer she searched, finding old newspaper clippings about the revolution, notebooks filled with random thoughts, journals and old documents. There was no trace of the letter Count Alexander had given him, as if it had never existed, as if she had imagined it.

Frustrated, she looked through his garderobe, finding nothing but clothes.

If I had something to hide, where would I hide it? she thought. Under the rug? Nothing. Behind the curtain? Nothing. Finally, under his mattress, inside the book Dmitry was reading, she found the mysterious letter.

My dear brother and sister-in-law,

I received no reply from you, so I'm sending another letter, this time through a friend of mine. Here I am, a free man at last, and all I do is work from morning till night, sometimes through the night. You were right to leave Petrograd when you did. We are on the brink of something great, but the price of greatness will be more destruction, more disorder, more lives lost. All is quiet in the city right now but as I walk through the streets, I can sense it. I can't go into detail but everything is in place. We are ready. I hope the country is, too. The house feels empty without all of you. Every moment of every day, as I work or try to sleep, I think of you. I hope you are safe in Kislovodsk. I would ask you to write but I know your letters won't reach me.

Yours always,
Nikolai

Trembling, tears in her eyes, Sophia read Nikolai's letter again and again, until she could open her mouth and recite it word for word. She memorised it like a poem, like a lullaby to hum to herself when it was dark and she couldn't sleep. When she heard the key turn in the front door, she hid the letter in the bodice of her dress and straightened the mattress.

'Sophia, there you are. I waited for you to come for lunch,' exclaimed Dmitry when he saw her in the corridor.

Her hand on her chest where the letter was hidden, she said, her voice flat, 'Regina is in town. I ran into her on my walk.'

'That's good. That will cheer you up, having her here.'

'She told me some interesting things.'

'What did she tell you?'

'Nikolai is alive. But you already knew that.'

His face seemed to deflate a little. 'I found out yesterday. I was waiting for the right time to tell you.'

'You found out a week ago at the Sudakovs'. That's when you received this letter.' She waved it in front of him but when he tried to take it from her, she quickly hid it. She had no intention of ever letting it go. 'Why did you lie to me? Why did you tell me the letter was from Count Butylov?'

'I didn't lie. That letter *was* from Count Butylov. Here it is.' He pulled another letter from his commode. She must have overlooked it when she was searching the room. The writing on this letter was nothing like Nikolai's writing, thin, large and leaning to one side. 'Question is, why were you going through my things?'

'Because I knew you were hiding something. Why didn't you just tell me your brother was alive? The minute you found out, why didn't you say something?'

'I should have. I'm sorry.'

He took a step in her direction, but Sophia moved swiftly away, storming off to her room and locking the door.

*

Regina and Sophia were strolling past the shops and the local library, where Sophia had been borrowing most of her books, no longer able to afford them, past the boys selling newspapers and shouting out headlines.

'I wish I never saw another newspaper again for as long as I live,' said Sophia. 'Every day, it's anarchy, uprisings, murder,

179

destruction, hunger and death. This is the country we live in.'

As if he overheard her, the boy screamed at the top of his voice, 'Murder on Anichkov Bridge! Twelve officers stabbed to death!'

Regina said, 'In Petrograd, you don't have to read the papers. It's right in front of you. Properties are attacked, people murdered for their political beliefs. The housing committee has meetings every day on how to protect Petrograd families, while people are arming themselves with guns and rifles and standing guard outside their houses, like it's war.'

'It *is* war! The revolution is war against all of us.'

'That's what I don't understand about the revolution. We had one type of power above us and they didn't like it, so they overthrew it. But now we have pointless committees for everything. And they control every aspect of our lives, just like before. It's so peaceful here, like a different life. We are lucky.' They came to a tall building with a large sign that said *Post Office*. 'Wait here a moment. I want to see if there are any letters for me.'

'Why would Valentin write to you so soon? And why did he stay anyway? He would have been safer here, with us.'

'He wanted to see if he could get our house back. He never gives up, my brother. But it's not him I'm waiting for letters from.'

'Who then?'

Regina blushed. 'Nikolai. I think he's very close to asking for my hand in marriage.'

Sophia stumbled on a rock and almost fell. When she regained her balance, she asked, 'What makes you think so? Has he said anything?'

'Not in so many words. But it's obvious in a million little details. How protective he is of me. How much he wants to help. How worried he is for me.'

He is protective of everyone, Sophia wanted to say. *He helps everyone. It doesn't mean anything.* She didn't say it to her friend because she didn't know if it was true. What if Nikolai did have feelings for Regina? What man wouldn't? Regina was beautiful and

180

smart. And, most importantly, she was free. She wasn't married to Nikolai's brother.

'When we said goodbye, he told me he'll come to Kislovodsk as soon as he can. Why would he come here if it wasn't to see me?' Regina smiled. 'This is it, Sophochka, I just know it. He is the man I'm going to marry.'

'I thought you didn't believe in marriage. You told me so when I was marrying Dmitry.'

'I don't believe in marriage of convenience. I believe in marriage for love. And I've never felt like this about anyone before.' She laughed with joy. 'Why are you looking so gloomy? Tell me you're happy for me!'

'I'm happy for you, Regina.' Sophia tried to muster a smile for her friend's sake but couldn't.

'I want this wedding to be the most memorable event of the season. Even in our present situation. I want people to be talking about it.'

'He hasn't asked you yet, has he?'

'He will,' Regina said confidently. 'And you can be my maid of honour, like we've always wanted. Just imagine, we will be married to brothers. I will have the same last name as you. Regina Orlova. Doesn't it sound wonderful? We'll be like real sisters!'

'We are like sisters now. But what about his political views? I know you don't agree with them. What would your Papa say if he knew?'

'Nikolai is from a good family. He is well educated, smart, kind and caring. If he'd got to know him, I'm sure Papa would have approved. Besides, in the current climate Nikolai's views are convenient.'

'Is that what you want? Convenience?'

Regina was oblivious to the note of sarcasm in her friend's voice. She practically danced on the spot. 'I always knew I would marry for love. I drove Papa crazy, refusing every suitor he found for me. I didn't want to end up like you, unhappy.'

'What makes you think I'm unhappy?'

'It's so obvious. When a woman is in love, her eyes sparkle. And yours never sparkled for Dmitry.' Regina turned her own sparkling eyes to Sophia. 'Look at me. I can't think of anything else. When I'm not with him, it's like a part of me is missing.'

'That doesn't sound very nice.'

'But then, when we are together, it's the best feeling in the world. I feel like flying. I want the whole world to know how I feel.'

'Have you told him?' asked Sophia, holding her breath.

'If he doesn't know, he must be blind.'

'Most men are.'

'I wish I could ask him to marry me myself. I don't understand why women can't. It seems so unfair. This waiting is killing me. The uncertainty of it. Will you help me? When he comes here, will you find out what his intentions are?'

'How do you want me to do that? Why would he tell me?'

'He'll tell his brother. Maybe he already has, in a letter. Please, will you ask Dmitry for me?'

'Of course.'

Regina disappeared through the doors of the post office and Sophia waited. When her friend appeared and announced there were no letters, she breathed out in relief. And instantly felt guilty. 'Don't worry. It's only been a couple of weeks,' she reassured her, hoping Regina wouldn't notice that her voice was trembling. 'Besides, the post doesn't make it here from Petrograd. You said so yourself. The whole country is in chaos. What's the point of even checking?'

'I guess I'm hoping for a miracle.'

At home, Dmitry was shaking his head over that day's newspaper. 'There was a Bolshevik uprising in Petrograd,' he said as soon as they walked in. 'They stormed the Winter Palace and arrested the Provisional Government. Kerensky is in hiding.'

'How could the Bolsheviks have arrested the Provisional Government? Kerensky has the army,' said Sophia.

'Not anymore. Most of the army has deserted. Soldiers and sailors, over two hundred thousand of them. The majority of Petrograd garrison support the Bolsheviks. I always said Kerensky is not up to the job. Where cruelty and action are required, all he does is talk and try to reach a democratic agreement. The government is like a lost child. The honeymoon is over. People are disillusioned with the revolution. It's time for action, for ruling the masses with an iron fist.' Dmitry clasped his own fist and shook it in the air. His eyes burnt with a passion, as if he was dying to show Kerensky how it was done. All this coming from a man who was too afraid to leave his house in Petrograd and ran at the first sign of trouble. 'While the Provisional Government discussed, analysed, planned and argued, the Bolsheviks acted.'

'Kerensky is no dictator. He is no Napoleon,' said Regina.

'He is weak. But Lenin and Trotsky are strong. And now we have another revolution on our hands. It says here all our property and fortune have been officially confiscated by the Bolsheviks.'

'What does that mean for us?' asked Sophia.

'Our house no longer belongs to us. Nor does our estate in the country. We will never see them again. In an instant, we have become poor.'

Sophia didn't want to think about it. Their house and country estate had long seemed like a distant dream, a distant past. All she saw was the tiny apartment where they lived, the white Kislovodsk streets, the mighty mountains. She realised she had an advantage over Dmitry. She had said goodbye to their old life a long time ago, while he still had hope. Quietly, not looking at her husband or her friend, she said, 'He did it. Nikolai did it.'

'Yes, but at what price?' said Dmitry.

Chapter 9

June–July 1918

Month after month, through blizzard and rain and the summer heat, first thing every Friday morning, Sophia accompanied Regina to the post office, where her friend would ask if there were any letters for her. There never were. Regina would post her own letter to Nikolai, praying that this once it would reach him.

'What do you write to him about?' asked Sophia one day in June. Everywhere she looked, she could see roses and tulips, their heady scent reminding her of summer trips to Kazan, of playing in the fields and watching the cows graze. Reminding her of Nikolai's face as he showed her the red tulips he had planted for his mother, what seemed like a lifetime ago in Petrograd. Sometimes, when she looked at the red and purple of the flowers, to match the red and purple of a Kislovodsk sunset, on every corner, in every garden, climbing up the wall of every building, she had to pinch herself to make sure she wasn't dreaming. It was like living inside a postcard, picturesque and breathtaking and completely alien. Despite the beauty around her, almost every night she dreamt of the grey skies of Petrograd.

'Everything and nothing. Yesterday I wrote about the sweet

pies you made. I told him I've never tasted anything like it in my whole life. And last week, I wrote how you refused to go in the water because you thought there were eels. Who knew you were such a scaredy-cat!'

'Not a scaredy-cat, just smart. You wouldn't be laughing if an eel bit you.'

'In this heat, I'll take the risk.' Regina waved her fan in the air. 'I'm a northern girl. Give me snowstorms and howling winds any day.'

'Do you write to him about anything other than me?'

'I tell him I'm waiting for him. That despite how hard it's been, I'm not going overseas until I see him. Anything to make him come here sooner. I wonder what's taking him so long.'

Day after day, week after week, Regina watched the road leading to their apartment block. When they had their meals on the balcony, she sat facing the street, jumping at every noise. Sophia, who watched that road religiously herself, pretended she didn't notice. She wrote her own letters to Nikolai, like diary entries every day.

Today we went swimming in the river and someone stole my shoes. I had to walk home barefoot.

Today Kirill got a new kitten. The kitten loves me but hates Kirill because his voice is too loud when he drinks.

Today I made Napoleon cake and had a slice with a cup of camomile tea and thought of you.

Today our house was searched – again.

She never tried to send the letters but hid them in a hollow of a tree in the nearby park.

Regina had been right. It had taken a couple of months but in February 1918 trainloads of Bolsheviks started arriving in Kislovodsk. They had set up committees and councils, issued decrees and overhauled the way the sleepy town operated. Suddenly, their little apartment on Kabardinskaya Street no longer felt like a safe haven. Once again, they were treated like the enemy.

'I was scared for my life last night. As they searched the place, they kept looking at me like they thought I was hiding something,' Sophia said to Regina as they walked hand in hand through Kurortnyi Park, admiring the beautiful grounds and the manicured lawns, watching the bathers in Semigradusnyi Spring on the right bank of Olkhovka River, laughing and splashing, carefree and full of joy, as if the arrests, searches and murders had not come to Kislovodsk on the Bolshevik trains.

'Did they take anything?'

'What's there to take? We have nothing left. It's the fifth search this month. My violin is gone and so are the pearl earrings my mother gave me. All I have is this one dress.' And her mother's portrait that she hid under her mattress together with the only letter they had received from Nikolai, only taking it out after dark, when the likelihood of another search was low. Her heart stopped every time another man dressed in black looked through her things. Slowly but surely over the last four months, the jewellery and silks had disappeared from their dinners and lunches, giving way to drab clothes and dim eyes. 'All Dmitry talks about is going overseas. We will always be pariahs in our own country. But to go overseas, we need special permission. And to get special permission, we need connections.'

'Funny how it's all about connections. Under the tsar, under Lenin, it's all the same.'

'Look at the workers and the peasants. Are they happier? Or are they still starving? Are they satisfied with their revolution?'

'They have no choice but to be satisfied. The Bolsheviks shoot them if they aren't.'

Taking short gulps of hot air, Sophia ran to the river and took off her sandals, hiding her face from the sun under her only hat which had lost its shape and no longer looked new or fashionable. She wanted to feel the water on her feet. What a nice summer it would have been, if only the revolution hadn't come to the Caucasus. Why couldn't it stay in Petrograd? It wasn't welcome

186

here, in their hiding place, among rivers and giant rocks, where they thought they were safe.

As she was about to put her sandals back on, a voice startled her. It was loud and harsh as it sang the Marseillaise, the hymn to the revolution she had come to loathe. Shuddering, Sophia looked up but couldn't see anything. Whoever it was, he was hidden by a bend in the road and a tall English oak. Even without seeing the man, Sophia knew he was drunk. The words were slurred, barely intelligible. The two women looked at each other and in a mute agreement turned back in the direction of home. They had seen enough drunken soldiers and sailors on the streets of Petrograd to know it was best to avoid them.

Sophia and Regina were too late. The man must have seen the movement through the bushes or heard the rustle of their dresses. In a few unsteady strides he was by their side, blocking their way. He wore a sailor's uniform and loomed over them like a dark shadow. His face was red, his nose large, his body thin and hunched over like a worm, his mouth stretched into a smirk. 'What a fine pair of ladies we have here,' he said, hiccupping and twisting his moustache. He made the word *ladies* sound like a dirty word, like it was something to be ashamed of. Sophia could smell the alcohol on his breath. Instinctively, she took a step back and bumped into Regina. As if by magic, a revolver appeared in the sailor's hands. The two women backed away but there was nowhere for them to go. 'Fine ladies like yourselves always have something special hidden away for a rainy day. And I'm going to search until I find it.'

Snorting with laughter, he placed his hands on Sophia's waist. She recoiled from him and said, 'We have nothing. Everything we had, has already been taken.'

'We'll see about that.' His hands moved up to her chest. 'And if you don't have any jewellery, there's always something else.'

'Get your hands off her, you beast,' shouted Regina. Sophia wished her friend would stay quiet. She had heard enough stories about trigger-happy drunken sailors to know better than to make him angry. The man's hands were in her bodice and his putrid breath was in her neck. She would have screamed from fear but all oxygen seemed to have left her chest. All she could do was pant. With a sharp movement the sailor pulled at the bodice of Sophia's dress. The material tore and she cried out.

'Don't touch her, I said!' Regina grabbed him by the arm, hanging on to him with all her weight, like a bullterrier off a rope.

The sailor shook her off easily and raised his gun. The muzzle pointed at Regina. The hand holding the gun was shaking but from such a short distance Sophia was certain he would not miss. 'No!' she cried, squeezing her eyes shut, her throat constricted in horror, afraid that at any moment she would hear a gunshot.

When the gunshot finally came, it sounded far away and seemed to take the sailor by surprise. The man looked away from the two women and some clarity flashed through his eyes. Without lowering his gun, which was still pointing at Regina, he pushed Sophia towards the bushes. 'Quick, I don't have all day. Either you come with me or your friend dies.' His words were lost in an explosion somewhere on the other side of Kislovodsk. A volley of shots followed. Her knees shaking, her heart in her throat, Sophia couldn't think straight. What did the explosions mean? Were the Bolsheviks blowing up Kislovodsk? And why?

Through the mist of her fear, Sophia heard another sound, like heavy rain on a cobbled alleyway. She realised it was horses galloping. As the sailor was pushing her into the bushes, half a dozen men appeared as if out of nowhere, balancing in the saddle like they had been born in it, sabre in one hand, rifle in the other. They surrounded the sailor, who in his shock had dropped his revolver and was cowering in the grass. After pausing for a moment, all but one man rode off, clearly in a hurry to be somewhere else. The remaining rider pointed his rifle at the shaking sailor. 'Harassing innocent women? Your mother must be so proud. Cursed revolutionaries …' The man spat on the ground with disgust. A bushy moustache and a beard hid most of his old and weathered face and he had on a uniform Sophia had not seen in a long time – that of the Imperial Army. He turned to the two women and asked if they needed help. All Sophia could do was nod. *Yes*, she mouthed. *Yes, please.*

Regina looked like she was praying. Her hands were clasped together and her eyes were closed.

'Please, don't shoot me,' cried the sailor. 'I didn't mean any harm. I wasn't going to do anything, I swear.'

'Oh, you were, if only we appeared five minutes later. Now scoot. I won't even waste a bullet on you. It isn't worth it.'

When the sailor started running in the direction of the baths, muttering *thank you* under his breath, the man in the Imperial uniform jumped off his horse and said to the two women, 'No honour, no respect. And they want us to believe in their revolution.'

Regina was the first to find her voice. 'Who are you people?' she whispered, her eyes wild.

'We are Andrei Shkuro's Cossacks.' As he spoke, more gunshots were heard somewhere in the distance. 'We are here to throw the Bolsheviks out, so that ladies like you can walk in the park and not be afraid.'

Sophia had heard of Andrei Shkuro, the legendary white ataman who was offered a high command in the Red Army and declined, preferring to hide in the mountains with his small squadron of Cossacks, biding his time. She was about to say something, to ask what they were doing in Kislovodsk, perhaps, but another explosion shook the earth under her feet and she couldn't get the words out.

'Don't be alarmed. We are blowing up the railway bridge to Pyatigorsk. Now the Bolsheviks can't receive any more reinforcements.'

Sophia shivered. 'Is it safe in the city?'

'We are shooting at the council buildings. The Bolshevik head-quarters. We won't hurt the civilians.'

'How many of you are there?'

'Enough to give them a fright they will never forget.' He bowed to the two women. 'Lieutenant Surikov, at your service. Please, allow me to conduct you home.'

They walked back through the park, past the flowers and the river, with the sun on their faces. The man led his horse, while the two women held hands, still trembling. Regina said, 'So you are the famous Shkuro's partisans we keep hearing about? I thought you were a myth.'

'We are not a myth, madam. We are the counter-revolution.'

'What is it that you are trying to do?'

'We will not rest until the power is back in the hands of the tsar. This is our first offensive on Kislovodsk. Believe me, it won't be the last. Today our mission is to empty the Bolshevik treasury and confiscate their weapons. Tomorrow we will drive them from the Caucasus. And then from the rest of Russia. We will not stop at anything.'

'Not even civil war?'

'Not even civil war.'

Although counter-revolution was something they had all been hoping for since the revolution had started, the thought of Russia plunged into another war, of years of bloodshed, hunger and misery, terrified Sophia. But then she thought, there was already bloodshed in every Russian city, and hunger and misery every-where you turned. How could it possibly get any worse?

As if reading her mind, the Cossack said, 'If civil war tears Russia apart, it will be on their conscience. What they did was treason. The only reason they got away with it was because they were successful. Had they been unsuccessful, the lot of them would have perished on the scaffold. Well, we are here to make sure they don't get away with it. And to restore order as God intended.'

At the door to their building, the Cossack saluted them, jumped on his horse and rode off in a cloud of dust. Sophia watched him disappear around the corner, while her heart trembled one moment with hope, the next with fear.

When she turned around, she saw the building manager Kirill watching them from the porch with an unkind smile on his face.

*

The four of them were having breakfast on the communal porch they shared with three other families. It was misty and cold that morning. The mountains wore clouds like beards and the sun was burning her skin. Sophia could hear the sound of distant thunder. Thunder or war? As she thought about all the things the Cossack had told them as he walked them home, the knife she was holding shook so badly, she couldn't cut the bread on her plate.

'Are you all right, dear?' asked Dmitry, taking the knife from her hand and helping her with the bread. 'You are so pale this morning.'

'Is it any wonder?' cried Nanny, hands flailing. 'That terrible man! If I met him, I would have killed him myself. Didn't his parents teach him anything? Where do people like this even come from?'

'The revolution seems to breed them by the thousand,' said Dmitry. 'Forgive me, my dear. I should have been there to protect you.'

'He had a gun,' said Sophia. 'What could you possibly have done against a gun?'

'He was like a rabid dog,' exclaimed Regina. 'I was certain for a moment he was going to kill us both. My whole life flashed before me.'

'Nothing like that could ever happen under the tsar,' muttered Nanny, patting her eyes with a kerchief.

'It wouldn't have happened if only you stayed home,' said Dmitry.

191

'I refuse to be a prisoner in this apartment. Or they might as well have won.'

'They have won or haven't you noticed? From now on I will go with you everywhere,' said Dmitry. 'I won't let you out of my sight. I will never forgive myself if anything happens to you.'

She opened her mouth to argue but before she had a chance, they heard a voice shouting, 'Breaking news! The royal family murdered. Read all about it!'

Over the fence Sophia could see the scrawny boy, seven or eight years old, walking with a proud swagger, knowing he was the bearer of the most important news and enjoying the attention. She froze in shock, while Dmitry threw a coin to the boy and got the paper, spreading it on the table. After a moment of silence, he said in a grim voice, 'They were shot in a cellar in Ekaterinburg in the middle of the night. Grown-ups, children, even the servants.' He pushed the paper away in disgust. It fell under the table and there it remained, while they sat in shocked silence, not looking at each other.

Nanny crossed herself and sank into a chair.

'I don't believe it,' said Regina. 'It's just Bolshevik propaganda, like everything else they print. They wouldn't dare. The whole world would condemn them. I'm sure the Romanovs are safe and well, wherever they are. And with the Cossacks here, the Bolsheviks won't stay in Kislovodsk for long.'

'Where are these Cossacks?' grumbled Dmitry. 'They flew in for a couple of hours and just as quickly they were gone. And nothing has changed.'

'Regina is right,' said Sophia. 'All they print is lies and fake rumours. What monsters are capable of something so horrible? It's simply not true.' Did she say it to convince them or herself?

Nanny whispered, 'But what if it is?'

No one answered. If it was true, life as they knew it was truly over. And not one of them wanted to believe it.

'Why would they kill them? Why do it now?' asked Regina.

'They are no longer a threat.'

'Remember, yesterday the Cossacks were wearing Imperial uniforms? They won't stop at anything to see the tsar back on the throne. The Romanovs *are* a threat to the revolution because people are ready to rally around them.' Sophia shuddered with horror at the thought of the royal family murdered in cold blood, including innocent children. She didn't want to believe it was possible. But in her heart, she knew that it was. The people who had marched through Petrograd, destroying everything in sight and murdering everyone who stood in their way, were capable of anything. They were certainly capable of eliminating the biggest threat to the revolution – the royal family.

When it was just the two of them, Regina whispered, 'I wish Nikolai was here. We'd be safe with him around.'

Sophia, who with all her heart wished the same thing, said, 'You heard the Cossack. It's civil war, Regina. No one is safe. Not even Nikolai could protect us.'

'What happened yesterday made me realise something. Life is short, especially now. I have to tell him how I feel before it's too late. Sometimes the only thing that gets me through the day is the thought of seeing him again. Do you know what I mean?'

'I know exactly what you mean.'

'When he kissed my hand goodbye at the station, he told me to take care of myself, that a better future would come. That sounded almost like a promise. A better future with him.'

They heard voices outside. A loud knock followed. 'Who could that be?' whispered Regina, paling. Nanny rushed to open the door. 'We are here to arrest Dmitry Orlov,' came an unemotional voice.

Dmitry appeared in the corridor, carrying two cups of steaming tea. Sophia wanted to shout to him to run and hide but even if he tried, there was nowhere to go in their tiny apartment, no secret room filled with books, cards, violins and hidden emotions, where they could keep him safe. Two scruffy men stepped through the door and positioned themselves on either side of Dmitry. Sophia gulped as they grabbed Dmitry by the hands.

'What do you want with me?' demanded Dmitry, not making an effort to pull away but standing up straight, looking his tormentors in the eye.

'You are under arrest for your connection to Shkuro and the Cossacks.'

'What? That's ridiculous! I've never seen or spoken to the man in my life. I am a law-abiding citizen and have done nothing wrong.' He was trying to pull his hand away but it was no use. The militia officers held him in an iron grip, their fingers like handcuffs around his wrists.

As he was led away, Dmitry glanced at Sophia one last time and her legs trembled.

'Wait! Where are you taking him?' cried Regina. The men didn't reply. The only sound in the little apartment was the front door slamming loudly behind them.

As if waking from a dream, Sophia ran through the door and after the men. 'Stop! He's done nothing wrong. Let him go!'

But it was too late. The carriage containing her husband was speeding away towards the gendarmerie.

*

Sophia spent the rest of the morning by the window, watching the empty road. Every time there was the smallest noise, she rushed to the door and flung it open. It was always the wind. Momentarily, it seemed, the sky went from blue to charcoal. The rain started and thunder clanged overhead. At first, she thought it was Shkuro's men returning to town. They would chase the Bolsheviks away and free Dmitry. She prayed for gunshots and explosions the way she had once prayed for peace, feverishly clasping her hands to her chest, her eyes to heaven. But for once, all was quiet in Kislovodsk.

Even though Regina and Nanny didn't leave her side, Sophia had never felt so alone.

'Don't worry. They will see Dmitry is innocent and let him go,' Regina repeated like she truly believed it. 'He'll be back in no time.'

'All they want is an excuse to get rid of us. And now they have one.' Sophia knew Dmitry was innocent. But in this day and age, being innocent didn't guarantee safety. She saw it happening every day to their friends and acquaintances. People imprisoned and shot without proof, without so much as a trial. The newly established regime saw danger everywhere. And it endeavoured to eliminate this danger at all cost.

'No need to panic just yet. Let's wait and see what happens,' said Regina, stroking her hand in small soothing circles.

Hour after hour passed and soon it was dark outside. The only sound was the rain pelting the roof of their building. What was going to happen to Dmitry? Was he going to be thrown in prison or sent to a labour camp or, worse, shot on the outskirts of Kislovodsk with his face to the wall? Like the royal family had been shot in their home in Ekaterinburg, without reason or mercy. If the Bolsheviks had no qualms about doing something so unspeakable while the world was watching and judging, what would stop them from shooting someone like Dmitry in cold blood when no one would ever know about it, not even her? 'Dima is so kind. He's never hurt a fly. He doesn't deserve this,' she whispered.

'Of course he doesn't, darling. Are you hungry? Can Nanny make you something to eat?'

'I can't think of food at all.'

'What I don't understand is, why would they arrest him for having connections to Shkuro? What does Dmitry have to do with the ataman?' asked Regina.

There was a noise at the front door and both women jumped to their feet, while Nanny unlocked it to see who it was. Sophia stood mutely in the corridor, her hand on her beating heart. Was it Dmitry coming back to them?

It was only the building manager Kirill. 'Can I help you?' Sophia asked, wishing the man would leave. This was not the time to discuss the rent they couldn't afford to pay or the window latch Dmitry had broken a few days ago.

But Kirill didn't mention the rent or the window. He looked straight at Sophia, like he wanted to challenge her to a fight, and said, 'I am here to inform you that you are to vacate these premises within two hours.' He stepped from foot to foot and cleared his throat. His left eye was twitching. Sophia could detect a faint smell of alcohol.

'You want us to leave? We have nowhere else to go. And it's almost night-time.'

'Don't worry, darling,' said Regina. 'We can stay in my room and wait for Dmitry there.'

Kirill focused his gaze on Regina, looking her up and down. 'This concerns you too. I want your room vacated at the same time.'

'I don't understand,' muttered Sophia.

'I don't abide traitors under my roof. And I don't want any problems with the authorities.'

'We are no traitors.'

'Your husband was arrested as one. The whole street saw it. Who wants that kind of publicity?'

'How dare you talk to us like this?' cried Regina. 'Don't you know who we are? And who you are?'

'As of November last year, everyone in Russia is equal, comrade.'

As Sophia watched the man pulling his moustache with satisfaction, like he was pleased with himself, she remembered seeing his face when the Cossack walked them home the day before. Suddenly, it all made sense. 'It was you, wasn't it? You saw us with one of Shkuro's men and told the authorities.'

'I don't know what you are talking about.'

196

'You should be ashamed of yourself. My husband is innocent and you have put him in terrible danger. If he is killed, his blood will be on your hands.'

'The authorities didn't think he was innocent. After yesterday's attack, they are eager to speak to anyone sympathetic to Andrei Shkuro.'

'Half of Kislovodsk is sympathetic to Andrei Shkuro,' said Regina.

'I can't have Shkuro's Cossacks visiting this house in broad daylight. I have a business to run. If you don't leave in two hours, the militia will escort you out.'

'Please, don't force us to leave,' pleaded Sophia. 'If my husband comes back, this is where he will look for us.'

'Don't worry, comrade,' said Kirill with an evil smirk. 'Your husband is not coming back.'

*

Distraught and not knowing where else to go, Sophia, Regina and Nanny moved to Princess Anna Sudakova's apartment that had mice and smelt of sweat. For all her haughty demeanour, Anna seemed to have it worse than the Orlovs. The apartment consisted of one bedroom with the bed taking up most of the space and a long dark corridor. They had to share their kitchen and bathroom with two other families. For a moment, Sophia felt sorry for Anna but then remembered that they had no place to stay at all. And Dmitry was gone.

When the three of them arrived, Anna's husband, Vladimir, placed some straw on the floor behind the bed. It wasn't soft or comfortable, and Sophia preferred curling up in a little armchair as she tried to sleep.

'He always told me I was the best thing that's ever happened to him. Now that he's gone, what will become of me? I'm all alone in the world,' she whispered to Regina, while doing her best to ignore the food she had brought her. 'It's God's punishment. God is punishing me for my sins.'

'What sins, darling? What are you even talking about?'

If only Regina knew. Sophia longed to tell her friend everything. She was suffocating with guilt.

Every day, Sophia wandered through the streets of Kislovodsk and remembered walking there with her husband. Despite Regina's warnings, despite danger lurking around every corner, Sophia couldn't remain inside the tiny apartment. As she walked, she saw Dmitry's shadow everywhere. Sometimes she would catch a glimpse of a tall man with broad shoulders and think it was her husband. She would break into a run, her heart racing, her breath catching. But invariably, the familiar shadow would turn into a stranger and the emptiness inside her would grow deeper.

Every morning she stopped in their favourite place, a small park on Podkumok River, overlooking the mountains. She sat on their favourite bench and thought of him.

A week after their first meeting, he had brought her a present. She faked excitement, expecting the usual flowers or jewellery or sweets. But it was none of those things. It was a live butterfly in a jar.

'What do you want me to do with it?' she asked, puzzled and a little taken aback. She held the jar in her hands, examining the exquisite creature through the glass. All colours of the rainbow were on its wings, which were trembling as if it was afraid. She thought she had never seen anything so beautiful in her entire life.

'I want you to set it free somewhere nice, where there are lots of flowers. Butterflies like flowers. In your garden, perhaps.'

'Can I keep it? It's stunning.'

'You can't keep her in captivity. She wants to be free.'

'She? You think it's a girl?'

'Of course. Look how beautiful she is. And she deserves her freedom.'

'Why did you give me something only to take it away five minutes later? That's not how presents work.' She pretended to pout, even though she wasn't upset, not in the slightest. This young boy was unlike anyone she had met before and she was secretly pleased with the gift.

'Because releasing this butterfly together will make us happy. Because we will always remember this moment.'

He was right. As she watched the butterfly flutter away, she felt hope, as if it were her, Sophia, flying to a new life, towards her future. And in a way, it was. Just like the butterfly, she was about to start a new life with this wonderful man.

The day before their wedding, Dmitry gave her a golden hairpin shaped like a butterfly, with emeralds for eyes and rubies for wings. Stunning, like the one they had released. 'Wear it tomorrow. I can't wait to marry you,' he said.

As they exchanged their vows the following day, she wore the butterfly in her hair and thought of the special moment they had shared. And she thought of it now, as she sat on their bench watching the Podkumok flowing towards the Kuma, without him.

She had always taken him for granted. She had never appreciated him. But now that he was gone, she missed him terribly.

At Anna's apartment she searched through her cases, finally finding the butterfly hairpin that had miraculously survived the searches and the requisitions, tucked away safely inside a kerchief. She stroked it lovingly. Its emerald eyes sparkled as brightly as they did on the day of their wedding. Trying not to cry, her heart hurting, she placed it in her hair.

The next morning during her walk, she stopped at a small church that she found tucked away between a bread store and a library. The church was empty. There was no priest or other parishioners. She was grateful for the solitude. She wanted to talk to God alone.

'Dear God,' she whispered, kneeling on the floor before Virgin Mary and Jesus. 'I promise I will be a better wife to Dmitry. I promise I will be loyal and true. Please, God, keep him safe and bring him back to me.'

As she was praying, she suddenly knew exactly what she had to do.

*

The streets of Kislovodsk were empty. It was a calm before the tempest, and she knew from experience it didn't bode well. It took her ten minutes of walking very fast, almost running, to reach the building where the Bolsheviks had established their headquarters when they took over the town. When she finally got there, she was shaking and out of breath. Clasping her fists to calm her heart, she asked to see the commissioner in charge of citizen arrests. The grim man behind the counter barely looked in her direction, telling her to wait in the corridor. There were no chairs to sit on, so she stood next to half a dozen women like herself, desperate to learn the fate of their loved ones.

A grey-haired woman with deep lines on her face dabbed her eyes with a kerchief. 'Mikhail went out for a walk two days ago and didn't come back. I don't know what happened to him and no one will tell me anything.'

'My little boy was arrested this morning. He's only sixteen. Today is his birthday. He's done nothing wrong,' exclaimed a woman who, except for her eyes, looked too young to have a sixteen-year-old son. She had an old person's eyes that had seen too much.

All around her, Sophia saw tears and mournful faces. She tried not to look at them, nor did she cry or share her story. She had a job to do. She wasn't leaving until she knew what Dmitry was accused of. She wasn't leaving until she had done her best to prove his innocence.

The hope she had felt in the morning dwindled, as one after another she watched the other women disappear behind the heavy wooden door, only to reappear a while later more distraught than before. It took six hours before it was her turn. Six hours of leaning on the wall and watching the swaying trees through the window. Finally, the door opened and a young man, almost a boy, invited her to come in. His eyes were cold, and when he asked how he could help, he sounded indifferent and impatient, as if he resented her for taking up his precious time.

Her voice cracked as she replied, 'My husband was arrested two days ago. Dmitry Orlov.' She took a deep breath. 'I want to know what happened to him.'

The man looked through his files, muttering, 'Orlov, Orlov. I recognise the name. Oh yes.' He watched Sophia in silence for a moment, as if trying to read her mind.

'There's been some kind of a mistake. My husband is innocent.'

'That is impossible, Comrade Orlova. We would never arrest an innocent man. And we don't make mistakes.'

Of course you don't, she thought bitterly. Out loud she said, 'He hasn't done anything wrong.'

'That's what you all say. And yet you would give anything to see the old regime restored.' He glanced at his papers. 'Dmitry Orlov is accused of plotting an overthrow of the government with Andrei Shkuro. Treason punishable by death.'

Sophia felt like all her breath had been knocked out of her as if with a fist. 'How can that be? Dima has never seen Shkuro or spoken to him. He would never plot against an established regime.'

'How do you know? Can you read minds?'

'He is my husband.'

'Wives are usually the last to know what their husbands are thinking.'

'We have no secrets from one another.' She blushed as the lie slipped from her mouth.

'We have eyewitness reports of Shkuro's right-hand man visiting the residence and meeting your husband.'

That Kirill, Sophia thought. 'It wasn't like that at all. My friend

201

and I had been attacked at Narzan Gallery. The Cossack helped us, then escorted us home to make sure we were safe. He didn't go inside and he never met my husband. We said goodbye at the front door.'

The man took off his glasses and leaned closer to Sophia. 'You walked from Narzan Gallery all the way to your apartment accompanied by a known criminal and didn't think of detaining him or alerting the authorities?'

'Detaining him? How?'

'These are wanted men, comrade, condemned to death. It is the duty of every citizen to report their whereabouts. The duty in which you have failed.' He waited for her to say something. When she didn't, he continued, 'What did he talk to you about? Did he mention their plans to take Kislovodsk and start a civil war with the view of overthrowing the government?'

'No, of course not,' Sophia exclaimed, doing her best to appear indignant and offended by his accusations, even though that was exactly what the Cossack had talked about that day. 'Why would he discuss it with us? All he did was ask if we were all right. It was just small talk.'

'Did he ask for your support? The support of your husband? How long did he spend at your house? Who else did he speak to?'

'No one, I told you. He walked us home and said goodbye at the door.'

'And why should I believe you?'

'Why would I lie?'

He chuckled but his eyes remained cold. 'You all lie. To save your life, to gain time. You say all the right things but in your heart you are all traitors. And we know it.'

'My husband has done nothing wrong. He never even saw the man. If anyone is guilty, it's me. Although God knows I meant no harm. Arrest me if you like. But let Dmitry go.'

The man reached for a little golden bell on his desk. 'Why can't we have you both?' He rang the bell. A moment later the door opened and an officer walked in. 'Take her downstairs,' said her interrogator.

'You are arresting me?' she exclaimed in disbelief. 'For what?'

'Being in contact with a wanted criminal is forbidden by law. You broke the law. I am fully within my rights to arrest you,' said the man, turning away from her. The audience was over.

She thought of another time, another grim office and wide table, another man with dead eyes and an angry smirk on his face threatening her with unspeakable horrors. This one didn't threaten, nor did he raise his voice but she was afraid nonetheless. Petrified. 'Please, we haven't done anything wrong,' she pleaded but it was too late. The door had shut in front of her, blocking her tormentor from view, and the officer was dragging her down the corridor to her cell.

*

In the cell, Sophia perched on her bunk and waited. It was all a misunderstanding, she was sure of it. Any minute now someone would realise they had made a mistake and release them. She wouldn't have to remain in the damp, cold dungeon for long. And so, she remained on the edge of the bed, ready to leave at a moment's notice.

'You might as well relax, dear. I've been here for four days and no one has come for me,' said one of her new neighbours, a tall woman with sad eyes.

'They arrested half of Kislovodsk this week. They don't have the manpower to deal with all of us,' said another woman. Before Sophia was brought in, they were playing cards. Now they were busy watching Sophia, as if she was the most interesting thing that had happened to them all week.

Without a word, Sophia lay back on the hard bed and closed her eyes. Had they really arrested all those people? Half of Kislovodsk couldn't possibly be traitors. Were they using Shkuro's invasion as an excuse to get rid of the nobility, to destroy the spectre of the old regime once and for all?

If that was the case, there was no point in trying to prove their innocence. In the eyes of their captors, they were already guilty, merely through the accident of birth. Having been born into the upper class, there was no place for them in the new Russia.

She should have listened to Regina and stayed home. Instead, she walked willingly into the bear's den and now here she was in a cell, her face turned to the wall, so that no one could see her cry. But what else could she have done? She had to help Dmitry. The other option, the safer option of doing nothing and hoping for the best, felt like betrayal. Like she had given up on him.

Exhausted, she drifted in and out of sleep, trying not to listen to the voices around her. But there was no escaping them. They reached her through the pillow she had placed over her head, filling her dreams with terror.

'They are running out of space in their prisons.'

'Don't worry. Plenty of space in Siberian labour camps.'

'They are barbarians who torture people. Prepare to be tortured.'

'Have you heard what they do to the Cossacks they manage to catch? They burn them alive. And then they burn their families.'

'Lucky they haven't caught that many. Shkuro is like a cat. He has nine lives.'

In the morning, Sophia woke up to a strong hand shaking her.

'Sophia Orlova? Follow me,' someone barked in her ear. She recognised the monosyllabic officer who had conducted her to her cell.

'Where?' she asked, still woozy from sleep but scrambling to her feet as fast as she could.

The man didn't reply, pushing her outside, ignoring pleas and enquiries from the other prisoners.

*

The officer took her to the familiar room, which was now empty. He told her to wait and closed the door, leaving her alone with her thoughts. They were not watching her. That was a good sign. Could she slip out through the entrance and onto the street? She glanced out the window at a group of people walking past with baskets in their hands. Freedom was so close. But what about Dmitry? How could she leave him here? She remained standing in the middle of the room, her back to the window.

A moment later, she heard footsteps. She stood up as straight as she could, expecting to see the man who had questioned her the day before. She would show him that even the night in the cold cell hadn't broken her spirit. She would explain one more time that they were innocent. And this time she would make sure he believed her.

The door opened. Dmitry stood in the doorway. Sophia rubbed her eyes, as if she couldn't believe what she was seeing. Then she cried out and ran to him. He looked like he hadn't slept in days. The stubble on his face made him appear older. There were black shadows under his eyes. At the sight of him, she started to cry. Mutely he pulled her into a hug and patted her back. 'Shh, shh,' he whispered.

When she raised her eyes, she saw a dark silhouette in the corridor behind him. Try as she might, she couldn't make out the man's face. 'You are here. You are safe. I didn't think I would see you again,' she whispered, placing her hand on Dmitry's rough cheek, pressing him close to her, her tears falling on his face.

'I didn't think I would get out of here alive. Those monsters were ready to shoot me for my connection with Shkuro. "What connection?" I asked them. But they refused to listen. All they hear is the sound of their own voice. If it wasn't for Nikolai, I would be on the next train to Siberia.'

Sophia's hands trembled as she glanced past Dmitry. There he was, standing behind his brother, wrapped in a dark cloak, a smile on his face, his eyes on her. Nikolai! She couldn't speak or move or think. Her mouth opened slightly and she took in shallow, nervous breaths, while Dmitry was clasping her hand and talking about his ordeal. And even as she cried with relief at seeing her husband again, her eyes were drawn to Nikolai and her heart was bursting.

'What are you doing here?' Dmitry asked her. 'You are the last person I expected to see.'

'I came here to tell them you were innocent. They detained me and I spent the night in the cell.'

Dmitry took her hand and pressed his lips to the tips of her fingers. 'My poor darling. You shouldn't have come here. You know it's dangerous. These people are not to be trusted.'

'I couldn't leave you here. What was I supposed to do?'

'You were supposed to stay safe and wait for me. That's all I want. For you to be safe.'

'I know. I'm sorry. What is going to happen to us?'

Nikolai said, 'The two of you are free to go. It was all a big misunderstanding.'

Dmitry's arms around her, Sophia watched Nikolai. How many times had she imagined this moment? Here he was, alive and well, his eyes twinkling with joy at the sight of her, and here she was, unable to say a word, shocked into silence by everything she was feeling. All she wanted was to reach out and touch him, to make sure she wasn't still asleep and dreaming about him, like she had dreamt about him every night for the last year. 'You are here, in Kislovodsk?' she finally said. She wished she could have a glass of water. Her throat felt so dry.

'I was assigned here as an army commissar. As of today, I am in charge of everyone who has been arrested in the last few weeks.'

Sophia couldn't take her astonished eyes off Nikolai. 'What happened to you? They told me you were dead. I went to visit you in jail and they said I was too late. Did they lie?'

'They didn't lie, at least not intentionally. They transferred me to another jail to be shot.' Sophia gasped and her hand flew to her mouth. He smiled. 'Don't worry. Here I am, alive and safe. Just before I was to be executed, there was another uprising. Suddenly, my jailers were gone and all my paperwork was lost. In all the chaos and confusion, everyone seemed to forget about me.'

'How long were you in jail after that?'

'A couple of months. After the failed Kornilov coup, the Provisional Government realised it wasn't us they had to fear, so they released us.'

'And how wrong they were!' said Dmitry. 'Look at them and look at you.'

'What was it like? The October Revolution?' asked Sophia. She moved closer to Dmitry, so he wouldn't see the expression on her face.

'With little resistance from the Provisional Government. Just like France in 1799, Russia was ready for a change long before the cruiser *Aurora* fired its victorious shot.' Nikolai sounded elated. And extremely pleased with himself. *And so he should be*, thought Sophia.

'You did it. You achieved the impossible,' she said. Every time she looked into his face, she wanted to cry.

Dmitry said, 'Yes and now what? Their first real test was the war with Germany. And what do they do? The Treaty of Brest-Litovsk is a disgrace. They gave up ancient Russian land and for what?'

'It ended the war for Russia, didn't it? And now we can concentrate on our internal reforms.'

'Don't you see what you've done? The country that hasn't been conquered raised its hands in surrender and agreed to atrocious terms as if it has lost. It's against tradition, against honour, unprecedented and shameful. What makes you think Germany will leave us alone and not occupy us?'

'We have another enemy to contend with. The enemy within. Men like Shkuro, Denikin, Kornilov and many others. That's why I'm here. My job is to make sure these men don't succeed.'

'Thank God you are here,' whispered Sophia. 'You saved us, again.'

'Yes, thank you, brother. We owe you our lives. We won't forget this,' said Dmitry. 'Now, let's get out of here, Sophia. I couldn't stay here another minute.'

Sophia couldn't agree more. She couldn't wait to leave this place. On the way back they stopped at Anna's apartment and when Regina saw Nikolai, she did all the things Sophia longed to do but couldn't. She hugged him close and asked a million questions, eventually, reluctantly, letting go of him but never straying far from his side. In their old apartment building on Kabardinskaya Street, Nikolai had a word with Kirill and assured them no one would bother them again. 'Thank you,' whispered Sophia, too afraid to raise her eyes to him.

'You are welcome.' He watched her with such warmth and affection, she wanted to cry. He looked like he was about to say something else but decided not to. Instead, he said his goodbyes, telling them he had a lot of work to do before catching a train to Pyatigorsk the next morning.

'Be careful out there, brother,' said Dmitry. 'Rumour has it, the Bolsheviks have been killing people on the trains and throwing their bodies out the window.'

'But not before cutting out their hearts, cooking them on their gas stoves and eating them for lunch? You shouldn't listen to rumours, Dima,' said Nikolai. 'I will come and see you soon. I need to talk to you all.'

In her little bed, her hand on Nikolai's letter, Sophia listened to Dmitry's snoring next door and Nanny's soft breathing coming from the dining room. Since she had found out Nikolai was alive, she waited for the day she would see him again. And now he was here and things were just like they had been in Petrograd – their future uncertain, the revolution in full swing, the storm cloud of civil war gathering over their heads, Regina wearing her heart on her sleeve for Nikolai, and Sophia wishing for the impossible.

Chapter 10

August–September 1918

After Nikolai left, time stretched before Sophia without end, like the steppes of the Caucasus. How to fill the hours? Where were her patients to take her mind off everything that she was feeling? She baked cabbage pies and sweet buns and waited. She read Chernyshevsky and waited. She spoke to Regina about Nikolai, even though she couldn't say his name out loud without trembling.

The only indication of the Cossacks' existence in the first weeks of August was the Bolsheviks' unabated anger. Unable to capture Shkuro, the revolutionaries were taking it out on the people of Kislovodsk. There were no more lunches or dinners for Sophia and Dmitry and Regina to enjoy because there was hardly anyone left to attend them. Anna Sudakova and her husband had been taken away one day, never to be seen again. Dmitry's friend, Count Alexei Strelnikov, had been arrested at the train station for trying to leave the country without permission. Anna's cousin, Count Alexander, had been arrested as he was sipping a cup of coffee at a hotel, in front of five of his friends, without a reason or an explanation. Grand Duke Boris Romanov, the cousin of Nicholas

II, who was living in Kislovodsk, was arrested and later released. And the question on everybody's minds was, who would be next?

Every wall and every tree sported posters promising a reward for Shkuro's head. Every day, the newspapers published stories of captured Cossacks and punishments inflicted on them. Sophia knew they were lying. The Cossacks were like the wind. Hidden away in the mountains, they were impossible to find.

One especially warm morning in August, Sophia was in the garden, her embroidery in her lap. Kirill's kitten, who had adopted Sophia as his surrogate mother, was by her feet, playing with the thread. Sophia laughed, every now and then, bending down and giving him a stroke. Suddenly he touched her with his paw, emitted a squeaky sound and ran off. Still smiling, Sophia watched as the kitten climbed up an apple tree. Seconds later, she heard the kitten's plaintive miaowing. It was clear – he was asking for help.

'I hate to say this to you but I told you so. You shouldn't have climbed that tree,' she admonished. 'And now you are stuck – again. Dmitry is not here. Who is going to rescue you this time?'

More pitiful sounds in reply. Sophia placed her embroidery on the table and approached the tree, looking up. 'How did you get all the way up there?' She sighed. Holding on to a branch, she pulled herself up. From here she could almost reach the kitten. 'Come on,' she called to him. 'Come down a little and I'll help you.'

But the animal remained on his branch, not moving, his eyes two burning coals of fear.

The kitten and Sophia were having a stand-off. He refused to come down even a little bit. And she couldn't climb any further.

Suddenly, she heard a familiar voice. 'What are you doing up there?' Under the tree, his hat in his hands, a smile on his face, was Nikolai.

So happy was she to see him, she forgot she was in the tree and let go of the branch, almost falling and holding on at the last moment. 'I heard that the Caucasus Mountains produce the best apples. Something about the altitude. I was testing this theory out.'

210

'Yes, but why are you up in the tree?'

'That's where the apples are. Would you like one?' She picked an apple off a branch, throwing it up in the air.

'No, thank you. The apples are still green. Are you planning to stay up there? Should I climb up and join you?'

'I'm coming down, as soon as I get the kitten. He's stuck in the branch above me.'

'Don't move,' he said, rolling up his sleeves with a comical expression on his face. 'I'll go up and get your cat.'

He climbed the tree quickly and efficiently and picked up the cat, carrying him to safety and placing him gently on the ground. With a short meow, the kitten ran off and hid under the porch. 'Do you need help getting down?' Nikolai called out to Sophia, who was still in the tree.

She blushed. 'I might need some help,' she said. 'Thank you. Why is it always harder on the way down? No wonder the naughty thing always gets stuck.'

'Does your kitten have a name?' he asked, lifting himself up and offering his hand to Sophia.

Leaning on him, she jumped down and dusted herself off. 'Yes, it's Kitten.'

'A great name for a cat. Suits him.' He grinned.

Happily, she grinned back. 'Why don't you come in? Nanny made some lovely sweet blinis. Dmitry is not here but Regina should be here soon. She'll be happy to see you.'

'I wish I could, but I don't have much time. My train to Essentuki leaves in …' he glanced at his watch, 'half an hour. And I need to talk to you.'

She had thought of this moment a thousand times, imagining all the things she would say to him and what it would feel like to see him again. But as she faced him, she was lost for words. 'When did you get back?'

'Three hours ago. I couldn't leave again without seeing you.'

Sophia glanced at Regina's window, hoping her friend was

211

busy with her needlework and wouldn't see them. She wanted Nikolai all to herself.

As if reading her mind, he said, 'Why don't you walk me to the station? I'll get someone to walk you back home afterwards.'

Her heart bursting with happiness, Sophia nodded. She couldn't talk.

Side by side, they walked through the familiar alleyway of poplars and pine trees. The sky was the colour of sapphire, a shade darker than in Petrograd. The grass was a vivid green, the sun brighter, the summer breeze warmer, the backdrop of mountains stunning, as if nature itself was experiencing life more fully here. Or was she only noticing it now because he was walking next to her? Everything seemed different when he was around. Better.

As they meandered past the post office and the library, Sophia asked what his plans were. Nikolai told her he was staying in Essentuki for two weeks and then in Kislovodsk for another three. And then he would return to Petrograd. 'The city is slowly returning back to normal. Trams are running again. Shops are reopening. Theatres and ballet, too. Everywhere you go, there are music and celebrations. Flowers are blooming on the Field of Mars. You would like it.'

'I wish I could see it again.' She missed the city of her birth. There was nothing in the world quite like it. 'Do you think it's safe to return?'

'That's exactly what I wanted to talk to you about. You, Regina, Nanny and Dmitry must leave Russia immediately.'

Sophia was thinking of walking through the streets of her childhood with Nikolai, while the sun set behind the Neva. Of being alone with him, of never having to say goodbye. Suddenly, he was talking about leaving. She wasn't expecting it. She watched him for a moment. 'Leave and go where?'

'Overseas somewhere. Paris, Milan, Vienna. Anywhere you like. But you can't stay here. It's not safe. This is just the calm before the storm.'

'You call it calm? This week alone we had our passports checked four times. I can't sleep for fear of another search. All our friends have been arrested.'

'That's nothing compared to what's to come. From what I've learnt, the White Army is getting stronger. Soon they will be here.'

'That's what everyone is hoping for. The nobility are waiting for the Cossacks to come to town and liberate them from the Bolsheviks. Everyone wants life to go back to normal.'

'Don't kid yourself. What we are facing is not an insurrection or an uprising that will soon be over. It's civil war.' She stumbled and fell. He caught her. 'War, Sophia. Do you understand? Fighting on the streets, people getting killed. Believe me, you don't want to be caught in the middle.'

'We've been caught in the middle since the beginning of last year.'

'That was nothing compared to what is about to happen. I can arrange for permissions for the four of you to travel to Paris. You will be safe in France and when things quieten down, you can come back.'

It had always been her dream to see Paris. Why was she suddenly so reluctant to go? 'What about you?' she whispered.

'I have to stay here. My work is just beginning.' Nikolai turned to her and took her hand. His eyes were burning. 'But if you want, you can stay with me. Let Dmitry go overseas by himself. I will make sure you are safe. I will look after you.'

All Sophia wanted was to be with him. If only it was that simple. 'I can't leave him. How can I leave him? It will kill him. I could never …' She fell quiet.

'I understand.'

Her heart hurt. *Take me with you*, she wanted to tell him. *To Petrograd or Essentuki, I don't care, as long as I am by your side.* But what she actually said was, 'I don't think you do understand. What I feel for you … I've never felt this way before. I never even knew I could feel this way. But I gave him a promise. I married him in a church in front of five hundred of our friends and family. In front of God. He's always been there for me. He's the most loyal husband a woman could want. How could I ever betray him?' They stood close to each other outside the station, while all around people were running, shouting, waving their hands. Carriages screeched past and dogs barked. Impatiently, she waited for him to say something. But before he could do so, they heard horses' hooves resound on the cobblestones. Sophia turned sharply and saw a squadron of Cossacks riding fast into the square before the station. Their uniforms were tattered and their weapons old and rusty but they had an air of superiority about them that made everyone pause and look. At the head of the cavalcade was a tall, broad-shouldered Cossack carrying a black standard with a wolf's head painted on it.

'It's Shkuro and his Wolves' Hundred,' exclaimed Nikolai.

'They are back,' whispered Sophia.

'Of course they are. They won't rest until the monarchy is restored or every single one of them is dead. Which is why I want you to leave Kislovodsk as soon as possible.'

A series of gunshots startled her, making her jump and momentarily forget what she was about to say. It was coming from the armoured train that had just pulled up outside the station. Sophia could see Red Army soldiers hanging from the open windows, aiming their rifles at the Cossacks. The bullets whizzed past and she felt the air around her move. Terrified, she turned to Nikolai.

She knew instantly something was wrong but didn't understand it at first. Nikolai stood motionless for a moment, as if suspended in time and place, and then he rose, his arms in the air, and started falling backwards. To her horror, she saw red on his tunic. Everything fell quiet. She no longer heard the shots or the shouts, no longer noticed civilians running past in a panic or more Cossacks arriving outside the station. 'Nikolai!' she whispered, throwing herself on him. 'Nikolai, can you hear me? What's wrong?' But he couldn't hear her. His eyes were closed. His face was pale. When she touched him, her hands felt damp. Lifting them to her face, she saw that they were covered in blood.

Stifling a scream of horror, she felt for his pulse. It was still there, thank God. He was breathing, barely. 'Please, hold on,' she cried. 'I will get you to safety.'

The train started moving, with the Cossacks riding after it and firing. A dishevelled man ran down the street, screaming. Sophia realised he was the conductor. 'Stop your fire. That train is filled with explosives. One bullet and the whole station will blow up, all of us with it.'

But no one paid him any attention. A moment later, Sophia felt the earth move under her feet. A wave of scorching hot air hit her. She cowered in the dust, hands over her ears. And then all hell broke loose. Women and children were screaming hysterically, while men cursed. Some people ran for their lives, while others froze, as if afraid to move. On the ground around them were motionless bodies – Cossacks and civilians.

A tall Cossack with a moustache rode forward and said, 'Ladies and gentlemen, you have nothing to fear. We are not here to hurt anyone. You are free to go and will not be harmed.'

Instantly, those sitting on the ground scrambled to their feet and dispersed. In the chaos of stomping feet and panicked voices, Sophia knelt by Nikolai, tearing his tunic open with superhuman effort, examining his chest where the bullet had entered, rolling her gloves into a ball and pressing hard to stem the bleeding, wondering what else she could do to keep him with her, to keep him alive, and all the while whispering, 'Wake up. Please wake up. I love you. Please, don't leave me. Not again.'

Her tears fell on his face, while his blood trickled all over her hands and dress. He didn't move. Covering his head with kisses, closing her eyes, she repeated, 'Please, God, save him!' over and over, like a woman possessed.

'Can I help you?' she heard. When she opened her eyes, she

saw a pair of military boots in front of her. They belonged to the tall Cossack who moments ago had spoken to the people at the station, promising them safety.

'I need to get him home,' she muttered.

The man whistled and two Cossacks appeared. He told them to conduct Sophia home and help her with Nikolai.

'Yes, Ataman,' they replied.

Only when he was out of sight and the two men lifted Nikolai, who remained unconscious, carrying him away from the station, did she realise that the man she had been talking to was Andrei Shkuro himself.

*

The men walked fast down the street. Sophia had to run to keep up. They tried to strike up a conversation, talking about their plans to overthrow the Bolsheviks. She barely noticed, like she didn't notice the blood covering her hands, face and dress. Squeezing Nikolai's hand, she whispered, 'Not long now. Please, hold on. Almost there.' The trip that seemed to take mere moments when she walked side by side with him through the poplars was now taking a lifetime.

He was so quiet in the men's arms. Why was he so quiet? She strained to hear if he was still breathing but couldn't tell for certain. Clasping her hands together, she prayed all the way down Kabardinskaya Street.

When they finally reached home, Sophia directed them to her room and asked them to place Nikolai on her bed. He didn't make a sound. She leaned over him, telling him everything was going to be all right, asking if he could hear her and checking his pulse. He was breathing, barely. His forehead was hot to the touch. His blood stained her white sheets and for a moment Sophia stared at the dark blotches, shaking with terror.

'Do you think we could have some vodka for our trouble?'

asked the taller of the two Cossacks.

'Sorry, we don't have any,' she replied. It was a lie. They had half a bottle in the cupboard somewhere. Dmitry wasn't much of a drinker, only touching the vodka on special occasions. And she didn't like the taste and never had any, not even on her birthday. But she would need it for Nikolai, to disinfect the wound, to take the edge off the pain. 'If you go to the kitchen, there might be some pies there for you.'

The men's faces stretched in disappointment at such an inferior substitute but they said goodbye and trudged to the kitchen.

Once the front door closed behind the two Cossacks, Sophia ran to the kitchen and fetched a bucket of water, some clean cloth and the bottle of vodka. When Nanny saw her, she gasped and her hand flew to her mouth. Her eyes like saucers, she stared at Sophia without a word. At first, Sophia didn't understand why and then she remembered – his blood was all over her. She quickly told Nanny what had happened and together they removed Nikolai's tunic, cleaned the wound as best as they could without touching the torn flesh, disinfected it with some vodka and applied a dressing. 'Please, God, let him live,' repeated Sophia. She wished she had gone to church more often, called on God more often, so He would recognise her voice among so many others. But more than anything, she wished she had Nikolai's skills, so she would know how to keep him alive.

She was in the kitchen, refilling the bucket with clean water from the jug, when Dmitry came in. Just like Nanny, he cried out at the sight of her. 'It's not my blood,' she said calmly, even though she felt anything but.

'My God. What happened?'

'It's Nikolai.'

Dmitry followed her to the room as she told him about the shooting. 'What were you doing at the station with my brother?' he asked.

'I was on my way to the market. We ran into each other.' She

217

didn't think twice about lying to her husband. Nor did she feel guilty. All she could think of was Nikolai.

'Is he going to be all right?'

'Of course he is going to be all right,' she snapped. She couldn't imagine the alternative and wouldn't think about it.

'He doesn't look so good.'

'He doesn't feel cold or clammy. He's going to be just fine.'

'He's burning up.'

'He was shot in the chest. I don't think the bullet exited. If it's still there, the wound could get infected.'

'Can you get the bullet out?'

'I've never done it before. We need a doctor.'

Dmitry volunteered to get a doctor, saying he knew someone on the other side of town. After he left, Sophia changed the blood-soaked sheets under Nikolai. Glancing impatiently at the clock, praying for the doctor to arrive, she sat by Nikolai's side, reading to him from Pushkin and Chernyshevsky, from Marx and Engels.

Amidst the noisy ball, in Hell
Of everyday distress,
I've seen you, but the secret's veil
Was covering your face.

She put her head next to his and whispered, 'Can't you see what your revolution is doing? An honest citizen can't walk down the street without getting shot. But you still believe in it, don't you? You still think it's for the greater good. Maybe when you wake up, you can tell me why. Now look what happened.'

She wrapped him in cool damp sheets to bring his temperature down, just as he would do to his patients in Petrograd. But it wasn't helping. His hands were like hot coals inside her trembling little hands.

Hours passed. Nikolai didn't move and only his heavy breathing could be heard in the dark room. Sophia jumped at every noise, hoping it was Dmitry and the doctor. But there was no sign of them. When the front door finally opened, it was Regina, coming to have dinner with Sophia and Dmitry. As soon as she saw Nikolai, she started crying and wouldn't stop. Sophia didn't cry. She had no time to cry. She was too busy thinking of ways to help him. Patting her friend gently on the hand, she said, 'He's still alive. That means the bullet didn't touch any vital organs. That's a good thing.'

'I will stay by his side until he's better,' stated Regina. She sank into the chair where Sophia had been sitting moments earlier. 'It would kill me if anything happened to him.'

'Nothing is going to happen to him,' said Sophia, trying to convince herself, not Regina.

Their heads together, their eyes on him, the two women sat in silence. The kerosene lamp burnt on the table, throwing wild shadows on the wall, playing on his face, making him look animated and alive, as if he was waking up. But he wasn't waking up.

'He is the only man I've ever loved,' whispered Regina.

'I know,' said Sophia. *He is the only man I've ever loved too*, she wanted to say. If only she could. What wouldn't she give to have the freedom to wear her feelings for Nikolai like a medal on her aching chest, the way her friend did.

'I wish I'd told him how I felt. What if it's too late and now he will never know?' cried Regina.

'I'm sure he knows, darling.' More lies, even as he lay in front of them, barely alive.

'No one ever made me feel this way. When he's with me, I forget about everything. I forget that I don't have a place in the world to call my own. I forget that I have no future. With him, I feel hope like never before.' Regina clasped her hands together. 'If I talk to him, will he hear?'

'He might do.'

'Please, wake up soon,' Regina whispered to Nikolai. 'When you wake up, I'll be right here, waiting for you. And I won't waste another second. From now on, no more secrets. I love you and

I want the whole world to know.'

Sophia wished Regina would leave, so she could be alone with Nikolai. Her heart thumping with guilt, she said, 'Let me change his dressing.'

Reluctantly, Regina moved away. Sophia removed the old dressing. Nikolai groaned. The wound looked angry and red but the bleeding had slowed down. It was a good thing, she told herself. She could barely breathe from fear.

'Please, help him,' said Regina. 'You've helped so many others. Save him, for me.'

'I'm so afraid. What if I do something wrong? Where is this doctor?'

The door opened. The two women looked up. Dmitry was standing in the doorway, his face grim. Even before he spoke, Sophia knew he didn't have good news. 'The doctor is no longer there. Either he was arrested, like so many others, or he moved. I tried to ask around, but no one knew anything. It's pandemonium outside. The Cossacks are back.'

'The hospital. We need to take him to the hospital,' cried Regina.

'That's where I went next, to see if there's a bed for him. The hospital is occupied by Shkuro's men. There are no doctors left there.'

'Who is looking after the patients?'

'I don't know. I was told to leave by a man who wasn't inclined to answer my questions.'

Sophia sat on the edge of Nikolai's bed, suddenly afraid. There was no doctor. She was all he had. Was she going to be enough?

'You need to remove the bullet,' said Dmitry, as if he knew about such things.

She tried to concentrate through the fog inside her head. She seemed to remember Nikolai talking about it once. What was it he had said? When one of his men was brought in with a gunshot wound, he bandaged it and left the bullet where it was. *A little bit of metal in his body won't hurt him. It will only make him stronger. But touching it could cost him his life.* Suddenly, she knew what Nikolai would do. 'I don't think we need to remove it. It could cause more damage and that's the last thing he needs.'

'Leaving it there could kill him.'

'Removing it could kill him just as easily. It could be near a blood vessel or a nerve or a vital organ. We have no antibiotics, nothing for infection. Touching the bullet is a major surgery and a huge risk.'

'What do you suggest?'

'All we can do is wait and hope he recovers.'

'And what if he doesn't?'

Sophia didn't want to think about it. She hoped she was right. But what if she wasn't? She couldn't bear that thought.

*

At night, the shadows danced on the sheets and the walls, and on Nikolai's face. He looked so peaceful as he lay motionless in her bed, like he was sleeping without a care in the world. But when she placed her hand on his forehead, she could feel the heat coming from his body. He was burning up and there was nothing she could do to help him. She thought she had felt helpless before, when her patients were dying at the hospital, when she watched her house ransacked, when Arsenii was killed in front of her eyes. But it was nothing compared to what she was feeling now.

What time was it? It felt like the middle of the night. Dmitry had finally convinced Regina to go home, thank God. She did so reluctantly, promising to be back first thing in the morning.

Sophia curled up in bed next to him and touched his face. She whispered his name, wondering, like Regina, if he could hear her. In case he could, she told him how much he meant to her and about all the things they could do together, if only she was free to be with him. 'We will walk by the Neva until morning. We will see the bridges go up and spend the night on the river. You will buy me chocolates and lemonade. I will play my violin for you. You will sing for me. We will be happy. Just get better.' It was wishful thinking. She knew Dmitry would never let her go.

She ignored the ever-present guilt, shut it away in the secret place in her heart where she kept all the heartbreaking things she never wanted to think about. She didn't ask for these feelings. She couldn't control them, just like she couldn't control the sun rising in the morning and setting in the evening behind the majestic mountains. It was meant to happen, for better or worse, and there was nothing anyone could do about it. Did true love make everything all right or was she being selfish, telling herself what she wanted to hear? She wondered if this was how her mother had felt when she had fallen in love with a man who wasn't her husband. Like it was meant to be? Like it was destiny?

Yes, and look how that had turned out.

She wasn't her mother. She couldn't help these feelings but she could help what she did about them. Even if her heart was breaking.

Sophia remained like this, with his hand in hers, and watched the candle burn out until it was dark in the room.

When she heard Dmitry's footsteps, she sat up. Under the cover she let go of Nikolai's hand.

'What are you still doing here? Come to bed. You can sleep with me tonight,' he said. His hand touched her shoulder.

'I'm a nurse, Dima. This is what I do. I sit with the wounded.'

'It's late. You need rest. There is nothing more you can do for him.'

'What if he wakes up? I don't want him to be alone in the dark.'

'Leave a candle burning and let's go.'

She had no choice but to follow him. In bed, she curled into a ball, as far away from him as possible. 'He's going to be fine, you know that, don't you? And even if he isn't, you've done all you could,' said Dmitry.

222

Sophia turned to the wall, but there was no escaping his arms around her or his mouth in her hair as he whispered how much he loved her. Like a convict with shackles around her ankles, she was entrapped by her husband's feelings. She lay very still and soon he fell asleep but she stayed awake, despite her tiredness, listening for noises and hoping for a miracle.

*

When the sun streaked auburn through the windows, Sophia was out of bed and by Nikolai's side. 'Good morning,' she whispered. 'Are we feeling better today?'

But he didn't seem to be feeling better. His forehead felt even hotter than the day before. Her heart sank.

Nanny walked in with a hot pie on a plate. 'Oh, Nanny,' Sophia exclaimed. 'How can I think of food at a time like this? His bleeding slowed down but his temperature is still up. And I have nothing to give him. Not even any herbs.'

'I know a healer who can help. I can take you to her.'

Sophia waited till Regina arrived. She didn't want Nikolai to be alone. Regina looked terrible, her hair a mess and her eyes dim. But unlike Sophia, she didn't say no to Nanny's pie and devoured it in the chair by Nikolai's bed.

'Check his dressing while I'm gone. If it needs changing, do so. Wrap him in damp sheets to cool him down,' Sophia told her.

'Of course.'

'Read to him. It's good for him to hear someone's voice and know there are people around. He loves Pushkin. And don't forget to check his temperature.'

Regina stared at Sophia for a few seconds and then said, 'I know what I'm doing. Don't worry. Go already!'

Nanny and Sophia set out when the sun was still low in the sky and it wasn't too hot. There was an expectant tension in Kislovodsk, not unlike the tension in Petrograd just before they'd left. Sophia recognised it and it filled her heart with dread. She knew from experience – nothing good could come of it. She walked as fast as she could, pulling Nanny behind her and every few minutes telling her to hurry. The older woman huffed and puffed, doing her best to keep up. 'Rejoice, child. Nikolai is back and he's alive. It's a miracle,' she said as they walked by the river past the spot where the drunken sailor had threatened Sophia and Regina.

'I couldn't lose him now, not when I just got him back. If he doesn't get better, I don't know what I'm going to do.'

'And what are you going to do if he does? What about Dmitry? What about your husband?'

'Please, Nanny, not now. I can't even think about it.'

As they walked past the town hall, they had no choice but to slow down. A large group of people gathered around a placard on the wall, reading what looked like an official announcement. Nanny and Sophia couldn't get close enough to see what it said. Mutely they stood, hoping the crowd would disperse.

'No more Bolsheviks!' exclaimed a man with a noble bearing and rags on his body. 'Finally, Kislovodsk belongs to Shkuro.'

Another man nodded happily. 'First the Caucasus, then the rest of Russia. The days of the revolution are numbered.'

Shkuro and his Cossacks did exactly what they had set out to do. They were true to their word – the Bolsheviks were gone. Sophia rejoiced at the news but fear for Nikolai outweighed her curiosity. Impatiently, she pulled Nanny by the arm and they continued on their way.

The small hut on the outskirts of Kislovodsk was barely visible from behind the overgrown bushes. Clean laundry hung on the fence that was rotting in places. Sophia could hear a dog growling, its chain rattling as it jumped and pulled. Somewhere, a rooster crowed. The garden was overrun with weeds and the house was leaning to one side. It looked abandoned and unkempt, and if it wasn't for the dog, Sophia would have thought no one lived there. Nervously, she stopped outside the gate.

'Don't be afraid,' said Nanny. 'Her name is Tonya. Tell her Katerina sent you.'

'Who is Katerina?'

'A friend of mine. She was sick with pneumonia and Tonya was the only one who could heal her.'

'You are not coming in?'

Nanny crossed herself and shook her head. 'I'm a Christian. We don't go to healers. What a sin.'

'Yet, you brought me here.'

'You need help. And Tonya can help you.'

Gingerly, Sophia opened the fence, crossed the yard, her feet drowning in dry yellow grass, ignored the dog snapping at her heels and pulling hard enough to rip its chain off, and knocked. All was quiet inside the hut. She waited for a few moments and turned to go. A part of her was relieved. She didn't believe in healers. But Nanny was right. She needed help desperately and didn't know where else to turn.

Finally, she saw a shadow through the window. A screechy voice, like nails on glass, asked who she was.

'My name is Sophia. I need your help.'

The door opened a fraction and Sophia found herself face to face with a tiny old lady with crooked fingers. 'You'd better come in.'

Sophia followed Tonya inside a small kitchen. When the old woman lit a candle, she saw that the house was as dirty on the inside as it was on the outside. It was bare of furniture, with bookshelves lining the walls from floor to ceiling, filled with sinister books, many of which had been banned under the tsar.

'What can I help you with?' the woman asked impatiently.

'My husband's brother has been shot. He has a fever that won't come down. We are afraid for his life.' The woman appraised her in silence. Sophia took a sharp breath and continued, 'Do you have anything for the fever? I have money. I will pay.'

225

Tonya continued to watch her without a word. Sophia shivered, feeling small under her gaze. When the old woman spoke, she sounded angry. 'Look at you. Your dress is old and torn but your hands are white. Haven't known a day of hard work, have you?'

'That's not true. I'm a nurse.'

'Gentry, are you? I know the likes of you. For centuries you exploited and used us for your own good. The glorious revolution soon put a stop to that. How does that make you feel?'

'Afraid,' said Sophia. 'It makes me feel afraid.'

'So you should be. You think Shkuro will help you? He has no chance. He's fighting against the tide that will soon swallow him up. My cards told me so.' The old woman cackled. Sophia felt goose bumps all over her arms. Nanny had been wrong about Tonya. She couldn't help her. The woman continued, 'All of you ought to be burnt. Russia won't heal until every last one of you is gone.'

'Please. I haven't done anything wrong. And a man's life depends on it.'

The woman shuffled into the corner and pulled down a weighty tome. Looking through it, she muttered to herself, 'I can always pretend to help and poison her instead. Poison the lot of them. Do my bit to help our glorious leader.' Her crooked finger shook and her eyes darted back and forth.

Sophia shuddered. She had two choices. Run for her life while she still could. Or stay and talk some sense into the old woman. She thought of Nikolai, burning up in her bed at home. 'The man who needs your help, he's not one of us. He's in the Bolshevik party. He was shot when Shkuro's men invaded Kislovodsk.'

The healer placed the book on the table and turned around. 'Is that so?'

'I'm telling the truth.'

'Who is he?'

'He is an army commissar sent from Petrograd to deal with Shkuro and his supporters. If you don't believe me, you can check for yourself. His name is Nikolai Orlov.'

'That changes everything.'

She walked to the stove and placed a pot on the fire, then fetched half a dozen jars, adding various herbs to the pot. Finally pouring in some water, she stirred the concoction for a few minutes until it was boiling. When it was ready, she transferred it into an empty jar and handed it to Sophia. 'This potion will take care of the fever.'

'What's in it?'

'A healer never reveals her secrets.'

'Thank you. And here is the money.'

Tonya pushed her hand away. 'Don't they teach you anything at your posh lyceum for girls? Witches don't accept money. And I'm a witch like my mother and grandmother before me.'

'How can I thank you?'

'Your necklace.'

'Excuse me?' Sophia's hand flew to her neck.

'Your crucifix. I want it.' The woman stretched her crooked fingers towards Sophia.

'My crucifix?' Nanny was right. A good Christian shouldn't see a healer. It was a sin and now she was paying the price. 'I've had it since I was a baby. Since the day I was christened. It belonged to my mother.'

'It's made of pure gold, isn't it? It will do.' Before Sophia could take another step back, the old woman ripped the necklace off her neck, making her cry out.

Still holding the jar, she backed out of the house. It was clear the old woman was mad. Could Sophia trust her? She knew some healers had incredible powers. They studied herbs and traditional medicine and the common folk called on them before they called on a doctor. But she also knew many of them were charlatans. And even if Tonya had any special knowledge, what would stop her from giving Sophia poison, just like she said? She certainly looked mad enough to do it.

As they walked home, Sophia's hand on her neck where her

crucifix had been, she decided she wouldn't give the potion to Nikolai. How could she give him something when she had no idea what it was? But when they returned, a frantic Regina met them. While they were gone, Nikolai's fever had got worse.

In the kitchen, Sophia examined the jar. The potion looked murky green. What secrets did it hold?

Hesitating only a moment, she poured herself half a glass and drank it. She spent the rest of the day tending to Nikolai. When in the evening she didn't feel sick, she poured the rest of the potion into a glass and spoon-fed it to him.

That night, she slept on the little chair next to him. In the morning, she was ready to fall from exhaustion, but when she touched Nikolai's forehead, it felt cooler. As she changed his dressing and cleaned his wound, she cried with relief.

Chapter 11

September 1918

The next couple of days brought little change to Nikolai's condition. Although his temperature remained down, he didn't regain consciousness. Sophia had made another trip to the healer and begged her for another jar of the magic potion. This time, the woman didn't make any accusations. She looked like she didn't even recognise Sophia, preparing the potion in silence and accepting money as payment. Her eyes were shifty, as if she was afraid of something. Sophia thought it was because her prediction hadn't come true. Shkuro's Cossacks had occupied Kislovodsk, taking all the major buildings in town – the post office, the hospital, the town hall and the train station – and they looked like they were here to stay. A couple of days later, life was already changing for the better. Little by little, Shkuro's men were releasing all those who had been imprisoned by the Bolsheviks. The Cossacks had torn down all the revolutionary propaganda posters and forbidden any Bolshevik material from being distributed. The newspaper from Petrograd no longer reached Kislovodsk. No more trying to avoid Dmitry as he read the terrible news at the dinner table.

Sophia never left Nikolai's side, while Dmitry hovered nearby, watching her every move. Every glance in Nikolai's direction, every affectionate gesture, every dressing she changed, every time she checked his pulse, Dmitry's eyes were on her. Sophia kept her gaze down as she performed her duties, a caring and efficient nurse and nothing more. But when Dmitry wasn't around and it was just her and Nikolai, she would whisper sweet nothings to him, talking of how they had met and of the hours they had spent together looking after the wounded in Petrograd. She would dream about the future. 'You'll get better soon and take me back to Petrograd. We'll find a small house on the river. I will learn to cook something other than pies. I will cook for you and we'll have children. I've always wanted a big family. We will go to Paris and Rome. We will go to Switzerland. You will show me the lakes and the waterfalls and the cities you love.' If only any of it was possible.

Sometimes his eyelids fluttered as if he could hear her. Or was it just her imagination?

Regina breezed in a few times a day, sat on the edge of Nikolai's bed, held his hand and spoke to him, then left to go for a promenade or to bathe in the river. Time and time again she invited Sophia to join her but she always said no. She was afraid the minute she left him, something terrible would happen to him. Nanny would walk in with trays of food, leaving them at Sophia's feet as she tended to Nikolai. Sophia would remember them hours later, when her stomach would hurt from hunger, and devour the pies and the potatoes and the home-made bread.

The city welcomed Shkuro's men with tears of relief. The Cossacks had once been part of the tsar's army. They still wore their old uniforms, if somewhat tattered and torn, and they still displayed their old standard. In the country ravished by the revolution, Kislovodsk was an oasis of old values and tradition, and the exiled gentry rejoiced. On her daily trips to the market, Sophia saw smiles instead of tension and fear. But one morning, as Sophia was making herself a cup of tea, having slept only sporadically in her chair next to Nikolai, she heard gunshots. They sounded far away at first but seemed to be getting closer. *What is it this time?* she thought with trepidation.

In the evening, Princess Anna and her husband, Vladimir, appeared on their doorstep. Gone was the haughty attitude and the straight back. Anna's shoulders were stooped and she looked older by years. Sophia hugged her. 'We were so worried when you were arrested. We didn't know what to think. Thank God you are back!'

'Shkuro liberated us personally. Everyone detained by the Bolsheviks was told they were free to go. What a relief!'

'Finally, some good news. And your cousin, Count Alexander?'

'It was too late for him. The cursed Bolsheviks had already taken him to Petrograd. Who knows what awaits him there. We were supposed to go too but Shkuro intervened just in time. The Bolsheviks treated us like we were singlehandedly responsible for the Cossacks' attacks in Kislovodsk. It made no sense.'

'Why do you sound so surprised?' exclaimed Vladimir. 'Nothing those people do makes sense.'

'We would have come sooner but we were too busy packing what little belongings we have left,' said Anna.

'Packing?'

'We wanted to be prepared. And a good thing too. Did you hear the shooting? The Bolsheviks are back. They are pushing Shkuro's men out.'

Sophia's hand flew to her mouth. 'It can't be.' She didn't want to believe it but in her heart, she wasn't surprised. Shkuro's presence in Kislovodsk was a temporary reprieve, too good to be true.

Vladimir said, 'On the contrary, it was inevitable. Shkuro took Kislovodsk with five thousand men. He has no heavy machinery, hardly any ammunition. He couldn't hold the town for long.'

'At least the two of you are free. Something good came of it,' said Dmitry.

'I will be forever grateful to the man,' said Anna. 'A gentleman through and through, the remnant of the old regime, so unlike the revolutionary brutes.'

Vladimir said, 'Now the monsters are back, we can't stay here. They could arrest us again at any moment. The Bolsheviks are out for our blood. They won't stop until there is no gentry left in Kislovodsk.'

'What can we do?' asked Sophia, suddenly afraid but not for herself. How could she keep Nikolai safe if once again the world was crashing down around them?

'We are joining Shkuro and his Cossacks and going into hiding. Many others are doing the same. Tomorrow evening everyone is meeting at the Grand Hotel and we'll follow the Cossacks into the mountains. I suggest you join us.'

'You are going to hide in the mountains?' exclaimed Sophia. Her eyes were on Princess Anna, a delicate flower of Petrograd society, born into fortune, brought up to enjoy the finer things in life, until recently living a life of luxury on the Neva. Although she had lost everything, she remained a delicate flower, uncertain and afraid. Princess Anna hiding in the mountains with the partisans? It was impossible.

Vladimir nodded. 'I would go to the far side of hell if it meant getting away from the Bolsheviks. After the horrors they'd put us through, the farther and more remote we are, the better.'

*

With a heavy heart Sophia watched as Dmitry threw their belongings into a trunk. Kislovodsk was supposed to be their saving grace, their refuge. Where would they go this time? Although the town had never felt like home, Sophia had fallen in love with the ragged mountains and bursting rivers, stunning green parks and fruit trees in bloom. They were supposed to wait out the revolution here, so that one day they could return home. And for a brief moment in time, they were safe. Leaving the town in the dark of night, running away into the unknown felt too much like admitting defeat.

And yet, to stay here was impossible. Since Shkuro's first attack in July, the Bolsheviks had treated them as enemies. Was Vladimir right? Were things going to get worse? Sophia thought of Nikolai's words at the train station just before he got shot. *What you faced up until now is nothing compared to what is about to happen*, he had said to her. She couldn't imagine living in fear for much longer. Nor could she take more searches or arrests or the sound of clamping boots in the corridor, followed by a terrifying knock on the door. They had to go, that much was obvious. Then why did it seem like the scariest thing she had ever had to do? With no destination in mind, it felt like stepping out of a window of a burning building and hoping there were some trees underneath to break the fall.

The packing didn't take long this time because they hardly had anything left. Late in the afternoon, Dmitry went out and soon returned with a horse-driven cart. He said he had been lucky to get one. Everyone seemed to be leaving. Everyone wanted one. Without a word, Sophia helped him load the trunks onto the cart.

'Before we go, I'll take Nikolai to a local hospital,' said Dmitry. 'It's bound to open again once the Bolsheviks are back for good.'

'And what if it doesn't? You will leave him here?' exclaimed Sophia, horrified. She couldn't believe her ears.

'He'll be fine. He's one of them, remember?'

'He's your brother, Dima. You want to leave him with strangers who don't care if he lives or dies?'

'The hospital staff will look after him. He needs professional care. We can't help him anymore.'

'It's a good thing Nikolai didn't think the same about us the night the revolutionaries tried to kill us on the balcony. Or when you were arrested. Your brother saved our lives more times than I can count. And you want to leave him behind? You should be ashamed of yourself.'

Dmitry didn't look ashamed. He looked annoyed. 'How can we look after him when we are running for our lives? We are no longer living a life of luxury in a mansion on Nevsky. The road will be hard for everyone. What if he doesn't make it? You will never forgive yourself. And what if we are in danger and need to move fast? He will only slow us down.'

'Is that what you are afraid of? That he will slow us down?'

'I have to think of you. Of your safety.'

'We can't leave him here. He's family.' She stood up tall, her hands on her hips, and glared at him with contempt.

'He's not your family.'

'I'm married to you, aren't I? And I'm not leaving without him.'

'It's not up to you,' said Dmitry, raising his voice ever so slightly.

'If he stays, I stay,' she said quietly but firmly.

'What is it about him? Why are you so devoted to him?'

'I would be a bad nurse if I left my patient to his unknown fate and fled. I am not leaving him here to die.'

'I'm with Sophia on this,' said Regina, appearing in the doorway, pulling her trunk, her face concealed behind a black veil, her hair a mess of unruly blonde curls. 'I'm not leaving without him.'

Dmitry barely glanced in her direction but didn't argue any further. Nor did he offer to lift his brother onto the cart. Nanny volunteered to help and the three women carried Nikolai down the corridor and through the front door, gently placing him inside the cart on top of a woolly blanket with a pillow under his head.

*

As they gathered around the cart, the skies turned grey and Sophia could hear the sound of distant thunder. Somewhere on the other side of Kislovodsk, machine guns sang their terrifying song. She barely looked up. She was getting used to the terrible

234

sound of war following her everywhere she went and that was the scary part, the unnatural part. She didn't want to get used to the unthinkable, to have it become her everyday reality. As Sophia threw one regretful glance at the tiny apartment that had been their home for over a year, she wondered what was going to happen to Kislovodsk. What was going to happen to all of them?

Nanny helped her lift the last trunk onto the cart. 'Where are your things, Nanny? I didn't see you packing. Your sewing machine is still in the room. You don't want to leave it behind. We might need it.'

'I'm not coming, dear.' Tears were running down Nanny's wrinkled cheeks. 'I'm too old to hide in the mountains. Too old to run.'

Sophia blinked her own tears away. 'You can't stay here all by yourself. It's not safe.'

'I'll be fine. I'm not of noble blood, remember? As far as they are concerned, I'm one of them.'

'How can I go without you? Whatever am I going to do?' It occurred to Sophia that she had never spent a day without Nanny by her side. Not a day. Through everything, Nanny had always been with her. When her own mother had turned her back on her, Nanny remained her rock, the one constant in her life. And now it felt like she was losing her. She put her arms around Nanny, placed her head on her chest and cried.

'We will meet again. Better times will come, and we will see each other,' whispered Nanny, kissing Sophia's cheeks.

Dmitry shouted that it was time to go but Sophia ignored him, standing mutely with her arms around Nanny, unable to tear herself away.

'This is not goodbye,' Sophia cried as she climbed into the cart. Her foot slipped and she almost fell but Dmitry was behind her and helped her up.

'God bless you, child,' said Nanny, making a sign of a cross over Sophia. 'For your kind heart, may He always protect you.'

235

Regina climbed into the cart and sat next to Nikolai. 'Will it be comfortable for him? Here, I took another blanket from my room. I'm sure Kirill won't mind. Let's put it under him.'

'You stole a blanket from Kirill?'

'Borrowed it. We need it more than he does. I have some pillows too.' She moved closer to Nikolai and placed his head on her lap. Sophia looked away. Suddenly, the cart seemed too small for the four of them.

As the horse started moving, Sophia turned around. The sun peeked through the clouds, igniting the apple trees and their apartment block, making them look like they were basking in late afternoon light. The mountains in the back framed it all like a picture. But she wasn't looking at the mountains or the apple trees or the apartment block. Her gaze was on the small lone figure on the porch, grey and stooped, waving goodbye. With tears in her eyes, Sophia raised her hand and waved back, wondering if she would ever see Nanny again.

*

The cart Dmitry was able to procure was not meant to carry people for long distances. It was meant to carry produce. It had a small wooden driver's bench, where Dmitry sat as he directed the horse through the narrow alleyways of Kislovodsk, just in case trying to avoid the main streets. And it had a large area in the back, where Nikolai was lying flat, his head in Regina's lap, his eyes closed and his breathing regular. Sophia perched uncomfortably next to them on the wooden planks.

Dmitry had never driven a cart before and it showed. The vehicle shook and weaved on the cobblestones as the horse stopped and started as if it could feel the uncertainty of the human who was trying to control it. When they went faster, the large wooden wheels screeched like they were about to fall off. No matter how much she propped herself with pillows, Sophia could feel every bump and every lurch. After twenty minutes, her legs and hips were killing her. She worried about Nikolai. Was he comfortable? He looked so still and serene, asleep in Regina's lap. His face was pale.

There was a sense of nervous unease on the streets of Kislovodsk, brimming with people from all walks of life, everyone strolling briskly, trying to get to their destination as fast as possible, as if the last thing they wanted was to stay longer than necessary out on the alien streets. The roads were flooded with automobiles and horse-driven carriages, with carts and bicycles, while somewhere in the distance machine guns barked and rifles responded eagerly, their thunderous dialogue making Sophia tremble with fear.

'We should have secured the trunks,' said Sophia when the horse lurched and the edge of one of the trunks hit her on the leg, making her cry out.

'Who knew the ride would be so bumpy,' said Regina, throwing a look at Dmitry. 'How far is the Grand Hotel? At this rate, we'll never get there. Not in one piece, anyway.'

Dmitry replied, his eyes frantic as the horse pulled, 'Feel free to do the driving if it will make you feel safer, ladies.'

'The Grand Hotel is not far,' said Sophia. 'I think we're almost there.'

'Thank God,' whispered Regina, rolling her eyes as the cart hit another pothole.

'But we are not staying at the hotel. We are moving on, remember? You better get used to this.'

'Maybe I *should* drive. I will do a better job than your husband,' said Regina. But she made no move to get up and her hands remained on Nikolai's shoulders.

Sophia touched Nikolai's forehead, then reached under the blanket and took his hand. It felt clammy and damp. She held it under the blanket until Pyatnizkaya Market, where they ran into Anna and Vladimir and followed their cart.

The white building of the Grand Hotel was like a beacon of

hope for all of Kislovodsk that evening. The park nearby was filled with carts and carriages. Hundreds of them were lining the streets. Hundreds more refugees were coming on foot, carrying what little possessions they had left. One man had a live chicken in his hands and a string bag behind his back. A woman had a screaming child on one hip and a sheet filled with clothes on the other. She walked heavily, like every step caused her pain. Not everyone had been lucky enough to procure a horse-driven cart.

Once upon a time, these people had been princes, counts and dukes. They had lived in mansions filled with expensive furniture and paintings, liveried servants, silks, satins and family jewels. They wore the latest Parisian fashions, spent their days hunting and nights dancing and socialising. A year later, here they all were, walking despondently to their unknown destination with their heads held low, rags on their bodies, stomachs empty and hearts heavy.

All around them, the street was abuzz with nervous voices. 'What is happening?' everyone wanted to know. 'What are we waiting for? Where are we going?'

No one seemed to have any answers, only questions.

As she watched the motionless procession of carts and carriages, like boats waiting for the dam to open, and the stream of pedestrians leaning under their worldly possessions and their fears, Sophia wondered what was in store for them. Were they moving towards their salvation or undoing? Two blocks away, someone's horse trampled a man and a large dog. A fight broke out. On the outskirts of the city, an explosion sounded. As she listened to the commotion, she thought, *I can't take much more of this. What's the point?* Running from the Bolsheviks, hiding her true self from Dmitry and Regina, day after day, minute after miserable minute, with no end in sight.

Sophia was hungry and weak with nerves. Her neck was sore, her hands trembled as she changed Nikolai's dressing and broke a small piece of bread to share with Regina and Dmitry. 'Here we are, on the run again,' she said quietly. 'Only this time we have nowhere to go.'

'Are we making a mistake?' asked Regina. 'To hide God knows where, to not know what tomorrow will bring. Look at all these people. The highest mountains in the world can't hide this crowd. Isn't it better to stay here, be what may?'

'Here we know exactly what tomorrow will bring. More searches, arrests and interrogations. It's only a matter of time before they come after us, like they came after so many others,' said Dmitry.

'Nikolai will protect us,' whispered Regina. All eyes turned to Nikolai, who remained motionless on the wooden planks. 'Papa always told me to take nothing in life for granted. That anything could be taken away from you at any moment. I didn't really understand what he meant, until now.' She closed her eyes. 'I miss him so much. Every time something happens, I want to tell him about it.'

'You'll feel like this for a long time. I still feel like this about my parents and it's been years,' said Sophia.

'A part of me is glad to see the back of Kislovodsk. Unlike you, I don't enjoy the river and the mountains. I prefer the theatre and the ballet. It's so provincial and uncivilised here.'

'You think where we are going will be less provincial and more civilised?'

Sophia knew Dmitry was right. They couldn't stay in Kislovodsk, torn by civil war, where all of them were under suspicion and no longer safe. Would they be safe where they were going? If only she could predict the future. When the order was finally given to move to Tambievskii Aoul to join the Cossacks there and the sad procession stirred to life, her heart raced with fear.

As the cart screeched and lurched, Nikolai groaned. Sophia wanted to take his hand, whisper something to him, give him comfort, but Regina was already doing all of it. The only thing left for Sophia to do was change his dressings and hope for the best. As she watched Regina's hand on his face, she thought, *It's for him. I can take anything, as long as he lives.*

*

It took hours to leave the city. Sophia expected to be stopped at any moment, dragged off the cart and asked to follow a man in black to a dark dungeon. If the Bolsheviks treated the accident of their birth as a certain proof of their loyalty to Shkuro, how would they view their attempt to join him in the mountains, to support him in his war against the newly established regime? She knew what it looked like – treason. She shuddered as she remembered the man who had interrogated her in Petrograd. If they were caught, was labour camp or a firing squad in store for them? And which was preferable? A quick and merciful death or a slow and painful one?

As the buildings gave way to rocky hills surrounded by shrubs and greenery, she breathed a sigh of relief. Hour after exhausting hour in the trembling cart and before they knew it, the hills grew in size, turning into a chain of sandy mountains that embraced Kislovodsk like a lover. The road had become narrow and steep, the terrace-like rocks leaning over them, and Sophia thought they were mad for even contemplating an escape here, in this unforgiving terrain. And yet, here they were, among a thousand others, inching their way up. But was it to freedom or a certain death?

She heard rumours that the Cossacks had joined them at the rear and were protecting the procession from a possible surprise attack by the Bolsheviks. But as hard as she tried, she couldn't spot them. When she looked back, all she saw was the sea of people, as lost and bewildered as they were.

On the right, a few metres from the cart, was a sheer drop so steep, Sophia had to stifle a scream the first time she noticed it. She had to force herself to look straight ahead, so she wouldn't see the deadly cliff. That, and Regina's arms around Nikolai.

'Please, be careful,' she whispered to Dmitry every time the cart hit a rock or an uneven patch of the road.

'Don't worry,' he would reply. 'I know what I'm doing.' But a second later, the cart would veer off to the right and Sophia would shut her eyes in panic, praying to God to protect them – *Our Father, who art in Heaven, hallowed be Thy name* – like a gloomy song accompanying their maddened journey.

When darkness fell, the carts stopped. People who were walking next to the carts sat on the side of the road, pulling out their meagre provisions, lighting their cigarettes and talking in hushed voices. No one seemed to know what to do next.

'Where are we?' Sophia asked wearily. She could barely sit up straight, let alone talk. Regina was asleep with her arms around Nikolai.

'Nowhere, I think,' said Dmitry, jumping off the driver's bench and sitting down next to her.

'Then why did we stop?'

'We can't travel in the dark. The roads are treacherous in the mountains. We'll have to wait till morning.' He pulled her closer. 'Are you tired? Hungry?'

She wanted to pull away but somewhere in the distance, a wild animal was howling. What was it? A wolf? A coyote? Were there wolves and coyotes here, in the mountains around Kislovodsk? She had no idea. Trembling, she allowed Dmitry to hold her. 'Too tired to eat.'

Dmitry looked into the distance, at the shadows of mountains looming overhead and the shimmering circle of the moon. 'When we were young, Nikolai and I dreamt of travelling in the Caucasus. Of seeing the mountains.'

'Your dream has come true.'

'The scenery is spectacular here, don't you think?'

'Yes. How far is it to Tambievskii? Will they have a bed for us to sleep in?'

'Will they have beds for a thousand people? I don't know.

241

I don't think so. But the moss looks comfortable. Better than sleeping on the wooden cart.'

Once, Sophia had the best Egyptian cotton money could buy. Now, she had no energy to get off the cart to sleep on the damp moss. Shaking her head, she stretched out on the wooden planks and closed her eyes. All around them, men and women prepared for the night. Someone started a campfire and the air filled with the scent of burning wood and baking potatoes. She could hear children crying and soft voices singing lullabies. Someone strummed a guitar. The melancholy sounds washed over Sophia like waves, making her want to cry.

'As my mother came out to hug me goodbye,
As the tears came to my father's eyes,
So I have set out.'

No matter how hard she strained her eyes, she could no longer see Nikolai's face but she could hear his breathing. The stars were like a silver carpet over her head, unlike anything she had ever imagined. The sky was bottomless black above her. She felt suspended in time and place, removed from her day-to-day reality, as if it was all happening to someone else. The deep voice of the singer, the pitiful sound of the guitar, the words of the familiar song, the smell of the fires, the darkness enveloping her and the fresh mountain air making her feel light-headed, she didn't even notice how she fell asleep.

She was woken at dawn by trumpets and horns, trombones and drums, and loud voices singing a military tune, stirring her to action, to stand and resist the enemy, to never give up and live each day as if it were her last. Sophia, who since March 1917 had believed every day would be her last, opened her eyes and wondered if she was still dreaming. For a second, she didn't know where she was. Her face felt damp to the touch and when she wiped it with the back of her hand, she saw that it was covered in mud.

Behind the cavalcade of carts, there was a large meadow. On that meadow were soldiers in Imperial uniform. A band was playing. The refugees were running towards them, hugging them, giving them bread and flowers, shaking their hands and thanking them with tears in their eyes.

'Where are we?' asked Regina, stretching and looking around. Nikolai's head was still in her lap, and her hands rested on his shoulders.

'I believe Tambievskii Aoul is just around the corner,' said Dmitry. 'We are closer than we thought.'

'This is Tambievskii?' exclaimed Regina, rubbing her eyes as if she couldn't believe it.

Dotted around the place, Sophia could see half a dozen huts. 'What did you expect?' she asked. 'Another Petrograd?'

A tall man in a dashing uniform stepped forward and addressed the refugees, welcoming them to the camp and inviting them to follow them to Bekeshevskaya Staniza near Beket mountain on the bank of the river Upper Kuma, deeper into the mountains and safer from the Bolshevik attacks.

'I know that man,' said Sophia. 'It's Andrei Shkuro. I met him in Kislovodsk at the train station.'

'Rumour has it, the Germans valued his head at sixty thousand roubles during the war,' said Dmitry. 'The man is a legend. If anyone can deliver Russia from the Bolsheviks, it's him.'

Sophia felt safer knowing they were under Shkuro's protection, even though the Cossacks were a sorry sight. Side by side walked ancient men with rifles their fathers and grandfathers had used to conquer Kuban from the Tartars. Next to them were children and women with slingshots. Their uniforms were in tatters but their eyes blazed with passion.

'We are ready to give our lives for freedom from the yoke of the Bolsheviks,' Shkuro said, concluding his speech. 'Our fight is just. We will not be conquered. Every day, hundreds of volunteers are joining our ranks. It is only a matter of time before we unite Russia under the royal standard once more.'

'How will you fight? You have no weapons,' someone from the

crowd shouted. Sophia turned around and recognised Vladimir, Anna's husband. She was pleased to see a familiar face.

'The Bolsheviks have weapons. All we need to do is take them,' replied Shkuro.

The Cossacks cheered and Sophia couldn't help but feel hopeful. These people had a goal – to bring the old regime back to Russia. And they would stop at nothing to achieve that goal. Being by their side made her feel like she, too, was part of it. She wasn't a soldier and she didn't know how to fight but she believed wholeheartedly in what they stood for. And she was here, among them, to give them her irrevocable support.

*

As they waited for the horns to blare, announcing it was time for the camp to move, they had some black bread for breakfast and a few sips of water. Their supplies were dwindling. From the cart, they could hear a gentle rustle of a river nearby. Sophia and Regina walked around the camp and saw the glimmer of water behind the trees.

'Race you to the river,' exclaimed Sophia, who was happy to be on solid ground again after hours on top of the shaking cart. She pulled Regina by the sleeve.

'Wait, what's the rush?'

While Regina walked slowly, Sophia danced impatiently on the spot, finally leaving her friend a few steps behind and running forward. Her neck and back ached. The skin of her face felt grimy. It was so good to stretch her legs, to move, to feel alive. The river was nothing but a small crystal-clear stream, navigating its way as fast as it could through the rocks and trees.

'I want to feel water on me,' cried Sophia, looking around. The bushes hid them completely. She undressed to her undergarments and stepped in the cold river, squealing with delight.

'Are you out of your mind? It must be freezing.' Regina backed away from the riverbank, as if she didn't trust her friend not to pull her in. But she didn't back away far enough. Within seconds Sophia was by her side, pulling her into the water. 'You are crazy! Let go of me. I'm still wearing my dress,' cried Regina.

'Take it off. It's a warm day. And the water is glorious.'

'Anyone can see us here.'

'Nonsense. They are all busy. Just pretend we are on the Neva like when we were children. Remember how happy we were?'

'We are not children now. And I don't know about you but I'm not happy.'

'That's because you are not in the water.' Sophia tugged on her friend's sleeve. 'Come on, there's nothing like a dip in the river to make us forget our troubles.'

'A dip in the river will add to my troubles. I don't want to get wet …'

But Sophia refused to leave Regina alone until she took off her dress and jumped in the water. The two women splashed and squealed. For a moment under the unblemished Caucasus skies, there was no revolution and no civil war, only a moment in time when they were carefree and young. Just like when they were children frolicking on the banks of the Neva, once upon a time, before it all went horribly wrong.

Afterwards, they sat on the rocks in the sun and dried their clothes. 'Maybe when Nikolai gets better, we can go back to Petrograd together,' said Regina dreamily. 'As his wife, I will be safe there.'

Sophia shivered in her wet undergarments. 'He hasn't proposed yet,' she reminded Regina.

'I know. But he will. And I'm ready to follow him anywhere, as long as there's a bed to sleep in. Another night under the open skies and I might go mad.'

'Maybe you should wait for the proposal before you plan your future together. I don't want you to get your hopes up and be disappointed.'

245

'I know it was meant to be. Otherwise I wouldn't feel this way about him.'

Sophia remembered Nanny's words. *When we love, we assume we are loved in return. We can't imagine it any other way.* 'If it was that simple, there wouldn't be so many songs and books about unrequited love.'

'Don't worry, I won't get my heart broken. I know how he feels. He doesn't need to say a word.'

From the moment Sophia opened her eyes in the morning until she fell asleep at night, she lied. When she glanced in Nikolai's direction and caught her husband's gaze, she faked indifference, looking away from the face she loved, so that her husband wouldn't know what was in her heart. Every time she poured Dmitry a cup of tea and broke their bread and changed Nikolai's dressing, she lied. She pretended to be a good friend and a loving wife, smiling at Regina, listening to her hopes and dreams, faking affection for her husband when they lay down to sleep side by side inside the wooden cart. But as she drifted off to sleep, she listened to Nikolai's breathing and her heart swelled with hope. Hope that one day the web of lies could be broken.

When their clothes were dry again, they refilled their flasks and ambled back to the settlement. A blaring horn greeted them when they arrived. 'What is that noise?' Sophia asked Dmitry, who was cooking a few potatoes on the hot ashes of someone else's campfire.

'A signal to start moving. Where have you two been? I was worried.'

The two women exchanged a glance. Sophia's hair was still damp but she knew Dmitry wouldn't notice. 'We went looking for supplies and brought some fresh water.'

'Perfect. I was just about to make some tea.'

He had a hat on his head to protect him from the sun. There was mud on his trousers and tunic that were falling apart at the seams. He no longer looked like the lord of the manor but like someone who belonged in these mountains. Where had he learnt how to bake potatoes and brew tea in an iron jar they had borrowed from Anna? Just like Sophia, he'd had everything done for him since the day he was born. She watched him with amazement as he put the potatoes on plates, cut up some old bread and poured the tea.

They finished their food in silence, while all around them the carts started moving. Slowly, reluctantly, as if remembering the hardships of the day before and unwilling to endure more of the same, the horses set out. How far was Bekeshevskaya Staniza? No one seemed to know. Everyone was blindly following their leader and not asking any questions.

The procession that was silent and grim the day before was alive with songs and music. The trumpets blared and the drums beat a cheerful tune. When they stopped for lunch, the Cossacks rode their horses around the camp, occasionally stopping for a chat. They had cheerful smiles and kind words for everyone.

'I thought we were hiding. With all this noise, the Bolsheviks will have no trouble finding us,' said Regina.

Vladimir, who had joined them for lunch with his wife, replied, 'They want the Bolsheviks to think they are dealing with a much bigger squadron. They are burning more campfires than they need, making noise, leaving traces in the mud to make it look like an army has been through here. With luck, the Bolsheviks will leave us alone and not engage.'

Vladimir seemed to have all the answers. Sophia was impressed with his knowledge, unlike Anna, it seemed, who shrugged and said, 'I can't take much more of this. Day and night on the road, with no end in sight. You convinced me to leave Kislovodsk and now what? Where are we going?'

'Now we follow everybody else and don't complain.'

'It helps if I have an end goal in mind,' Anna said, pouting. 'Why did I even listen to you?'

'I don't know why, my dear. Usually you don't. But you know

what the end goal is – to rid Russia of the Bolsheviks.'

'That could take years,' said Sophia. She felt weary, like she had been on the road for a thousand days, not just two.

Anna turned to Vladimir. 'You want me to spend years living in a wooden cart under the open skies? What did I marry you for? I should have listened to my mother.'

'Stop grumbling, woman. Leaving Kislovodsk might have saved our lives. Do you want to go back to jail?'

In silence, they watched as a military band marched past, followed by a cavalry unit, leaving more traces in the mud.

While Sophia agreed with Vladimir, she understood Anna perfectly. This seemingly aimless journey with no destination in sight was enough to break anyone's spirit. She was dirty and sweaty, the joy of their impromptu swim that morning nothing but a distant memory. The skin of her bare arms was turning red in the sun and her hat did nothing to protect her face.

'Look on the bright side,' said Dmitry. 'So many things could have gone wrong and didn't. We haven't been caught. We haven't been arrested. We still have food. And it's not raining.'

'The rainy season will come,' said Sophia. 'And we barely have any food left. What are we going to do when it runs out?'

'Let's cross that bridge when we come to it. What I'm trying to say is, it could have been worse. We are lucky to have escaped in one piece. Unlike many others. Unlike Anna's cousin Alexander. Unlike Count Alexei. I bet they would give anything to swap their prison cells for fresh air and freedom, for mountains and open skies. Look around you. Isn't it glorious?'

Out in the open, he was like a different man. Sophia didn't recognise him. 'I'm glad you're enjoying being homeless,' she said. But Dmitry was right. She was lucky because Nikolai was still alive.

Regina's hand was on Nikolai's cheek. 'Why isn't he waking up? It's been days. What's going to happen to him?'

'He's lost a lot of blood. His body needs to recover. He'll wake up when he's ready,' said Sophia.

'You really think so?'

'I know so.' She tried to sound convincing for her friend. 'His fever is gone. His wound is no longer infected. He's doing well.'

'I hope you're right. If anything happens to him, my life will be over.'

How could Sophia tell her friend the truth? She didn't have the heart to say to her that the life she had imagined for herself was all in her head. Instead, she gritted her teeth and pressed Regina's hand in a reassuring, deceitful gesture.

At night, a terrible noise woke her. The moon was shining its cold light on the little settlement, while the stars were indifferent observers to the human drama unfolding underneath. Sophia heard frightened voices all around her but couldn't see anything beyond darkness. At first, she thought it was the Cossacks with their trumpets and drums but then she heard gunshots and realised Shkuro's plan to scare the Bolsheviks away with their supposed numerical superiority hadn't worked. All they had done was alert them to their whereabouts. A volley of gunshots from the mountains was answered every now and then with a few shots from the Cossacks. Short on artillery, they were saving every bullet.

'Into the cart, now,' shouted Dmitry. 'And get down.'

As she climbed into the cart, Sophia heard more gunshots and this time they seemed closer. Too close for comfort. She threw herself on Nikolai, wanting to protect him, while Dmitry was still on the ground, trying to talk some sense into Regina.

'I can't move!' wailed Regina. 'Go without me. I'll stay here.'

'We are out in the open here. If you don't hurry, they will cut us all down one by one.'

'No,' cried Regina in panic. 'No! Why are they shooting at us? We are civilians.'

'Like they give a damn. The minute we joined the Cossacks, we became their enemies. And the Bolsheviks will do anything to stop us.' Dmitry was trying to push Regina forward but she was hysterical and refused to move. 'Pull her up by the arms,' he shouted to Sophia. But before Sophia could do anything, she felt the cart tremble and lurch forward. With a panicked neigh, the horse bolted, taking Sophia and Nikolai with it, leaving Dmitry and Regina behind. Petrified, Sophia wanted to scream but couldn't. Her mouth opened, her hand flew to her mouth but she remained silent as branches of the nearby trees slashed her face. She could hardly breathe as the horse dragged the cart through the forest. Soon they were off the road and running over rocks, the cart propelled high into the air every time it hit one. Screaming with frustration and fear, Sophia crawled to the front of the cart, wondering if she could stop the horse from running. It seemed impossible but she had to try. Nikolai's life depended on it. The trunks were moving around freely, hitting Sophia's legs and arms, making her cry out. With a superhuman effort she pulled her body up and grabbed the side of the cart but it lurched to the left and she hit her head on something hard.

Her last thought before everything went dark was *Nikolai*.

*

When Sophia came to, an eerie silence greeted her. No gunshots, what a relief! But no voices either. Only the trees whispered in the wind and birds whistled happily on their branches, while the horse grazed on the grass that was peeking defiantly through slabs of rock. They were in a large clearing, surrounded by small pines, like dwarfs reaching their crooked fingers for Sophia and Nikolai.

Where were they? And where were the others? Her heart pounded with fear for Dmitry and Regina. Her wrist throbbed and her head hurt. Wincing, she placed the palm of her hand on Nikolai's forehead. The sun was in her face and she blinked. How far did the horse drag them? Suddenly, something caught her attention. She wasn't sure what it was at first and then she realised – Nikolai's eyes were open and he was looking at her. She blinked again, wondering if she was imagining it. Shielding her eyes from the sun, Sophia watched him. She *was* imagining it – here he was, with his eyes closed. It must be her tired brain, giving her what she longed to see. 'Nikolai! Can you hear me?' Her heart racing, she shook him.

'Of course I can hear you. What are you doing, trying to pull my arm off?'

His voice sounded rough, like he was recovering from a cold. But he was awake and talking to her! She took a deep breath. 'Welcome back. You slept forever.'

'My chest hurts. Like it's on fire …' He tried to sit up but couldn't.

'Don't move. You need to stay still. You were wounded. Don't you remember?'

'The last thing I remember is walking to the station with you. I was worried about missing my train to Essentuki …'

'You missed your train all right. I'm sorry.'

'Where are we?'

'In Shkuro's camp. Dmitry and Regina are here somewhere.'

He touched his head and grimaced as if he was in great pain. 'What else have I missed?'

'Not much,' she said, smiling. 'How are you feeling?'

'Like I've been hit with a ton of bricks.'

'Are you hungry? I can give you a piece of bread.' She sat him up and broke the bread into tiny pieces, feeding it to him. He swallowed the bread, breaking into a cough. She gave him a few sips of water from her flask. 'I'm so glad you're feeling better. We didn't know if you would ever wake up.'

'What are we doing with Shkuro?'

'Running from the Bolsheviks.'

'But I *am* the Bolsheviks.'

'Don't tell anyone or we'll be in real trouble.'

Suddenly, Sophia felt so happy. She didn't know where they were or how to get back. She didn't know if the Bolsheviks were lying in wait behind the next bend in the road. They hardly had any provisions left. And yet, she felt like she was exactly where she was supposed to be. She wanted to leap in the air and dance a mad tango with him across the clearing into the rest of their lives.

After breakfast, Nikolai slept with his head in her lap and she watched him, the way his chest rose and his lips trembled, the way his stubble was growing into a beard. She stroked his head, his rough cheeks, caressed his face with the tips of her fingers. 'Everything will be all right,' she whispered, her arms around him. 'Everything will be all right.'

But they couldn't remain in the middle of nowhere forever. When the sun was high in the sky, she regretfully placed his head on a pillow and moved to the driver's bench, pulling on the reins. She had seen Dmitry do this countless times but hadn't paid much attention. How did one drive a horse? Was it even possible? The animal was large and strong and seemed to possess a mind of its own. Was it true that horses were like dogs? Could they smell her fear? She wished she knew the horse's name. 'Here, girl. Good girl!' she said, making a noise with her tongue. 'Forward! Go-go-go. Please, go!'

Miraculously, the horse obeyed. Slowly, it lifted its head and made a step forward. But the cart resisted. 'There's something wrong with the cart,' she said to Nikolai, who was still sleeping and didn't seem to hear. 'I hope it's still in one piece.'

Making sure he was comfortable and his neck was supported, Sophia jumped to the ground. The horse seemed content to chew on the grass under its feet. Careful not to come too close to its hind legs, she inspected the cart. The wheels didn't seem broken and nothing else looked out of place. As she walked around the cart, she noticed one of the back wheels was stuck behind a large rock. 'That's easy to fix,' she muttered, grabbing the rock and pulling it. And pulling and pulling. The rock didn't give in.

Sophia took a sip of water and observed the rock. For a moment she wished Dmitry was here. He would know what to do. But he wasn't here. The only person she could rely on was herself. Once again, she tried to heave the rock out of the way, and once again, it refused to give way. When her fingers were ripped to pieces by its uneven surface, she stopped and looked around. Under one of the pine trees she spotted a large branch. She ran across the clearing and fetched it, placing it under the rock and using it as a lever. Little by little, centimetre by centimetre, the rock gave way. It took a quarter of an hour but soon she was able to push it aside. 'Thank God,' she whispered, standing up straight. Her neck, back and arms were hurting, her hands were bleeding, but the cart was free.

She climbed back onto the driver's bench and picked up the reins. 'Here we go,' she whispered. This time, the horse and cart moved forward easily. Without turning around, she said to Nikolai, 'I don't know where to go. And I don't know how this thing works.'

'The horse? You steer it much like a bicycle,' came a voice from the back.

'I thought you didn't know how to ride a bicycle?' She smiled at the memory of the two of them on a picnic blanket, sharing the cake he had baked for her, what seemed like a lifetime ago.

'I don't. Where are we going?'

'To find the camp. We are a tiny bit lost but we'll be fine. We need to get back, to make sure the others are safe. They must be worried about us too.'

They had the remainder of yesterday's potatoes for lunch. She changed his dressing. Side by side they sat on the floor of the cart, looking at the forest that stretched towards the horizon and seemed to have no end and no beginning. 'What a fright you gave us!' Sophia said. 'Don't ever do that again.'

'Wouldn't dream of it. Did the Cossacks shoot me?'

'I think it was the Bolsheviks. They opened fire from the train. But it was mayhem at the station that day. I was so afraid for you; I hardly remember what happened. Two Cossacks helped me carry you home.'

'How bad was I?'

She thought of the long hours of watching over him, not knowing if he would live or die, of his burning forehead under the palm of her hand. 'Not too bad.'

She packed their food away and they set out. There was no road nearby, only rocks and trees and the mountains looking down at them. Every time the cart hit a rock, Nikolai groaned. When Sophia asked how he was, he assured her he was fine. But his face was pale and his eyes were closed. She propped two pillows under his head, placed a thick blanket underneath and tried to move as slowly as possible but the cart still lurched and jumped on the rocks.

Beyond every bush, Sophia hoped to see the settlement. But there was no sign of it. After an hour on the road, she could swear they were moving in circles. Every tree and rock formation looked familiar, like they had passed it a hundred times before.

She stopped when she heard the murmur of a stream behind the underbrush. Checking on Nikolai, who had fallen into an uneasy sleep, she jumped off the cart and ran to the river, where she splashed some water on her face and refilled their flasks. Was it the same river Regina and she had frolicked in the day before? If they followed it, would it lead them back to their original location?

Craving water on her body, Sophia undressed to her undergarments and dove in. What was it about being in the river that made her feel like she was flying through time and space, without an aim, without a care in the world? The water washed everything away. Here, she could be herself. She could forget about the past and not worry about the future. As she floated on her back, she wondered where this river was running to so swiftly, as if it was in a great rush. Did it end in the mountains somewhere, just ceased to be, like so many things in life? Or did it feed into a lake or the Black Sea? If she swam downstream, would she reach Georgia or Armenia? Would she end up somewhere where there were no Bolsheviks and no revolution? And was there such a place in Russia?

Long after the revolution finished reconstructing Russian society, this river would continue to rustle through the rocks. Long after the Red Army soldiers stopped marching, rifles in hand, and the Cossacks stopped hiding away in the wilderness, the green giants of the Caucasus Mountains would loom over this forest. It was a reassuring thought. It made her realise that all her troubles were temporary, that everything was temporary, except the beauty around her.

Sophia swam gracefully against the current, her long limbs moving swiftly, her wet hair clinging to her face. All of a sudden, Dmitry and Regina seemed far away, like a distant memory of a different life, a dream that melted away in the early morning mist. It was just the two of them alone together under the southern skies. Sophia and Nikolai. When she glanced up, she saw him watching her from the cart. So much emotion was in his face, she gasped and stopped paddling for a moment. Could he see her near-naked body through the water? Careful not to slip on a rock, she climbed out, concealed by the bushes, and got dressed behind a pine tree, tying her hair up in a bun. Then she ran to him through the trees, asking if he was all right and if he needed anything.

'I would love a swim,' he said. 'You looked like you were enjoying it.'

'You can't swim. We have to keep you dry and warm. Doctor's orders. The water is freezing. What?' she prodded. 'Why are you looking at me like that?'

'You in that river. I've never seen anyone so beautiful.'

She blushed and didn't reply, climbing onto the driver's bench, nudging the horse forward and following the river. It soon disappeared without a trace, but on and on they rode, and after a few hours she was ready to give up. Soon it would be dark. They were lost and alone, and little by little her hope of finding the settlement was dwindling. What would become of them? How long could they continue like this, spinning blindly in circles, while all around them danger lurked? But to be with him, to be alone together, to not have to hide anymore! To look at him openly and not see the suspicion on Dmitry's face. To not see Regina's arms around him and her adoring eyes crying for him and her adoring lips whispering to him. To have him all to herself, even as they were about to perish in the wild, wasn't it worth it? To no longer live her life of lies but to watch him with truth in her eyes.

When the sun went down, she started a fire and sat next to him. The flame cracked peacefully. The potatoes were roasting. 'The sunsets are spectacular here,' he said. 'Unlike anywhere else I've been.'

'Have you been to many places?'

'Hundreds.'

'I've never been anywhere. Where is your favourite place in the world?' She wanted to take his hand in hers but didn't dare.

'Sardinia. It's a small island in the Mediterranean and if I had a choice, I'd be happy to live there for the rest of my life. The place is incredible. It has amazing pale sand and turquoise sea. White houses like clouds line the shore. In spring, so many flowers bloom in Sardinia, the whole island turns purple and red. And people are always smiling because they know they live in Paradise.'

'My mama and papa went to Sardinia when I was a little girl. They brought a doll back and I remember thinking how happy they were and how in love. The doll didn't last. Regina accidentally tore its head off a few months later. The happiness didn't last either. It was the last carefree summer I remember.'

'What happened?'

'Mama went to our estate in Kazan one day and never came back. She met a man there, ten years younger than her and broke. She thought it was true love. But he was only after her money.'

'Oh no.'

'Papa waited and waited for her to come back. But as the years went by and he realised she wasn't planning to, he melted away in front of my eyes. The doctors said there was something wrong with his lungs but I knew better. He died from a broken heart. He never stopped loving my mother.' She felt like crying but his calming hand was on her hand. She closed her eyes, blinking the tears away.

'What happened to your mama?'

'Her lover left her and a few months later she died too. She was all alone. We didn't find out until much later.' Her voice broke and she couldn't continue.

'I'm so sorry. You must miss them so much. Is that why you married Dmitry? Because you were lonely?'

'It was my father's last wish to see me married to Dmitry. How could I not?' She thought of the day of her wedding, seeing her father's proud smile and thinking she was doing the right thing. 'My father told me not to marry for love. All love does is break your heart, he said to me.'

'Do you agree with him?'

'I did back then. Seeing what happened to my parents, how could I not?'

'What about now?'

She was quiet for a long time. The fire burnt out and darkness fell. She listened to the silence that was interrupted once in a while by a screech of an owl or a distant howl of a wild animal. Finally, she whispered, 'Imagine if I had lived the rest of my life and not known this feeling?' She pressed her head into his shoulder. 'Why did you take so long to come to Kislovodsk?'

'At first, I couldn't leave Petrograd. After October, it was impossible to get away.' He hesitated. 'Afterwards, I didn't want to get in the way …'

'In the way?'

'Between you and Dmitry. I was hoping if I wasn't around, things would get better between the two of you. He's my brother. And he loves you.'

257

'Then why did you come back?' She barely breathed as she waited for his answer. What if he did come back to marry Regina? What if right now, lost in the mountains together, she would find out that his love for her was an illusion, something her imagination had conjured?

'I had no news from you. With the civil war looming, I had to know you were safe, so I volunteered for this job.'

'That day in Petrograd, when they told me you were dead, I felt like my life had stopped. I didn't want to go on. I didn't care if I lived or died.'

He pulled her close. She inhaled his smell, placed her head on his chest and listened for his heartbeat. He said, 'I'm sorry you had to go through that. After I got released, I wrote to you almost every week.'

'We didn't receive your letters,' she whispered.

'You told me before that you could never leave Dmitry. And I respect that. But I'm not myself when I'm around you. I seem to lose my mind whenever you are nearby.'

I do too, she wanted to say to him. *I do too.*

Nikolai was so close to her, if she moved her head slightly, she could touch his lips with hers. And more than anything she wanted to kiss his wonderful lips. It would be like the first time, she realised, because she had never kissed a man she loved. 'You must be so tired,' she whispered. 'Go to sleep. Get some rest. Tomorrow we have to find the settlement or we'll have no food left. What will we do then?'

'If we run out of food, you'll have to go out and hunt.'

She didn't know if he was serious or if he was teasing her. 'Hunt what? What animals live in these mountains?'

'Birds, mostly. Foxes, badgers. Hedgehogs.'

'Hedgehogs?'

His smile was wide on his face. He *was* teasing her. 'I'm not tired yet. Tell me everything that happened after you left Petrograd. Start from the beginning.'

She told him about the journey south and the long months of thinking he was gone, of their hopes to live the rest of their lives quietly in Kislovodsk and how these hopes had been dashed one terrible day when the revolution came to the Caucasus. And she told him of a hollow tree in the park not far from their apartment where she had hidden her letters to him. They fell asleep side by side, with her head on his shoulder. In the morning, she was the first to wake up. Leaping to her feet, as if afraid her husband would see her with Nikolai, she ran to the river, had a quick swim, this time unobserved, then started a fire and cooked some oats in boiling water, waking Nikolai and feeding him. Bringing a bucket of water from the river, she washed his face and hands. The wound on his chest didn't look as red and angry as before. When he spoke, he sounded more like his old self.

In circles, they moved in their cart, through trees and rocks, small and large. Another hour of futile searching, another break for food. Is that what the rest of her life was going to be like? Moving blindly through forests and mountains, in search of a place to call her own.

After lunch, they found a small trail and followed it for a couple of hours, not sure where it would lead. When Sophia was about to stop for the day, they arrived at a clearing. She heard a dog barking and saw a small hut half-hidden behind a fence. Looking over the fence, she spotted a dozen chickens pecking the ground and a goat chewing on a dry twig. A scruffy old man sat on the porch, staring into the distance.

'You two are a day late,' he cried out to them.

'A day late for what?' asked Sophia with a friendly wave, relieved to see another living soul.

'Your comrades went past here yesterday.'

'Our comrades? So they *were* here?'

'A thousand of them descended on my house like locusts. I gave them all the food I could spare. Now I have nothing to share with you.'

259

'We don't need anything, thank you. Just tell us how to get to Bekeshevskaya.'

As the man drew a map, he mumbled, 'Young people today. Fighting, revolting, never happy with their lot. Why not live your life peacefully? That's why I'm here, in the mountains, far from the hustle and bustle. You can't find peace like this anywhere.'

'You helped the Cossacks. You don't support the revolution?' she asked. His hands were rough and his face lined. He looked like a peasant or a farmer, just like thousands of others who had marched past her house in Petrograd, demanding change and firing their rifles.

'I helped people who were hungry and tired. I don't care if they are the Cossacks or the Bolsheviks. Personally, I'm not on anyone's side. I'm too old to care. What does it matter who's tsar, if it's Nicholas or Lenin, as long as I have my fresh air, clean river, goats and chickens? As long as the sun rises in the morning and goes down at night.'

The old man's map was impossible to read but his verbal directions were detailed enough. After a couple of hours in the woods, they saw huts, carts and people. Sophia should have felt elated but didn't. As the sun set and she pulled the cart closer to the settlement, she told Nikolai it was too dark to look for the others. The truth was, she didn't want to go back just yet. She wanted one more night with him before she had to lie and pretend and act like he meant nothing.

Chapter 12

October 1918

She watched him in the near dark and prayed the morning wouldn't come. Why couldn't they stay in the mountains? They could build a life here, like the man they had met who gave them the map. If they had clean air, freedom and each other, what more could they possibly need?

But to abandon Dmitry without a word or an explanation, to leave him forever wondering what had happened to her, mourning her for the rest of his life and never having the closure he needed to move on? She couldn't do it. He had been a good husband to her. He deserved better. Even her mother hadn't vanished into thin air. She had done so with a polite smile and a wave goodbye. Not that it made it any easier.

In the morning, Sophia walked through the settlement, past people, carts and horses. There were a few fires burning here and there and someone was strumming a guitar. Last time she had seen Regina and Dmitry, they were under Bolshevik fire. She remembered that moment so clearly – bullets flying past, Regina screaming hysterically and refusing to get into the cart, Dmitry shouting. What if something bad had happened to them? As terrible scenarios whirred through her head, Sophia tripped and sank to the ground, her eyes on the never-ending carts.

'Are you all right, my dear?' She heard a voice behind her. A warm hand touched her shoulder.

She turned around and saw an old lady leaning over her with concern. Her bearing betrayed her noble birth, even if her clothes were torn and muddy. Sophia assured her she was fine and, getting back up, asked about the attack two days ago.

'The Cossacks soon put a stop to that. They chased the Bolsheviks all the way to Kislovodsk. Took their weapons and food.'

'The Bolsheviks never came back?'

'Not yet,' said the old woman quietly. 'But people are afraid for their lives. The Bolsheviks killed twenty of us and wounded a dozen more. They are in the tent over there.' She waved her hand in the direction of the mountains. 'No one knows what to do with them. Imagine, so many people and not a single doctor or nurse among them.'

Thanking the woman, Sophia made her way to the tent. The wounded, all men, were in a bad shape. Their wounds hadn't been cleaned or dressed properly and even at first glance she could tell they were getting infected. It was dark in the tent. She lit a candle and looked into every face but didn't find them.

Dmitry and Regina were not among the wounded. But what if they were among those who had been killed that day? Unsteady on her feet, she stumbled out of the tent into the morning sunshine, making a promise to herself to come back and help the wounded men as soon as she could. As she shielded her eyes from the sun, she heard the sound of a horse's hooves on the dusty road and saw a weary man in Red Army uniform, with a red stripe across his upper arm and a red star on his cap. Sophia wondered what he was doing here, in the enemy camp. People were gathering around him, eyeing him with curiosity. If he felt intimidated or uncomfortable, he didn't show it. 'I am looking for the ataman, Andrei Shkuro.'

Two dozen children, barefoot despite the cool weather, pointed and shouted. Sophia came closer to hear better.

'The Cossacks are half a kilometre down this track, at the other side of the settlement,' said a man with a scar across his face, pointing behind him.

But before the Red Army soldier had a chance to turn around, Andrei Shkuro appeared, riding his horse. Despite the early hour, he was dressed in full uniform. 'I am Andrei Shkuro. And who may you be?'

'The Government entrusted me with a mission to find you and let you know that if you give up, you and all of your men will be spared. You will be offered a position as the general in the Red Army.'

'The last I checked, we haven't lost yet. Why would I give up?'

'Russia is on the brink of becoming a great power. It's about to step into the future. Why are you fighting to pull it back into the dark ages?'

'Russia is on the way to a catastrophe and we are fighting to save her. My men rely on me. Russia relies on me.'

'Is it your final decision?'

'Absolutely.'

The messenger lowered his head. 'In that case, I have another message for you. We have your wife. If you don't comply, she'll be shot.'

All colour left the ataman's face but he didn't flinch. 'Please, tell the commissars that women have nothing to do with this war. If the Bolsheviks touch as much as a hair on my wife's head, I swear I will kill the families of all high-ranking Bolsheviks I can find. As to giving up, thousands of Cossacks entrusted their lives to me. I will not let them down. As long as I live, I will not lower my weapons. I will fight you and the likes of you until the day I die. Justice will be restored. The power will return to the hands of the royal family, where it belongs.'

The messenger was about to say something else, but Shkuro

turned his horse around and galloped swiftly away, leaving a cloud of dust in his place. An angry buzz accompanied the messenger as he left the camp but no one tried to stop him.

Sophia was watching Shkuro as he disappeared behind the rocks, amazed at his cool in the face of such terrible news, when she heard someone call her name. When she looked up, she saw Regina running towards her. 'Thank God,' whispered Sophia, embracing her friend.

'We thought we lost you,' exclaimed Regina, pulling away slightly and touching Sophia's face as if to make sure she was real and not an apparition. 'We looked everywhere for you after the attack. Dmitry is beside himself. They've been riding back every day, searching the area where you disappeared.'

'We are fine. Just fine.'

'And Nikolai?'

'Nikolai is awake.'

Regina's face lit up with joy. 'Come, I'll take you to Dmitry. Wait till he sees you! He'll be so happy.'

Sophia followed Regina to Anna and Vladimir's cart only a few metres away from where she had stopped for the night. She must have walked past them earlier that morning and didn't notice.

'They won't dare touch Shkuro's wife if they know what's good for them,' Vladimir was saying as he poured tea into a clay mug. 'The man's reputation precedes him. They know his word is law. If he said he will kill their families, nothing in the world will stop him.'

Dmitry, his back to Sophia, didn't say a word.

'It's the Bolsheviks you are talking about,' said Anna. 'They act first, think later.' She turned to Dmitry. 'Tea, Dima?'

'No, thank you, Anya.'

'You have to eat something. Not eating won't bring Sophia back. And you need your strength. Are you going back to look for them today?'

'What else can I do? I can't give up on her.' Dmitry sounded defeated and spent. 'I can't help all the bad thoughts running through my head. She could have been killed by the Bolsheviks. She could have been attacked by a wild animal or dashed on the rocks. Out there, anything could happen. I want to hope but with every day that passes it's getting harder and harder.' He wiped his brow with the back of his hand.

Sophia froze to the spot, unable to move, to call out to him, to let him know she was safe. Here he was, wondering how he would go on without her. And here she was, unable to think of anything but Nikolai.

Regina climbed into the cart. 'You shouldn't think like that. And you definitely shouldn't give up. They could come back any moment.' She winked at Sophia, who remained on the ground, watching them.

Dmitry barely glanced in her direction. His head was low. 'Do you really believe that?'

'Oh, I do!' she exclaimed, a mischievous twinkle in her eyes. 'I really do.'

'If they were alive, they would have been back by now.'

'How much do you want to bet that I'm right?'

'This is not a game, Regina.'

Anna and Vladimir noticed Sophia and smiled. Regina waved. 'Sophia, why are you taking so long? Come up right now.'

Sophia lifted herself up into the cart.

Slowly, as if unable to believe his ears, Dmitry turned around. At the sight of his wife, his mouth flew open and his eyes grew wide. Practically knocking Vladimir off his feet, he rushed to her side. In seconds, she was in his arms. There were tears in his eyes. 'Where have you been all this time? Where have you been?' he kept repeating, kissing her hair, her cheeks, her lips. 'I didn't know where else to look, what else to do.' Then he took a step back and looked at her closely, as if to make sure she was still in one piece. 'Don't ever scare me like this.'

'We are back safely. I'm fine.'

'What happened? One minute you were there, the next you were gone.'

'The gunshots spooked the horse and it took off. I hit my head. When I came to, I had no idea where we were or how to get back.'

'You are lucky to be alive,' said Regina, crossing herself. 'It's a miracle.'

'It really is! You're safe now. You're here. That's all that matters,' whispered Dmitry, pressing her to him so hard, for a moment she couldn't breathe.

His eyes were on her, happy and relieved. But Sophia couldn't meet his gaze. She was finally back where she belonged, with people who loved her. Then why did she feel like crying?

*

Sophia couldn't look at Regina as she was reunited with Nikolai. 'Thank God you are feeling better. We were so afraid for you,' Regina repeated, practically dancing on the spot. She plumped up his pillows and asked him if he wanted anything. She read to him from her diary, telling him everything that had happened since they saw each other last. She played someone else's guitar to him and sang soft gypsy ballads in her husky voice. She fed him food Sophia cooked and water Sophia fetched. All Sophia could do was change his dressing, without so much as a glance in his direction, because Dmitry and Regina were watching her every move. Just like before.

It pained Sophia to see the love for Nikolai on her friend's face. The only thing that made it bearable was that in Nikolai's face she saw nothing for Regina. He was polite and friendly, like he was with Nanny or his own brother. But when Sophia was nearby, his eyes filled with warmth. It cost all the energy she possessed to remain detached, to not betray what was in her heart. It was as if the last two days had never happened. As if she had imagined the blissful hours under the mountain sky with him.

As the only nurse around, Sophia volunteered to look after the wounded. Little by little, just like in Petrograd, their needs took over until she had nothing left – no strength to think or do anything else. Now she had an excuse not to be around while Regina whispered sweet nothings to Nikolai as if they were a married couple.

Sophia begged her friend to join her in the tent as she cleaned the infected limbs and changed dressings. Was it because she needed help or because she didn't want to leave the two of them alone? Regina refused, saying Nikolai needed her. 'I'm fine,' said Nikolai, smiling at Sophia, who didn't raise her eyes to him. 'Go! Those people need you more.'

But Regina never strayed two paces away from him.

Most days, Sophia arrived in the tent long before breakfast and didn't leave until it was time to go to sleep. She survived on scraps of food the wounded didn't finish and drank water from the stream nearby. She had no supplies, nothing to disinfect the wounds or take the pain away. Nothing to stop the infection. All she could do was sit next to the wounded and hold their hands. And often, a kind word and a reassuring smile were enough. Just like Nikolai had told her what felt like a lifetime ago, knowledge made a good doctor but kindness made a great one.

'What are your plans now that you are better, brother?' asked Dmitry one morning, as Sophia was getting ready to leave for the day.

'Once I can walk again, I have to make my way back to Kislovodsk. I have a lot of work to do in town.'

Dmitry's face brightened, as if it was exactly what he wanted to hear. 'I bet they are missing you in Kislovodsk.'

'But not till he's better,' said Sophia sternly. 'He needs his rest.'

Dmitry read to Nikolai from the Bolshevik newspaper that got delivered to the camp every day, albeit with a week's delay. 'It's lucky we left Kislovodsk when we did. Just listen to this! Mass arrests and shootings every single day, like in Petrograd. Glorious revolution indeed.' Dmitry glared at his brother. 'Can you believe what they are saying about Shkuro?'

'What are they saying?'

'That he was captured and killed and his boots were sold at an auction.'

'How much money did they fetch?' asked Sophia, watching the ataman on a meadow nearby, putting his Cossacks through military exercises.

'Every word they print is a lie,' said Dmitry with disdain.

'They do it for a reason,' said Nikolai. 'Every day, hundreds of volunteers arrive to join Shkuro. The counter-revolution is like an avalanche, hurling down the hill, collecting strength. But if people believe Shkuro's been killed, they will stop supporting him.'

'If Shkuro is gone, there will be someone else to take his place. Russia's had enough of the revolution. We want peace. We want security. You are right, brother. Stopping the counter-revolution is like stopping an avalanche. Impossible.'

*

In the third week of October, when the air was crisp and the wind howled in the mountains, what Sophia had feared finally happened. They ran out of provisions. Every morning she awoke with an empty feeling in her stomach. She would make soup that was nothing but grass, old cabbage and water. They would sit down to eat, speak of the revolution and the counter-revolution, sing and play the guitar, Vladimir would tell jokes, and Sophia would jump to her feet and rush to the tent to check on her patients, her stomach still empty.

Dmitry, like many others in the camp, had learnt how to catch fish in the river. They used nets and fishing rods but because there were so many of them, he often returned empty-handed. But sometimes he came back with a whole trout or chub and it felt like they were having a feast. They shared with Anna and Vladimir and, in turn, sometimes Anna and Vladimir shared with them.

One morning, Sophia was dragging her feet, trying to put off going to the hospital tent. She loved being a nurse and seeing the gratitude and joy on her patients' faces, but here in the mountains, her helplessness was like hunger – it never left her for a second.

'I wish we brought our books,' she said to Nikolai. Where was everyone else? Dmitry was by the river with his fishing net. Regina was helping Anna, who had a cold. 'Then I could read to you.'

'Just tell me a story,' said Nikolai, smiling at her. She smiled back. For once, she could watch him openly, without fear. 'Or recite a poem.'

And she did. She knew Pushkin and Lermontov practically by heart. As she spoke of wounded hearts and sleepless dreams, of white sails taking you away where no one could ever find you, she couldn't help the tears from falling. She was hoping he wouldn't notice. 'Hey,' he said, his hand on her cheek. 'What's wrong?'

Sophia wiped her face. 'I'm so afraid for them. I do everything I can but they are just not getting better. Tim's fever isn't going down. His wound is infected. He screams in his sleep and he screams when he's awake. I feel like any moment he could die. But what can I do? I have no medicine to give him.'

'I'll help you. I'll take a look at the wounded.'

She brightened a little. 'How? You can't even get up yourself.'

'That's where you're wrong. Yesterday I managed to walk around the cart, leaning on Regina's arm. She didn't tell you?'

'No, she didn't. That's fantastic! But walking around the cart and walking to the hospital tent are two different things. It's on the other side of the camp.'

'Get someone to carry me.'

She asked two men to carry Nikolai to the hospital tent on a stretcher. As he examined her patients, he looked almost as white as they did, like he was about to collapse at any moment. He must have been in terrible pain but not a tremor in his hands and not a frown on his face betrayed it. From the other side of the tent, she

269

watched him lean over Tim and say something, while his skilful hands changed his dressing. Once Nikolai was done, there was an expression on Tim's face Sophia had not seen before. Instead of a gloomy despondency, there was hope. Nikolai had that effect on people. Was it the doctor in him? Or was it because he cared?

'You are being too hard on yourself,' he told her. 'Without you, these men would have died. You are doing your absolute best.'

'Then why do I feel like what I'm doing is not enough?'

'That's our curse and our blessing as doctors. We always want to do more. We are never satisfied. Tim will be fine. Others too. Thanks to you.'

Nikolai stayed with her all day, lying on one of the unoccupied beds in the tent. Every time she had a moment, she walked over to him and asked if he needed anything. *No*, he would reply. *But the man in the bed by the entrance is calling for you.* They were always calling for her, asking for food, water, a kind word. As she flitted from bed to bed, her step wasn't heavy and her heart was light. Nikolai was with her. She no longer felt alone in her battle for these men's lives.

It was dark when they returned. Regina met them with her hands on her hips. 'Where have you been all day?'

'In the hospital tent, just like every other day,' said Sophia wearily. She was ready to fall down with exhaustion.

'And Nikolai? I came back and he wasn't here. I didn't know what to think.'

'Nikolai was with me.'

'You took him to the hospital tent with you? Are you out of your mind? He's unwell. What were you thinking?'

'It wasn't Sophia's fault,' said Nikolai with a grin. 'She needed help. I volunteered.'

'You need rest or you won't get better.' Regina spun to face Sophia. 'You told us so yourself.'

'I've rested long enough. Any more rest and I will go insane,' said Nikolai.

Regina's anger seemed to deflate a little. 'You took him to the hospital tent full of infections.'

'They have gunshot wounds, Regina, not TB. It wouldn't hurt if you joined me once in a while. I could do with the help,' said Sophia.

Regina huffed but didn't reply.

'My brother ought to marry you after all this is behind us, Regina,' said Dmitry, shaking water off his boots and spreading his fishing net over the cart to dry. 'The way you care for him.'

'You think so?' Even in the near dark, Sophia could see Regina blush. She looked immensely pleased.

'I hope my wife looks after me with equal zeal if I am ever wounded.'

'Of course I will, darling.' But when she said it, Sophia didn't look at him.

'That's settled then. Regina and Nikolai will get married and the four of us will live in our cart, happily ever after, picking mushrooms and catching fish for dinner. Speaking of which, I had a great day on the river today. Caught more than ever. Stop bickering, join me by the campfire and I will cook some for us.'

'That's lucky,' said Regina, still flushed from Dmitry's teasing. 'We finished our last oats yesterday.'

'I heard the Cossacks raided a Bolshevik village and came back with a cow,' said Sophia.

'I heard that too,' Regina replied. 'And went to see if there was anything left for us.'

'Let me guess,' said Nikolai. 'There wasn't.'

She shook her head. 'With all those mouths to feed, it was gone before they even finished carving it.'

After dinner, as they watched the stars like diamonds above their heads, Dmitry said, 'Do you know what we need? Music.'

The fire was crackling, throwing shadows over their faces. Sophia thought it was too warm for October. They would not be able to sit like this in Petrograd, outside under the sky, with

271

a shimmering moon over their heads. Sighing, she said, 'If only I had my violin.'

Dmitry replied, sounding happy and relaxed, 'Look behind you.' She turned around. The string bag he usually took with him when he went fishing was on the grass near the cart. 'In the bag,' he added, pointing.

Sophia opened the bag and saw a violin. Amazed, ready to cry, she held it gently, like she would a small child. It wasn't the expensive instrument she was used to, but it could play music and, miraculously, it was in tune. 'Where did you get it?'

'Bartered two of our fish for it.'

'You should have kept the fish,' said Regina, always the practical one.

'Yes, but fish would be gone in no time. Music we'll have forever.'

Reverently, Sophia brought the violin to her chest, closed her eyes and started to play. Beethoven's Fifth Symphony filled the air, and suddenly she was no longer outside of Kislovodsk, surrounded by the Caucasus Mountains like they were her jailers, but in Petrograd, a little girl with not a care in the world. When she opened her eyes, she saw Nikolai's face. He looked mesmerised by her, as if all of his heart's desires were right in front of him and he longed to reach out and touch them. She felt light-headed, from the music, from the mountain air that was too pure for a city girl, from his eyes on her in the dark. For a moment, the world faded away and it was just the two of them.

*

Nikolai had been right about her patients. Tim's fever went down and soon he was able to sit up in bed by himself. Every time he saw Sophia, he thanked her with tears in his eyes. His wife never arrived empty-handed and always had a present for Sophia, a string of onions or a small fish or a cup of mushrooms. Some of her other patients were able to leave the tent and join their families, and suddenly she had a little time on her hands. She went mushroom picking with Anna, leaving Nikolai alone with Regina and trying not to think of the two of them together.

Having grown up in a mansion in Petrograd with everything done for her, Sophia knew nothing about mushrooms. 'Can you eat this one?' she would ask.

'You can. But it will be the last mushroom you ever eat,' Anna would reply, snatching the mushroom from Sophia and throwing it away.

'Why is that?' asked Sophia, looking at the mushroom with regret. It was large and would have made a great addition to their meal that evening.

'Because one bite can kill you.'

'How do we know which ones are safe?'

'Trial and error?' suggested Anna, her eyes sparkling with mischief. Sophia knew she was teasing her. She reached for another mushroom and placed it in her basket, only for Anna to throw it on the ground and stamp on it, shaking her head.

Eventually, Sophia learnt. Like she learnt to identify the medicinal herbs Nikolai told her to bring. As she walked through the woods, looking for pine sap, poppy and goldenseal, she thanked God for Nikolai, who knew exactly what her patients needed. She would collect bilberries that looked like blueberries but tasted sour like lemon. No one liked them but she put them in everyone's tea because Nikolai told her it was good for the immune system. One spoon for each of them but two spoons for Nikolai, who was quickly regaining his strength.

There were days when Sophia would walk around for hours and not find any mushrooms. But once she had come across a valley with so many of them, she filled her basket in five minutes. Often, she would climb on a rock, look around and gasp. The view was not fit for humans, she thought. It was made for gods. The valley basking in timid autumn sunshine, the mountains standing guard like mute soldiers, their uniforms the translucent clouds and morning mist, the dark-blue ribbon of a river twisting its way east, and for a moment Sophia would forget where she was going as she took it all in.

One morning at the end of October, when Sophia returned from the forest, having collected a dozen large porcini mushrooms for dinner, she was about to climb into the cart when she heard Regina. The intensity in her voice stopped Sophia in her tracks and she paused to listen.

'Nikolai, are you awake?' Regina whispered urgently. 'I brought you something to eat. The partisans raided another Bolshevik village. There's some bread and even a little bit of chicken. Of course, there wasn't enough for everyone, but I told the woman in charge of the food that we have a wounded man who needs to eat. She didn't want to give me any. She said everyone here needs to eat.'

'What did you do to change her mind?'

'I promised her a large fish. Let's hope Dmitry manages to catch one. I made some chicken broth for you. When was the last time you had chicken?' She sounded so pleased with herself, so happy. Just like Dmitry had said, Regina was playing the role of the perfect wife like she was born to it.

'What about the others? Maybe Sophia would want some? She looks so thin, always with the wounded, looking after them, not looking after herself.'

'I got the chicken for you, not Sophia. She's not recovering from a gunshot wound. You are.' Regina no longer sounded chipper. There was a jealous note in her voice.

'Thank you.'

Sophia heard the sound of a spoon hitting a plate. Regina said, 'I wanted to talk to you about something.' She fell quiet, as if gathering her thoughts or searching for courage. Sophia, who was about to climb into the cart, paused. 'When are you going back to Petrograd?'

274

'As soon as I'm better and my work in Kislovodsk is done. A few weeks, maybe.'

'Take me with you!' exclaimed Regina. Sophia knew she was eavesdropping on a private moment. She wanted to walk away but couldn't. It was as if an invisible force pulled her towards the cart. Her guilty heart pounding, she continued to listen.

'Take you with me where?'

'To Petrograd. I miss the place where I grew up. I want to go home. And I can't bear this nomadic lifestyle any longer. Without a roof over our heads, freezing and dirty, not knowing where the next meal is coming from. I don't know how much more I can take.'

'It's still not safe in the city. Especially now, with the civil war looming. You saw what it was like. You were lucky to get away. Why would you want to go back?'

Regina's voice trembled. 'I want to be where you are. The months I spent apart from you were hell. And when you got shot …' She fell quiet, as if waiting for him to say something. When he didn't, she added, 'I don't care if it's dangerous, as long as I'm with you.'

Nikolai cleared his throat. 'Regina, if I ever gave you the wrong idea, I'm sorry. It's never been my intention. I can offer you my friendship but that's all.'

There were tears in Regina's voice. 'I've never felt this way about anyone before. I know you feel the same. A woman can always tell.'

'I'm sorry, I don't. You are a wonderful woman. You will make some man very happy one day. But I'm not the one.'

Sophia moved deeper into the shadows, wishing she could disappear altogether. Her heart was breaking for Regina, who whispered, 'You just need more time. If you get to know me better, if we are together, you'll feel differently. How can you not? If this wasn't meant to be, why would I feel this way about you?' Sophia knew her friend well. She knew Regina never gave up. And she always got her way. But not this time.

'Believe me, it's not meant to be.' Nikolai's voice was warm but firm.

'You don't have a wife or a sweetheart. Your heart is free. Why don't you give me a chance? What have you got to lose?'

'My heart is not free. I'm in love with someone. I'm sorry.'

Trembling all over, her hand on her chest, Sophia listened to Regina as she demanded to know who the woman he was in love with was. All she could think of was, *What are we going to do? Here we are, without a place to call our own, on the run, in hiding, besieged and surrounded. How can we find our way without breaking the hearts of the people who love us?* Was it possible to build happiness on someone else's sorrow? Her mother couldn't do it. Could Sophia and Nikolai?

*

Nikolai and Sophia sat side by side in the cart, their heads close together, their arms touching. Dmitry was fishing. Regina was with Anna. After their ill-fated conversation the day before, Regina seemed to be avoiding Nikolai and who could blame her? She barely spoke to anyone and looked gloomier than ever. Sophia felt an overwhelming sadness for her friend, who deserved the best and was the best, but there was nothing she could do to help her. She couldn't even offer a word of encouragement. After all, she wasn't supposed to have eavesdropped on Regina's confession.

'Guess what Anna gave me this morning?' Sophia said to Nikolai after they finished their fish.

'A kitten?'

'No, she didn't give me a kitten. What would we do with one?'

'We would call it Kitten and spend our days rescuing it out of trees.'

'No, it's not a kitten.'

'A piece of bread?'

'No one in the settlement has any more bread. Try again.'

'Golden earrings?'

She shook her head, laughing. 'Do you give up?'

'A book?'

'How did you know?' She reached behind her and placed the book in his lap.

'I guessed.' He laughed with pleasure. 'Chekhov, my favourite.'

'Are you comfortable? Would you like me to read to you?'

'I'm not comfortable. This pillow is too hard. Here, that's better.' He moved closer and put his head in her lap. 'Now you can read to me.'

Sophia opened the book on her favourite story, 'The Lady with the Dog', about two married lovers irresistibly drawn to each other. As if seeing it with new eyes, she read page after page, amazed that something built on a lie could feel so true. A few times she stumbled on words and had to start the sentence anew. If you were trapped in an unhappy marriage and found true love, did you follow your heart? Did you owe yourself and your loved one a chance at happiness? Or did you stay loyal to your spouse, the man or woman you promised to love and cherish for the rest of your life, forsaking all others? Was true love a fair justification for betrayal? Chekhov seemed to think so. What did Nikolai think? His eyes were closed and he was listening intently, not saying a word. Unable to get past the heartbreak on the page, Sophia stopped reading.

Her fingers were threaded through his fingers. She was deathly afraid someone would walk past and see but couldn't bring herself to pull her hand away. 'Enough reading. Let me help you up. We'll go for a nice walk around the cart. What do you think? Exercise is the best medicine. A wonderful doctor once told me that.'

'What a wise man.'

Sophia helped him down. His face went pale as soon as his feet touched the ground but he grinned and said, 'It feels so good to be moving again. Let's walk faster.'

'You can't walk fast. Be careful. Lean on my shoulder. Wait, not so fast.'

Nikolai leaned heavily on her arm and, groaning, took a few steps. It hurt her shoulder to support his weight but she tried her best not to show it. The smile on his face was worth it. He tripped on a rock and would have fallen but she pulled him up. Their eyes met. His hand pressed hers gently as if to say *thank you*. A few seconds passed and still they were unable to look away from each other. The sun was in his face, making him squint. His beard made him look like a forest dweller, like he belonged in these woods, a long cry from the sophisticated young man she had met in Petrograd. She thought he had never looked more handsome. A wave of pure happiness washed over her, the likes of which she had never known before. She smiled, all her worries forgotten, Dmitry, Regina, the revolution, all flying out of her head without so much as a goodbye.

When Sophia finally tore her gaze away from him, she saw Regina watching them from a distance, her face twisted.

*

The next morning, a wall of water came down steadily from the skies that were no longer cobalt but charcoal. Sophia had never seen rain like this before. Sure, it rained in Petrograd. Often in autumn, it drizzled for weeks without a reprieve. But this was different. There was no place to hide, no hope it would ever end. The sunshine of only a day ago seemed like a long-forgotten dream.

Without a roof over their heads, the refugees struggled to cope. Sophia, Regina, Dmitry and Nikolai continued to sleep inside their cart, wrapped in tarpaulin. As the rivulets got under her clothes and her boots filled with water, Sophia looked into the darkness and dreamt of her warm and comfortable bed on Nevsky Avenue, her soft pillow and cosy blanket. She longed for her bed in Kislovodsk, cheap, hard, with a saggy mattress that smelt of mould. But dry! After a day and a night of this, she no longer remembered what dry felt like. All she could hear was the rain and all she could think of was Nikolai. If she turned to her side, she could see him in the light of the fires, his face peaceful as he slept.

Once, he opened his eyes, saw her looking at him and smiled. He reached his hand to her and whispered, 'Courage!'

But then Dmitry stirred and pressed her harder to himself. And Nikolai turned away.

The four of them were like a family splintered and torn, trapped together without a chance of escape. Regina barely spoke to anyone. By the time evening came, Dmitry was too tired to talk. And Sophia wanted to talk to Nikolai but couldn't, not after she had seen heartbreak on Regina's face at the sight of the two of them together.

They had their meals in the rain and lived their days and nights in the rain. During breakfast one morning, Sophia said, 'I saw a nice cave when I was picking mushrooms yesterday. It's spacious, with the softest moss growing inside. Maybe we could sleep there from now on. We'd be dry and comfortable.'

'Yes, let's move there today!' exclaimed Anna. 'I can't bear this for another moment. I look like something that lives in a bog. I feel like I could never get dry. I wouldn't wish this on my worst enemy.'

'Do you ever stop complaining, woman?' exclaimed Vladimir. Turning to Sophia, he added, 'Do yourself a favour and stay away from caves.'

'Why?' Sophia wanted to know.

'Bats. There are so many of them around. And they love caves.'

'I don't mind bats, if it means being warm.'

'You will mind if a thousand of them swoop in on you while you sleep.'

'They don't bite, do they?' asked Anna with hope.

'They do bite,' said Nikolai, who was propped on two pillows and chewing an old baked potato. 'And what's worse, they spread rabies.'

'Rabies?' Anna's eyes widened in horror.

'It starts with a fever and mild headache and leads to paralysis, confusion, paranoia, hallucinations and, finally, death,' said Nikolai. Everyone was mute for a moment, staring into their plates. 'Vladimir is right. Stay away from caves.' Nikolai smiled at Sophia warmly. She smiled warmly back and looked quickly away, in case Regina was watching.

'Don't mind my brother,' said Dmitry. 'He dropped out of medical school but not before learning all the things a gentleman should never say to ladies at breakfast.'

'Who would have thought a cave filled with rabid bats would seem like a wonderful place to live? What have we been reduced to?' Anna said. 'I wish we'd never left Kislovodsk.'

'Believe me, we are better off here, in the rain. Cold and hungry but alive,' said Dmitry. When the rest of them barely had the energy to get up in the morning, he whistled under his breath and mended his fishing net with a smile on his face.

'You look chipper this morning,' said Sophia.

'And why not? I'm alive. I'm free. And you are back safely. While you were gone, I made a bargain with God. I promised I would never complain, as long as I have you. Because that's the only thing I need to be happy – you.'

Sophia looked away from him, her heart skipping with guilt.

Here in the Caucasus, far from civilisation, she wished she could pretend nothing bad could happen to them. As she gathered mushrooms in the rain and cooked in the rain and tried to sleep in the rain, as she hid her true self from Dmitry and Regina but showed it to Nikolai every time their eyes met, she could no longer imagine a different life. Unfortunately, the Bolsheviks never let her forget that she was living in a country torn by civil war. Small Red Army squadrons harassed their flanks regularly and quickly dispersed when the Cossacks retaliated. In the last five days, there had been five surprise attacks. Ten people had been killed. Ten civilians, men and women who had never held a weapon in their lives. Once again, the hospital tent filled with the wounded and Sophia was running off her feet, trying to help as many of them as she could, while thinking of those who had been killed, her heart breaking. She didn't know them personally but she had seen them around the settlement. She had nodded to them in greeting and they nodded back. Suddenly, they were gone, and she couldn't help but wonder if she or her loved ones were going to be next.

Shkuro and his men didn't let the rain stop them. While Sophia and the others tried to sleep, the Cossacks mounted their horses and rode to war, to blow up bridges and rail tracks, to organise uprisings in various regions, to raid Bolshevik households for food and ammunition. They were like owls, active at night, sleeping during the day. But no matter what they did, it wasn't enough. The partisans and the refugees were starving. Wet to the bone, their uniforms hanging off their exhausted, malnourished bodies, mud on their faces, they were a pitiful sight. Shkuro had plenty of men – eight thousand Cossacks and their numbers were growing every day as new recruits arrived. But hardly any of them had weapons. They armed themselves with sticks and stones and went out fighting the well-equipped Bolsheviks. Many of them never came back because sticks and stones didn't measure up to rifles and machine guns.

One morning, when there was a brief reprieve from the rain, Sophia said to Regina, 'Did you hear the rumours? Shkuro got in touch with General Denikin on his radio. We can expect reinforcements at any time.' The two women were sitting on a rock, attempting to start a fire. It wasn't working. The twigs were too damp. Sophia had tried to strike up a conversation with her friend a few times, but Regina never responded. Only her eyes flashed daggers every time she glanced at Sophia.

Undeterred by her friend's silence, Sophia continued, 'Our food situation is getting worse. With winter coming, there won't be any mushrooms left.' She lowered her twig and contemplated her friend. What was it in her face? It was as if she wanted to ask her something but couldn't. It was as if she already knew the answer. 'Are you all right?'

'I'm fine. Everything is fine.'

'Nikolai was able to walk three times around the cart unsupported. Isn't that wonderful?'

Regina nodded but didn't say a word, her anguished eyes on Sophia.

*

Every day, Sophia had to fight the rain, hunger and sheer exhaustion. There were some mornings when she thought she couldn't do it anymore. She didn't want to move from the wooden floor of their cart, while the rain seeped under her clothes and sadness seeped inside her heart. But her patients needed her. The only thing that got her through the day was the look on their faces when they saw her.

Sophia and Regina heard the bell when they were walking back from the river, having replenished their water supply. Everyone was ordered to move to yet another location because there was no grass left for the horses to graze on. Regina said, 'Another move. How much more can we take? What's the point?' Her face was smudged with mud and her wet hair hung around her face like seaweed. She looked small and fragile in her oversized coat.

'The point is to live,' said Sophia. 'Success is in running.'

'How long do we run for? Are we going to do this for the rest of our lives? At what point do we stop?' Regina sounded weary, like she was ready to give up. And who could blame her?

'You haven't eaten anything at breakfast. You're looking so

thin. We still have some stew left from yesterday. Why don't you have some?'

'I'm not hungry.'

'We never talk anymore. We wake up and spend our days looking for food, we fall asleep next to each other but we never have a moment to talk.'

'You are busy with your patients. We barely see you. Besides, what's there to talk about?'

'You don't seem like your usual self.' Sophia wanted Regina to confide in her, like she would back in the old days. But those days were forever gone. So much had changed and suddenly there was a wall between them Sophia didn't know how to breach.

'This hasn't been easy on any of us.'

'No, it hasn't. But look at the bright side. We are still alive. And we have plenty of drinking water.'

'Too much if you ask me,' said Regina, wiping raindrops off her face.

'Sometimes we have fish. It could have been worse.'

'We have nothing, Sophia. Nothing to return to. Nothing to look forward to. The revolution took it all.'

'We still have each other. I feel needed at the hospital tent. Dmitry is enjoying his fishing. I've never seen him so passionate about anything. And Nikolai is recovering. We have so much to be grateful for.'

At the mention of Nikolai, Regina's face fell. 'Maybe you have a lot to be grateful for. But not me.' She slowed down and turned to Sophia. 'What does it feel like to have both of them love you so much? Does it make you feel special? Important? Superior to everyone else?'

'What are you talking about?'

'Nikolai told me he's in love with someone else. It's you, isn't it?'

'He's my husband's brother. What are you even saying?'

'What a hypocrite you are. All this time you've been secretly in love with him and lying to me.'

'What makes you think …' Sophia fell quiet. To live her life in deceit from dawn till dusk, hide her true self from her husband and her friend, lie by omission every waking moment was one thing. But to lie to Regina's face was something else entirely. She couldn't do it.

'Even now, you're still lying to me. What for? Look at the way we live. We're under attack every day; we are hungry, wet and cold. There is no hope for any of us. Nothing matters anymore. Why can't you just tell me?'

'There's nothing to tell.'

'It's written all over your face. I must have been blind not to have noticed.'

'I don't know what—'

But Regina didn't let Sophia finish. 'You know very well what I'm talking about. Otherwise, you wouldn't look so guilty. Come on, look at me and tell me you have no feelings for him. See if you can deny them to my face.' Sophia looked at the ground, at the small stream of water rushing past. Regina nodded, satisfied. 'I thought so. Don't think I didn't notice the way your face changed when I spoke about my feelings for him. The way you look at him and the way he looks at you. I just didn't to believe it.'

'I haven't done anything wrong,' whispered Sophia.

'You justify yourself; you tell yourself love makes it all right somehow. But it doesn't. You are a married woman, Sophia. Every time you look at him, every time you think of him, every time you talk to him, you are betraying someone. How do you live with yourself? If you didn't seduce him with your feelings and the promise of your love, maybe I would have stood a chance.'

'I never meant to hurt you.'

'All you do is hurt people and you are not even sorry. I've never met anyone more selfish. If you don't think you've done anything wrong, why don't you tell Dmitry?'

'There is nothing to tell,' repeated Sophia, her head down.

'Tell him you don't love him. Tell him you love his brother.'

'I don't want to hurt his feelings. Why would I be so cruel?'

'Because it's the right thing to do,' shouted Regina. 'He deserves better than your lies. Like I do. But it's not his feelings you care about. It's yours. And I promise you, you will pay for this. If I can't have Nikolai, no one can.'

Before Sophia could say anything else, Regina stormed off, the water in her bucket spilling as she walked.

Chapter 13

November 1918

When Sophia woke up in the morning, Regina was gone. She wasn't at the river or on their meadow looking for mushrooms. Finally, Sophia found her on Anna and Vladimir's cart, a needle in her hand, mending an old dress.

'Did you sleep here? Come back. You don't need to leave,' said Sophia.

'I'm fine right here, thank you.'

Sophia noticed how much weight her friend had lost since leaving Kislovodsk. Her face looked thinner and her cheekbones were more pronounced. Her eyes were dull. She moved closer to Regina and lowered her voice. 'I didn't mean to lie to you. Can't you see, I wasn't trying to hide it from you. I was trying to hide it from myself. I was trying to convince myself it wasn't real.'

'It isn't real. You imagined it all because you feel trapped with Dmitry and are looking for a way out. You wouldn't know what love was if it hit you on the head.'

'And you would?' exclaimed Sophia.

'I'm a free woman. I'm not breaking anybody's heart.'

'You can't help who you fall in love with,' whispered Sophia.

'But you can help what you do about it.'

'I'm loyal to my husband. I haven't done anything to betray him.'

'Your every thought is betraying him.'

Sophia returned to her cart, leaving Regina alone with her sewing. As she was feeding Nikolai, she heard the military band, drums beating a cheerful tune and trumpets screeching. Sophia looked up to see columns of men marching past, wearing royal uniforms and carrying royal standards. They were old men on malnourished horses but they had weapons and heavy artillery. Everyone ran to meet them. Women greeted them with tears in their eyes, giving them food they couldn't spare and waving their kerchiefs. Children ran after them as fast as they could, squealing with excitement.

Nikolai said, 'The reinforcements Shkuro's been waiting for. General Pokrovsky and his men.'

'There are thousands of them,' Sophia whispered in awe, fighting the urge to follow the women, to dance with delight and throw flowers at the soldiers' feet.

'Now that they are here, the civil war is well and truly under way,' said Nikolai grimly.

Sophia knew he didn't approve but as she watched the jubilant faces of everyone around them, as she listened to the speeches welcoming the general and his men to camp, as she looked at the beloved royal standard she thought she would never see again, her heart trembled with hope.

Not only their way of life, but their property and livelihood had been taken away by the Bolsheviks. Their identity had been stolen. These people were fighting to bring this identity back. They were risking their lives to return to the old regime. How could Sophia not welcome them with joy?

*

The next morning, Sophia didn't wait for Regina but went to get water herself, bleary-eyed and shaking from the cold, her clothes clinging to her skin like wet snakes. At night, enough rain had been unleashed on the pitiful settlement to fill a large lake, perhaps Lake Ladoga, where her father used to take Sophia when she was a child. There was no reprieve from the rain or hunger, no matter how much time they spent in the forest foraging for mushrooms and berries or waiting by their fishing nets for fish. At the edge of the settlement, she saw a large crowd gathered in a semicircle, watching a dozen wooden structures that as if by magic had sprung up overnight. Like ghosts, they reached their skinny arms to the leaden sky as thunder erupted overhead. Off every terrifying structure hung a rope, and at the end of each rope was a noose.

At first, Sophia didn't understand what she was looking at. And when she finally realised, she recoiled in horror.

'Gallows!' she exclaimed. Surely, she was wrong. Why would there be gallows at Shkuro's camp? Was she still sleeping? Was it a terrible dream from which she would soon awaken?

But she wasn't sleeping and it wasn't a dream.

A man to her right said with a satisfied nod, 'General Pokrovsky is a big fan of hanging.'

'Hanging who?' she whispered.

'The Bolsheviks they catch. Traitors. Anyone who's against us.' While women looked away in disgust, the man shook his fist and shouted, 'No mercy for the enemies! Pokrovsky will soon show the Bolsheviks what we're made of.'

Feeling faint and unsteady on her feet, Sophia staggered away. She wished she had walked a different way to the river, so she wouldn't see the terrible contraptions groaning in the wind. She knew there were a few prisoners at the back of the settlement, their arms and legs bound – the Bolsheviks captured during skirmishes or raids on villages. Never in a million years had it occurred to her that these people could be killed. They were no enemy soldiers. They weren't German or Bulgarian or Turkish but Russian. Their only crime was that they believed in the revolution. Like Nikolai.

That day, the gallows stood empty and abandoned. But the next morning, when Sophia walked past, she saw limp bodies swaying in the wind. She cried out in horror. For the rest of the day, she did her best to avoid the terrible sight. But every time she closed her eyes, she could still see the lifeless faces and bodies of the victims.

She had no sleep at all that night and it had nothing to do with the cold or the rain or Regina's cruel words.

*

To avoid the gallows, Sophia started walking through the other side of the settlement, where General Pokrovsky had a tent all to himself, large and pompous, with the royal standard swaying over it. It wasn't a tent; it was a portable palace. His soldiers slept in the mud or on wet grass, covering themselves with pieces of tarpaulin, while their horses grazed nearby. Not the general. He was safe and warm inside, hidden away from the never-ending rain.

Sophia looked at the majestic tent with longing, wishing she could step inside for just a moment, to remember what it was like to not be wet or freezing cold. The mansions of the past seemed like something out of another life, with cosy fires burning in their fireplaces, servants in red liveries bringing refreshments, and couples waltzing the night away in the dance hall. As she watched the tent, the flaps flew open and a familiar shape appeared. To her surprise, Sophia recognised Regina.

Not believing her eyes, Sophia called out her name. Either Regina didn't hear or she didn't want to talk, because she increased her pace and disappeared in the crowd.

When Sophia returned, Dmitry was cooking a stew of herbs

and mushrooms on the campfire. With so many people fishing, they hadn't seen fish in days. 'Now that Pokrovsky is here, do you think we'll be able to go back to Kislovodsk?' asked Sophia as they sat down to eat. The rain was like tears running down her face.

'Now that Pokrovsky is here, it's only a matter of time before they throw the Bolsheviks out and we can return,' said Dmitry confidently. 'And then who knows, maybe we can go to Paris and wait there until it's safe to come back to Russia.'

'Russia is divided. They are tearing it apart,' said Nikolai.

'They didn't divide it. You did. The Bolsheviks and the revolutionaries. Were you hoping Russia would take it lying down?'

'You think the Bolsheviks are monsters. But look at your commander. He hangs our people without a trial, without so much as a second thought. His favourite saying is, a hanging in the morning is good for the appetite. This is the man you pin your hopes on.'

'You told me once yourself, you can't make a revolution without upheaval. And I'm telling you now, you can't make a counter-revolution without upheaval either.'

'You want Pokrovsky to come to power in Russia? You really think he will give up this power willingly to the royal family? Or will he take it for himself? Under his rule, what will Russia become?'

'What has it become under Kerensky, under Lenin?'

'We are working to unite Russia for the greater good of the working class.'

'What Russia needs is a strong leader. She is like a drowning ship. Pokrovsky and other generals – Kornilov, Denikin, Wrangel, Kolchak – are just what she needs to steer her to safety.'

'You mean dictatorship,' said Nikolai.

Dmitry had his boots on and his fishing net in his hands. 'I would stay and talk but I have a wife and a wounded brother to feed. I will let you have the last word.'

When Sophia and Nikolai were alone together, she said, 'Do

you want to go for a walk around the cart? How are you feeling?'

'Good as new,' said Nikolai. 'I think I can hop around the cart on my own today.'

But when Nikolai stood up, he flinched and cried out in pain, leaning on her shoulder. Slowly, they walked in small strides. 'You look so lost this morning. What are you thinking?' asked Nikolai.

'All of it scares me. The Bolsheviks scare me. Pokrovsky scares me. Even Shkuro scares me, and he's the nicest of them all.'

'Not so nice when he has a rifle in his hands. Shkuro has a fierce reputation.'

'They all seem intent on killing one another, while innocent people like us are caught in the middle. I'm so tired of it all. All I want is peace.'

'Peace and remaking the world for the better often don't go together. Just look at France. The French had decades of upheaval after the revolution.'

'If you are trying to make me feel better, it's not working.'

As Sophia helped him up to the cart, she thought, *He still believes in the revolution. After everything, he hasn't lost his faith. He is still hoping for the best. How can that be, when the rest of us have no strength left to believe in anything?*

*

Another sleepless night, drenched from the rain, unable to get warm or dry, her stomach hurting from hunger. Another grey morning, when Sophia walked slowly to the river to fill up their flasks, her head turned towards the mountains and the forest, away from the gallows. Was it her imagination or did more skeletal structures pop up in the night?

When Sophia returned, she heard loud voices. It wasn't unusual to hear voices in the settlement. With nearly a thousand people living together in close proximity, there was always someone shouting or arguing or playing music, even in the early hours before the sun was up. But this time she was certain the voices were coming from their cart. The only word she could make out was *Nikolai*. When she approached, she saw Dmitry talking to two men in Imperial uniforms. Pokrovsky's soldiers.

One of them reached into his pocket and said to Dmitry, who looked flushed and unkempt that morning, 'I have a warrant for his arrest.'

Sophia didn't understand. Whose arrest? Who were they talking about?

'My brother has done nothing wrong. Why would you arrest him?' demanded Dmitry, blocking the man's way.

The soldier leaned closer to Dmitry, forcing him to take a step back. He was a giant of a man and looked down at Dmitry when he said, 'Either you take us to Nikolai Orlov or we'll arrest all of you.'

'No,' whispered Sophia. It was like déjà vu. The last time it happened, Nikolai had nearly been killed and she didn't see him for over a year. She expected Dmitry to stand up to the men and try to stop them but he didn't. Faced with two rifles, he simply stepped out of the way and let them climb into the cart. She rushed to their side. 'You arrived here a week ago with your weapons and your horses. What makes you think you can march in and harass innocent people? What gives you the right to arrest anyone?'

'Just following orders,' replied one of the men. The other barely looked in her direction. All his attention was on Nikolai. He poked him with his boot and when Nikolai opened his eyes, he demanded, 'Are you Nikolai Orlov?'

'Who wants to know?'

'We have a warrant for your arrest.'

Sophia grabbed the man by his sleeve and pulled with all her might. 'Nikolai is wounded. He can't walk unsupported. He needs rest and medical attention. I'm a nurse looking after him and I forbid you …' Her voice cracked. 'I forbid you from taking him anywhere.'

'Believe me, madam, where he's going, he'll get plenty of rest.' The man sneered, shaking her off.

She cried silently, while they lifted Nikolai and dragged him away. She wanted to scream, to roar like a wounded animal and wrestle him out of their clutches. But she knew there was little she could do against two strong, armed soldiers.

Sophia and Dmitry didn't look at each other as the soldiers led the limping Nikolai to the fenced-off area behind the settlement where prisoners were kept, while the horrifying gallows screeched in the rain. As if waking from a dream, Sophia ran after them, shouting to them to stop. They didn't even glance her way. Like marble statues, they were intent on executing their orders, without pity or emotion. And there was Nikolai, resigned to his fate. Their eyes met. 'Don't worry, Sophochka,' he whispered. 'It will be all right.'

When she returned, shaking and afraid, Dmitry was still there, sitting on the edge of the cart, staring into the distance. His fishing net was in his lap and he was busy untying the knots. As if nothing had happened.

'Why are you behaving like nothing is wrong?' Sophia exclaimed. Dmitry turned to her and opened his mouth to reply but she interrupted. 'Why didn't you stop them? You were just standing there.'

Dmitry shrugged, his face long and mournful. 'Stop them how? They had a warrant. They were following orders.'

'You didn't even ask any questions. Why did they arrest him? What are they going to do with him? Where are they taking him?'

'Where they are taking everyone they've arrested, I suppose.'

Her insides were numb with fear. She could barely talk. 'They take them to the gallows,' she whispered.

'I'm sure it's a misunderstanding. Nikolai hasn't done anything wrong. Sooner or later they will let him go.'

'Sooner or later? And in the meantime, you are going fishing?'

'What do you want me to do?'

'Go to Shkuro. Go to Pokrovsky. Demand an explanation.' Impatiently, she tapped her foot on the ground.

'What makes you think they would talk to me?'

When he didn't make a move to get up, she whirled around and walked away, throwing over her shoulder, 'If you don't do anything to stop this, I will.'

At the edge of the meadow she paused, hoping he would follow. He didn't.

*

With a heavy heart Sophia walked as fast as she could towards Shkuro's camp. Unlike Pokrovsky, the young lieutenant general didn't have a tent of his own. He slept on the grass among his soldiers, wrapped in tarpaulin. Sophia found him alone under a large oak tree, leaning over his maps and tracing something with a red pencil. When he heard her footsteps, he looked up and smiled. She thought it was a good sign. He had a good smile, kind and open, one that inspired trust. Encouraged, she moved closer.

'Good morning,' he greeted her. 'I'm glad you're here. I wanted to thank you for all the work you are doing with the wounded. We are lucky to have you.'

'Just doing my job.'

'How can I help you this morning?'

Clearing her throat, stumbling over her words, she told him what happened. 'I don't understand why they would arrest him. He's done nothing wrong. I was wondering if you could help,' she concluded.

'I'm afraid there's not much I can do. General Pokrovsky is my superior. He doesn't take orders from me. I take orders from him.'

'But why did they take Nikolai? What do they want with him?' exclaimed Sophia, on the verge of tears. She pinched her hand to control her emotions. More than anything she needed to stay calm. Nikolai's fate depended on it.

'Someone came to General Pokrovsky directly and told him Nikolai holds an important position with the Bolsheviks. Of course, the general couldn't have a Bolshevik commissar among us. He was concerned your brother-in-law would report important strategic information back to the Bolsheviks if he remained in the camp.'

'Nikolai is weak and wounded. We took him with us because he was unwell. He is no danger to anyone.'

'I'm afraid the general doesn't see it this way. He has his own methods of dealing with the enemy.'

'Methods you don't agree with.'

'That might be so. But the general has little regard for my opinion. Or anyone's for that matter.'

'Nikolai is no enemy. He is a hero. He saved our lives. Without him, my husband and I wouldn't be here. Nikolai is recovering from a gunshot. I'm his nurse. He needs around-the-clock medical care. Please, can you talk to the general for us?'

'I'll see what I can do.'

In a daze, she walked back to the cart. It seemed smaller without Nikolai and Regina. She sat next to her husband in silence. Dmitry lit a cigarette and asked, 'Where did you go?'

'I didn't know you smoked,' said Sophia, moving slightly away.

'Vladimir shared his cigarettes with me. It takes my mind off things. Want one?'

Sophia shook her head. 'I went to see Shkuro.'

'Any news?'

'Nikolai was arrested as a Bolshevik commissar. That's all he told me.'

'How did Pokrovsky know about Nikolai?' Dmitry's shoulders were tense, his skin looked grey in the rain. 'Other than you and me, no one knows who he is.'

'You, me and Regina,' whispered Sophia.

For a moment, she watched the hustle and bustle of the settlement, women running after their children and singing quiet lullabies, men playing their guitars and starting campfires. It was almost lunchtime. The smell of potatoes baking in hot ashes filled her nostrils. Not far from here, in the prisoner camp, together with the Bolsheviks captured the day before, was Nikolai. And somewhere on the other side was Pokrovsky's tent. One word from him and Nikolai would be released. She wondered what it would be like to have that kind of power, to have the right to decide if someone lived or died. Did it make him feel important, like God? Or did he stay awake at night, haunted by lifeless faces?

She jumped off the cart and started walking. 'Where are you going?' Dmitry called after her. She didn't reply.

She found Regina sleeping on Anna and Vladimir's cart. Wrapped in her cardigan, she looked so peaceful, Sophia was almost sorry to wake her and give her the bad news until she remembered it must have been all Regina's doing. *How could you?* she wanted to scream to her friend of twenty years, her friend for most of her life, by her side as long as she could remember. *You loved him; how could you do this to him?* Hell hath no fury like a woman scorned, she thought. In her mind, she could still hear her friend's words. *If I can't have Nikolai, no one else can.* She looked at Regina, whom she loved like a sister, whom she trusted more than anyone, with all her secrets but one, and realised she didn't know Regina at all because the woman she knew could not have condemned an innocent man in cold blood.

Regina opened her eyes. It took her a few seconds to notice Sophia's pale face. When she did, she shuddered and sat up. Was it Sophia's imagination or did she look guilty?

'What are you doing here?' Regina muttered.

'I saw you a few days ago, coming out of General Pokrovsky's tent,' said Sophia, looking straight at her.

'Yes, and?'

'I didn't realise you two knew each other.'

'He was an old friend of my father's. They were in the military academy together. I haven't seen him in years.'

'What did the two of you talk about?'

'Nothing much. The past. The present.' Her face lit up. 'The man is a visionary. He hates the Bolsheviks. He swears to rid Russia of every single one before the year is over.'

'I heard his methods are somewhat extreme.'

'What does it matter, provided they are effective? If anyone can bring the old regime back, it's General Pokrovsky.'

Regina acted as if she didn't know. For a moment, Sophia couldn't find the right words to tell her. Finally, she said, 'Nikolai was arrested this morning. Someone told Pokrovsky he was a Bolshevik commissar.'

'Nikolai was arrested?' Regina paled. She didn't speak for a few moments. Finally, she whispered, 'What are they going to do to him?'

'What they do to all the Bolsheviks they capture, I suppose.' Sophia didn't take her hostile eyes off her friend.

'We have to do something. We have to stop them,' exclaimed Regina. Was it an act? She had always been a good actress. When Sophia didn't reply, Regina cried, 'Wait, you think it was me? You think I told Pokrovsky on Nikolai?'

'He rejected you. You couldn't take it. You told me yourself we were going to pay. And a few days later, I see you leaving Pokrovsky's tent. I don't believe in coincidences.'

'I love him. I would never do anything to hurt him.'

'This is your revenge. You should be ashamed of yourself,' cried Sophia, turning around and walking away, no longer listening to Regina.

Lies. Every word coming out of her mouth was lies.

*

And then the unthinkable happened. A messenger from Shkuro told her Nikolai would be hanged in the morning with the other Bolsheviks that had been captured the day before in the nearby

297

villages. When Sophia heard, her legs buckled under her. She would have fallen if Dmitry didn't catch her. She wanted to run back to Regina and shout, 'Look what you've done! Because of you, Nikolai is going to die.' If only she could run or shout. She was a quivering mess on the floor of the cart, silent tears rolling down her cheeks, while Dmitry bustled around her, asking if she wanted anything, if she was hungry or thirsty. As if she could think of any of that now that her life was over.

This time tomorrow, Nikolai would be gone. And there was nothing she could do to help him. 'It's all my fault,' she repeated.

'How is it your fault, my dear?' asked Dmitry, stroking her head like she was a child.

'If I didn't insist on bringing Nikolai with us, none of this would have happened. If only I'd listened to you.'

'Don't blame yourself. You couldn't have known it would turn out like this.'

'I'll never forgive Regina. How can anyone be so heartless? She might as well have killed him with her own two hands, delivering him straight to her friend Pokrovsky.'

'I'm sure she did it in a moment of anger and now regrets it. And it's something she will have to live with for the rest of her life.'

'You think you know someone. And then they do something like this.'

'Maybe it wasn't her. Maybe someone else recognised Nikolai and told the general.'

'I introduced them. They met at our house.'

'Don't beat yourself up. Why don't you try to sleep? Everything will seem brighter after you get some rest.'

'You think if I get some sleep, I will feel better about the fact Nikolai will be killed at dawn tomorrow?' She glared at him.

How Sophia got through the day, she didn't know. If anyone asked what she did, she wouldn't be able to say. Dmitry fed her, even though she refused to eat. And he brought her water, even though she said she didn't want it. He talked about his brother, and it was comforting to know that someone else was feeling what she was feeling. It was as if the load she was carrying was a little bit lighter because Dmitry had a similar one on his shoulders. He held her but she barely noticed. She was delirious with grief, not quite asleep but not awake either, not wanting to be awake.

When it was dark and Dmitry was sleeping peacefully by her side, Sophia wriggled out from under his arm and ran in the direction of the makeshift prison. She told the sentry Nikolai was her brother-in-law and she had to see him. She lied and pretended she had Shkuro's permission. The sentry waved her through, his face blank and indifferent.

Without so much as a tree or a piece of tarpaulin to cover them from the rain and the wind that howled like a wild animal through the night, a dozen prisoners were huddled together under the rifles of their jailers. At first, Sophia couldn't see Nikolai. Only when she walked around the little group, the sentry close behind her, did she notice him in the damp grass, his arms and legs bound. He lay on the dirty straw with his eyes closed but she knew he wasn't sleeping. Who would be able to sleep, knowing what was in store for them in the morning? She whispered his name but he didn't hear her. It took all her self-control not to cry out and run to him.

'You have five minutes,' said the sentry. She barely heard him. All she could see was Nikolai. Her heart breaking, she sank to the ground next to him, touching his forehead, lifting his hand to her lips and kissing it. He felt hot to her touch. His fever was back.

Nikolai opened his eyes and reached his hand out, stroking her face. Mutely, they watched each other in the dusk. 'I didn't think I would see you again,' he whispered.

'How can I not come and see you? What are you even saying?'

'I didn't think they would let you.'

'How can they do this to you? How is it possible?' She hid her face in her hands and cried.

'Shh, not so loud,' he said, pointing at the other prisoners and the sentry mere steps away. But she didn't care if anyone heard her. She didn't care if they arrested and handcuffed her, locking her up.

'You haven't done anything wrong and they are threatening to hang you in the morning. They are barbarians, monsters.' She shook, hysterical.

He stroked her back gently. 'It's war. These things happen in war.'

'Even in war, there are rules, there must be a trial.'

'Pokrovsky's cruelty is legendary. He doesn't value human life, whether it's his men or the enemy. And sooner or later it will be his undoing.'

At the mention of Pokrovsky, Sophia clasped her fists in anger. She hated the man, even if he was trying to bring the old regime back to Russia. He wasn't human, he was a beast. 'What can we do to stop this?'

'There is nothing we can do. We have to accept it.'

'Accept it? Never! What they are trying to do, it's against the law, against common decency.'

'It's their camp. They make the law and they don't give a damn about decency.'

'I'm going to kill Regina for doing this to you.'

'Regina?' He pulled himself up on one elbow, looking into her face. 'What does she have to do with any of it?'

'She's the one who has told Pokrovsky about you. When she found out about us, she lost her mind. She was crazy with anger and jealousy. And then she did this.'

He shook his head. 'I don't think it was her. She doesn't strike me as cruel or vindictive.'

'If not her, then who? Who else knew about you?' Nikolai had no answer to that. 'Well, I'm not giving up. I won't stop at anything. I already spoke to Shkuro. I will speak to him again. I will go to Pokrovsky if I have to. There is still time before dawn.' The thought of what awaited them at dawn made her gasp.

'You won't do any of it or you'll put yourself in danger. If Pokrovsky knows you are in any way sympathetic to someone like me, it will be you under guard with your hands bound. You can't help me but you can help yourself.'

'I love you. I've never loved anyone before. I can't lose you now.' He was quiet and in his eyes she saw something resembling amazement. 'What? Why are you looking at me like that?'

'That is the first time you've said it to me.'

'You're wrong. I've said it to you before.' *As the bullets whistled past and people ran for their lives, she leaned close to him and held his head, feeling life slowly seeping out, his blood on her dress, on her face and all over her hands. Please, don't leave me, she had whispered.* And now, as she clung to him as if her life depended on it, she repeated, 'Please, don't leave me. I can't make it without you.'

'I love you too, Sophia. Do you hear me? I've loved you from the first moment I saw you. I want you to know that.'

She had dreamt of hearing these words since the day they met. But now that he'd said them, they brought her no joy, only heartache. It sounded too much like he was saying goodbye. And she couldn't take it.

'Time,' cried the sentry. She trembled, pretending she didn't hear. She didn't care if they dragged her away kicking and screaming and the whole camp saw it. She didn't care if her husband saw it. Nothing mattered anymore. 'How can I help you? How can I keep you safe?' she whispered, desperately clutching his hands to her chest and covering them with kisses.

The flames of the sentry's torch were playing on his anguished face. There were tears in his eyes when he said, 'Stay safe and do your best to survive, for me. Look after yourself, for me. That's how you can help me.'

'Yes, but who will look after you?'

'Let's go,' shouted the sentry, making a move towards her. It reminded her of another time, another place, another prison when she didn't want to say goodbye. Sophia had been forced to leave and spent months thinking he was dead. Did he come back to her just so she could lose him again? It didn't bear thinking about.

Only when a pair of hands lifted her and a harsh voice ordered her to move did she let go of him. And still Sophia hesitated, watching him in the light of the torch, trying to commit his face to memory, knowing it was the last time she would see him before he walked to his death in the morning.

The sentry dragged her away, leaving her on the side of the road a hundred metres from the prison, and there she remained until dawn, cold and alone, not knowing where she was or what to do next. During the night, she heard gunshots nearby but paid them no attention. Someone shouted in fear, there was another voice frantically screaming to stay down, to take cover and stay safe. She didn't move, praying the Red Army would take over the camp and make it all go away – Pokrovsky and his men with their bloodthirsty and unthinkable justice. If the Bolsheviks came here, they would liberate the prisoners, Nikolai included. For the first time in her life she prayed for the revolutionaries to win. But it wasn't to be. Soon the noises quietened and the camp fell back into uneasy sleep.

Sophia couldn't bear thinking of what was coming at dawn, six hours away, five, four … And yet, she could think of nothing else. The night was torture but she prayed it would never end because morning would bring unspeakable horrors with it.

Chapter 14

November 1918

When the terrible day of Nikolai's execution dawned, Sophia dusted herself off and staggered back to the cart. As she was passing the prison, she slowed down, hoping to catch a glimpse of Nikolai through the trees. As hard as she tried, she couldn't see him. The rain had stopped and the air was still. The gallows were silent like terrifying shadows. When she saw their silhouettes, red from the rising sun, waiting patiently for their prey to arrive, she bent over in the grass and clutched her stomach. For a few moments she remained there, too sick to move.

Dmitry was still asleep when she pulled on his sleeve. He jumped to his feet, his eyes wild, asking what the matter was. She didn't reply, just watched in silence as his face twisted in realisation. He glanced in the direction of the gallows and just as quickly looked away. 'Is it time?' he asked. She nodded, unable to talk, trying very hard not to fall apart just yet. Afterwards, she could fall apart. But until it was over, she would do everything in her power to stop the unthinkable from happening.

The rising sun turned the mountains orange, like they were volcanos spitting out hot lava intent on destroying their little settlement. *If only*, thought Sophia, changing into her one dress that wasn't torn and muddy and tying a black shawl around her head. She was going to throw herself on her knees in front of General Pokrovsky as they led Nikolai to his execution.

Dmitry was busy with the campfire. 'Let me make you a cup of tea, dear.'

She shook her head.

'Please, eat something.'

She couldn't.

'We should go. Or we are going to miss it,' he said finally.

Her knees trembled so badly, Sophia couldn't take a single step on her own towards their horrific destination. She wanted to delay the inevitable, to put it off forever. She had to lean on Dmitry's arm as she stumbled towards the gallows. Without a word, they stood in a small crowd of onlookers, while a dozen soldiers in Imperial uniform milled around aimlessly. There was no sign of the prisoners or Pokrovsky. Trying not to look at the gallows, empty nooses at the ready, with Dmitry holding her up, she waited with trepidation.

The sun was barely up, its cold rays peeking from behind the mountains, when the condemned were brought in. Hands bound behind them, faces white in the pale morning light, they walked slowly, as if they, too, were trying to delay things. Time and time again, they tripped over and rose to their feet, looking fearfully at the guards who carried whips and shouted at them to hurry along. 'Keep walking!' they screamed, riding their horses in circles around the frightened men. 'We haven't got all day. Let's get it over and done with.'

Get it over and done with! Sophia gasped, recoiling from the spectacle, wishing she was blind and deaf so she wouldn't have to see and hear. Wishing she could get struck by lightning or a blunt object and lose her memory, so she would never have to remember this day. But she suspected the pitiful figures would be etched into her memory for as long as she lived. She didn't want to look at them as they stumbled past, didn't want to see Nikolai's beloved face, minutes away from death. She closed her eyes and searched for a memory of the two of them together.

As the men walked past, she opened her eyes and forced herself to peer into every face. Nikolai wasn't among them.

She blinked and looked again. She couldn't see him.

Had he been delayed? She glanced in the direction of the prison, expecting to see another group of prisoners. But there was no sign of him.

'Is that all of them?' demanded the officer in charge of the execution.

'Yes, sir,' replied one of the guards.

'Let's start.'

The condemned were told to stop in front of the gallows. Sophia couldn't look at their terror-stricken faces, at their collapsed bodies or the vicious grins of their tormentors. She turned away.

Dmitry was almost as pale as the men waiting to die. 'I don't see Nikolai,' he whispered. 'Where is he?'

The guard shouted for the prisoners to step forward. Sophia couldn't take it. Without a word to Dmitry, without so much as a glance in his direction, she turned around and ran towards Shkuro's camp. Shaking, barely intelligible, she asked the ataman if he knew anything about Nikolai. He didn't. As the settlement woke and people greeted one another, sitting down to breakfast and warming themselves on their campfires, she left Shkuro's camp and walked past the place where she had seen Nikolai last. It was deserted. She knew where most of the prisoners were – on the gallows, ropes around their necks. But where was Nikolai?

Not knowing where else to turn, Sophia made her way across the settlement to Pokrovsky's tent. Soldiers sat in a circle in front of it, laughing, drinking, washing their faces with water, breaking off chunks of bread and chewing loudly. She approached one of them and asked timidly if she could speak to the general.

Pokrovsky scared her. On a couple of occasions she had seen him, he seemed like a devil of a man with his height and his moustache and the glint in his eyes. Would she be able to look in those eyes and enquire about Nikolai? And didn't she promise Nikolai to stay away from him? It didn't matter. She needed answers and it seemed Pokrovsky was the only one who could give them.

'The general is away, my dear,' replied the soldier with a wink. 'Why don't you stay here and wait for him, keep us company?'

'All right,' she said.

'But before I can let you into the camp, I have to search you. To make sure you are not carrying any weapons. The general is a very important man. We can never be too careful now, can we?'

His hands went around Sophia's waist. She could feel his breath on her neck. She took a step back. 'Will he be gone long?'

'All day and possibly all night. But don't worry, we'll find ways to make the time go faster.'

Her heart in her throat, Sophia pulled away from him and ran towards the river, the soldiers' laughter ringing in her ears. For a long time, she remained on the rock where she had often sat with Regina. What she had feared so much hadn't happened. Nikolai wasn't among the prisoners executed that morning. It could mean any number of things. For some reason, his execution had been delayed and he had been moved elsewhere. Was it possible he had been pardoned? She didn't dare let hope inside her heart. Besides, if he'd been freed, wouldn't he have found them by now to let them know everything was fine? Something else must have happened. She remembered the disturbance the night before, the gunshots and the shouts. What if he'd been killed? The more she sat and watched the water rush past, the more she felt suffocating dread envelop her like a cloak. Fighting a sudden premonition, she rushed to the hospital tent. If he had been wounded, would they bring him here? Or would they leave him in the woods to die?

All the beds in the hospital tent were full. Six people had been wounded in the Bolshevik attack the night before – five men and one woman. She barely glanced at the woman, who was unconscious, and walked from bed to bed, looking into the men's faces.

'Nurse Sophia, can I please have some water?' she heard from one of the beds. It was Matvei, one of her patients.

'In a minute, Matvei,' she replied grimly.

'Nurse Sophia, please could you wash my face? I feel like I'm burning in hell.' That was Danil, recovering from a shoulder wound.

'I'll be right with you,' she said to him, ready to break down. Nikolai wasn't there.

As she gave Matvei some water and washed Danil's face, the woman on the bed in the corner groaned. Sophia heard a soft voice, barely a whisper. 'Sophia, is that you? Please, help me.'

She thought she recognised the colour of the hair and the shape of the head. In two strides she was by the bed. Regina's tormented eyes met hers. 'What happened? Why are you here?' whispered Sophia, her hands fidgeting, fixing her friend's bedding and checking her pulse.

'Last night …' Regina was talking with difficulty, wheezing with every breath she took. 'When the settlement was attacked, I was walking … I got shot.'

There was a spot of red on her dress. Someone had bandaged her chest but they had done so carelessly. The wound looked infected. Regina was like a ghost on her white pillow, her skin sallow, lips pale and trembling.

'Please, don't talk. You need to lie very still. I'm going to clean the wound and take a look at you. I have a couple of shots of vodka left for an emergency. I think this qualifies, what do you think? Do you want some, for the pain?'

Regina shook her head.

'Are you sure? When I disinfect the wound, it will hurt.'

'Nikolai …' Regina croaked.

Sophia perked up. 'What about him?'

'He's a doctor. He can help me.'

'I don't know where he is. But I'm here now and I'll look after you. You will get better soon. Everything will be just fine.' Regina felt clammy and cold. She fainted as Sophia was cleaning the wound. 'I'm sorry. For everything,' whispered Sophia as she bandaged her friend's chest.

She didn't think Regina could hear but she opened her eyes and looked straight at her. 'You are the best friend I've ever had. My whole life you were like a sister to me. I love you.'

'I love you too,' replied Sophia, her cheeks damp, her heart aching.

'I don't blame you for loving Nikolai. You couldn't help it, just like me. When he told me there's someone else, I was so angry. But I'm glad it's you. You are the best person I know. If he can't be happy with me, I want him to be happy with you.'

'Thank you,' said Sophia. 'Now relax and try to breathe deeper. Yes, just like that.'

'I don't feel so good,' Regina said. 'What is going to happen to me?'

'You need to rest. Whatever you do, try not to move.'

'As if I could. Sophia, am I going to die?' Regina's eyes were dry and staring.

'Of course you are not going to die.'

'Then why do I feel like every part of me is broken? All I want is to close my eyes and let go.'

Sophia sat on the edge of Regina's bed. Her hand was on her friend's forehead. 'Close your eyes and have some sleep. You know what Nikolai says. Sleep is the best medicine.'

'He does say that. I want to see him one more time. I want to tell him what he means to me …' The candle burnt out. It was dark in the tent. More than anything Sophia wanted to see her friend's face but all she could make out was the pale outline of her hair. Regina coughed and spluttered. Sophia fetched her a glass of water. It was a few minutes before Regina could talk again. 'It wasn't me, you know? I didn't tell Pokrovsky about

Nikolai. I could never do something like that.'

'I believe you, darling. And I'm sorry for what I said earlier. Please, don't talk. You'll need your strength.'

'I didn't tell Pokrovsky,' repeated Regina. 'But I told Dmitry.'

'Told him what?'

'About you and Nikolai. That the two of you love each other.'

Regina slept and Sophia sat next to her for a while, holding her clammy hand and staring into space.

Only three people knew about Nikolai – Sophia, Regina and her husband. And Dmitry had every reason to wish his brother harm.

*

One of Shkuro's soldiers approached Sophia as she was leaving the hospital tent. 'The ataman wants to see you,' he said. She wondered what Shkuro was going to tell her. Had Nikolai been killed in last night's attack? Had the hanging been moved to a later date? Had he been wounded? As she followed the messenger to Shkuro's camp, she felt like she was walking to her own execution.

The ataman greeted her with a smile. 'I have good news for you,' he said.

'You do?' She held her breath.

'Nikolai was pardoned yesterday. It seems your friend has the magic touch with the general that I don't.'

'My friend?'

'Regina. She asked the general for compassion and he relented. To be honest, I'm surprised. He is not a compassionate man.'

'Regina did this?'

'From what I've heard, Regina's father had once saved Pokrovsky's life. And when she begged the general to spare Nikolai, he couldn't say no. Your brother-in-law will be banished but he won't be hanged.'

'Thank God,' whispered Sophia, wanting to fall to her knees and pray. 'Where is he? When can I see him?'

'I will let you know.'

'How can I ever thank you?'

'Don't thank me. Thank your friend. And if I were you, I would take Nikolai away as soon as possible, before the general changes his mind.'

As she rushed back to the hospital tent, she cried with relief. Thanks to Regina, Nikolai was going to live! And here she was, blaming her friend for everything. She was going to apologise for her suspicions and tell Regina that her love for Nikolai had blinded her, that she should have known better, that she would spend the rest of her life making it up to her. They could go back to Petrograd together, the three of them. With Nikolai to protect them, they would have nothing to fear from the Bolsheviks. One thing Sophia knew for certain. They couldn't stay another day in these mountains where bullets whizzed past and people you trusted betrayed you.

But no, Sophia wouldn't think of her husband just yet. First, she had to talk to her friend.

Inside the tent, the wounded were groaning, shouting, calling her name, reaching for her, like ghosts grey and terrifying in the dark. Ignoring the arms trying to grab her, Sophia walked straight to her friend's bed. Regina was in the same position as before, her skin translucent in the light of a candle. Something in the stiffness of her neck alerted Sophia straightaway that something was wrong. Even before she touched her, she knew Regina was no longer breathing. Blinded by tears, she searched frantically for her friend's pulse and couldn't find it. Regina was gone.

Kneeling by her friend, Sophia placed her hand on her forehead. She was stupefied, unable to move or take her eyes off Regina's body. Sometimes in the light of the candle a shadow ran over Regina's face and then it seemed that her friend was back, that she was alive. Every time it happened, Sophia jumped to her feet, shaking Regina gently and touching her face, but it was no use. Her eyes remained closed, her hand was cold.

310

'I'm so sorry,' Sophia whispered. 'I'm sorry I doubted you. I should have known better. I'm sorry I thought the worst of you.'

She tried to think of her life before Regina and couldn't. Her best friend had always been by her side, her one ray of sunshine, her perfect partner in crime. Once, when they were six or seven, Sophia had broken her father's favourite vase. She cried for days, waiting for punishment but it never came. Later, she found out Regina had gone to her father and pretended she was the one who had broken the vase. When Sophia thanked her, Regina said, *It's the least I could do. He's not my father. I knew he wouldn't punish me.* And when Sophia asked why Regina didn't tell her, her friend replied, *Good deeds should remain a secret or it might seem like you expect something in return.* And even now, many years later, while Sophia had been seething with hatred and suspicion, Regina had been secretly working on her last good deed.

'I wish things were different. I should have been honest with you from the start. I didn't want to hurt your feelings, so I lied. It was wrong. You deserved the truth and I'm so sorry.'

Sophia continued talking but her friend could no longer hear her.

*

Sophia couldn't stay in the dark hospital tent another moment. She stumbled outside, oblivious to the voices calling for her.

Her heart aching with guilt and sadness, Sophia stopped at the river where the two of them had spent so much time together. She sat on their favourite rock and took off her boots, dangling her feet in the water. It was freezing but she didn't care. She remained like this for a long time, thinking about her friend and Nikolai and her husband. Once again, she was delaying the inevitable. If she could, she would have turned around and ran, all the way to Nikolai, as far away as possible, because she never wanted to set eyes on Dmitry again. She didn't want to face him and have her

311

suspicions confirmed because then she would have to accept them as truth and live with it. And she didn't know how to live with it.

Slowly, Sophia made her way back to the settlement. She saw Dmitry as soon as she turned the corner. He was sitting on a log, mending his fishing net. Like nothing was wrong in the world.

'There you are, my dear. I was beginning to worry,' he said, putting the fishing net down and smiling with affection. Getting up to his feet, he approached her and drew her into a hug. She stood without moving. Only her eyes flashed as she stared at him in silence.

Did he look like someone capable of the most terrible betrayal? He knew about her feelings for Nikolai. How could he not? He wasn't blind. Why hadn't he said anything? Never, not once, had he reproached her. And now here they were, and she didn't know what to say.

'Anna came by. She told me about Regina. I'm so sorry, darling. I know what she meant to you. Why don't you sit down?'

Sophia slumped down on a tree stump and watched his familiar face, trying to read between the words.

'I'll be right back, dear.' He walked away but soon reappeared with a pot and two cups. 'It must be such a shock. First, Nikolai. Then Regina. My poor darling.'

'Nikolai's been pardoned. He will be banished from the settlement but his life will be spared.'

If Dmitry was shocked or upset, he didn't show it. 'That's wonderful news! I knew they would see reason. My brother didn't do anything wrong. Where is he now?'

'You knew they would see reason? But you were hoping they wouldn't?'

He poured their tea. Without looking up, he said, 'What do you mean, Sophochka? Why would I be hoping that?'

She looked into her cup of tea and didn't reply.

*

312

It was a beautiful day, finally a break in the rain, when they laid Regina to rest. The rising sun behind the mountains looked like a crown on a giant's head. There was not a cloud in the sky. The whole camp came to say goodbye to Regina. Sophia didn't realise how many lives her friend had touched, how many people she had helped. Anna was crying. Others too. But Sophia's eyes were dry. She had no more tears left, only suffocating sadness. Now more than ever, she needed her best friend. She wanted to share her heartbreak and her fears with Regina the way she had shared with her for most of her life. But it was impossible. And it broke her heart.

After everyone else had left, Sophia and Dmitry stood quietly together. He put his arm around her. Gently she moved away.

'I know what you did,' she said quietly. She was too tired for affliction or confrontation. Too much was broken inside her. There was darkness in her soul, despite the cheerful sunshine that seemed to scream of hope and joy and better things to come. All she wanted to do was get her things, her small trunk of what little clothes she had left and her mother's painting, and leave, never to see him again.

Dmitry didn't seem to hear her. 'Do you want anything? Let's go back and I'll make you something to eat.'

He turned to go, taking her hand. She didn't move. 'Wait!' Sophia exclaimed. He stopped. With surprise she noticed that her hands were trembling. 'I need to talk to you.'

'Of course, we'll talk. After you have some rest and once you have something warm in your tummy. Let me feed you. Let me look after you.'

'It was you, wasn't it?' The words came out like an angry hiss, like she was a cat snarling at a deadly enemy.

'I don't know what you are talking about. You are not yourself. You are hurting, you just lost your best friend. Why don't you have a sleep while I cook you some fish?'

'Your own brother, Dima. How could you?' He turned away

313

but not before she saw the expression on his face. Everything she didn't want to see was there – guilt, anger and heartbreak. What little hope she had melted away. She clasped her fists as tight as she could, willing herself not to cry. A sudden realisation chilled her. 'It wasn't the first time, was it?' He didn't reply and didn't look at her. She continued, 'I've been wondering about this for a while. Back in Petrograd when the Provisional Government was looking for Nikolai. They had us in their custody and let us go. Why?'

'I don't know why. They got what they wanted and didn't need us anymore?'

'They mistrust anyone who is opposed to the revolution. They use any excuse to get rid of people like us. They let us go because you told them where your brother was. When they came back to search our house, they knew exactly where to look.'

'I don't know what you are talking about,' he repeated, still not raising his eyes to her.

Sophia walked over to him and pulled him by the arm, forcing him to look at her. 'He saved your life twice. And this is how you repay him?'

His voice shook when he spoke. 'He was trying to take my most precious possession from me.'

'I'm not a possession. I'm not an object.'

'I couldn't lose you. What was I supposed to do? If you were in my position, can you honestly say you wouldn't do the same?'

Sophia turned away from him, unable to take the expression on his face. 'I would never condemn my brother to a certain death.'

'I would do anything for you, you know that. *Anything*. I can't live without you. You thought I didn't notice what was happening, but you were wrong. I saw it all. I thought it was one-sided, an infatuation that would soon pass. But then Regina opened my eyes. Of course, I wasn't surprised. In my heart I already knew.'

'So you decided to go to Pokrovsky and get rid of your own brother once and for all?'

'He was trying to take you away from me.'

'He wasn't trying to take me away. I'm not a toy.'

'How could you do this to me? I trusted you. How could you?'

'We didn't ask for it. We didn't plan it. It just happened. We didn't mean to hurt you.'

'Everyone I love leaves me. First my brother, then my parents. And now you. I couldn't let you go.'

'Even at the price of your brother's life?'

'He is the most selfish person I know. Always does what he wants, never thinks about other people. He destroyed our family. There were four of us against the world. But it all changed the minute he turned his back on us with his revolutionary nonsense. My mother never forgave my father for banishing Nikolai. She left for the countryside and I hardly saw her. My father threw himself into his work. I hardly saw him too. At the age of twelve, I had no one, because of Nikolai.' Dmitry's voice was bitter, his eyes two angry slits. 'His betrayal didn't come as a surprise. I didn't expect anything better from him. He always did what was best for him. What came as a surprise was you. Why did you hide it from me for so long?'

All blood rushed to her face. 'I wasn't hiding anything. We didn't do anything wrong.'

'You withdrew from me completely after you met him. You changed.' He took a step towards her and she backed away. She was struggling to breathe. He grabbed her hand. 'I was a good husband to you. I did my best. Other men take mistresses and have families on the side, but I was always true to you. I never betrayed you, not even in my thoughts. Why couldn't you love me? Wasn't our marriage worth something?'

She pulled away from him. 'You call it a marriage? Look at us. We are like strangers living together. When was the last time you asked me how I was and meant it?'

'I don't need to ask. I know. You are my wife. I know you better than anyone.'

'You don't know me at all. And you never wanted to know me. As long as I play the role of the perfect little wife and don't interfere in your business, you are happy. I'm like a porcelain doll you purchased at the market, an object to show off to your friends.'

'I don't understand. I thought you were happy. You had everything you needed, right here with me. I loved you more than anything in the world. We were planning to start a family. What was missing?'

I never loved you, she wanted to say but didn't because, despite everything he had done, she didn't want to be cruel. 'Can't you see? I was torn between the two of you but I had given you my word. I was going to stay with you. I could never break the promise I made you on the day we were married.'

His face brightened. He looked at her with affection. 'I believe you. We can leave Russia and start a new life somewhere far from here. We can forget everything that happened. We can embark on a new adventure together. Just you and me.'

'I can never forget what you did to Nikolai. If you can throw your own brother away so easily, how can I ever trust you?'

'Don't you understand? Everything I did, I did for you. Including this.' Sophia was shaking from anger and couldn't talk. Encouraged by her silence, Dmitry added, 'I will forgive you for loving him if you forgive me for what I've done. We can start over.'

'Forgive you? Never!' Horrified, she staggered away from him.

'Please, don't walk away from me,' she heard.

Sophia didn't turn around. What he wanted from her, she couldn't give him. Instead of forgiveness, kindness and love he was asking for, all she had for him was bitterness and resentment. He wanted pure gold and all she had was small change. She ran as fast as she could, she didn't know where, hearing his words over and over in her head. *Everything I did, I did for you.*

What happened wasn't just his fault. It was hers too.

*

Sophia waited impatiently for Shkuro to come back from one of his missions, so she could ask him about Nikolai. She still didn't know where he was and the uncertainty was killing her. At the hospital tent, she checked Danil's temperature and brought Matvei a glass of water. She changed two dressings and wrote a letter to Kislovodsk for a man who had lost his fingers. She was about to leave when she heard a groan. It was coming from the bed in the corner where a man was sleeping. She approached the bed, thinking a new patient must have arrived that morning. It was dark but for a small candle burning on the ground next to the bed. In the light of the candle, she saw the man's face and gasped. It was Nikolai!

Sophia dropped the candle and it went out, plunging the place into darkness. She sank to her knees next to him, stroking his face, bringing his hands to her lips, kissing his fingers one after another. She spoke to him softly because she didn't want to disturb him. 'What have they done to you? Look at you. You've lost so much weight. Your chest looks infected. But it's all right. It's all behind you now. I will look after you. I won't leave your side until you're better. I love you.'

His eyelids trembled. 'And once I'm better, are you going to leave me?'

'No, of course not,' Sophia whispered, relieved that he heard her, that he was well enough to make jokes.

'Good. Or I'm never getting better.'

'I thought you were sleeping? You need your sleep.'

'And miss your declaration of love?' In the near-darkness, she saw that Nikolai was grinning. She grinned back, her heart aching. 'What is happening? Where am I?' he asked.

'In the hospital tent. They are letting you go. You are free.'

'I don't understand. Why would they let me go?'

'Are you complaining?' He pressed her hand and for a moment she forgot what she was about to say, so happy was she to see his face and know he was safe. 'You were right about Regina. She didn't betray you.'

'I know.'

'Do you know who did?'

He nodded.

'Why didn't you tell me?'

'I didn't want to come between you two.'

'Even after everything he's done?'

'He's your husband. And my brother. Nothing will ever change that.'

Sophia told him they had to hurry. To thank her for tending to the wounded for the last few months, Shkuro offered to give them a cart, some weapons and food. They had to get away before Pokrovsky changed his mind, even though it wasn't the general Sophia was worried about, it was her husband. Something told her Dmitry wasn't going to let them go easily. He betrayed his brother once. What was to stop him from betraying both of them when they were on the brink of escaping? 'We have to leave at dawn tomorrow.'

'We?'

'I'm not letting you go on your own. The minute my back is turned, you get in trouble.'

He took her hand and pressed it to his lips. For a long time, they were silent. 'What about Dmitry?' he asked finally.

'I can't stay with him after what he's done. I could never look at him the same way. I hope one day he'll forgive me.'

'He might forgive *you*,' said Nikolai. 'But he'll never forgive *me*.'

'What makes you think that?'

'Because I know what it's like to love you. I could never forgive anyone for taking you away from me.'

*

The morning was misty and cold. Here in the mountains in November, Sophia could feel winter's icy breath in the air. Fog was like cotton wool draped around the tops of the mountains, making them look even more formidable and impenetrable, as if they were telling Nikolai and Sophia to stay away, to not even try to cross this unforgiving terrain on their own. Before they left, Sophia went to see Anna, who told her Dmitry had been looking for her. As they said goodbye, she hugged the woman who through adversity had turned from a mere acquaintance into a true friend. They promised each other to take care, to write, to stay alive, to see each other again, in another world, a better time. As she waved to her friend, Sophia wondered if that time would ever come.

She watched Dmitry through the branches of a bush as he disappeared in the direction of the river. *This might be the last time I see him*, she thought. And as she thought that, she felt nothing, not even a sliver of regret. That chapter of her life was over. A new chapter was about to begin.

Sophia waited five minutes to make sure Dmitry didn't come back, then ran across the clearing to the cart she had once shared with her husband, Regina and Nikolai, collecting some of her personal belongings: her books, the painting of her mother, pillows and blankets for Nikolai. She was about to walk away but then paused, thought for a moment and pulled the butterfly hairpin out of her hair, leaving it on the bench.

Finally, the cart Shkuro had given them was packed and ready to go. Nikolai was in the back and Sophia was in the front, holding the reins, just like before. But unlike before, there was a sense of finality in their departure. She knew they were never coming back, that they were on the brink of an exciting adventure and they were embarking on it together. The thought filled her with nerves and happiness.

'We don't have much food,' she said as the horse moved slowly forward, leaving their old life behind.

'Don't worry, with the rifle Shkuro gave us we can hunt. We are not going to starve.'

'What do you mean, *we*? I'm not hunting. I could never hurt an innocent animal,' she exclaimed, squinting in the sun.

'But you could eat an innocent animal if someone else killed it?' She could tell he was teasing. Even without turning around she knew he had the widest smile on his face.

'I don't even know how to use a rifle. I could fish though. Or pick mushrooms. I'm good at that.'

'So let me get this straight. You are happy to hurt an innocent fish but not an animal?'

'For you, yes. I would hurt a fish for you. To make sure you don't go hungry.' She let the reins drop for a moment, turning around and smiling at the expression on his face. 'Now, do we have everything? Weapons? Maps? I don't want to be lost in the wilderness like last time. What? Why are you looking at me like that?'

'Like what?'

'Like I said something wrong.'

'You didn't say anything wrong.'

'Then what is it?'

'You don't want to be lost in the wilderness with me? Last time we were lost in the wilderness together, it was the happiest few days of my life.'

'Mine too,' she whispered, as he shook his head, muttering, 'Women' and giving her a look filled with such affection, it made her heart hurt.

When they turned around the corner and could no longer see the settlement, Sophia felt like singing at the top of her voice. She felt light like a bird, like she would take off into the sky at any moment, carried on her happiness, with the weight of her guilt and her doubt no longer pulling her down. As the last carts disappeared from view, she felt like she was leaving all her troubles in the past, travelling full speed towards her future. What was it going to bring? It didn't matter because she was with him. She was not afraid of anything when she was with him.

While Nikolai slept, she concentrated on the road in front of her, on avoiding the larger rocks, on the horse's hooves hitting the ground, regular like a heartbeat. This early in the morning, away from the settlement, with nothing but mountains around them, it was the only sound she could hear. That and the trees whispering in the breeze. Suddenly, she heard something else. A fast tap-tap-tap, like a typewriter under impatient fingers. It sounded threatening, almost alien in this peaceful place. A horse galloping, she realised.

Sophia let the reins go slack in her hands and the cart came to a stop. Turning around, she tried to see where the sound was coming from but couldn't. Were they being pursued? Had Pokrovsky changed his mind, just like Shkuro suspected he might? She shouted to Walter the horse, 'Go-go-go, trot-trot-trot' and for once he obeyed, as if he could sense the urgency of what was happening. But no matter how hard he tried, they could not compete with a man on horseback, riding as fast as he could.

The next time she turned around, she saw a cloud of dust on the other side of the valley. This cloud was getting closer and closer, and bigger by the minute. Soon a rider emerged from the dust, spurring the horse on, his head bent low. Sophia let go of the reins. There was no point in trying to outrun him. It was clear the horseman was after them and he wouldn't stop until he caught them.

Nikolai sat up. 'What is happening?' A gunshot was his answer. The rider lifted his weapon and was shooting in the air.

'We'll find out soon enough,' said Sophia, her face pale, hands trembling, trying to hide from Nikolai how afraid she was. After everything they had been through, they finally had each other. She couldn't bear to lose him now, when they were so close to freedom.

It took a few minutes for the rider to reach them. They were the longest minutes of Sophia's life.

Only when the man approached and stopped in front of them did she recognise him. 'Dmitry! What are you doing here?'

A part of her was relieved. They were not pursued by Pokrovsky after all. Nikolai was not going to be wrestled away from her and taken back to prison, to be hanged in the morning. But another part of her was terrified. Hadn't Dmitry told her he would never let her go? And here he was, with a gun in his hands and a crazed look in his eyes. After all these years together, she realised she didn't know her husband at all. She didn't know what he was capable of and couldn't predict what he would do. 'A gun, Dima? Really?' she said quietly. 'Is it necessary?'

'Did you think I would let you leave with him?' He laughed, the familiar sound she knew so well, only this time it sounded sinister and unkind. There was a hint of madness in his face and Sophia shuddered. For the first time in her life, she was afraid of her husband.

For a few moments they faced each other in silence, Dmitry on horseback, his face like a dark cloud threatening thunder, Sophia with reins in her hands, petrified, and Nikolai, who lifted himself up and was watching his brother.

Dmitry was the first to break the silence. 'He can leave if he wants. I don't care what he does. But you are coming back with me.' His eyes were cold and emotionless but his voice trembled.

'I am not.' She tried to sound brave, even if she didn't feel it.

'You are my wife and will do as I say.'

'Despite what you seem to think, you don't own me. I'm not a possession. I can make my own decisions.'

Dmitry waved his hand, as if dismissing her. 'You are upset right now. You are not thinking clearly. Come back to camp and we can talk.'

'She already said no,' said Nikolai.

Dmitry pointed the gun at his brother. His voice became shrill. It was a stranger's voice. Sophia didn't recognise it. 'Stay out of it. This is between me and my wife.' His eyes burnt with a passion she had never seen before. He turned to Sophia. 'If you don't come with me this instant, I will shoot. I'll finish what Pokrovsky

322

has started. Then you will be mine again.'

'I will never be yours. I never was.'

'Because of him. Once he's gone ...'

'Not because of him. Because of us. You and me. The two of us are responsible for what happened to our marriage.'

'And now, without him, we'll have another chance.' Slowly, without taking his eyes off Sophia, Dmitry cocked his gun and pointed it at Nikolai. Sophia's hand moved towards the rifle on the bench next to her. But she knew it was no use. She could never shoot Dmitry, even as he threatened them.

Nikolai looked straight at his brother. He didn't flinch, nor did he look afraid. 'I'm sorry it has come to this, Dima.'

'You are sorry, you wife stealer, the man who had turned his back on everything we believe in? We were so happy, Sophia and I, until you came along and destroyed everything.'

'It was never my intention. We didn't ask for this. I did my best to stay away ...'

'You were sniffing around her from day one, like a dog in heat.' Dmitry waved the gun in the air. He was screaming now, his words coming out slurred as if he were drunk.

Sophia said, 'You can kill us both, Dima. It won't change anything. Our marriage is over. I'm not coming back with you.'

'The moment you saw him, you lost your mind. It's like he cast some kind of a spell over you. And I know exactly how to break it.' He raised his gun until it was level with Nikolai's head.

'Remember that day a week before our wedding when you gave me a live butterfly?' Sophia asked softly.

Dmitry shuddered as if stung by a bee. When he spoke, his voice sounded strained, like there was a fish bone stuck in his throat. 'Of course I do.'

'Remember what you said to me that day?'

'What does the butterfly have to do with this?' he interrupted angrily.

'You said, even a butterfly deserves to be free.'

323

His eyes flickered with warmth, as if the memory brought back the old Dmitry, the one who would do anything for her.

'You have to let me go,' she added, stretching her hand to him, as if she wanted to touch him, through all the pain, through the space between them.

'I love you. How can I let you go?' he asked, lowering his gun.

'If you truly love me, how can you not? I made my decision. I love Nikolai. I want to be with him. I hope one day you can forgive us.'

Dmitry's face fell. Suddenly, he looked shattered, like a vase that had been cracked and hastily put together. Like he was about to collapse any minute. He took aim at Nikolai, and as he was about to pull the trigger, Sophia's mouth opened in a silent *No!* Her body began to slide. She was about to throw herself between Dmitry and Nikolai, between Nikolai and the bullet, when Dmitry turned the gun around, pointing it at his own head. 'Don't!' shouted Sophia.

Dmitry didn't. With a furious cry he threw the gun on the ground, turned around and galloped away.

*

Sophia and Nikolai were alone in the steppe, the little horse-driven cart moving slowly through the rocks. It was so peaceful here, so serene, it was hard to believe that somewhere nearby people were fighting for power, struggling, shooting and revolting. Kislovodsk seemed like a universe away. Petrograd, too. Here in the mountains of Caucasus, the world ceased to exist and it was just the two of them under the star-studded sky, searching for a way back but hoping they wouldn't find it. Not just yet.

Sophia was on the driver's bench, holding the reins. Nikolai was watching and teasing. 'Can your cart go any faster? We could walk quicker to Kislovodsk.'

'You can't walk,' she said. 'And until you can, sit back and enjoy the ride.'

'I can't walk but I can hobble. We could hobble quicker to Kislovodsk.'

'Do you want to get there quicker?' She turned around. He was sitting up with a straight face but his lips were trembling like he was fighting a smile.

'I'd be happy if we never got there at all,' he said. 'I think we should stop.'

'Yes, you're right. Let's stay here. We could build a hut and live in the mountains. Have chickens and goats. A kitten called Kitten and a dog. Like the man we met on the way to Bekeshevskaya, remember? He seemed happy, away from civilisation.' Away from the revolution, she wanted to add.

'Yes, he did.' His eyes twinkled. 'But I meant, stop for the night. It's getting late.'

They found a spot by the river and sat on the grass together. He started a fire and she boiled some water for their tea. They broke the bread Shkuro had given them. The moss was soft and inviting after a day of travelling. The air was crisp. She was thankful it wasn't raining. Thankful for so many other things too. For the unfamiliar feeling of freedom, as if metal chains had fallen off her shoulders. For being alive. For being with him. She put her head on his shoulder and whispered, 'What is that noise? It's too loud to be the river. Yet, it sounds like water falling.'

'It *is* water falling.' His arms were around her. He was nuzzling her neck. 'I believe it's a waterfall.'

A waterfall! She wriggled free, jumped up and ran towards the sound.

'What are you doing?' he called after her. Sophia didn't reply, in awe watching the wall of water coming down strong from a giant rock. She reached her hands out, felt for the water. A second later, the palms of her hands were wet, her face and hair, and the front of her dress. She squealed in excitement. He shook his head in amusement. 'No, you don't. I know what you're thinking. It's November. Too cold to swim.'

How she wished it was summer! She wanted to feel the water on her bare skin, experience the power of it as it fell from its great height. She lifted her face to the waterfall and stood still for a moment. 'Isn't it magical?' she cried. 'I've never seen a waterfall before. I will never forget this moment!'

'Magical, yes,' he replied. 'You're right. One never forgets one's first waterfall.'

Sophia stretched her arms out and danced on the spot, like a child without a care in the world. On and on she twirled, away from the pain and the heartbreak of the last two years, away from the bad memories, of her husband's pale face as he pleaded for her to stay, of Regina's trembling lips as she took her last breaths, towards freedom and a future with the man she loved. Softly, she sang under her breath, while the water was a cascade of silver beads behind her. When she looked up, she saw Nikolai, as mesmerised and awe-struck as she was, except his eyes were not on the waterfall but on her. He rose to his feet with difficulty and slowly approached her. A moment later he was pulling her close, his lips in her damp hair. Touching her neck softly, he took the clips out of her hair and when it was loose around her face, falling down her back like the waterfall, he ran his fingers through it like a comb. Turning her around, he kissed her.

She lost her footing because her head was spinning and because the rock they were standing on was slippery. But his arms were tight around her waist and he didn't let her fall. Not taking his lips away, kissing her like he needed her lips to live, he guided her to safety, to the soft moss and the whispering river.

Cold water on her face, his warm lips on her lips, and before she knew it, he was leaning over her, his eyes twinkling. 'Careful,' she whispered. She was afraid to touch him. Afraid to cause him pain. 'You are still recovering. I don't want to hurt you.'

'Don't worry. You won't hurt me.'

Nikolai undressed her, slowly and gently. Although it was November and unusually chilly, Sophia felt like she was burning inside. She needed to jump into the waterfall to cool off or she might catch on fire. But most of all, she needed his hands on her. She was afraid of what was happening. Afraid he would stop, afraid he would continue, like she was a virgin on her wedding night and it was her first time. As he held her close, she realised that it might as well be. It was the first time she touched someone she loved and was touched by someone she loved.

Afterwards, she relaxed in his arms, a blanket over them, drowsy and content. Her lips were on his cheek, while her fingers traced his beard. Her eyes were on the sky overhead. 'Regina often said the moon here is twice the size of the moon in Petrograd. There are twice as many stars. And the air smells differently here. It smells of freedom and hope.' At the thought of her friend, she tried hard not to cry. She wouldn't cry here, alone with him, at the start of the rest of their life together.

'I'm sorry about Regina. I wish I could thank her for saving my life.'

'I wish I could thank her for saving you for me. There is so much I want to tell her. And now I never will.'

'Whatever you want to tell her, she already knew.'

They hardly slept at all that night. They had all the time in the world but after everything they'd been through, it didn't feel like it was enough. Under the open skies of Caucasus, with the river by her feet and nothing but the waterfall like a Beethoven symphony to accompany them, possessing nothing and yet everything, for the first time since March 1917, Sophia felt like she truly belonged.

Epilogue

He was skin and bones. If there were mirrors in the camp, he would not have recognised himself. Nothing was left of the groomed young man who had once lived on Nevsky Avenue with a sprawling marble staircase and an army of valets running to execute his every whim. When he touched his face, his cheeks felt hollow under his fingertips. His mouth had gaps in it where teeth had once been. His clothes hung off his withered frame. He was a shadow of his former self. Years spent in the Gulag could do that to a man. They made one disappear, and not just physically. He wore a grey prison uniform. He toiled from dawn to dusk, in the rain, snow and bitter cold. He had become immune to hunger. Here in the Siberian wilderness, he barely knew who he was.

He was on his bunk with his eyes closed, his broken body aching. In mere hours, he would have to be up again, to start another gruelling day that would stretch in front of him without an end in sight. Day after miserable day of living his worst nightmare. Somewhere in the distance he heard the metal gate cough and slide open. Drifting in and out of sleep, he didn't pay any attention to the sound of approaching footsteps.

'You have a visitor,' he heard the harsh voice of the guard.

He opened his eyes with interest. It was rare for anyone to have visitors in the camp. Which of his comrades got lucky this evening?

The guard was looking directly at him. 'Orlov, do you hear me? Sort yourself out and follow me.'

He got up slowly. In all his time here, no one had come to see him. It didn't surprise him. He had no one left in the world.

Silently, he followed the guard down a long and winding corridor. In a dimly lit room, at a square cast-iron table, sat a woman with his back to him. Something in the way she turned her head seemed familiar. He stared.

When he saw her face, he recoiled from her like she was a ghost. He thought she had died in the mountains for sure. Sometimes he mourned her. Other times, when his worst got the better of him, he told himself she got what she deserved, for deserting him and turning her back on him. He never thought he would see her again. And yet, here she was, alive.

'Guard!' he shouted. 'Take me back. I don't want to speak to this person.'

The woman stood up, her hand resting on her belly. She was heavily, uncomfortably pregnant. 'Dima, please. Just hear me out.'

Their eyes met. 'What are you doing here?'

She glanced at the guard and lowered her voice. 'Please, sit down, so we can talk.'

Reluctantly, he crossed the room to the little table and sat in the uncomfortable metal chair, his hands clasped in front of him. Not saying a word, he waited.

'My husband found out where you were and …'

'Your husband? Last time I checked, you and I were still married.' He spat out the word *married* like it was a curse. 'In church, no less. What God hath joined together, let not man put asunder and all that. You made a vow. Was it just meaningless words from you?'

If his bitterness and animosity bothered her, she didn't show it. 'Nikolai is here on business and I thought I'd come and visit. To see how you were doing.'

'Are you here to gloat?'

'Not at all. We want to help you,' she whispered, leaning closer.

'How did you find me?'

'My husband has connections. He's Lenin's right-hand man. So when we heard that you'd been arrested, along with the other refugees, we made enquiries. If all goes well, we can get you out of here.'

'Your husband …' He sneered as he said that. 'He must be a big man now. Does it make him feel important, to have power of life and death over someone? Does it make him feel like God?'

'Think what you like. I'm not here to fight. You don't belong here, in a camp for political prisoners. You are the most apolitical person I know.'

'Tell that to the Bolsheviks.'

'The civil war is over. We can help you leave this place.'

When she said *we*, it was like a slap across his face, an acknowledgement that she no longer belonged to him and never would. That she had left him behind as if he meant nothing. His chest hurt and he hated himself for it. 'After everything I've done, you want to help me?'

'I never forgot what you said to me. Everything you did, you did out of love for me.'

He laughed mirthlessly. 'You're wrong. I never loved you.'

'You are family. The only family we have left in the world.'

'What a turncoat you are. Accepting the new regime because it's more convenient for you. Becoming one of them.' He looked her up and down with disdain.

'And I suppose you are proud to be imprisoned and sent from labour camp to labour camp for your beliefs? If you had a chance, wouldn't you make a different choice?' He had to admit that yes, he would. 'I'm too tired of fighting, running, hiding away,' she continued. 'I want to live a normal life, to be with Nikolai and

330

have a family.' She looked away from him. 'There is a new order in Russia. Nothing we can do about it, other than accept and make peace. Besides, Nikolai believes in it. And I believe in him.'

Everything in Sophia's appearance displeased him. Her modest dress that covered her knees, her round stomach, her shiny hair, her clean nails, the contentment in her eyes. She hadn't known a day of hard labour in her life. She didn't lift rocks or mine gold, day after excruciating day. He didn't want her help. But he knew he needed it because it might be his only chance. Leave this place or die. That was his choice. 'Tell your common-law husband I accept. But under one condition.'

'What is it?'

'That I never have to set eyes on either one of you again. Guard, we are done here.'

'Wait,' she said quietly. 'I brought you something. Nanny made some sweet pies.'

The expression on her face made him pause. She looked like a lost little girl. Something stirred inside him, a warm recollection of what had once been. 'Nanny? Not you?'

'I don't bake anymore. Don't have the time. Before I fell pregnant, I volunteered at the hospital. And now I sew and knit for the orphans.'

'Are you happy?'

She lowered her eyes, as if she was embarrassed. 'I'm happy.'

'That's all that matters.'

Accept and make peace, he repeated to himself as the guard led him back to his bunk, while she returned to her peaceful life, to his brother who loved her more than anything in the world. Like he had once loved her.

A Letter from Lana Kortchik

Dear Reader,

Thank you for choosing *The Countess of the Revolution*. I am so excited to share this story with you.

This novel is very personal to me. My grandfather often spoke of his great-grandfather, who was a revolutionary, just like Nikolai. After the Polish uprising of 1863, he was sent from Warsaw to Sakhalin, where he spent ten years in a labour camp. I grew up hearing stories about him and always knew I wanted to write this book.

The Russian Revolution of 1917 was a watershed moment in Russian history. It turned every Russian's life upside down, rich or poor, peasant or noble. The revolution ended the rule of the Romanov dynasty and led to the world's first communist government, as well as a civil war that cost ten million lives, mostly civilians.

Although this book is fiction, the events it describes are not. It also features two real people. Lieutenant General Andrei Shkuro, the infamous White Ataman, dedicated his life to fighting the Bolsheviks. After the White Army had been defeated in 1920, Shkuro lived abroad, primarily in France and Serbia. During the Second World War, he sided with Nazi Germany, hoping it would destroy the Soviet Union and the Bolsheviks. In 1945, Shkuro was detained by British forces in Austria and handed over to the Soviet authorities. He was executed by hanging in 1947. Just like Shkuro, Lieutenant General Viktor Pokrovsky, known for his cruelty and penchant for hanging prisoners, couldn't let go of his dream to see the Bolshevik regime gone, even after the defeat of the Whites. He emigrated to Bulgaria in 1920 and was killed in 1922 by Bulgarian police while resisting arrest for the murder of a Bolshevik agent.

As I researched the period of the revolution and the civil war, I read dozens of memoirs and diaries. The one that stood out and had the most influence on this story was the diary of Mathilde Kschessinska, the most famous Russian ballerina at the time, who during the Revolution immigrated to Kislovodsk and France. She was the mistress of the future Tsar Nicholas II of Russia prior to his marriage and later the wife of his cousin Grand Duke Andrei Vladimirovich of Russia, and her experience of the Revolution is absolutely fascinating. Andrei Shkuro's memoirs were also an invaluable source, shedding light on the Civil War in the South of Russia.

I hope you enjoyed this story. I'm always happy to hear from my readers and would love to know what you think. Please feel free to reach out by leaving a review or contacting me via my website or social media.

Thanks,

Lana

Twitter: https://twitter.com/lanakortchik
Facebook: https://www.facebook.com/lanakortchik/
Instagram: https://www.instagram.com/lanakortchik
Website: http://www.lanakortchik.com/

Sisters of War

Can their bond survive under the shadow of occupation?

For fans of *The Tattooist of Auschwitz* and *The German Midwife* comes this unforgettable tale of love, loss, family, and the power of hope.

Kiev, 1941: Watching the Red Army withdraw from Ukraine in the face of Hitler's relentless advance, sisters Natasha and Lisa Smirnova realise their lives are about to change forever.

As the German army occupies their beloved city, the sisters are tested in ways they never thought possible. Lisa's fiancé Alexei is taken by the invading army, whilst Natasha falls in love with Mark – a Hungarian soldier, enlisted against all his principles on the side of the Nazis.

But as Natasha and Lisa fight to protect the friends and family they hold dear, they must face up to the dark horrors of war and the pain of betrayal. Will they be strong enough to overcome the forces which threaten to tear their family apart?

Daughters of the Resistance

Ukraine, 1943

On a train from Ukraine to Germany, **Lisa Smirnova** is terrified for her life. The train is under Nazi command, heading for one of Hitler's rumoured labour camps. As she is taken away from everything she holds dear, Lisa wonders if she will ever see her family again.

In Nazi-occupied Kiev, **Irina Antonova** knows she could be arrested at any moment. Trapped in a job registering the endless deaths of the people of Kiev, she risks her life every day by secretly helping her neighbours, while her husband has joined the Soviet partisans, who are carrying out life-threatening work to frustrate the German efforts.

When Lisa's train is intercepted by the partisans, Irina's husband among them, these women's lives will take an unimaginable turn. As Irina fights to protect her family and Lisa is forced to confront the horrors of war, together they must make an impossible decision: **what would they be willing to lose to save the people they love?**

Be swept away by this heart-wrenching novel of love, resilience and courage in World War II, from the author of *Sisters of War* **– perfect for readers who loved** *The Tattooist of Auschwitz* **and** *The German Midwife*.

Acknowledgements

Being able to share this book with the readers is a dream come true. None of it would have been possible without the help and support of so many.

I would like to thank my family for always being there for me. Thank you to my mum for sharing the family history that inspired this book, and for the hours of babysitting. Thank you to my husband for his love and support, and to my beautiful children for filling every day with joy, laughter and cuddles. Everything I do is for you.

Thank you to my amazing agent, Mark Gottlieb, for believing in me and holding my hand every step of the way.

Thank you to my fantastic editor, Belinda Toor, for making this book the best it could possibly be and for making me a better writer. Thank you to Rebecca Jamieson for her insightful feedback, and to everyone at HQ and HarperCollins360 for working so hard to bring this book to the readers. A special thank you to HarperCollins design team for creating this stunning cover. I love it so much!

Finally, I would like to thank all my readers around the world for buying my books, reading, reviewing and spreading the word. Thank you to all those who have reached out to let me know how much they enjoyed my stories. Your words mean the world to me.

Dear Reader,

We hope you enjoyed reading this book. If you did, we'd be so appreciative if you left a review. It really helps us and the author to bring more books like this to you.

Here at HQ Digital we are dedicated to publishing fiction that will keep you turning the pages into the early hours. Don't want to miss a thing? To find out more about our books, promotions, discover exclusive content and enter competitions you can keep in touch in the following ways:

JOIN OUR COMMUNITY:

Sign up to our new email newsletter:
http://smarturl.it/SignUpHQ

Read our new blog www.hqstories.co.uk

𝕏 https://twitter.com/HQStories

f www.facebook.com/HQStories

BUDDING WRITER?

We're also looking for authors to join the HQ Digital family!
Find out more here:

https://www.hqstories.co.uk/want-to-write-for-us/

Thanks for reading, from the HQ Digital team